THE BEAST
IN HIM

Also available

SUN, SAND, AND SEX

THE MANE EVENT

Coming soon

WHEN HE WAS BAD

THE BEAST
IN HIM

SHELLY LAURENSTON

BRAVA

KENSINGTON PUBLISHING CORP.
http://www.kensingtonbooks.com

BRAVA BOOKS are published by

Kensington Publishing Corp.
850 Third Avenue
New York, NY 10022

All Kensington titles, imprints and distributed lines are available at special quantity discounts for bulk purchases for sales promotion, premiums, fund-raising, educational or institutional use.

Special book excerpts or customized printings can also be created to fit specific needs. For details, write or phone the office of the Kensington Special Sales Manager: Kensington Publishing Corp., 850 Third Avenue, New York, NY 10022. Attn. Special Sales Department. Phone: 1-800-221-2647.

Brava and the B logo Reg. U.S. Pat. & TM Off.

ISBN-13: 978-0-7582-2037-0
ISBN-10: 0-7582-2037-5

First Kensington Trade Paperback Printing: April 2008
10 9 8 7 6 5 4 3 2 1

Printed in the United States of America

THE BEAST
IN HIM

Prologue

True, he was drunk. Very drunk. His daddy's idea of a proper send-off for his youngest boy before the United States government owned his ass for the next few years. But just because he shouldn't have had those last four tequilas, didn't mean he didn't know they were tracking her.

They were always tracking her. Always screwing with her. From what he could tell, she didn't even stay at the house anymore. Her foster parents didn't care as long as the checks kept rolling in. So she mostly lived out in the woods like a wild child. Except she wasn't a wild child. Just a poor kid who'd had the unlucky misfortune of getting on the wrong side of his baby sister.

He caught their scent and immediately knew where they were heading—to the high school. They'd find her under the bleachers. She hid under there a lot. She could hide anywhere when she needed to. Unlike the brawnier She-wolves, her kind's body type was small and wiry, like all wild dogs.

By the time they made it into the gymnasium, he already stood in front of the bleachers. He didn't have time to find her and get her out; he'd have to stop them here.

"Hey, Bobby Ray," Bertha, also known as Big-Boned Bertha, cooed. His sister, at sixteen and already six feet tall, was still smaller than Bertha. But she was tougher and Bertha learned early on not to mess with Sissy Mae Smith. She learned the hard way. Now she took it out on the smaller, weaker Omegas of the town. Yet, she seemed to have a special hard-on for this one girl. This one girl with no protection, no family, and no Pack. A dog among wolves. The Lord could be cruel when He set His mind to it.

"I know why you're here, Bertha. And I want you to take your friends and go."

"Oh, come on, Bobby Ray. We won't hurt her none." Bertha squatted down to look through the slats of the bleachers. "Is she in there? Come on out, Jessie Ann. We just wanna say hi."

"I said you need to go."

Bertha stood up, damn near as tall as he was, and tossed her hair back. "Why aren't you at your party, Bobby Ray?"

"Once my daddy starts putting my brothers into headlocks and telling them they only live 'cause he didn't kill 'em in the crib, it's time for me to go."

She stepped closer to him. "You really going to join the Navy tomorrow?"

"Already joined, darlin'. Tomorrow I get on the bus." *And the hell out of here.*

"You'll be missed," she said low, for him only.

"My momma says that too." He put his arm around her shoulders and steered her back toward the doors. "Look, you take these guys out of here. I'm waitin' on somebody."

"Who?"

"A friend who's going to hook me up with the best 'shine in three counties. But he's not coming in if he sees an audience. So why don't you head back to the party and I'll meet you there." He forced a smile. "And then we'll have a party of our own."

"Okay. See you in about an hour?"

"Sure," he lied, feeling almost guilty if he hadn't known she'd come there to beat up a ninety-five-pound girl.

Bertha kissed his cheek and motioned to the other wolves to follow her out. The bunch of them were already pretty drunk. A few more drinks and they'd all pass out, and by the time they woke up in the morning, he'd be on a bus and gone from Smithtown forever.

Once their scent faded, Bobby Ray turned around and headed back toward the bleachers.

"It's okay, Jessie Ann. You can come out now." He waited for her to answer, but it seemed she was still scared. He caught her scent, so she was around somewhere. "Come on, Jessie Ann, you know you have nothing to worry about with me. I'll walk ya home." At least he hoped he could. That tequila was starting to hit him pretty hard.

"Dammit, Jessie Ann, I don't have time for this." He walked around the bleachers and crouched down to see under them. He felt a little wobbly from all the liquor, so he reached out and lightly put his hand against the metal of the bleachers.

"Don't!"

Small brown hands grabbed hold of his shoulders and yanked him back. They both hit the floor as the bleachers slammed down like a set of dominoes. If he'd been under there, he'd have been crushed to death.

The silence after the deafening sounds of all that slamming metal stunned him.

"You did that." Bobby Ray looked over his shoulder at Jessie Ann Ward. She was a cute little thing, but a tad innocent for his tastes. Big, wide brown eyes, a cute little nose, and full lips that promised all sorts of things he felt pretty confident she'd never be able to deliver on. She kept her long curly hair in two ponytails, and you could easily see the many colors flowing through each strand. All wild dogs had multiple colors in their fur and, when human, in their hair. Brown, gold, blond, white, and black all on one head made it hard for Jessie *not* to be noticed.

Still, he'd had the hots for her since the first time he saw her, but Jessie Ann was the kind of female who you mated with, not simply made out with. And he had no intention of getting trapped in this town. Another Smith male with a Pack of vicious sons and a mate who didn't know if she loved him or hated him, probably both.

"I could have gotten killed," he growled.

"Don't snarl at me," she growled back, pulling herself into a sitting position. "It wasn't for you anyway."

"No, it was for them. And do you think you would have ever forgiven yourself if they'd actually gone under there?"

"They wouldn't have. It was just to scare 'em off. I'm tired of being hunted like a gazelle."

He stared at her and finally saw all the bruises on her face and neck, probably going well down her torso and legs. They'd caught up with her again. Dammit. He did try to protect her, but there was only so much he could do, and Sissy Mae simply wouldn't call off her She-wolves. Not even seventeen and she already had her own Pack. The females her own age followed Sissy around town like the Second Coming. He had no idea what happened between them, but Sissy made it clear she thought of Jessie Ann Ward as their own Pack Omega. Problem was, Jessie Ann didn't much like that position. So she fought back when most Omega wolves would have taken it until it was over. But she wasn't wolf. She was wild dog. And if she had her own Pack . . . but the wild dogs were dying out. The young adults had been hit by a vicious strain of influenza that could only be passed between them when shifted. It had wiped out more than half of the adult breeders before their own doctors could get a handle on it and come up with a vaccine to stamp it out. The damn thing had left a lot of elderly grandparents raising pups and a lot of orphans. Orphans like Jessie Ann.

Tragically, like the full-blood wild dogs in Africa, Jessie's people were becoming extinct. Which meant she had no one except him watching out for her. And once he got on that bus tomorrow, she wouldn't even have that.

"Jessie, you've gotta learn to take care of yourself." Without thinking, Bobby Ray reached out to touch her cheek and she reared back from him, which hurt his feelings. Especially his drunk feelings. "I wouldn't hurt you."

She scrambled back from him. "I know that." If she did, then why did she keep moving away from him? Annoyed, he grabbed hold of her ankle, holding her still. "If that's true, why are you running from me?"

"I'm not running." But she desperately tried to get him to release her leg.

"Then stop fussin'!" he snapped. When she didn't, he yanked her over and somehow yanked her right onto his lap.

She gasped in surprise, her arms around his neck, her thighs on either side of his hips. For a little thing, she sure did feel good there. He rested his hands on her hips. Bobby Ray knew he should push her off, but all he wanted to do was bring her closer.

She stared down into his face, those brown eyes devouring him on the spot. Yeah, he knew when a female wanted him, and to his utter surprise, Jessie Ann Ward wanted him. He watched her gather her courage; then she moved in, her lips lowering toward his. He could feel her sweet breath against his mouth and he could easily imagine how hot the kiss would be. He knew she'd taste wonderful and would respond to him like no one ever had before.

He also knew kissing her would be the dumbest thing he could ever do. So, too drunk to temper his actions, he shoved her off his lap, wincing when she hit the floor hard.

Bobby Ray ran his hands through his hair. Sometime tomorrow all his hair would be gone. "We . . . we can't."

"We can't what?" she snarled, pushing herself to her feet. "*You* grabbed me." She stood and he could see she wore one of her *Star Wars* T-shirts. She must have ten of those and ten of her *Raiders of the Lost Ark* tees. A real nerd, Jessie Ann.

"Don't be mad, Jessie Ann. It's not—"

"Forget it." She glanced at the small watch on her wrist. She had a weird thing about time, which he found fascinating since no one else in town did. "I gotta meet my friends at Riley's." A comic-book store in the next town over.

"I'll walk with you." He didn't like her being out there on her own.

"No, I don't need you." She practically spit that in his face; then she grabbed her oversized backpack filled with her nerdy books and papers and hauled it onto her shoulders. For such a small thing, he had no idea how she managed to haul that bag around.

"It's too dangerous for you to walk over there at this time of night."

"I'm meeting my friends." Her friends. All male. He often caught their scent lingering around her. He saw them once when he and one of his buddies went to the comic-book store on a whim. She was in the back with five other guys playing some game that involved a board, paper, and many-sided dice. He sensed dragons were involved and that's pretty much where Bobby Ray lost interest. Dragons, swords, fairies—all that stuff seemed pretty stupid to him. But he hadn't liked her being around all those full-human males. He liked it even less now.

She turned to walk away but stopped and glanced at him over her shoulder. "Good luck, Smith. You know, tomorrow. You're gonna be great." Then she took off running. He didn't bother going after her. Wild dogs were wicked fast, and he was way too drunk to keep up.

Instead, Bobby Ray lay back against the floor and closed his eyes, figuring a few hours of sleep would have him right as rain. Of course, all those dreams about one small She-dog with innocent eyes and a wicked mouth only managed to drain him and make him wish things were different. But they weren't. Not until he got out of Smithtown and changed his life for good.

Then maybe, just maybe, he'd have something to offer a spunky little wild dog who could haunt a man's dreams and his heart.

Chapter 1

Sixteen years later

"Well, how bad is it?" Smitty asked, handing Mace Llewellyn a hot cup of coffee.

"Bad. Really bad. I can't sleep. I barely eat. I'm terrified they're going to come in the middle of the night and burn the house down." He shook his head and sipped his coffee, unable to continue.

"How much longer?"

Mace took a deep breath. "Another month. But she's talked about not going back. A few months ago I thought that would make me happy; but not now. It horrifies me."

Smitty winced. "Isn't there something you can do?"

When his friend only looked away, Smitty bumped his shoulder with his own. "Fess up, hoss. What did you do?"

"You don't understand," Mace stated desperately. "I had to do something. It's not just us I have to think about, but the baby."

"What did you do?"

Unable to look Smitty in the eye, "I called her father."

"And?"

"They'll be calling her back to duty next week." Shaking his head, "I had to do something, Smitty. It was out of hand."

"I understand, hoss."

"No, you don't. She's turned friend against friend, neighbor against neighbor, wives against husbands. Husbands against tennis coaches. She's started fistfights in the middle of Saks Fifth Avenue. When she's bored—I fear for the world."

Smitty sipped his coffee and marveled at how one cop on maternity leave could destroy an entire Long Island town. Before Dez gave birth, Mace put her in a four-bedroom house in Northport with the hope that if she liked it, she'd rethink living in Brooklyn and, even more important, risking her life every day as a New York City Police detective. But soon after the baby was born, Dez started acting strangely. She never spoke about work, and Mace would come home to a full-cooked meal and a smiling wife more than happy to cater to his every whim. Then the long walks around the neighborhood with the baby and the dogs started. By the time Dez returned home, thirty-year-old marriages were over. Tennis coaches shot at or slapped around at the country club. Dez wouldn't say anything when Mace asked her about it, but she'd offer him a slice of home-baked lemon meringue pie. That was around the time the man stopped sleeping.

"Does she know?"

"I don't know. They were going to call her today, give her the weekend, and bring her in on Monday—but I've been afraid to call home."

Smitty didn't blame his friend. Sure, they may have been Navy SEALS together, caught in the middle of firefights, invading foreign countries, doing whatever their government asked them to do. But not once had they ever felt a fear equal to having a smiling Desiree MacDermot-Llewellyn ask you if you wanted salt for your potatoes.

"Well, we've got a few more hours here at least."

Mace finished off his coffee. "Thank God. I can't go home. . . . She made me pot roast last night." He crushed the empty coffee cup. "Inhuman. The woman is inhuman."

Smitty finished off his own coffee and tossed the remainder in a trash can. He glanced at the TV screens. They'd set up cameras everywhere they could think of. This being their biggest job to date, Smitty wanted it going off without a hitch. So far, the team had stopped at least fourteen people trying to sneak into the party. When Mace told him a couple of months before they'd been offered a job as party security, Smitty's head nearly exploded off his body. Security for a party or rave were for guys who had criminal records and couldn't become cops. It sure wasn't for the well-armed team they'd assembled since Smitty and Mace opened their business. Then he heard about not only the party but the party throwers. This wasn't some bullshit event, but a computer geek's wet dream. The major players in computers—millionaires to billionaires—from around the country came to the party and had for the last five years. Getting an invitation something you could almost put on your résumé. The amped-up security was to protect the serious heavy hitters that even Smitty, who could give a shit about PCs except when he needed to send an e-mail or download some porn, recognized.

Within a few days it went from "that bullshit job we have to do" straight into an all-hands-on-deck event. Thankfully, they now had the manpower—former military-trained shifters looking for a new life among the civilians. So far they'd hired only three full-humans, and they were Dez's best friends.

"We better go back inside." Mace pushed open the back doors. "You guys okay?" he asked the two males and one female monitoring the screens and keeping in close contact through headphones with the entire team.

"Yup," the female answered as she quickly flipped through channels, those gold leopard eyes picking up everything.

"Good." Mace slammed the doors after Smitty jumped out and the two headed back to the party.

They quickly checked on front-door security and walked inside the building, a four-story brownstone the company that hired them owned. They weren't a big company but apparently quite

powerful. Computer and database security specialists or whatever. To be quite honest, Smitty really didn't care. Their money
was green enough, and they had lots of it.

Smitty and Mace stepped into the main ballroom and glanced
around.

These people definitely knew how to throw a party. This wasn't
some mere—and boring—black-tie event. This was a geek party
to the nth degree. Hardcore tech music, old-school video games
lining the walls, an insane amount of food and liquor—all free—
and a hot waitstaff dressed up like those disturbing Japanese an-
imation girls. He'd never seen so many girl school dresses paired
with garter belts before in his life. Yeah, these people definitely
knew their audience.

"Smitty?"

Smitty faced his business partner.

"This is Sierra Cohen. Miss Cohen, this is my business partner Bobby Ray Smith."

Smitty shook the female's hand and sized her up at the same
time. *Yum. Jackal.* There weren't a lot of jackals in the world,
but the few he'd met were damn cute.

Using his most charming smile, Smitty asked, "So, this is
your business, Miss Cohen?"

"Oh, no. No, I'm just a hard-working employee. The owners
aren't very comfortable with the general public. So I'm kind of
the face of the company."

"I can see why, darlin'."

She gave a throaty laugh and took a step closer. "I have to
say, Mr. Smith—"

"Smitty, darlin'. Everybody calls me Smitty."

"Smitty, I have to say I was very glad to find . . . uh . . . *our*
kind with a security business. I know my employers felt much
safer with your team than with the full-humans we usually hire
for this event."

"Well, we are available for any security needs you may have.
Actually, any needs at all."

He had to bite the inside of his mouth to keep from laughing when he caught Mace rolling his eyes in disgust. Before Detective MacDermot came along, it would have been an ugly fight between the two friends to see who got this little honey into bed first. But now that the big-headed lion had mated and married the lovely and big-breasted cop, poor Smitty was all on his own.

"That's very good to know. I'm sure there's something you can take care of for me later tonight."

"Any chance," Mace cut in, "you two can put a hold on this lovefest until the job is done?"

"Don't mind him, darlin'. He's married."

Mace snarled and Sierra looked at him in confusion. "Married? Why?"

"Because it made my sister want to set herself on fire."

Smitty laughed, clearly remembering the way Missy Llewellyn growled and snarled her way through the ceremony. Then Sissy Mae, Dez, and Ronnie Lee, Sissy's best friend and next in command, spent the entire day torturing Missy. Definitely fun to watch.

"My employers are big on marriage," Sierra added absently. "Marriage and pups."

"Aren't we all big on our pups and cubs?" Mace asked, although he looked like he really didn't care what her answer might be.

"Sure. But they're *really* big on their pups. Anyone gets too close and they get really *tense*."

Smitty frowned. "Wolves?"

Sierra shook her head. "No." She turned and nodded toward the enormous doorway. "Wild dogs."

Surprised, Smitty watched Sierra's employers walk into the room. There had to be about ten of them and, he guessed, not the full Pack. They wouldn't leave their pups alone except with other dogs they trusted.

Seeing them immediately reminded him of a sweet little She-dog he used to know. And, like her, they weren't large like the other shifter breeds. In fact, wild dogs were the only breed that shifted into a smaller animal. As human, the men weren't usually taller than five-ten or five-eleven and the women five-eight or five-nine. They were wiry and lanky, and watching them move, Smitty guessed they were a lot stronger then they seemed.

Another wild dog burst through the doors and made a beeline toward Sierra. She was gorgeous—Asian with almond-shaped brown eyes and full, sexy lips. Her dark hair reached to her waist and she exuded sex appeal.

Unfortunately, she was marked. Smitty could smell it on her a mile away.

"Sierra, you need to get up onstage," she said with a country lilt he hadn't heard in a long time from anyone not in his Pack.

Sierra nodded. "I'm on it." Her hand brushed Smitty's arm, letting him know she'd be back.

After she walked off, dark brown eyes locked on him and Mace. "Gentlemen."

"Ma'am," Smitty answered back. "How y'all tonight?"

The female raised one eyebrow. "Y'all making fun of my accent?"

"No, I thought you were making fun of mine."

Her expression changed quickly when she smiled. "Where you from?"

"Tennessee."

She pointed at herself. "Alabama."

"Well, it's nice to meet you, Alabama."

They shook hands and laughed while Mace looked about two seconds from jumping out the closest window.

"I'm Maylin. But everybody calls me May."

"Bobby Ray Smith. We're handling your security tonight."

"Oh, that's right. The shifter-run security company. I have to say I was quite surprised to find a Smith this far north. I'm from just outside Smithburg myself, and I never thought y'all would cross the Mason-Dixon line."

"Well, too many Alpha Males and not enough territory. Figured it was time to see what else was out there."

She glanced at Mace. "Your kin can't be too happy with you working with a cat."

"They tolerate him more than you'd expect."

May started to say something else but stopped when the music cut off and Sierra walked out onto the stage at the front of the room.

"Hello, everyone. I'm Sierra Cohen." Catcalls and whistles followed her statement and Sierra dismissed it laughingly with a wave of her hand. "I'm the VP of Promotions. And I wanted to thank you all for coming tonight."

Sierra continued to ramble for a bit, and May grabbed two glasses of champagne off a tray passing by. She offered one to Smitty, but he waved it off. "Sorry. On duty. Need to keep a clear head."

"I thought wolves just had to stay away from tequila."

"If he drank tequila," Mace muttered, "you'd find him passed out on the dance floor by now."

Smitty glared at him. "So now you decide to contribute to the conversation?"

Onstage, Sierra's voice rose. "So without further ado, let me introduce the CEO of Kuznetsov Security Systems . . . Jessica Ward."

Smitty's head snapped around and he watched Jessie Ann walk out onto that stage like she owned it. Maybe she did.

The applause Sierra received upon her entrance was nothing to Jessie Ann's reception. It sounded like they were at a rock concert with the reaction she got.

She didn't look anything like the Jessie Ann he remembered, all gangly limbs and lots of bruises. She'd finally put on some weight and it fit her perfectly, giving her some sexy curves. She'd cut her hair so it rested on her shoulders, straightened it, and dyed it one single color—dark brown. No jeans and sci-fi tees either. Instead, she wore a simple blue silk dress with tiny little straps barely holding it up and five-inch heels strapped to her feet. She looked mature and polished . . . and nothing like the Jessie Ann he remembered. He almost mourned the loss of that know-it-all geeky Jessie Ann. He'd always liked her raw edges and weird behavior. It made her different from everyone else

around him. Now she looked like any other important CEO—
gorgeous but average.

Jessie Ann stood in front of the mic and waved at the roaring
crowd.

When they quieted down a bit, she said, "It's the shoes, isn't
it?" Then she turned her foot in a bit so they could see it from
the side.

The crowd went even wilder. Clearly, she knew her effect on
this mountain of male geeks. But Smitty could see the predators
in the room watching her too—when they should be doing their
damn jobs.

Jessie waved her hands again. "Okay. Okay. Look, I don't
want to take up a lot of your time. 'Cause this is a party. But I
did want to echo Sierra's sentiments and thank each and every
one of you for coming tonight. Each year this party gets wilder
and better, and that's down to you guys. As usual, every cent we
raise goes to the Kuznetsov Foundation, and all that money is to
help orphans and foster kids find permanent placement in loving homes. Other than that—"

A blond-haired wild-dog male sidled up to Jessie Ann, cutting
her off. When he began to whisper in her ear, Smitty decided he
didn't like the wiry little bastard.

Jessie leaned back, eyebrows raised. Smitty remembered that
haughty expression quite well.

"Is that really necessary?" she asked.

The male nodded and she sighed, turning back to the mic.

"Phil here has asked that those who use our gaming room
tonight, if you lose, please don't throw your mouse, controller,
or cards across the room. And those who win, please don't
dance around the loser singing, "I won. You're a loser." The crowd
burst out laughing and Jess shook her head, a good-natured
smile on her face. "Anyway, have a great night and thank you."

The crowd burst into applause, and Jessie Ann strutted off
the stage.

May turned back to him, one glass of champagne empty, the
other half filled. "That's our Alpha."

"Your Alpha?" Jessie was someone's Alpha? Smitty had a hard enough time thinking of Jessie as a CEO, much less the Alpha of a Pack. Of course, they were dogs. Much easier to handle a bunch of dogs than wolves probably.

"Yup, has been for nearly sixteen years now."

That didn't make sense. She'd barely been sixteen herself sixteen years ago. And except for Jessie, there'd been no wild dogs in Smithtown.

"Are you sure? Jessie Ann should have been in school."

May almost choked on her champagne. "If you have any sense, my wolf friend, you will *not* call her Jessie Ann."

"But I always called her Jessie Ann."

Mace gazed at him. "You know Jessica Ward?"

"I went to school with her. Sissy Mae mauled her on more than one occasion." To May, he said, "But I'd like to not mention that if possible."

"Gee," she giggled, "I wonder why?"

"Wait." Mace faced him. "*You* know Jessica Ward?"

"Why do you say it like that? I know lots of people."

"Yeah, but they're not Jessica Ward."

"What the hell does that mean?"

"I'm just saying, Smitty—she's a little out of your league."

His wolf pride threatened, Smitty snapped back, "As a matter of fact, that little gal had a huge crush on me at one time."

Mace snorted. "Yeah, sure. I can see that—in a parallel universe."

Before the two males could get into it, the female they spoke of worked her way through the dancing crowd and over to May.

"How did I do?" she asked.

May gave her a thumbs-up and handed over her nearly empty glass of champagne. Jessie Ann finished it off and dropped it on the serving platter of a passing waiter.

She looked at Mace and smiled in surprise. "Mace Llewellyn!"

"Hi, Jessica."

"Oh, my God! When did you get out?"

"Over a year ago."

She went up on her toes and gave him a brief hug that had Smitty's eyes narrowing. "I'm so glad you're okay. You are okay, right?"

"I'm fine. Great, actually."

"I'm so glad to hear that. I just saw your sister at a charity ball a few weeks ago, but she didn't mention you were home. Actually, she didn't mention you at all."

Mace's answer was to laugh.

Laughing herself, Jess shook her head. "Ahh. I see little has changed there." She glanced at Smitty and began to walk away. Then she stopped and looked back, her eyes growing wide.

"Oh, my . . . Bobby Ray?"

"Jessie Ann."

"Wow. Look at you." She stepped in front of him and gave him a quick, rather unsatisfying hug. "I can't believe it. You look great."

"You too."

"I see your body finally grew into that head."

At least May had the decency to try to stifle her laugh. Unlike Mace, who let it ring out over the room. Treacherous bastard cat.

"Yup, I sure did."

"You went into the . . ." She snapped her fingers trying to remember. "Marines? Right?"

Mace laughed harder.

"Navy."

"That's right. Sorry. It's been a lot of years."

"I see that."

"So why are you here exactly?"

Smitty gritted his teeth but answered politely, "I'm partners with Mace. We own the security company handling your party."

"That's nice." But she didn't seem to mean it or care. Her eyes had already started scanning the room.

The male wild dog from the stage placed a glass of champagne in her hand.

"Was I right about the shoes?" he asked with a big smile.

"Let it go about the shoes."

"Think you can dance in them?"

"Of course. Why?"

"I wanna swing you over to Don Lester." *The billionaire?* "See if we can tag team him."

"Why? We're having dinner with him next week."

"Yes, but I want to do this now."

"Why don't you do this yourself?"

"One, I'd look stupid dancing alone. Two, he likes *you*."

"If you hadn't insulted his wife . . ." she muttered before swigging back half a glass of champagne.

"That was an accident. I wish you'd all let it go."

Jess handed her glass to May, who promptly finished it. It seemed the dogs weren't squeamish about sharing.

"Mace, I'll talk to you later. There's some work I think I can get you guys."

"Sounds great."

Brown eyes focused on him and Jessie again leaned in and gave Smitty a small hug. "It was great seeing you again, Bobby Ray. We should keep in touch."

But before he could even debate whether it was worth getting her number, she was off dancing with some wild dog to tag team a billionaire.

May gave them both a brief smile before moving off toward the rest of her Pack.

Mace nodded his head. "Oh, yeah, man. She is *so* into you."

He glared at his friend, feeling uncharacteristically angry, and snarled, "I knew that time you were laid up in the hospital after that firefight I should have put that pillow right over your head."

The rest of the evening was uneventful and went slowly. Painfully slow. All Smitty wanted to do was go home and sulk in peace and quiet. Instead, he found himself watching Jessie Ann work a room rather than doing his job. Thankfully his staff did theirs and they had no problems. As a business, the night was a screaming success. Smitty, however, couldn't seem to enjoy it. He even blew off the hot little jackal's blatant proposition. A proposition he normally would have been all over.

The last of the vans headed off back to the company's office parking lot, leaving him and Mace.

"What are you grinning at?" Smitty asked while leaning against his car.

"I'm grinning because I'm happy. Tonight went perfect. I have some leads on other jobs, lucrative jobs, and my wife is going back to her job come Monday. I didn't think that would make me happy, but it does."

Smitty shook his head and smiled. "Is she still out in Northport?"

"Oh, hell no. She's back at our Brooklyn place. Which is where I'm headed. I didn't want her out on the Island any longer. I fear for her safety. As it is, I'm sure the town burned our house down by now. To ensure we would never return."

Before the two friends could part company, the side door opened and the wild-dog Pack walked out. As late as it was, they still seemed to be filled with tons of energy. They discussed going to an all-night diner for a late dinner–early breakfast. Jessie Ann led the way, wrapped in a fur coat, strutting toward the corner. One of the males caught up to her and put his arm around her shoulders, whispering something in her ear. She laughed and pushed him away.

They walked to a big, black Hummer and pulled the doors open, piling in. Jess opened the front passenger side door but stopped and looked around, her eyes finally finding him and Mace. She smiled and waved.

"Thank you, guys! It went great."

"You're welcome," Mace answered for them. All Smitty could manage was a wave. Then the Pack closed the doors and the Hummer drove off.

"You all right, Smitty?"

"Yeah, I'm fine. Just thinking about how much little Jessie Ann has changed."

"People change. It happens."

"Yeah, you're right."

But he liked his little Jessie Ann. More than he'd realized. And now she was gone forever.

Jessica Ann Ward sat in the passenger side of one of the Pack's Hummers and stared out the window. She knew it was coming, she simply didn't know when. Leave it to Phil to break the ice.

She heard him turn in his seat to face his wife, Sabina.

"Golly gee, darlin'," he said in what had to be the worst rendition of a Southern accent Jess had ever been forced to listen to. "You sho' look good in them fine shoes."

"And you are . . . I can't quite place you," Sabina responded in her Russian accent that was suddenly that much thicker.

"Why, I'm the young man you once had a big ol' crush on and I've now grown into a manly buck of a wolf. Don't you remember?"

"Um . . . no."

Finally, Jess couldn't take it anymore. She burst out laughing, her Pack joining with her.

"Shut up! Shut up! Shut up!" she playfully yelled at Phil. "I wasn't that bad."

Danny, May's husband, stopped at a red light. "When you walked over, he was like this." He held his hands out at least eleven inches apart. "But when you were done, he was like this." He held his forefingers about two inches apart.

Jess covered her face with her hands, her laughter causing tears to flow down her cheeks. "Stop it!"

"Sweetie, it went brilliantly," Sabina cheered. "You crushed him." She always said that sort of thing with so much relish. And Phil always looked so turned on by it.

"What y'all missed," May added, "was all the chest thumpin' he was doin' with that big cat."

"Big is right," Phil agreed. "Now *that* was a big head."

May laughed in disbelief. "I can't believe you said that about his head."

"Well, it was large!" Jess argued to the four people she was closest to in the universe. The original members of their forty-strong Pack.

"I mean that thing was huge. I'd sit there . . . under the bleachers . . . hiding, terrified . . . and I'd think to myself, 'If he tips his head to the side, will he completely fall over? Like the Elephant Man?'"

"Oh, my God, Jess!"

"What? You ask a lot of weird questions when you're hiding under bleachers."

Danny found a fabulous parking spot right outside the diner.

"You guys think I'll see him again?"

"No," they answered in unison.

Jess sighed in relief. "Good." She waved at her outfit. She'd borrowed the dress and fur coat from Sabina, but unfortunately, she'd paid good money for the shoes.

"I can't keep this up on a regular basis. And I hate these shoes. My feet are freezing and I fell on my ass in the bathroom."

"Those shoes make that outfit," Phil complained. "So suck it up."

"Give me my sneakers, May."

"You're going to put sneakers on with that dress?"

"When did you become Karl Lagerfeld?"

Phil leaned into his wife. "They're being mean to me, my love. Destroy them."

"I'm hungry," Sabina said. "I want waffles and I want them now. Or someone will pay dearly." She looked at Phil and they all knew she meant that "someone" was him.

"Okay. Okay. My little Russian love bug. Calm yourself."

While the others got out of the Hummer, Jess pulled on her sneakers. Yeah, it was over. No matter how good Bobby Ray Smith might look, she was over her little "wait until he sees me now" moment.

Christ, though, the man did look good. Tall with mile-wide

shoulders and his entire body rippling with muscles under his black midlength leather jacket, black turtleneck, and black jeans. And those watchful, amber eyes staring out under that dark brown hair, most of which reached to his collar. Probably a relief after so many years in the military.

Yeah, the man still looked damn good.

She wished she could say she truly had no idea he'd be attending this party, but her Pack never did business with anyone they hadn't thoroughly investigated. And although she knew Mace through his sister and their mutual charity activities over the past five years, it wasn't until Danny gave her the information on his business that she saw Bobby Ray Smith's name listed as his partner.

At that point, she knew what she had to do. As childish and ridiculous as it seemed even to her, she couldn't resist. And, as always, her Pack had been more than willing to join in.

But now it was over. She'd showed him exactly how far she'd come, and it felt great. Yet, she had more important things to deal with now, moving Bobby Ray Smith officially into her past.

Although there definitely remained a part of her that still wished she'd gotten a chance to kiss him that night in the gymnasium. Just so she could stop wondering what it would be like. By now she felt certain she'd built it up to gargantuan proportions the poor man could never live up to.

The passenger side door opened and Jess grabbed hold of Danny's hand so he could help her from the huge vehicle. Now that she was back in her normal footwear, she didn't need the help, but she wouldn't turn it down either.

Laughing and happy, the Pack walked into the diner to feed.

Chapter 2

Smitty sat back and watched the high-powered activity of the busy kitchen. He always loved hanging out at this restaurant. The chef, first cousin of the Van Holtz Pack Alpha Male, always made him feel welcome and, more important, fed him.

"So how's the business?" Adelle Van Holtz asked as she handed a waiter two plates of food.

"It's okay. We're getting more clients. Had a big job last night that worked out well."

"Good. Good. I told my brother about you guys. He may have some work for you." She reached around him and grabbed a bottle of water. "As you know, the Van Holtz Pack doesn't like to sully our fingers with common wolf activities."

"The Smiths are all about the common wolf activities. And being sullied. So we're more than happy to help. Especially if it involves my favorite restaurant," he finished with a wink.

The Van Holtz Steakhouse restaurant chain had been neutral ground for shifters for years, although cats didn't come by very often. Yet every breed of wolf or canine could come and indulge their need for rare steak and hang with the other wolves. Only problem, the Van Holtz Steakhouse was in no way cheap. So Smiths didn't come very often since they didn't exactly roll in money like the Van Holtz and Magnus Packs did.

"I'll keep that in mind," Adelle said with a smile. "Now tell me what's wrong, baby boy?"

Smitty liked Adelle a lot, the two of them becoming impossibly tight after she'd hired Smitty to beef up her restaurant's security and figure out which of her staff had been stealing from her. It turned out to be the arctic fox busboy.

At least twenty years older than him, Adelle wasn't as snobby as most Van Holtzs, and she really knew how to cook up a steak. She had a mothering streak a mile long, and she loved to baby Smitty. With his momma in Tennessee and his sister a pain in the ass, he sometimes needed that.

"What makes you think something's wrong?"

She reached up and stroked his cheek. "You know you can't hide anything from me. Is it a She-wolf problem?"

"Nah." He kind of wished it was. She-wolves were real simple to understand if you followed three simple rules: Don't irritate them, don't stare them down unless you've got a death wish or you're sure you can take them, and don't irritate them. You followed that simple logic, you'd do just fine. But Jessie Ann wasn't a She-wolf, and there was nothing simple about that woman. Not a damn thing. "Just met an old friend last night and she acted like she didn't even know me."

"Well—"

"And how could she not?" he continued. "I'm amazing."

Adelle patted his chest. "That you are."

After the job and breakfast with Mace, Smitty didn't get back to his apartment until well after six A.M. He'd stripped and dropped into bed, expecting to be asleep within seconds. Instead, he'd stared up at his ceiling for a good hour wondering how Jessie could so easily forget him. True, it wasn't like they spent every hour of every day together when they both lived in Smithtown, but he was closer to her than he was to most anybody else except his sister. He'd even listened to her when she'd go on and on about some book she read. The fact that he'd endure conversations about elves and dragons and guys with swords still amazed him. But he'd done it for Jessie Ann.

Hell, maybe she was still mad. He knew females could hold a grudge like no other. Especially predators. Maybe she hadn't forgiven him for walking away, for leaving her alone in Smithtown. But what else could he do? It's not like the Navy would have let him bring a sixteen-year-old girl with him because "my sister and her friends use her like a chew toy."

What annoyed Smitty even more? That he cared. He cared whether Jessie remembered him. He cared that she might have been hurt when he left. Why the hell should he? But dammit he did, and he could hear his daddy as if the man were standing right next to him: "You always were a big pussy, boy."

A waiter stopped in front of Adelle and she quickly examined the tray full of food. She nodded and sent him on his way. "So you hot for this little chickie?"

Rearing back, Smitty shook his head. "Lord, no. She's just a friend. Someone I used to be close to, but I could never . . . we could never . . ." He shook his head. "No way."

"Huh. Flustered. I've never seen you flustered before."

"I am not flustered. You took me by surprise is all."

"Of course. That must be it." Adelle patted his shoulder. "You want another steak? It'll make you feel better." He'd already had two.

"I could eat again."

She smiled and grabbed a plate off the tray of a passing waiter.

The waiter stopped. "That's for table ten."

"So?"

"They've been waiting for forty-five minutes." Saturday nights were the busiest nights for the Van Holtz restaurants, yet Adelle didn't move any faster or do any more than she did on the slowest night of the year.

"Are they important?"

Now Smitty laughed. "Adelle."

"What? It's a valid question."

The waiter leaned close to Adelle and whispered, "It's Jessica Ward, boss."

Smitty blinked in surprise. "Jessica Ann Ward?"

"Yeah." The waiter grinned. "Another one of her first dates if I'm guessing right."

Pushing past the two females, Smitty opened the door and glared across the restaurant.

"I really don't know why the woman bothers," Adelle sighed behind him. "She has to be the pickiest canine on the planet. She's had some hottie-hots in here and she leaves 'em standing at the corner—alone—every time."

Smitty spotted the "couple"—he almost choked on that—immediately, his eyes narrowing when he saw the bastard take Jessie's hand.

Didn't she know she had to be careful in this day and age? The scrawny bastard probably just wanted one thing from her and she didn't even realize it.

"What's wrong, baby boy?"

"Nothing. Give 'em their food."

"You don't want it?"

"No, thanks, Adelle."

Adelle shrugged and placed the plate back on the tray.

Yup, Phil was right again. Sherman Landry of the Landry wild-dog Pack was really boring. Almost painfully boring and with a case of OCD the likes she'd never seen. And hoped to never see again.

He adjusted the butter knife on the table for the fourteenth time in the last forty-five minutes, and asked, "So do you have any plans for the long weekend coming up in a couple of weeks?"

Uh-oh.

"As a matter of fact, I do. With my Pack."

"Oh." He looked so disappointed. Like a Labrador that just got his bone taken away. "And the charity ball at the museum?"

Good God, Jess! Think of something. Something! She couldn't do this again. Not again. Dating was hard enough, but dating a guy this irritating was asking too much of her.

To be honest, Jess didn't know why she bothered anymore. She'd been dating wild dogs solidly for the past year. Some of them coming from Europe and Asia to take her out. Most of them were nice, but none of them got her all sweaty and squirmy. And the thought of breeding with any of them left her cold. Jess would admit it, she was ready. Ready to have her own pups. Her own mate. She'd helped raise her Packmates' kids for fifteen years, and it was time she had her own little nightmares to contend with. But the thought of Sherman Landry's obsessive-compulsive nature helping to raise any of her kids did nothing but make her feel a little ill.

"I'm going with my Pack."

"Of course," he said, his disappointment evident. It wasn't the first time he'd had that tone when talking about her Pack. As much as they didn't like him, Jess sensed he didn't like them either.

Too bad for him. Her Pack meant too much to her to bring in someone who'd cause nothing but problems between them.

"Yeah . . . well." Since she had nothing else to say, Jess wiped her mouth on a linen napkin. "I'll be right back. Need to go to the ladies' room."

She stood up, forcing a smile when he stood up as well. Say what you would about Sherman, he was definitely polite.

Jess walked toward the back until she hit the ladies' room, which she always called "the marble palace." She brought nearly every date to this restaurant because she knew even if the date sucked, the filet mignon was always perfection.

As she washed her hands and used the thick paper towels to dry them, she realized she couldn't put in another hour on this date. She'd finished her steak, now Sherman wanted dessert. And all she wanted was to get back to the office. The last week of preparation for Friday night's party had put her behind, and she realized now this Saturday date had been a huge mistake.

She pulled her cell phone out of her way too small purse—she'd give anything to have her backpack with her—and sent Phil a text message. It was a simple one:

GET ME THE FUCK OUTTA HERE!

Confident her friends would come through with no further prompting, Jess dropped her cell back into her bag and spun around—right into the brawny chest of some guy. A guy in a ladies' room.

Letting out a strangled scream, she started swinging. As usual, it wasn't pretty, much more a flailing wildly. She'd never been a very good fighter when human.

But the man caught hold of her, pinning her arms to her sides. Her fangs slid out and she started to go for his neck when she heard, "Jessie Ann! Would you calm down!"

Shocked, she leaned back and stared up into the face of Bobby Ray Smith. Damn him! Why did he have to look so freakin' good?

"What the hell are you doing?" she demanded. "Why are you in the ladies' room?"

"Can't a man use a ladies' room if he feels like it?"

"No, he can't. And do you mind getting your paws off me?" He did and Jess stepped back, but her ass hit the sink. Trying to look casual and not fall on her ass, she sauntered around him and tossed out her paper towel.

"How long were you standing there anyway? Or is this some weird kinky shit you've started doing since you joined the Marines?"

"The Navy, Jessie Ann. I joined the Navy."

"Whatever."

Bobby Ray looked at the door, then back at her. "Did you not know I was in here with you the entire time you were washing your hands—and mumbling to yourself like my crazy Aunt Ju-ju?"

Dammit. She really had to work on the talking to herself thing. "I knew."

"But not until you turned around."

"Look, I've got a lot on my mind. I can't be aware of everything constantly."

"But . . ." He looked so adorably confused all she wanted to do was punch him in the face. "You're one of us. How could you not know I was right behind you?"

"I—"

"You couldn't scent me? Hear me? Are you still that oblivious?"

How did he manage to do it again? Turn her into a sixteen-year-old? She clearly remembered getting these long lectures from him about being safe and aware of what was going on around her. "You can't live your life in them books, Jessie Ann," he'd always tell her. Like she'd want to spend a second of her day facing her reality. She usually received these lectures while she hid under bleachers or up in trees. The leopard family that lived near Smithtown territory thought she was "just the cutest thing" because she actually knew *how* to climb trees.

But that was a very long time ago. She wasn't that battered little girl hiding from a bunch of ravening She-pups. She was Jessica Ann Ward, CEO of Kuznetsov Security Systems and Alpha Female of the Kuznetsov Pack. And yet, here she stood, getting lectured to by this giant-headed mangy wolf.

Sure, she could yell at him. Scream at him even. But that wouldn't register with Bobby Ray Smith. No, there was only one way to get under a Smith's skin. Especially *this* Smith.

"Look, Bubba Ray—"

His eyes narrowed to glowing-amber slits. "It's *Bobby* Ray, as you damn well know. My daddy is Bubba."

"Bubba. Bobby." She gave a dismissive wave. "Sweetie, does it really matter?" For a brief second, she though he might hit her.

When he didn't, she patted his shoulder. "It's really sweet of you to care. Really. But I actually have someone waiting for me and," she wrinkled up her nose and whispered, "not to tell you your business, but shouldn't you be watching the front door? I wouldn't want you to get fired." When he stared at her with his mouth slightly open, she innocently asked, "You *are* restaurant security, right?" Frighteningly entertained, Jess rubbed his sweater-covered bicep a bit. "Well, I do have to go. You take care now, Bobby Joe."

Jess walked to the door and pulled it open. As she stepped into the hallway, she heard him growl, "It's Bobby *Ray*."

Smiling and feeling like she'd won the lottery, Jess sauntered back to the table. Before she could sit down, her cell phone went off.

She flipped it open. "This is Jessica?"

"I'm calling to rescue you from a fate worse than death. Dessert with Sherman the Dull."

"Oh, my God. Are you sure?"

"Yes, I'm sure he's really dull—just like I warned you he would be," Phil went on smugly. "You never listen to me."

"Okay. Okay. I understand. I'm leaving right now."

Jess closed her phone and gave Sherman her best pout. "I'm so sorry, Sherman. But I have to run. Trouble at the Pack house."

"Of course, of course." He stood and she waved him back into his seat. "My car is waiting outside. You have dessert and I'll talk to you later." She thought about kissing him on the cheek, but the thought made her wince, so she patted him on the shoulder instead. "Thank you for a lovely dinner." Then she headed for the door. The maître d', whom she knew on a first-name basis, already had her coat on his arm. She snatched it from him, rolled her eyes at his grin, and charged out of the restaurant. Her driver already had the car door open and she practically leaped inside.

"Home?" her driver asked.

"Nah, office. I've gotta salvage this crappy evening somehow."

Although torturing Bobby Ray Smith would definitely go down as the highlight of her night . . . if not her year.

He didn't move until Adelle walked into the bathroom and tugged on his sweater. "Are you all right, Bobby Ray?"

"She called me Bubba. She keeps thinking I was in the

Marines." He finally looked down into Adelle's concerned face. "*Has the universe gone insane?*"

He paced away from her. "I mean, this is Jessie Ann, for God's sake. Little Jessie Ann Ward. I used to have to coax her out from under the bleachers like a squirrel from a tree. She was insanely in love with me, and now she's calling me *Bubba*?"

"Uh, Bobby Ray, there are women waiting to use the bath—"

"And for her to stand there and act like I was some sort of pest she was trying to wave off her food is just too much. She *adored me!*"

Adelle shrugged. "I guess she grew out of it."

But he hadn't grown out of it. How the hell could she?

Raising her hands at his glare, Adelle stepped back. "Why don't I, uh, reroute the ladies outside to the men's room and you take your time . . . snarling. In here. And when you're ready, there's a forty-ounce cut of steak and a bottle of tequila waiting for you in the kitchen."

Then she turned and fled the room. Snarling, like Adelle said he could, Smitty stalked over to the bathroom sink. He stared at himself in the mirror. Fangs. His fangs were out! He let a woman get to him so much he'd unleashed his fangs? The universe *had* gone insane!

"This is so not over," he told his reflection. "Not by a long shot."

There had to be a reason Jessie Ann Ward kept treating him like dog shit on her shoe, and he'd sure as hell find out why.

Chapter 3

"**Y**ou *called her Spot?*"

His sister looked up at him in surprise. Probably because he never yelled. At her or anyone else. But no wonder Jessie Ann had looked right through him the last two nights he'd seen her. Who wanted to remember being called Spot?

"Lassie had been done, darlin'," his sister said as an explanation.

He didn't know how this particular event became a monthly one. Meeting with Mace, his sister, Sissy Mae, Ronnie Lee, Ronnie Lee's mate Brendon Shaw, and Mace's wife Dez for Sunday brunch at the Kingston Arms, Shaw's hotel. This specific dining room was hidden away from full-humans and catered mostly to their kind. A neutral space for all breeds. And the best damn French toast a body could ever have.

"It wasn't just that, Sissy Mae," Ronnie reminded her. "It was also her hair. All those colors in one head. It was tragic. It didn't look punk or anything. It just looked stupid."

"She's a wild dog," Smitty growled out, trying his best to control his growing rage. A rage he rarely, if ever, used. "All wild dogs have those colors unless they dye their hair."

"Then she should have dyed it. 'Cause all she did was make herself a big ol' target."

"I don't get it," Dez said around a spoonful of oatmeal and

her son hissing in her arms. "What's the difference between you guys and the wild dogs?"

As quick as it came, Smitty felt his rage slip away. Dez did have that effect on him. She so easily fell into momentous shifter faux pas that she never failed to amuse him. Sometimes it was like watching a train wreck.

It took a moment, but Dez suddenly realized she had the attention of the entire room. Her mate leaned back in his chair, arms folded over his chest, waiting with a smile to see how she got out of this one. Glancing around, Dez shrugged. "What?"

Sissy opened her mouth to say something, but Ronnie cut in before Sissy said something that would damage what had turned into a very healthy friendship among the three women.

"We're wolves," Ronnie Lee explained simply. "The wild dogs are, literally, dogs."

"Some say the first dogs," Mace added helpfully while stealing bacon off his wife's plate.

Sissy Mae pushed her empty plate away. "Forget all that. Why did you bring her up anyway, Bobby Ray?"

"I met her at that job we had Friday night." He couldn't mention last night's meeting. Not even to Mace. He still couldn't believe it. She'd called him Bubba. She might as well have spit in his face.

Mace shook his head, smiling as his son hissed and swiped at him when his father took toast off Dez's plate. "Forget it, Smitty. You are so out of her league. She barely remembered you."

Sissy and Ronnie exchanged glances.

"Out of whose league?" Sissy asked. "Jessie Ann's?"

"She may have been Jessie Ann when you knew her. But she's Jessica Ann Ward now. And you, my hillbilly friend, don't stand a chance."

Dez sat up a little straighter. "Are you guys talking about Jess Ward? Christ, I haven't seen her in ages."

"*You* know Jessica Ward?" How Dez put up with that superior lion tone, Smitty had no idea. Without fangs or claws, she couldn't exact her revenge during hunts, the way Smitty often did.

"Yes, Captain Ego, I know Jessica Ward."

"I love when she calls him that," Sissy laughed.

"We worked together a few years ago." Dez grinned down at her son. "A bunch of us were sorry when she left. She was so damn good at her job."

Eyebrows raised, Sissy said, "Don't tell me that frightened little rabbit was a cop."

"Not a cop. Technician. Computer tech specifically. She was good, but she left to start her own business. And now she's richer than God." Dez looked at Smitty. "Mace is right. She's so out of your league."

Smitty gave his best pout. "Why are y'all trying to hurt me?"

"Because it's fun?"

"It's easy."

"I love it when you cry."

Smitty sighed. "Forget I asked."

"So how did your date go?"

Jess rolled her eyes at May's question. "I don't want to discuss it."

May grimaced. "That bad?"

"That boring."

"I'm sorry, sweetie."

Jess stood and took her breakfast plate to the sink. "It's not your fault. We're just not a good match."

As she rinsed her dish, Jess said casually, "And I saw Bobby Ray Smith last night at the restaurant."

"Oh?" May asked, just as casually. "What happened?"

"Well"—Jess dried her hands and turned—"I guess you could say—"

The sight of forty wild dogs standing in the Pack kitchen, appearing suddenly simply so they could hear her response, stopped the words dead in her throat.

Phil motioned to her. "Every detail. Leave nothing out. Go."

And she did "go." Right to the front door and freedom.

Smitty motioned to Dez and she happily placed her son in his arms. "All I know is . . . Jessie Ann is still damn cute."

"And so not interested."

Smitty glowered at his friend. "Did you actually have to sing that?"

"Bobby Ray always had a thing for the damsels in distress."

"Oh, save me, Bobby Ray," his sister mocked. "I'm so weak and frail."

"Save me, Bobby Ray," Ronnie joined in, "I'm trapped under the bleachers—"

"—in a tree—"

"—in the school venting system . . ."

The two lifelong friends looked at each other and said in unison, "*Again!*"

Ignoring the She-heifers idiocy, he asked over their laughter, "When did she leave town?"

Still chuckling, Ronnie thought a moment. "It was right after Big-Bone fell off that mountain."

"Man, she must have been so drunk," Sissy said. "She broke both her legs and some ribs. Took her days to heal," she added with true pity.

Smitty said, "Her Packmate said she'd been their Alpha for sixteen years."

"It's possible. I know she left before the end of our junior year."

"Wow. Alpha of a dog Pack," Sissy sneered. "Wonder what ya gotta do to get that job?"

"Be the best ass sniffer?"

Dez shook her head. "You two are *mean*."

"What can I say? She brings out the worst in us."

"Actually," Ronnie reminded Sissy, "everybody brings out the worst in us."

"Good point."

Smitty sighed, a little sad. "Y'all don't think she left because of me, do you?"

He'd asked it honestly, knowing how he'd protected her and all. But the hysterical laughter he got back did nothing but insult him.

"There's nothing to tell. I saw Bobby Ray for like five minutes."

"She lies," Sabina accused. "But we will break her."

They pushed Jess into a chair and Sabina snapped her fingers. They placed it in her hand and she held it in front of Jess's face.

Jess snorted. "You really don't think that'll work on—"

"Dark, *dark* chocolate," Sabina told her softly. "Walnuts. Fresh from the oven."

Sabina held Jess's favorite brownies under her nose. They'd been baked, along with cookies, for an early afternoon trip to the zoo.

She reached for the pan, but Sabina yanked it back. "Oh no. Not unless you tell us *everything* about your five-minute meeting with the wolf."

"Fine," Jess agreed, her mouth watering. "But I get the whole pan."

"If you think your hips can handle that, my friend."

"When are you going to pick up the final check?" Smitty asked Mace.

Mace, finally sated, leaned back in his chair and put his arm behind his wife's chair, stroking her shoulder. "Forget it."

"I'll come with you."

"For-get-it. I'm there to do business. Not have you sniffing around her like a dog in heat."

The cub in his arms, Butthead, aka Marcus Patrick Llewellyn, smiled up at him and reached for his finger. You could actually feel small claws right underneath his skin. Yet, they wouldn't make a real appearance until Marcus hit puberty. Still, you didn't need to see those claws to recognize the animal within. He may

have his mother's gray–green eyes, but this wonderful little boy—
and Smitty's godson—still had the cold, hard expression of a
predator. Just like his daddy.

Smitty smiled at Dez. "How are you holding up, darlin'? I
know it's not easy raising one of us."

"Good. The cheetah nanny helps, though. But the first time
he snarled, I had a bit of a panic attack."

"She screamed and threw him at me."

Dez scowled at Mace. "I did not throw my son at you. I just
handed him over and walked quickly from the room so I could
scream into a pillow in our bedroom."

"I found her under the bed with the dogs."

"I was getting their toys, you big-haired bastard." She looked
back at Smitty. "It's just taking some getting used to. The snarling,
the hissing, the purring. Then I have to deal with it from the
baby. . . ."

"Ha, ha," Mace stated dryly.

"When do you go back to work?" Smitty asked because he
loved seeing the way Mace's entire body tensed with panic.

She gave a deep sigh. "Tomorrow. They asked me back early.
Said they were desperate. I thought about telling them no, but
Mace said I shouldn't risk my job." She rubbed her husband's
thigh and gave him that sincere, loving look that always made
Mace want to run for his life. "You're so wonderful about all
this, honey."

"Uh . . . yeah. Thanks."

Mace turned toward Shaw and asked him about the hotel,
and Smitty watched Dez, Ronnie Lee, and Sissy Mae all exchange
suspiciously smug glances.

"Hey," Smitty said, "did you three plan—*ow!*"

The entire room looked at him and he gritted his teeth
against the sudden and brutal pain in his foot where Dez had
stomped on him under the table.

"What's the matter with you?" Mace demanded, almost sounding like he really cared.

Smitty shook his head while Dez gently brushed his hair out of his eyes. "I think the poor baby got a leg cramp, huh?"

He nodded this time, unable to speak as she ground her heel into the upper part of his foot.

"You don't hunt enough," Mace accused, already turning back to Shaw. "That would work those cramps out, ya know."

Dez kissed his cheek and hissed in his ear, "You say a word—they won't find your body for months."

Wolves were a smart breed and always knew when a predator meaner than them was near.

Still holding the baby, who seemed quite happy with the vicious side of his momma, Smitty promised, "Not a word."

Jess dropped onto the couch beside the sixteen-year-old boy reading a book and trying to pretend she wasn't sitting next to him.

She opened her laptop and booted it up. "You weren't up to zoo time today?" she asked him.

Jonathan DeSerio, Johnny, shook his head, his eyes focused on the book in front of him. Until his head suddenly snapped up and he hurriedly said, "Unless you want me to go. I can next time."

For three years after his mother died, child services bounced Johnny between foster homes. For reasons no one but other shifters understood, the full-human families the city stuck him with simply didn't like having him around. They found him odd. And with reason. He wasn't really human, not completely.

Finally, a division of Child Protective Services that handled mostly shifter cases discovered Johnny. They tried to place him with one of the local wolf Packs, but none of them would take him. So CPS finally came to Jess and asked if they could place him with her Pack. They were all canines after all.

Jess didn't hesitate taking him in. And she'd worked hard to make him feel at home, but he continued to fear they'd send him away. Like all the others had. Johnny still hadn't realized he wasn't going anywhere. They wouldn't suddenly decide they didn't like having him around and kick him to the curb. Wild-dog Packs didn't work that way. Once you were in, you were in. Kind of like the Mafia except without the blood oaths and murders for hire.

"If you don't want to go to the zoo, Johnny, you don't have to go."

"Okay."

After a few minutes of silence, she asked, "So have you hear—"

"No."

"I wouldn't worry—"

"I'm not."

"Okay then."

Johnny had applied for an extremely prestigious summer music program that his violin teacher recommended. It was brutally competitive and only the best got in. Jess had faith, but clearly Johnny didn't. But that was okay. She had enough faith for both of them.

May and Danny's daughter Kristan walked into the living room, looking adorable as always in her pink, faux-fur–lined jacket and mini-skirt with the full-length leggings to keep her warm.

She glanced down at Johnny. "Are you still sitting here?"

"No," he said with dry sarcasm, not even bothering to look up from his book. "This is just my hologram. I'm actually in Utah."

Jess snorted. So far, Kristan had been the only one able to get Johnny out of his shell. She did it mostly by annoying him; but hell, if it worked, it worked.

"He was sitting in the exact same spot when the brats went off for zoo day," she informed Jess.

"Why didn't you go?"

"Hello? A little too old for that."

"One is never too old for the zoo."

Kristan rolled her eyes. "Whatever. I'm going to the diner. You wanna go?"

Jess stared at Johnny but realized he didn't understand Kristan spoke to him. She shoved her elbow in his side and his head snapped up from his book. "Huh?"

No wonder Jess liked the kid so much, he was a male version of her.

"Diner," Kristan pushed. "For dinner. Burgers. French fries. Lots of ketchup. Then we can hit the arcade or a movie or something. Unless you want to stay here with the old people."

"You do know I'm not afraid to hurt you, right? And don't be out late," Jess said with a mock glare, which merely elicited the usual eye-rolling-boredom-sigh universal among brats . . . er . . . children.

"Yes, *mom.*"

"I guess I can go." Johnny looked at her and Jess shrugged.

"Your choice, kid."

Unsure, Johnny stood, his book still firmly in hand.

"You're bringing that tome with you to the restaurant? I can assure you I'm much more interesting than some crappy old book."

"Hey!" Jess warned. "Watch your mouth when you speak of this book. It's *Lord of the Rings.*"

"Your obsession with elves is really unhealthy."

When Johnny simply stood there, dumbstruck, Kristan gave that put-upon sigh again, grabbed the book from his hand, and tossed it to Jess. "I'll even introduce you to some hot full-human girls. They're total sluts."

"*Kristan Jade!*"

"Sorry, sorry." Kristan grabbed Johnny's hand and dragged him toward the front door. "See ya, Aunt Jess."

Johnny looked back at her, and Jess couldn't help but enjoy that particular look of fear on his face. No panic, no despair, just a deep abiding fear of what a perky She-dog might be up to. Definitely progress.

"Have fun," Jess called after them before turning back to her laptop. Her Pack had whined—literally—when she said she should go into the office. So her compromise? She'd work from the couch.

At least that way she could join in later for a little after-dinner fetch.

Jess had no idea how long she'd been working when her cell phone went off. Thinking it might be Johnny or Kristan, she immediately answered.

"This is Jess."

"Hey."

She frowned. "Hey . . . who is this?"

"It's Smitty?"

Jess's eyes crossed. Still persistent as a pit bull. "How did you get my number?"

"Can't really tell you that."

"Oh!" she said with a huge amount of cheeriness. "Okay."

She slammed the phone shut and tossed it onto another couch across the room. "Asshole."

Smitty stared at the disconnection message on his phone in horror.

"She hung up on me."

Ronnie patted his leg. "I'm sure she didn't—"

"*On me!*"

Brendon Shaw burst out laughing. "You know, I never really paid much attention to Jessica Ward before. But I have to say . . . I'm starting to really like her."

Punching her mate in the arm, Ronnie said, "Remember our *many* discussions about when to speak and when not to when it involved the Smith wolves? This is one of those not-speak times."

Smitty looked at his sister comfortably resting on a leather love seat. Brendon Shaw's apartment had big, comfortable furniture, and to the cat's great annoyance, the wolves did love to come on over whenever it suited them and lounge.

"I'm Bobby Ray Smith," Smitty said simply to his kin.

"You are," Sissy agreed. "But apparently that don't matter much to little Jessie Ann."

"I know," Shaw said, still laughing. "Let's all go around the room and say what our names are. 'Cause that makes the differ-ence."

"Man, you are an asshole," Smitty snarled, looking for a fight and maybe just finding it.

"Oooh. Those are mighty fightin' words from a guy who just got shot down by a Rhodesian Ridgeback."

Ronnie let out a sigh. "You never know when to shut up."

Smitty stood. "Is there something you want to say to me, boy?"

"Not really." Shaw stood. "Just like your little nongirlfriend there, I have absolutely *nothing* to say to you."

And the last thing Smitty heard before he unleashed his claws and felt fangs bury into his neck was Ronnie Lee screaming at him, "*Just not his face, Smitty!*"

Chapter 4

"No."

Smitty stared at the lion. "No what? I didn't say anything. Did I, Mindy?"

Mace glanced at their executive assistant. "Don't involve her."

Mindy, a seriously hot cheetah hired by his sister, shook her head. "Do you two actually have time for this?"

"You're not going," Mace said again.

"Why would you want to?" Mindy asked, pulling folders out of her desk. "He's going to pick up a check, not stop by a whorehouse."

"He wants to see if Jessica Ward really has no interest in him."

Mindy snorted. "That dog is loaded. No," Mindy stated flatly, "she has no interest in you."

Smitty put his hand to his chest. "Mindy, you don't have to be jealous, darlin'. You know my heart belongs to you."

"Which my wife greatly appreciates."

"You're not going," Mace said again. "Jessica Ward can bring us some high-level clients. I don't need you and your dick fucking it up."

"Now, hoss, that just hurts."

Mace's eyes narrowed. "Look, hillbilly, you're not going and that's that."

"Really? Well, with you gone, that means I can get on the phone, call sweet Dez, and tell her how much you love her and need her and how much you love her pot roast and how you really, in your heart of hearts, want a little housewife cooking and cleaning for you when you get home. A little housewife waiting. Just. For. You."

"All right, fine! You can come." Mace gritted his teeth. "You . . . *bastard*."

He stormed out and Smitty sauntered after him.

"You are *mean*," Mindy laughingly whispered.

"Just doin' what I gotta do to make things happen, darlin'."

Because he was determined to see Jessie Ann Ward again. And nothing, especially not a big, surly cat, would get in his way.

The Kuznetsov office building stood in the middle of Greenwich Village. A prime piece of real estate that would only go up in equity. They'd taken over an old multifloored warehouse and turned it into the coolest office in a twenty-block radius. Each floor managed or handled different parts of the business, but the top floor belonged to the Pack. Only those invited to the floor ever made it up there. The Pack simply couldn't take the chance of a full-human seeing something they really shouldn't see. So if you weren't on the list at the front desk, you didn't get in.

When their lunch arrived, Jess had no other option but to join in with her Pack and eat since they stood outside her office singing "Feelings" until she did. Cruel but effective. So while Phil played a computer game, May and Sabina surfed porn sites, and Danny zipped around the office on his skateboard by holding their dogs' leashes and letting them run, Jess ate her tuna on rye and wrote e-mails on her laptop.

"Danny," she said as Danny flew past her, "any word on the Bander account?"

"Weasel says it took him less than thirty minutes to get past their security. It was way too easy."

"Bring Weasel in. I want to talk to him." Weasel wasn't an actual weasel but a full-human who could hack into damn near anything. Jess figured out long ago it was best to work with the same guys she wanted to keep out of the systems her company secured. Hackers didn't usually ask for much—a couple of bucks, sometimes bottles of tequila or Jack Daniels, or computer equipment. And Jess had always gotten along better with the full-human geek males and females than the hoity-toity types whose money she took.

"And walk the dogs, Danny. Since you're using them for your own amusement."

"Will do."

The dogs looped around Sabina's desk in the back of the office and dashed down the last aisle toward the already open front doors. Jess had no idea how Danny did that. Of course, with her clumsiness factor, skateboarding with her dogs was a very quick way to break both her arms.

She watched Danny drop into a crouch so the wind resistance wouldn't slow down the dogs. A few more feet at top speed and once they hit the door, they'd ease off so that by the time they reached the elevator, Danny and the dogs would cruise right inside.

But about ten feet before the doorway, Jess suddenly smelled the dogs' fear as ripe and powerful as their bad breath. Then the two of them dashed off in separate directions. The power and suddenness of their move yanked Danny back and off the skateboard, which went airborne and slammed right into the head of the non-Pack male walking into the room.

There hadn't been many places in this big wide world that Bobby Ray Smith hadn't been able to charm his way into. Especially when there was an unattached female manning the front doors. But the pixie-like brunette with the adorable squeaky voice could not be charmed. Never rude, she still would not let him simply head to the boss' offices.

"I'm so sorry, sir, but you're not on the list," she'd told him in no uncertain terms. "No, can't call. They'd put you on the list if they wanted to talk to you," she'd insisted. "I am sorry, sir."

All said with a big grin and perfect white teeth.

Of course, Smitty wasn't the kind of guy who ever gave up. He was still trying to convince her to let him head on up when the elevator doors opened and a bleeding, battered Mace Llewellyn had to be helped into the lobby by one tiny little She-dog and several of her tiny little Pack.

"*What the hell happened?*"

"It was an accident!" At least she looked distressed by the situation. Even better, she looked like the Jessie Ann he remembered. Gone was the polished, pristine, *boring* Jessica Ward he'd seen on Friday and Saturday, and in her place was the geeky, "I'm still wearing my hair in ponytails" beauty he'd always liked. "We forgot he was coming up for the final check."

Smitty stepped in front of them, stopping their progress, and grabbed a handful of Mace's hair. He lifted the big cat's head and examined him closely. Not completely knocked out, but Mace was damn close with blood oozing down his face. "Well, good Lord, woman. What the hell did you hit him with, anyway?"

Jess cleared her throat. "A skateboard."

"Excuse me?"

She shook her head and kept moving forward. "You need to get him to a hospital. He was definitely out cold for a couple of minutes there." She stepped outside the building and glanced around. "Where's your car?"

"There."

"That's a 'no parking' space."

"You're going to argue that with me now?"

Smitty remotely unlocked the doors. Grabbing hold of Mace by his jacket, he lifted him away from Jessie and shoved him into the car, causing the man to moan a bit.

Jessie's Pack quickly retreated to the warmth of the lobby, watching them from behind the glass doors, leaving only Jessie standing outside in the cold. She twisted her hands in front of her. "I'm so sorry about this." She looked at Mace. "God, you don't think he'll have permanent brain damage, do you?"

"You'd never be able to tell if he did."

She scowled at Smitty. "Is this time to joke?"

"If you're that worried"—he opened the back passenger door—"come with us."

"Huh?" She glanced back at her Pack before shaking her head. "No. No. That's not necessary."

"You want him to pay the bills for this?"

"Of course—"

" 'Cause personally I'd like to avoid any legal problems stemming from this little episode."

"What? You'd sue—"

"Now, now, darlin'. Let's deal with Mace first." He gave her his best earnest look. "He's all that matters right now."

"But—"

He pushed her into the truck and closed the door, enjoying his good luck. True, his best friend had been wounded, but sacrifices sometimes had to be made.

Chapter 5

He's not quite sure how it happened. One second he was in an elevator heading up to a dog den for the final check from his company's recent job, secretly enjoying the fact that Smitty couldn't get past the front desk. The next he was flat on his back looking up at a bunch of dogs staring at him, horrified.

Two hours later, he had a face full of stitches and a raging Desiree, who had somehow backed a predatory male wolf into a corner.

Mace had to admit he was enjoying the show.

"Well, where the hell were you?"

"Uh . . ." Hands in his front jean pockets, Smitty glanced over at Mace. His big dumb dog eyes pleading for help, but Mace only grinned, ignoring the pull of stitches.

When Dez looked at Mace over her shoulder, his face dropped into an expression of pure pain.

"Look at him!" She shoved Smitty by the shoulder. "Look at that face!"

"It'll heal in a couple of days."

Oooh. Wrong answer.

Dez turned those gorgeous gray-green eyes on the wolf, and Mace watched Smitty do what any sensible predator would do in a situation like this . . .

Plot to run away.

"He'll heal? Is that what you said to me?"

"Well—"

"Because what if this wasn't some simple facial lacerations? What if someone had pulled a gun or put a knife to his throat?"

"Yeah, but—"

She took a step closer. At least five inches shorter than Smitty, she still would make any male wary. After the baby had been born, Mace really worried that side of his Dez had gone away. But one day back at her job and she was tougher. More dangerous.

Mace found it so hot.

"When he goes to work, I'm assuming you're protecting each other. That you're protecting *him*."

"Yeah, but he's king of the jungle."

Mace watched those eyes he loved so much narrow dangerously. Her hand curled into a fist. And Mace knew Dez had at least two guns on her.

Smitty swallowed, probably wondering who could move faster—Mace's money was on his woman and her ability to draw her weapon. Then the hospital door opened and Smitty took his chance.

"It's not my fault." He pointed at the wild dog who'd just walked into the room. "It's hers."

Dez spun around, nailing Jessica Ward to the spot. But after a moment, the two women grinned, squealed, and ran into each other's arms for a big hug.

"Jess!"

"Dez! Oh, my God, girl. How are you?"

"I'm fine. Fine." Dez pulled back. "Look at you, Miss Too Rich to Remember Her Friends."

"Oh, yeah, right. I was at the Christmas party at Moriharty's. Where were you?"

Dez smirked and nodded toward Mace. "I'd just bred his little demon seed."

Jess gasped in surprise. "You're a mother?" That question

was followed with another squeal that had both Smitty and Mace covering their ears in agony.

When Mace could hear again, the women were huddled over Dez's wallet and pictures of Marcus—and her dumb dogs. He glanced at Smitty, who mouthed, "Asshole." In response, Mace gave him the finger.

"So what happened?" Dez asked after the pair had gushed over how beautiful Marcus and those dumb dogs were.

"Bobby Ray is right," Jess admitted. "It was my fault. I forgot Mace was coming to the office, and Danny was doing his usual lunch thing by letting our dogs take him around the office on his skateboard. They love doing that. Anyway, with a lion suddenly appearing in the office, they got a little spooked."

Dez turned accusing eyes on Mace. "*You scared her dogs?*" she yelled.

"Wait. How did this become my fault?"

Jess stood around chatting with Dez until two more lions, mocking Llewellyn mercilessly, showed up. One of the big cats she knew: Brendon Shaw. Her company had done work for him on more than one occasion, she'd seen him at a few social events over the years, and the Pack's much-loved Long Island property butted right up against Marissa Shaw's and the Stark hyena Clan's territories.

With Shaw came his brother. Not as big but just as handsome. She'd never met him before, but he seemed pleasant enough.

The problem wasn't the brothers but the fact that Brendon brought flowers for Mace. As a joke sure, but Jess couldn't find it funny. Since her allergic reaction to flowers could be considered colossal. She had small zipped cases in her backpack and key strategic places she frequented that held her allergy pills, nasal spray, and even an inhaler for those worst-case scenarios. Unfortunately, she hadn't brought her backpack or coat with her. So she had no way of stopping one of her bouts unless she left the room in the next ninety seconds.

Not wasting any time, she whispered good-bye to Dez with promises to see her another time for lunch or dinner, before making her escape.

She pressed the button on the elevator and checked her e-mail from her phone. The elevator doors opened and she stepped inside. She pressed the ground floor button and went back to her phone. A rude reply from a rude client had her seeing blood red, and she immediately began typing a seriously vicious reply. Once she hit send it suddenly occurred to her the doors hadn't opened. She glanced up and realized the floor numbers didn't seem to be moving either.

"Took you long enough."

Startled by the low voice—and damn him that sexy slow drawl—Jess snarled and slammed her back against the opposite elevator wall.

"Jesus, Mary, and Joseph! Don't sneak up on me like that, Bobby Ray!"

"Sorry, darlin'. Didn't mean to startle you into blaspheming. Though I'm never quite sure how you don't know when someone's standing right next to you. We're supposed to have enhanced skills."

"I was taking care of something."

"So I could see. Man, those little fingers move fast."

"They're not little."

He grabbed hold of her right forefinger and lifted her hand. "Like a leprechaun's hands."

Trying not to notice how good his rough fingers felt on hers, she snatched her hand back. After all these years—and with her at a cool five feet nine inches—Smitty still called her small. Of course, compared to those linebackers he called She-wolves . . .

"They are not like a leprechaun's hands! Now, is there a reason you stopped the elevator?"

"I see you still have your allergy to flowers," he said, stunning her that he actually remembered after all these years. "Is that why you left the room without talking to me?"

"Talk to you?"

"Yeah, remember? I told you I wanted to talk to you."

"Okay." Resigned to her fate, Jess waited for him to say something. After a good three minutes of mutual staring, she realized that wouldn't be happening. "And what would you like to talk about, Bobby Ray?"

"First off, feel free to call me Smitty. Everyone does now. And second, I wanted to talk about you."

"What about me?"

"I'd like to know what you've been doing all this time. Where you went. How you got here."

Truly perplexed, she asked, "Why?"

" 'Cause I'm interested."

Jess gave a short shake of her head. "No."

"No?"

"No."

She hit the elevator button and the doors opened on the same floor, but Bobby Ray—Smitty—hit it again and the doors closed.

"What are you doing?"

"Trying to talk to you."

"I said no."

"Why not?"

"Is your sister in town with you?"

"Yeah, but—"

"And Ronnie Lee Reed?"

"Yeah, she is—"

"Then I have nothing to say."

She hit the elevator button again and so did Smitty. "What do they have to do with anything?"

"They made my life hell. For all I know, you guys are just setting me up for some cruel joke. I'll end up walking down the street like in *Carrie*, wearing a prom dress and covered in pig's blood."

Smitty shook his head. "I don't understand anything of what you just said."

"Yeah, I know. We've never spoken the same language."

"You mean English?"

"No, geek. Now if you'll excuse me . . ." Again, she hit the button. And again, so did he. "Would you stop doing that!"

"Then stop trying to rabbit away from me."

Frustrated and getting kind of worked up being trapped in such a small box with one testosterone-saturated male, Jess crossed her arms over her chest and braced her legs apart. "What do you want, Smith?"

He stared at her for a long moment before finally saying, "I thought we could hang out."

"Hang out?"

"Jessie Ann, we were friends. I'd like to continue that."

"Friends?" Now Jess stared. "You *are* setting me up. Did your sister put you up to this? Little more torture for the dog. For Spot?"

"I didn't know she called you that. And just leave her out of this. I'm talking about you and me spending some time together."

"Forget it."

"Why?"

"Because I'm not an idiot."

"Jessie Ann—"

"It's Jessica. Or Jess. No one calls me Jessie Ann."

"Except me."

"Look, are you letting me out of here, or do I have to start screaming for help?"

"If you don't want to go out with me, fine. But know that I'm not setting you up for anything. I wouldn't do that to you, Jessie Ann. You of all people should know that about me."

Smitty pushed the button once more and walked out when the doors opened. Jess stared after him and, with a sigh of great annoyance, followed.

Smitty stepped off the elevator and ignored the sighed, "Smitty. Wait."

Forced to use extreme measures and manipulations to get this difficult woman to give him what he wanted, Smitty utilized the hurt walk-away. It didn't work on his sister, but Ronnie Lee fell for it every time.

He headed toward Brendon and Mitch, who stood a few feet away raiding the vending machines, but he wasn't remotely surprised to feel Jessie's hand grab the sleeve of his jacket.

"Smitty, hold on a sec."

He raised his eyebrows to Shaw and Mitch before facing her. "What?"

"I wasn't trying to hurt your feelings."

"Then you did a mighty good job."

"Are you actually . . . you're serious? You're really upset?"

He just stared at her, making sure his expression didn't change. A cool move he'd learned from Mace years ago. Cats did have interesting skills, if you were willing to learn.

"Aw, Smitty, I wasn't trying to—"

Jessie stopped and looked over Smitty's shoulders at the two cats standing there doing what they all did so well . . . staring. And eating.

"Can I help you two with something?" she asked, obviously more than a little annoyed.

"No," Shaw answered. "We're fine."

"You just keep talking," Mitch added. "This is fascinating."

"No, fascinating is what I'm gonna do to that pretty face—"

Smitty grabbed Jessie's arms and pulled her back down the hallway toward the elevators. He'd forgotten about her temper. The girl could get mad at a bag of donuts.

"Now, now, Jessie Ann. Just calm down."

"I will not calm—ooh! Chocolate." And like that, Jessie wandered over to the nurses' station desk to look over bars of chocolate someone had out to sell for their child. She never did stay angry long.

Smitty remembered how it had taken him a while to figure out Jessie wasn't some flaky pup wandering from thing to thing, like most dogs, looking for a new smell or something to eat. Once she focused on something, absolutely nothing would distract her. But you had to be interesting enough to hold her attention; otherwise, she'd wander away in the middle of a sentence.

The thought that he might not be interesting enough to hold little Jessie Ann's attention had his back teeth grinding. He simply wouldn't allow her to dismiss him so easily. He wanted answers, dammit, and he'd get them.

Determined, he walked over to the desk and leaned against it while Jessie talked to the nurse manning the station.

"How much?" she asked.

"Dollar a piece. My son's class is trying to take a trip to DC this summer."

Jessie dug into her jeans pocket and pulled out a ten. "Here. I'll take five."

"Let me get you change."

"Nah, put it toward his trip."

The nurse smiled. "Thank you."

"You're welcome."

Carefully selecting from the bars in front of her, Jessie quickly had her five. She handed one to Smitty. "Caramel," she said simply.

She walked away and he stared at the candy in his hand. After all these years she remembered his favorite chocolate? He glanced at the stack left. There were chocolates with caramel and nuts. Caramel, nougat, and nuts. White chocolate with caramel. On and on it went. But he'd never liked any of that. He'd only liked chocolate-covered caramel.

Slowly, Smitty turned and looked at Jessie Ann. Really looked at her.

She was a bit taller now. Easily five-nine or so. Small for a wolf or most cats, tall for a full-human. Her jeans were everyday. No low riders with her underwear showing. She wore jeans to lounge in, not to entice. Her sneakers had seen better days, but she always liked to wear them until they literally fell off her feet. Her sweatshirt had COMIC-CON blazoned on both sides with a date nearly five years ago. And while standing in front of the elevator, she silently pretended her chocolate bars were

Samurai swords. He knew this because she took up a stance you'd see in any bad American remake of a great Japanese Samurai movie.

Unable to resist, he said softly, "Jessie Ann Ward, what are you doing?"

Startled, Jessie snapped to attention, lowering her arms and her chocolate "swords," and answered back, "Nothin'."

Smitty grinned. He'd forgotten how much he'd always enjoyed her. With her brains came her wackiness, and he enjoyed them both.

Sauntering over, Smitty said, "Come over for dinner tonight." She opened her mouth and he quickly promised, "Only me and you. No Sissy. No Ronnie Lee. No anybody."

Her adorable face scrunched up with indecision. "Smitty, I don't know—"

Now walking around her, "I'll make my momma's key lime pie. . . ."

"Nice try . . . but no."

"Fried chicken. Yams."

"I hate yams."

"Come on, Jessie Ann. What do I need to do to convince you—"

"Not be you."

An explosion of laughter behind them had the pair glaring at the two cats who quickly turned to examine the soda machine.

Jessie looked back at him. "Look, I know you're used to getting your way, but I'm not in the mood to play. I got a lot of—" Her phone rang, cutting her off. "Damn." She looked at the caller ID. "I've gotta go."

She pressed the elevator button. It opened immediately and Jessie stepped inside. "It was nice seeing you again, Smitty. Any more bills come up regarding Mace, just call our office. You'll be on the phone list—only."

Smitty watched the doors close. Did she really think it would be all that easy?

"Dis-*missed!*" Mitch said next to him.

"Brutally ignored," Brendon added. "That must have hurt. Deep inside."

Sure, he could agree, but that wouldn't work. And they were too big as human to take them on directly. But they forgot he had four older, much meaner brothers.

Smitty put his head down and let out a dramatic, shaky breath.

"Oh, bruh, come on. She's just a girl. Not even that cute."

"Yeah," Brendon agreed with his sibling as the pair moved closer to see if Smitty was crying. "You can do so much better."

Even as he grabbed the brothers by the backs of their necks and slammed their big lion heads together, he appreciated their sentiment.

Heading toward the stairs and Jessie, Smitty tossed over his shoulder at the felines lying on the floor, "Thanks, y'all. That was sweet."

Chapter 6

Jess ended her call and raised her hand; a cab stopped right in front of her. She'd just pulled the door open when a strong hand clasped around her bicep. Without thinking about it, she snarled, "Get your own damn cab, motherfuck—"

"Jessica Ann!"

Startled, she looked up at a still smirking Smitty. Christ, she couldn't shake this wolf to save her life! "What now? And get off me," she snapped, yanking her arm away.

"Since you won't have dinner with me, I thought we'd get some coffee."

And before she could tell him no, he had her by the scruff of her sweatshirt, dragging her to the Starbucks on the corner.

Although she welcomed the warmth once inside since she'd left her coat at the office, she still couldn't believe the nerve of Bobby Ray Smith.

"Two regular coffees," he said to the girl behind the counter.

"No." If she was stuck here, she might as well get what she wanted. "Grande latte with nonfat milk, extra hot."

"Latte? What kind of wuss drink is that?"

"Besides annoying me, is there something you specifically want?"

"Yup."

She waited for him to tell her what that was, but, as usual, he left the "yup" hanging there . . . all alone. Annoying her beyond all reason.

"What, Smitty? What do you want?"

"Are you always in this much of a rush?"

"Yes, I have things to do."

"Even the Lord takes a break."

"Yeah, well, the Lord doesn't have my overhead."

Smitty grabbed the two drinks, and when he pulled her to a back table that's when Jess realized he still had a good grip on her sweatshirt.

"You know, I can walk without your assistance."

"Don't want you running out on me again. I know how fast you move."

He pushed her into a chair and sat across from her.

"Here's your fou-fou drink." He placed it in front of her. "And my manly regular coffee." He sipped it and made a satisfied "ahhh" sound that made her want to twist his nipples off.

"What do you want?" she asked yet again.

"Let's start off easy. What do you do?"

"What do I do about what?"

"I see 'easy' is still lost on you. I mean, what do you do, Jessie Ann? What pays for your precious overhead?"

"Systems security."

"Which means what exactly?"

She went to stand up and she saw him tense. Would he actually chase her down? Would she mind?

"Stay," she commanded before walking over to the counter that held all the necessary condiments for coffee drinkers. She grabbed a handful of brown-sugar and saccharine packets, wood stirrers, a metal container holding cream, and napkins, but the napkins were really for her since she had a tendency to wear her liquids as much as drink them.

Sitting back down, she placed the creamer on the table. "This is your company. See how it's unprotected? All alone in the big bad world. And look, it's saccharine coming to attack." Jess placed several of the blue packets down, aimed toward the creamer. Then she broke the sticks in half and gave them swords. "See? They're armed and dangerous." She placed the brown-sugar packets between the creamer and the saccharine. "But look! It's the sugars coming to protect us!" Now, thoroughly enjoying herself, she gave the sugar packets swords too. "Saccharine charges"—she moved the packets forward—"but the sugars battle them back with skill and the darkness within us all. They're not afraid to kill and destroy in the name of justice—and cold, hard cash."

Jess grinned, extremely pleased with her presentation. But when she looked up at Smitty, he sat there with his elbow on the table, his chin resting in the palm of his hand, and he was staring at her.

"What?" she demanded. "That's not clear?"

Dang but she was cute. Cute as hell. Even when making absolutely no sense with her sugar packets and little sticks. "No, it's not clear."

Rolling her eyes, she sat back in her chair like a disgruntled child. "We create security systems for companies to protect them from your run-of-the-mill hackers to hardcore identity thieves," she quickly rattled off. "We do hard coding, create software, and can even train a company's IT people to help a company protect themselves. We have a lot of overseas clients, and the government has used us on occasion to train their people or to give advice. But we make them nervous, so they won't give us any clearance. I blame Danny. But that's another story. There? Happy now?"

"Why didn't you say all that in the first place?"

"I gave you swords and a battle. A hero and an enemy. A defenseless damsel in distress. I gave you the makings of a terrific tale to tell your children."

"All right then."

"Forget it." She glanced at her watch. "Look, I've really got to—"

"Lord, Jessie." He reached across the table and grabbed her hand, pulling her arm out until he could look at her watch. "That's a lot of watch for a little gal. What do you need it for?"

"To tell time."

"I've seen admirals with the same watch. You planning on attacking those deadly saccharine packets by sea?"

Her eyes narrowed the tiniest bit and Smitty wondered how long before she decked him.

"Is there anything else you want?" *That's a nicely loaded question.* "Or can I go now?"

"Sure, you can go."

"Thank you," she said in an exasperated sigh. Then she pushed her chair back and stood.

As Jessie walked past him, he added, "I understand you're afraid."

Not surprisingly, she froze in her tracks. Even when he had to coax her from trees, Jessie would get insulted if he even suggested she might be afraid. To her, hiding in trees and under bleachers was merely a preventive measure that any sensible person would do. "Excuse me?"

"You're afraid. I completely understand." He patted her hand like he would his grandmother. "It's all right. You go on now."

She took two steps back until she stood right next to him. "Afraid of what?"

"Of your feelings for me. That's why you're fighting me so hard."

"I do not have feelings for you—other than hatred."

"Now, Jessie Ann, we've always been honest with each other. Just admit you still want me—after all these years."

She threw up her hands. "I'm walking away from this conversation."

He figured. But he simply couldn't help himself. It was such fun torturing her.

Smitty jumped up and followed after her. As he reached the door she'd already gone through, she was suddenly back, her small body slamming into his.

"What's wrong?"

"Uh . . ." She looked back and then shoved him onto a small couch. Sitting down next to him, she grabbed his arm and yanked it over her shoulders. "Now just sit there and look pretty."

A few moments later, three men walked through the door. Two were full-human, but the one whose eyes locked on Jessie . . .

Immediately, Smitty recognized the wild dog from Saturday night.

"Jessica! Hello!"

Jessie smiled and it had to be the fakest thing Smitty had seen since he went to Los Angeles on a business trip. "Sherman. Hi!"

Her forced cheeriness made Smitty's back teeth ache, but the dog seemed to buy it.

"What are you doing here? Shouldn't you be hard at work as always?"

"Oh, I was. I was." Jessie waved her hand dismissively. "But I was just taking a little break with my . . . uh . . . friend here."

"Now, Jessie Ann, don't play coy." Smitty nuzzled her neck. "You know I'm your boyfriend now."

As Jessie went tense all over, the male dog went from big and dumb to resentful in a heartbeat—like Smitty had dug up his favorite bone from the backyard. Didn't he get that Jessie had no interest in him? How could she? The woman deserved better than some scrawny dog. Unfortunately for the dog, he wasn't "getting it," forcing Smitty to make it clear as crystal. So when that resentful doggy gaze moved from Smitty teasing Jessie's neck to his hand, Smitty let his hand drop—right on Jessie's breast.

Jessie let out a sharp breath, and the dog asked, "Well, Jessica. Why don't you introduce me to your boyfriend?"

"Of course." Jessie casually took the hand lying on her breast with hers and when she curled her fingers into his palm, she unleashed her claws.

Smitty grunted, but that was all. He'd kind of seen that one coming. But, dammit, it had been for her own good. And he'd go to his grave saying that.

"Sherman Landry, this is Bobby Ray Smith. Bobby Ray, this is Sherman Landry."

The dog already had his hand out for Smitty to shake, but it fell back at his side as he stared at him. Smitty had seen it before. That look. A look of fear and panic. And he knew the next words that would come out of the dog's mouth.

"You're a Smith?"

"Yes, sir."

"Of the Smith . . . *Pack?*"

And there it was. A Smith could be any ol' body. But a member of the Smith Pack, one of the direct bloodline, brought out all sorts of reactions from other shifters. Some looked down on them and others looked horrified. That one small phrase, "Of the Smith Pack?" followed Smitty around like stink on a pig.

"Yes, sir, I surely am of the Smith Pack. The Tennessee Smiths."

"I see. Well, it's very nice to meet you. Jessica, can I speak with you for a second?"

"Well, as you see—"

"Now."

This had been what she'd been trying to avoid—time alone with Sherman Landry. Like most obsessive dogs that chased the same car every day, went after the same cat, slammed into the same mirror because they didn't seem to grasp the only other dog in the room was themselves, Sherman wouldn't quite give up on her. She really wished he would. He'd sent flowers to the office that morning, even though she'd told him about her allergies. How could Smitty remember sixteen years after the fact, but this idiot forget after two days?

He grabbed her hand and pulled her outside Starbucks into the cold, completely oblivious to the fact that she had no coat in ten-degree weather. Then he started rambling and she had a hard time focusing. Not merely because of the cold, but really because a tit grab had never felt so good before and Smitty hadn't even squeezed.

"I'm not sure what the problem is, Sherman," she snapped, too cold to bother being polite any longer.

"Jessica, do you know who you're sitting with?"

"Well, since I just introduced him to you, I have a vague idea."

"I don't mean who he is. I mean who he is." A physicist with several government contracts under his belt and a tenured position complete with his own lab at the local, blindingly expensive small university, Sherman still had the amazing ability of sounding like a complete idiot.

"And who is he?"

"He's a Smith. I thought he was just a wolf, but he's a Smith. What are you thinking?"

I'm thinking the man can palm my breast anytime. "I'm not sure what you mean. What am I thinking about what?"

"Jessica"—to her great annoyance, he took her elbow and led her farther away from the coffeehouse—"Smiths are, at the very least, not good for a woman's reputation."

"My reputation?" Had she actually portaled to another time and dimension? Where women actually had to worry about their reputations.

"I know. I know. You don't think about those things, but you need to. Smiths are infamous womanizers."

She'd never call Smith males "womanizers." Although she would call them whores.

"I see."

"And," Sherman said in all doglike seriousness, "they're dangerous, Jessica. Unstable. Even other wolves avoid them."

"I had no clue." Sure, she could explain to Sherman how she'd grown up around Smiths and knew them better than most. She could also explain how Smitty and she used to be friends. But all that would require her to spend more time with the man, seconds of her life she'd never get back.

Forcing herself not to glance impatiently down at her watch, she said, "I'll talk to my Pack about it."

"Of course. Because God forbid you should move without their permission."

It was the venom with which he made that statement that had

her eyes narrowing to slits. Her Pack only wanted her to be happy. For instance, they sure as fuck wouldn't let her stand out in the cold so they could lecture her.

The coffeehouse door opened and Smitty walked out, heading right toward them. She hadn't been this relieved to see the man since he dragged Bertha off her while she was pummeling Jess's face.

Smitty glanced down at her, and she knew he'd immediately caught on to her rapidly growing anger. Taking her arms, he pulled them around his waist and pulled her in tight to his body. His jacket and body heat kept her warm; his embrace kept her from tearing out Sherman Landry's throat.

"Everything all right out here?" Smitty asked.

"Yes," she said out loud. Under her breath, she added, "Make him go away."

"Leave it to me," he muttered back. "Well," he said clearly, for the entire street to hear, "we're going to go home now and have some hot and dirty sex."

Jess let out a startled gasp and tried to pull back, but Smitty held her tight against him.

"Yup," he continued, "we're gonna go have some nasty, dirty, whore sex."

Even with her face buried in his—very nice smelling—chest, Jess could still sense when Smitty locked his sights on Sherman.

"And you're not invited."

"Jessica," Sherman tried again, "maybe we should—"

"Son," Smitty drawled, "don't make me show you how much of a Smith I truly am."

Sherman cleared his throat. "I'll speak with you another time, Jessica." She heard his footsteps heading back to the coffeehouse.

When Sherman opened the door, Smitty tossed out, "Just don't call her when we're having sex—which will be constantly!"

Jess waited long enough for Sherman to get inside before she yanked away from Smitty and followed up with a solid fist to his chest. The pain that radiated up her arm afterward, she ignored.

"*What is wrong with you?*"

"Nothin'," he said, looking confused. "Why?"

Smitty wasn't sure what he enjoyed more. Torturing that scrawny dog—and he had tortured him. The poor guy didn't know whether to be horrified or jealous of Smitty and Jessie going at it. Or had his pleasure come from torturing Jessie Ann? All that was fun, but what he enjoyed the most was having Jessie Ann plastered up against him. She nuzzled real nice, even when she didn't mean to.

At the moment, however, she looked real cranky.

"I was helping like you asked."

"You were being a dick," she said while looking down at the giant watch on her wrist. "And you were enjoying every damn second of being a—oh, my God! I've gotta go."

She ran to the corner and hailed a cab, but before she stepped inside, she ran back over to him.

"One other thing."

"Yeah?"

She slid her hand under his jacket and twisted his nipple until his eyes watered.

"Touch my tits again without permission and I'll rip this off." She glanced at her watch again. "Ach! Now I really do have to go."

Jessie turned and ran back toward the waiting cab. Sure, Smitty could have let her go, but to be honest, he'd never been so damn entertained by a woman before. "So how do I get permission?"

She spun around, jumping back when she realized he stood right behind her. "Stop sneaking up on me! And you don't get permission."

"Why not? You said I was pretty."

"Look, Smitty, while I appreciate your doglike persistence,

you need to know that nothing you do or say will change my mind about this. You're part of my past, and these days I'm all about my future. I don't have time or room in my life for you and your casual chats. Understand?"

"Sure."

"Good."

" 'Cause I always love a challenge."

He'd caught her with that when she was halfway in the cab. With one foot in and the other still braced against the curb, she stared at him. "What challenge?"

"You're challenging me to get you back into my life."

"No, I'm not."

"Your exact words were 'I challenge you, Bobby Ray Smith, to get me back into your life.' "

"I never said that."

"That's what I heard." The beauty of wolf hearing. You heard only what you wanted to, made up what was never said but should have been, and the rest meant little or nothing.

"Is there something wrong with you? Mentally?"

"Darlin', you met my family. You've gotta be more specific than that."

"That's it. I'm leaving. I can't have this conversation with you. I can't—"

He saw it immediately. The way her entire body tensed, her eyes focusing across the busy city street, locking on something in the distance. She went from exasperated to on point in less than five seconds.

"What's wrong, Jessie?" He followed her line of sight but didn't see anything that stuck out to him.

"Nothing," she said, her eyes still staring across the street. "I need to go." She went up on her toes and absently kissed him on his cheek. He'd bet cash she wouldn't even remember she did it.

She stepped into her cab and closed the door. She didn't look back at him, didn't acknowledge him in any way. That wasn't like her. Even if it was to give him the finger, she'd do or say something before driving off.

Smitty turned and stared at the spot Jessie'd been staring at. But he still saw nothing that made him feel tense or worried.

So what the hell had worried his little Jessie Ann?

As soon as Jess stepped off the elevator, her friends made a run for it. They got away except the one she wanted to catch anyway.

"Jess! Be reasonable!" She dragged Phil into her office by his collar and slammed the door. She had about ten minutes before the others would sneak back in. She had to make this fast.

Phil, however, was busy defending his actions of deserting her with a crazy hillbilly wolf. "We figured we all didn't need to go to the hospital with you."

"Shut up about that. I've got a question for you."

"What?"

"Do you remember Walt Wilson?"

Phil thought for a second. "The name sounds familiar . . ."

"Kristan's biological father." And the man who'd unceremoniously dumped an eighteen-year-old Maylin because "That thing inside you ain't mine."

"Oh. Him," Phil sneered. "What about him?"

"I think I saw him."

"In New York?"

"No, in space."

"Okay. Sarcasm a little unwarranted."

Jess paced to the big window behind her desk. She rarely looked out it. She rarely had time.

"You sure it was him?"

"No, but I think it was. I saw his picture once in May's photo album. She kept only one picture of him so Kristan would know what he looked like." She frowned. "He's lost a lot of hair for a wolf. Got a giant receding forehead."

"I don't think foreheads can recede."

"You're gonna argue this with me?"

"Whoa. Is all this tenseness about Walt Wilson?" Phil grinned. "Or about that big ol' country wolf?"

When Jess pretended to lunge for him across her desk, Phil wrapped his arms around his chest. "Not the nipples!"

"Track Wilson down," Jess told him. "If he's in town, I wanna know."

"Okay."

"I find the timing of his appearance a little suspect, Phil."

"I was thinking that."

"And I won't have Kristan hurt. Not by this asshole. But keep your mouth shut until we know something."

Phil walked around the desk and stood beside her, mimicking her stance. "What else is wrong?"

"Wilson is a bigger problem than any of you realize." She let out a breath. "He's a Smith. Distant cousin or something. I'm not sure of the bloodline, but it's there."

"Great. Just great."

"Yeah, you know how the Smiths are about family. And if they think we're crossing him—"

"Let's not go there yet. I'll see what I can find out and I'll be discreet."

"Good."

"Besides, I wouldn't worry." Phil grinned. "We've got the Smitty hookup now."

"I'm not asking him to go against his family, you bonehead."

"Awww. You're protecting him. Is love in the air? I bet you just need a little help from me to get this thing moving. Just trust the love doctor to—and don't throw anything at my head!"

Jess put the five-inch pewter dragon statue back on her desk. "Don't irritate me, Phil."

"Yes, ma'am. But you know Wilson may just be here to see the kid." Phil shrugged. "Maybe he already has."

"I thought about that." Jess sat back on her desk. "But she's either with Keith"—Sabina and Phil's oldest boy"—or her sisters."

"You don't think they'd cover for her?"

"No way. No one's stupid enough to cover for Kristan's crazy ass."

* * *

Johnny moved his book to the side so the waitress could put down his burger and fries. He'd never been big on the fantasy stuff. He liked westerns and murder mysteries. But Jess went on and on about Tolkien's work, and to shut her up, he grabbed one of the many copies from the many bookshelves all over the Pack house. Johnny had to give it to her, though, the book was really good. He'd enjoyed the movies, but Tolkien's written word spoke to him on another level entirely.

"Hello? Calling bonehead." Annoyed, Johnny pulled his gaze away from the book and into the pretty face of Kristan Jade Putowsky.

"What?"

"I need you to do me a favor."

"Not on your life."

He returned his focus to the book, but Kristan's hand slapped down over it, covering the page. "Please?"

"What?"

"I need you to cover for me."

"Cover for you?"

"Yeah, you gotta go rehearse or practice or whatever, right?"

Every weeknight, Johnny spent three to four hours practicing on his violin. Jess had actually rented him rehearsal space at a nearby music studio.

"Yeah. So?"

"If they ask later, just say I was with you. You usually get home around nine, right? I'll meet you out front at nine."

"Forget it."

"Come on, Johnny. Please?"

"No."

"I'd cover for you. I'll owe you one. I promise."

"Why?"

"Why what?"

"Why do you need a cover?"

"Can't you do this for me without asking a bunch of questions?"

"No."

She leaned over the table and he caught her scent. That scent drove him crazy. *She* drove him crazy.

"Johnny, come on. Please."

It had to be a guy. He knew a few at their school who'd give their left nut to be with her. He definitely didn't like the thought of her with another guy. Any guy. But she showed him absolutely no interest, and alienating her now didn't get him any closer. At least this way, if he covered for her, they could remain friends. Important with them living together and all.

He stared into those brown eyes and realized he could deny her nothing, fool that he was.

"Nine o'clock. At the corner. You're a minute late and you're screwed."

Kristan squealed and kissed him on the cheek. "Thank you!"

Spoiled princess. He should hate her. She'd grown up loved and cared for with a Pack that adored her. But he didn't hate her. If anything, he had it for her bad. But the way her father, Danny, watched him, that would never be happening unless Johnny decided living wasn't one of his favorite things to do.

Resigned to a life of sexual frustration until he was old enough to go to college and get away from Kristan Putowsky, Johnny went back to his book and his burger.

Jess, already wearing the headset that went with her office phone, simply hit the answer button without even bothering to look away from the e-mail she was drafting on her computer.

"This is Jessica."

"So you going to tell me what happened earlier or do I have to guess?"

Shocked, Jess stared at the phone display. "How the hell did you get my personal number?" It wasn't listed and only the Pack had it. Even those in the building couldn't contact her through this particular line, and it wasn't billed under her own name. In fact, more people had her personal cell phone number than her private business line. That was the only reason she answered it at nine o'clock at night anyway.

"I can't really answer that," Smitty replied.

"Well, lose it. And stop calling me."

"I can't help you, Jessie Ann, until you tell me what's going on."

"Who asked for your help? I'm relatively certain I never asked for your help. And I never will."

Besides, as irritated as she was from hearing that slow drawl and sweet-as-molasses voice on her private phone line, she still wouldn't drag Smitty into this, whatever "this" was. The Smith credo was a simple one. Family first. Pack second. Everyone else dead last. If you were a blood relation to the Smiths, they'd come from all over the States to step in on your behalf. For that reason alone, the other shifters gave the Smiths a wide berth. Just one Smith was dangerous, but a whole swarm of them would be lethal.

For one Smith to go against that for an outsider would bring the wrath of Bubba Smith down on Smitty's head. She couldn't do that to him. He and his father had a difficult relationship. She wouldn't add to it.

Jess rubbed her eyes. Wait. Why did she give a shit about Smitty's relationship with his father? Had she lost her mind? She was getting sucked back in. Back into the insanity known as the Smith Pack.

"I appreciate you wanting to help," she said, trying a different tack with him. "But there's nothing I need help with. Everything is fine."

The pause that followed was long, and for a moment she thought she'd lost the connection.

Until Smitty said, "You're lying to me, Jessie Ann. And I'm gonna find out why."

"And why is that? Because you clearly need a hobby—and a girlfriend?"

"No, because that's what friends do for friends. We help each other out. And no matter what you think, we're still friends."

"What planet are you living on anyway?"

"I don't know. But it's nice. There are fire hydrants everywhere—and bunnies!"

Jess snorted, fighting hard to keep in her laugh. Damn him! He always could make her laugh. Like when he'd found her hiding in an air duct that time after the Friday homecoming bonfire. She'd planned on staying there the whole night until the liquor wore off with Sissy's She-bitches. But he'd coaxed her out with jokes and the promise of one of those giant Hershey bars. Then he made sure she got home safe.

Years later and he was still trying to protect her. Except now she didn't need it.

"I've gotta go, Bobby Ray." She was glad he couldn't see her face. Her smile would do nothing but prompt his continued efforts. "Don't call me again. Don't try and 'help' me. Just get on with your life—and be happy."

When he didn't say anything, Jess disconnected the call, glanced at her watch, and went right back to work.

Smitty walked back to the surveillance truck, Jessie's last words to him playing again and again in his head.

His sister sat on the edge of the truck floor, her back against one of the open doors. They had a job this evening involving some foreign businessmen, but so far all had been calm. The perfect job, really. Low on danger, high on payment.

"Break time?" he asked.

Sissy sipped coffee and nibbled on coffeecake. "Yes, I'm not lazing off."

"I just asked."

"It was the way you asked." Sissy watched him for a moment. "What's the matter with you?"

"Nothing. Why?"

"You've got a weird look on your face."

"Can I ask you a question?"

"If you must."

Smitty took her coffee and sipped it. "Do you care if I'm happy?"

"No." Sissy took her coffee back. "And get your own."

"Fine." He swiped up her slice of coffeecake, and as she made a wild grab for it, he shoved the entire thing into his mouth.

"There," he said, making sure he spit crumbs at her. "I got my own."

Chapter 7

Smitty had just begun to sign paychecks when Mace walked in his office.

"Do you know anything about this art museum job that just called?"

"Nope. What art museum job?"

"They want us tonight."

"Not enough time," Smitty answered, not looking up from the paychecks in front of him.

"We need to make enough time."

"Why?"

Mace laid a slip of paper on top of the checks he'd been signing.

Smitty stared. "Huh. Look at all those zeroes."

The cat grinned. "Yeah, just look at 'em."

"Where'd this job come from anyway?"

"An old tiger who's on the board for the museum told me he was strongly urged to hire us for tonight's charity event."

"Urged?"

"*Strongly* urged."

"By . . . ?"

Mace shrugged, already walking off to start pulling the team together. "Some guy named Phil."

Smitty stared down at the checks still needing to be signed. "Phil who?"

Jess took off her coat and handed it over to the girl behind the counter. Then she did what she'd been doing for the last hour—she tugged down the hem of her dress again. If you could call it a dress. It was more of a slip for an underdeveloped twelve-year-old.

"I can't believe you talked me into this damn dress," she muttered to Phil, slamming him with her shoulder. "I'm at a charity event, but I feel like I should be offering fifty bucks for a hand job and hundred bucks for a half and half."

"No, sweetie. The way you look? It should be a hundred bucks for the hand job and three hundred for the half and half."

Jess glared at him so hard that eventually he started to squirm.

"If it helps, the shoes look great."

Tossing up her hands in exasperation, she stormed off into the main area of the museum. The sooner she got in and mingled, the sooner she could get the hell out.

Smitty smiled an apology and quickly walked away from the full-human female who'd just offered to give him a blow job in the bathroom. Good Lord! These rich women were . . . *scary*. He'd had all sorts of interesting offers in the last two hours from women dripping in diamonds and platinum. One woman propositioned him with her husband only a few feet away. Smitty got the distinct feeling that if he'd taken her up on the offer, the husband would have been in some other room watching. Well, whatever got your rocks off. Although Smitty never could figure out why you'd marry someone if you were willing to share her.

He walked up to Mitch and let out a breath. "Have you been—"

"Offered sex every time I turn around? Yeah. I tell ya, full-human females have their place."

"Dez is full-human and Mace had to work to get her. I think

it's a money thing. The more money they have, the less vulnerable they feel. We're just cocks, son, and don't you forget it."

"I don't. And I don't care, but I learned the hard way you don't fuck around during work. It leads to all sorts of trouble."

"Ain't that the truth."

Marissa Shaw, Mitch's older sister, Mace's twin, and one of the stranger lionesses Smitty had known, slid to a graceful stop in front of the pair.

"Smitty."

"Marissa, darlin'. You are looking gorgeous this evening."

She reached up and petted his cheek. "Aren't you just the sweetest canine." She glared at her brother. "Loser."

"Fat ass."

The pair snarled at each other before Marissa walked away.

"I thought you two were getting along better."

Mitch stared at him blankly. "We are. Can't you tell?"

Smitty shook his head as his eyes swept around the giant room. They were in the Italian Renaissance room. Whatever. It paid well.

"Holy mother of God."

Smitty's body tensed, anticipating trouble. "What? What's wrong?"

"Nothing. Not a goddamn thing."

Following Mitch's avid gaze, Smitty turned and his entire body tensed. "Lord help me."

Jessie Ann walked into the room with her four friends behind her. Apparently, the rest of the Pack banged out of this little event. Of course, as much as the tickets for this cost per person, Smitty didn't blame them for not including the whole gang. Still, Jessie had definitely come up in the world—right along with her skirt length.

Good Lord! What was the woman thinking? It was a freezing New York night, and dammit, there were decency laws! Where the hell was the rest of that dress? And why wasn't she in her jeans, tennis shoes, and T-shirt? Why was she damn near naked?

"Think if I asked her nice she'd marry me?"

"Get control of yourself, cat. We're on a job."

"I quit." Mitch started to walk over there and Smitty yanked him back by the hair.

"Sweep the area, son, before I get cranky."

"Fine, but you don't stand a chance in hell either. If memory serves, she shot your ass down like a jet over enemy territory."

"Sweep. The. Area."

With one last look at Jess that almost got him popped in the face, Mitch walked off.

Smitty thought about going over there that second, if for no other reason than to throw a coat over her, but he knew better. Jessie was a "runner." One of those dogs that would take off running for no real reason and suddenly find themselves in Utah. So, taking a deep breath, and with one last look at those legs, he buried himself in the crowd of people.

Jess had been listening to the conversation between Marissa Shaw and the head female of the Stark hyena Clan for the past ten minutes and she was starting to get really pissed. Her Pack knew it too. They stood around her, waiting for her to do something. True, the whole thing wasn't any of her business, but still . . .

"So this canine your brother is living with," said Madeline Stark as she shoveled yet another pâté-covered cracker in her mouth. "Does she sit on command? Fetch his slippers? Roll over and beg when appropriate?"

Madeline's four boneheaded sisters and cousin continued snickering, sounding like that cartoon dog Muttley.

What Jess found really funny was that they were all neighbors. The Pack's Long Island property butted right up against Marissa Shaw's and the Stark Clan's territories. Yet, they never got along. True, the Pack tolerated Marissa to a degree, but they never tolerated the Starks. Wild dogs hated hyenas.

Jess's eyes focused on the back of Madeline's neck as she continued to mock the canine universe. She had her light brown hair swept up off her shoulders and in an elaborate knot on her head. Giving Jess all that long neck to play with.

Facing her Pack, Jess started coughing. Phil caught on first, grinning and turning toward the table. His wife joined him, the pair taking a small white cocktail napkin and shredding it. Still coughing, Jess stepped closer to Phil and he placed the tissue in her hand. Danny glanced around and then poured water on the shreds, getting it good and wet.

Jess turned back around, still supposedly hacking up a lung. She walked up behind Madeline and let out a cough that had Marissa tensing and looking at her. That's when Jess let that wet, messy napkin fly. It hit the back of Madeline's neck and the woman froze in mid-mock.

"Oh!" Jess said, clearing her throat. "Oh, my God! Madeline! I'm so sorry. Here, let me help you clean that off."

Horrified, the woman reached back and touched the wet tissue on her neck. Unable to see it, she could only *feel* it. As soon as her fingers brushed it, her body began to shake and she retched violently before she took off running toward the bathroom, her sisters and cousin following behind. Following and laughing hysterically.

Jess looked at Marissa. "Well, that'll be awkward next time we're all out on the Island, huh?"

Marissa, who always seemed an unpleasant woman and was definitely not friendly, stared at Jess for several long seconds before her lips turned up and she grinned. Then she started laughing and couldn't stop. She quickly walked over to two lionesses from the Llewellyn Pride, Mace's sisters Serita and Allie. Between bouts of hysterical laughter, she spoke to them until all three women were laughing.

May handed Jess a glass of champagne. "You had way too much fun with that, sweetie."

"I did, didn't I?"

Could it legally be considered "stalking" if he watched her for her own good? She was blowing fake lugies at hyenas, on her third glass of champagne, and wearing those killer shoes. What else could Smitty do but keep an eye on her?

He would say, though, that the dogs knew how to enjoy what would otherwise be a painfully dull party. They seemed to be entertained by the simplest things, and at times, they seemed to have the sexual maturity of thirteen-year-olds based on the way they giggled over a rather well-endowed statue. Of course, that could also be the champagne.

Smitty leaned against the wall and checked in with his team. All seemed well, although he no longer found that surprising. They were becoming a well-oiled machine, and a few more jobs like this and they might actually finish out the year in less debt than they already were. In a couple more years, he might be able to come to events like this as a guest rather than as staff.

His eyes strayed back to Jessica. Once again, she hadn't noticed him. Truly. No "faking that I haven't seen him" either. She really hadn't seen him. The woman was completely oblivious.

Some old Latin music came on and the same blond wild dog from Jessie's party the week before took Jessie's hand and pulled her into some rather good dance moves. Smitty's eyes narrowed. What was it with that guy and "dancing" with Jessie? Seemed more like an excuse to get his paws on her. Although, Smitty grudgingly had to admit, the man did seem loyal to the blond female he kept hanging around. Maybe it was a dog thing.

The blonde spun Jessie out and then expertly pulled her back in, before having the nerve to dip her. Smitty briefly wondered how many of the men there were trying to look up Jessie's dress.

That was it. He had to say something. The woman was a menace to herself!

Champagne in hand, Jess pulled away from her Pack and headed toward the buffet table, debating whether she felt like eating standing up or not. You'd think for ten thousand bucks a plate they'd have a sit-down dinner. Still, she'd have given them the money anyway. For a kid's charity, she could do nothing less. Pushing through the crowd, amazed at the turnout, Jess stopped when a male voice called her name.

"Jessica! Jessica!" She cringed and turned to face Sherman

Landry. She'd completely forgotten he'd probably attend this event, but Phil and Sabina had insisted she needed to come.

"Hi, Sherman." When he stood in front of her, she gave him a big forced smile. "How are you?" she asked.

"Fine. Fine. And you?"

"I'm fine."

"And your wolf friend?"

Lie, Jessica. Lie! "Oh, he's around here somewhere."

"I assume you had to pay for his ticket."

Jess didn't answer; instead, she used her forefinger to rub away the sudden tic in her left eye.

"You don't see many Smiths around these kinds of events," Sherman continued. "They're much more your beer and NASCAR crowd."

Jess's eyes narrowed, suddenly envisioning Sherman not as a true wild dog but one of those pampered pups sitting on a pillow. A bichon frise or a papillon. Imagining him with bows in his hair did make her smile.

"I love NASCAR," she admitted, hoping the truth would make him go away. "It's fun, the people are nice, and it has fast cars. I love fast cars."

"Yes, yes. Nothing like watching people drive in a circle." Before Jess could say anything—like "fuck you"—Sherman stepped back as far as he could in this crowd and smiled appreciatively. "Jessica, I must say you look gorgeous."

"Thank you." She'd kill Phil.

"You take my breath away."

"Sherman, that's very sweet. Thanks."

He cleared his throat. "I was wondering . . ." Another throat clear. "About us going out again. For dinner?"

"Dinner? Um . . ." *Think of an excuse. Think fast!* "Uh . . . Smitty." She took in a deep breath. "I can't 'cause I'm seeing Smitty." *There. That'll work.*

"Jessica, seriously." He stepped closer. A little too close. "I've discussed this with my sister and we both understand a girl has needs." His sister? He'd talked about this with his sister? Suddenly, Jess felt a tad ill. "And wolves are perfect for the short term. But you're not getting any younger."

Wait. Did he just say that to me? No, no. He couldn't have.

"You have to think about the future of your Pack. I'm sure you'll want to breed pups of your own. *Normal* pups. Not hybrids. I believe you and I have much to discuss in that area."

Jess stared at him. She couldn't help it. Apparently the presence of Smitty had pushed Sherman's hand. Instead of romance, though, she got the word "breeding" tossed at her.

"Jessica . . ."

He moved in closer, and to her horror, she thought he might kiss her. But her phone rang and she yanked it out of her tiny designer purse with an urgency she'd never felt before.

"Phone! I must answer my phone."

"Yes, but—"

"Bye now." Jess turned and walked away, answering the phone at the same time.

"Yes?"

"Hi, Jess. It's Bets." Her assistant. Someone would be getting a quarterly bonus for saving her wild-dog ass from more breeding discussions.

"What's up, Bets?"

Betsy went into a litany of problems with one of their accounts while Jess headed toward the bathrooms. This problem was not normally something that would work its way up to Jess, but the client was pissed and she brought in a lot of serious money and other important accounts. It would not be in their best interest to ignore this woman.

"Can you put me through to her?"

Standing outside the ladies' room, Jess leaned against a wall and waited for her call to be patched into a very nice office in Detroit.

Once she had her, Jess went into her usual soothing spiel. She'd gotten really good at it. Must have had something to do with working with cops for a few years. They'd come busting into her department, anxious, annoyed, and usually pissed off at some ADA, wanting to know what she'd found on some scumbag's computer. At that point, Jess had two options: get pissy right back, which a lot of her coworkers did, or soothe. She soothed, and to this day she still had friends on the force who watched out for her, her company, and her friends.

As Jess listened to her client and made lots of "I absolutely agree with you" noises, she turned and realized she had the females of the Stark Clan standing there, glaring at her. Their eyes glowed in the low light of the narrow hallway.

"Think that was funny, did you?" Madeline practically snarled.

In answer, Jess held up one finger. "Give me a sec, hon," she whispered, "until I'm done with this client."

The hyenas blinked in shock. They always expected some first attack from her. She wasn't a wolf. She only did a first attack when her pups were in danger. Then all hell broke loose. But some bullshit show of strength? That could wait.

"Hey. I'm speaking to you."

Jess smiled and nodded in agreement. They hated when she did that. She saw a fang, but then Marissa Shaw came up behind them and slammed her hands against Madeline Stark's back.

Now lionesses? Yeah, those big cats were all about the first attack.

Jess stepped back and out of the way of the yearly fight that would most likely ensue between the females. While she did, she continued to keep the conversation going with her client. Living with her Pack, one learned to multitask.

"You gotta problem, bitch," Marissa growled, baring enormous fangs. "You can bring it to me."

"So says Jane of the Ghetto."

Jess winced. That was a dumb thing to say. Marissa wasn't exactly ashamed of her humble upbringing, but she didn't take it well when some rich heifer mocked her about it either.

Marissa grabbed Madeline around the throat and shoved her. Madeline stumbled back. Jess tried to move out of the way, but she didn't move fast enough and the hyena slammed into her, sending Jess flying out the back exit door. She hit the opposite wall, a surprised grunt exploding out of her as the exit door slammed shut.

"Jessica? Are you all right?" her client asked with genuine concern.

She took a calming breath. "Uh . . . yes. Sorry about that. I, uh, stubbed my toe on my desk."

"Oooh. I hate when I do that."

Her client went on, now much calmer. Letting her ramble, Jess walked to the door and pulled. It didn't budge. She pulled on the handle again. Nothing. She'd locked herself out.

Dammit!

"I feel so much better now that I've spoken to you, Jessica. Thank you."

"No problem. Anytime, you know that." She did her best to control her chattering teeth. "We'll contact you in the morning, okay?"

"Yes, thanks again." The client disconnected the call and Jess wrapped her arms around her body.

"Okay," she muttered to herself. "This dress. Bad idea in winter." As were the goddamn shoes. Trying not to fall on her ass in the disgusting alley, Jess started to walk toward the opening leading to the street. As she reached the end, she saw two females standing by a piece of shit Buick. They seemed to be in quite an agitated discussion. Normally Jess wouldn't notice or care, but she scented they were wolves. Wolves she didn't recognize. She recognized all the local wolves and now the Smiths, but new wolves on an already small island asked for trouble.

As she approached the mouth of the alley, the two women stopped talking and those cold wolf eyes focused on her.

Uh-oh.

*   *   *

Smitty grabbed hold of Madeline Stark while Mitch grabbed his sister. Not easy since both females had decided to shift. In the middle of a full-human party no less. *Has everyone lost their goddamn mind?*

He shook Stark. "Shift back. *Now!*" She did and suddenly he had a naked hyena in his arms. Man, he could find much better ways to spend a Tuesday evening. He shoved her toward the bathroom. "Get dressed." He threw clothes at her, but he had no idea if they belonged to her, her sisters, Marissa, or Mace's sisters Serita and Allie, who'd delighted in joining the fray.

Mitch pushed his still-shifted sister into the men's bathroom across the tiny hallway since he knew better than to put her in an enclosed space with the Starks. The other two lionesses followed Marissa in, and as soon as the door closed Mitch had to walk away, laughing before he even got five feet.

Smitty glanced around. The reason he found this little fight before it got truly ugly was because he saw Jessie Ann head down this hallway to the bathroom and the Starks follow her. Now he had no idea where she'd gone.

He knocked on the men's bathroom door. "Y'all seen Jessie Ann?"

"Who?" a trio of voices answered back.

He rolled his eyes. "Jessica Ward?"

"She was here a few minutes ago," Marissa answered.

Dammit. Where did she go? He needed to find her. Now.

He simply couldn't get that vision out of his mind of that runt dog practically salivating all over her. At least the males in Jessie's Pack had some wiry strength to them. Landry could get his ass kicked by one of Smitty's three-year-old nephews.

Well, she couldn't have gone far.

He stroked his chin and glanced around until his gaze finally settled on the back exit door. The one that locked automatically.

Smitty grinned. He sure did love his job.

Jess stood at the end of the alley, her gaze locked on the two females. One of them with a horrible red dye job snarled and advanced. Jess snarled back, unleashing her claws and bracing her stance. If this got ugly, she'd kick off the shoes. If it got really ugly, she'd shift. That was always a last resort, though, when out in the open like this.

But before the female could get close, the other She-wolf grabbed her arm and yanked her back, shoving her toward the car.

"Not yet and not her," she heard her whisper. Jess had wild-dog hearing. She could hear a pin drop a mile away if she needed to. "Get in," the She-wolf ordered. The redhead started to argue, but the other one slapped her and pushed her toward the car.

Gee, as difficult as her Pack could be, Jess never had to bitch slap one to get her way. Even the Smith females didn't slap. You either complied or they mauled. There was no in between in the Smith universe.

The two females got in the car and pulled away from the curb; Jess let out a relieved breath.

"Jessie Ann?"

Jess screamed and turned swinging. Unfortunately, it was much more of a flailing than any kind of actual fighting moves and Smitty easily caught her arms.

"What are you doing?" he demanded calmly.

"Beating you senseless?"

He let out that annoyed sigh she remembered so well. The same one he gave her when she fell out of a tree after Sissy and her She-wolves chased Jess up there in the first place.

She glanced down at the big hands gripping her biceps to hold her steady. "Do you mind letting me go?"

"Sure you can handle the basics of walking and talking at the same time, darlin'?" She bared fangs and he quickly pushed her away. "A simple yes would have gotten the same sentiment across, ya know?"

"Why are you here?"

"My team's here for additional security coverage for the museum. Good thing, too, with lions and hyenas fighting in the hallway."

Jess chuckled. "Good point." She motioned to the door. "Since you're security, can you let me back in?"

Smitty stared at her. "Do you have a ticket?"

She blinked. "It's inside with my coat."

"Sorry, darlin', I'm not really authorized to let you in if you don't have a ticket."

Jess took a steadying step. "I'm sorry. What?"

"We're only letting in people who have their tickets. You don't. Sorry."

Jess's teeth began to chatter and she desperately rubbed her arms. What exactly was wrong with this man? Yesterday all he'd wanted to do was "help" her. Now she couldn't get him to open the goddamn door when she was freezing to death. "Tell me you're joking."

"Jessie Ann, you know how serious I take my job. I can't let anyone into the party without a ticket."

"You son of a—"

"Now, now, Jessie Ann. No call for that kind of language."

She threw her hands up. "Fine. I'll just go walk around the entire goddamn building and go in through the front. Hopefully I won't die from exposure on the way."

"Nah, you know our kind don't die that easy from the cold." She ignored him and turned to walk away. "They won't let you in either," he said to her back.

She stopped. "Why not?"

"You don't have a ticket."

She spun on her heel, shocked she didn't fall on her ass in these goddamn shoes. "*Bobby Ray Smith, I swear to God*—"

Still calm, he cut in and said, "Don't blaspheme at me, Jessie Ann."

"It's Jess-i-ca!" she nearly screamed. "Not Jessie. Definitely not Jessie Ann."

He shrugged. "I like Jessie Ann." It was his calmness that had her crazed. That calm, in-control Smitty air. His brothers didn't have it. His father definitely didn't have it. So Smitty must have gotten it from his mother. But right now it made Jess want to take off her shoe and stab him in the eye with the five-inch heel.

He glanced at her hand. "You can use your phone. Call one of those friends of yours to bring your ticket."

"They're not carrying their phones. Their phones are in their coats."

"Why wouldn't they have their phones?"

She held up hers, gripping the small device so tightly she had the feeling she'd crush it. *"Because I'm carrying mine!"*

"No need to yell, Jessie Ann."

"I can't talk to you." She spun around yet again and started to walk away.

"Of course," he said behind her, "maybe there's something we can work out."

"And what would that be?" she bit out even as she kept walking.

"You go out with me tomorrow."

Again, Jess stopped in her tracks. To her utter disgust and self-loathing, her heart leaped in her chest. "A date? You're having me freeze my ass off because you want a date."

"Not a date," he said right by her ear and she nearly jumped ten feet straight up.

How does he do that?

"Just two friends hanging out."

Of course. Because why would Bobby Ray Smith go out with "little" Jessie Ann Ward? Her leaping heart tripped and took a nice plunge off Depression Mountain. This had all to do with his ego and nothing to do with her. Sixteen years and she still wasn't worth . . . *Oh, forget it.*

"My friends don't let me freeze to death."

"I'm sure you're not as difficult with your friends as you are with me. Just say the word yes and I'll get you right inside, darlin'."

"You're a bastard."

"I'm a Smith," he said simply.

"What's the difference?"

"To many there is none." His grin was slow and so damn charming she wanted to slap it right off his face. "One word, Jessie Ann. Yes. And I'll take you inside."

"That's blackmail."

"That's an ugly word. I prefer extortion."

She couldn't even feel her toes. The thought of walking around the entire goddamn building to get back inside made her cringe. Especially in these stupid shoes. Never again would Phil get her in shoes like these.

"I'll never forgive you for this."

"Doesn't sound like a yes to me."

"Fine. Yes."

Smitty immediately took off his jacket and put it around her shoulders. It smelled like him, and she kind of wanted to growl and rub it all over her body.

He walked her back to the door, and as he opened it May nearly tumbled out since she had her hand wrapped around the inside handle.

"Jess! There you are. We've been lookin' everywhere for you, girl."

"I had to take a call," she growled.

May looked between her and Smitty. "All right," she said before scampering away like the weak-willed mutt she was.

As Jess stepped into the warmth of the museum, Smitty said in her ear, "I'll pick you up tomorrow at your office. Around six." Smiths didn't do specific time. What did "around six" even mean? "So make sure to add me to that little office list of yours."

She snatched off his jacket and threw it at his head.

"Asshole!" she raged before she stormed off to gather up her Pack and go home.

* * *

Smitty pulled his jacket back on.

Ha! Got her. Did she really think she could outmaneuver him? Hello? Military training. Smith training. Those two things alone made him the most wily and vicious of the predators.

He'd take her out to dinner and they'd have a nice long discussion about where she'd been for the past sixteen years . . . and about how to properly dress for these sorts of events. Then he'd find out what the hell she was hiding from him. Yup. That worked as a plan. He'd get his old friend back if he had to drag her kicking and screaming into his life.

To Smitty, this did not seem pathetic.

A strong hand landed on his shoulder as Marissa leaned on him for balance so she could slip on her pumps. She started to say something when Jessie Ann charged back into the hallway. She threw herself into Smitty, pressing her back into his chest. She wrapped his arms around her waist and snarled, "Now look pretty."

Five seconds later, Sherman Landry appeared at the end of the hallway. His smile faded as soon as he saw Smitty. And he looked downright terrified of Marissa.

With a despondent sigh, he gave a half-hearted wave. "Bye, Jessica."

"Bye," Jess said with an over-the-top glee. When Sherman walked off, she spit out between her teeth, "Asshole."

A good minute passed before Jess realized she still had Smitty's arms around her. Slowly, her face lifted and she looked up at him. Unable to help himself, Smitty let that smile come in all its glory. His daddy had the same one and it had caused his mother to go after the old bastard with the ax they kept in the backyard more than once.

Thankfully, Jessie didn't have an ax on her.

"Get off me!" She pulled out of his arms. "Bastard."

"See ya tomorrow!" he said with the same cheer she'd told Landry good-bye.

She stormed off, spinning on those deadly heels to give him the finger with both hands, before disappearing altogether.

Marissa rested her chin on Smitty's shoulder. "I must say, Smitty, you do have an interesting way with women."

"Self-taught," he said with pride, grinning when Marissa laughed.

Chapter 8

It took Jess the rest of the night and most of the day to remember the Buick. The Buick those two She-wolves outside the museum had driven away in. It struck her as strange when she saw it; now she remembered why. All those long discussions when she'd just met a still-sobbing May about her boyfriend's Buick and all the "making out" that went on in that backseat. Could the guy still be driving around in the same car? And if it was his car, who were the She-wolves? They worried Jess but didn't scare her. Not after living among the Smith wolves for two years.

Her big problem was whether to tell the rest of the Pack. When she had a few minutes, she'd grabbed Phil, but that quickly degenerated into one of their arguments where they kept saying the same thing but continued to argue anyway.

Unfortunately, Jess and Phil didn't know Sabina stood in the doorway until she barked. And she had one of those annoying, high-pitched yelping barks too.

Jess and Phil cringed, knowing Sabina had busted them royally.

Watching them closely, she shrewdly sized them up like she did everyone else. "What are you two so heatedly discussing?"

Jess faced her friend and answered, "Our torrid affair?" That probably would have been more believable if she hadn't phrased it as a question.

"Your torrid affair?"

"Yeah, me and Phil. For years now. Hot and heavy. Right, Phil?"

He stared blindly at his wife and Jess had to hit him in the chest to prompt a response. "Right. Sure. Hot and heavy."

Sabina folded her arms over her chest. "You two are pathetic. Pathetic liars. Now tell me the truth." When they remained silent, she added, "Tell me. Or I shift and so begins the peeing."

A female dog who lifted her hind leg on a whim—this was not an idle threat.

Jess held up her hands. "Okay! Okay!" Might as well just deal with it. "Let's grab the others and get this over with."

"You've gotta tell her."

"Why can't it wait? Until she gets home?"

Kristan rolled her eyes. "Honestly! You'd think I was dragging your dumb ass to the gas chamber." And she *was* dragging him because he refused to go on his own.

Pulling Johnny into the building, she smiled at the woman behind the front desk. "Hiya, Paula. Are my parents and Jess upstairs?"

"They sure are. Go on up, hon."

"Thanks." The big goofus started to slow up, but she yanked harder and pulled him all the way to the elevator doors. "I swear! You're being such a drama king about this."

She glanced at the man waiting for the elevators while keeping a firm grip on Johnny's arm. His scent reminded her of Johnny's, and based on his size, she realized they were the same breed. And, man, was he way cute!

The doors opened and the wolf stepped inside. She followed but had to keep dragging Johnny. The wolf pushed the top-floor button and the doors closed.

"So who are you going to see?" she asked, knowing he'd only be allowed to head upstairs if the Pack wanted him up there.

"Jessie Ann."

She snorted and got a raised eyebrow for her trouble. "We all call her Jess," she explained.

"I knew her a long time ago when she was just Jessie Ann."

"I'm Kristan. This is Johnny."

"Nice to meet y'all. I'm Bobby Ray Smith, but y'all can call me Smitty."

She laughed a bit. "You sound just like my mom. The accent."

"So you're May and Danny's daughter."

She liked that he didn't assume because she was Asian she was automatically Maylin's daughter. "Yup."

Kristan glanced up at Johnny, surprised he hadn't said anything yet. But she had no idea she'd find him glaring at the wolf—the much *bigger* wolf—like he really believed he could take him on. Just great. *Now* his testosterone decided to kick in?

Smitty stared back at Johnny; although his body lounged casually against the wall, his eyes let her know he was feeling anything but casual. "Is there a problem, hoss?"

It was a low growl, but one from Johnny's gut. Startled into action, Kristan stepped between the two, her hand against Johnny's chest.

"So," she said way too eagerly, "what was Jess like back then? Did she always have her nose in a book? I bet she did. She has like a ton of books. Stuff you couldn't pay me enough to read. Boring, boring, boring. But I do like—"

"Christ," Johnny snapped, "stop babbling."

She knew that would work. Johnny hated when she rambled. But most important, she'd defused a situation she wasn't really in the mood to deal with.

She briefly wondered if the skill was built into her DNA. Her mom could do the same thing.

Smitty stepped out of the elevator, working hard not to smile. The kid wouldn't appreciate it much if he did. Smitty wasn't mad. He had no reason to be. At that age, challenging adult wolves was normal. A rite of passage. It was also a right of passage to get your ass kicked by adult wolves. Of course, being around a Pack of dogs, this might have been the first time the kid had felt the desire to take on a male he didn't even know. Obviously it was the first time little Kristan had witnessed it.

Together, the three of them walked into the office.

Pairs of desks facing each other ran down the middle of the room. Only one office sat tucked away in a corner. Although it had a door, you couldn't call it private since it was made completely of glass. The door, the windows looking in . . . all of it glass.

Toys and games littered the floor. He could see paused computer games on some terminals, and there were several televisions set up with the high-end game consoles attached. Posters for the *Stars Wars* trilogy, *Lord of the Rings* trilogy, *Logan's Run, Raiders of the Lost Ark*—every geek movie ever made—decorated the walls. They also had full-size standing displays from *Star Wars, Xena: Warrior Princess,* and *Star Trek.*

And Smitty'd thought Mace had gone overboard by investing in those quiet eight-by-ten pencil drawings of the seaside for their front office. How these wild dogs got anything done, Smitty would never know.

"That's weird," Kristan said softly. "Where is everybody?"

It did seem strange, with it not even being six yet, that no one would be around.

Smitty wouldn't put it past Jessie Ann to run out on him, but he didn't see the rest of her Pack running with her. Of course, he'd always heard that wild-dog Packs were uncommonly close.

He scented the air and walked to the back of the office, the two pups trailing behind. The back door led to a long hallway that appeared to still be under construction. Jessie's scent went down the hall, past bathrooms and storage rooms, until he hit another doorway. Smitty pushed through and walked down the ten flights of stairs.

One door led out. A fire exit, he would guess. He could hear their lowered voices stop abruptly when they sensed someone on the other side of the door.

Smitty went right up against it and he could hear whispering from the other side—and sniffing. Grinning at the pups, Smitty loudly barked, "*What are y'all doin'?*"

First, they screamed in surprise. All of them, male and female, screaming like a bunch of girls. Then they started laughing and didn't stop. Smitty finally opened the door and found them sitting on the ground, laughing as only dogs could.

Goofy. That was the best word he could come up with for them. Goofy.

"So," he said to all of them, but with his eyes on Jessie, "anything I can help y'all with?"

Chapter 9

Okay, yeah, she'd lied to him. And they both knew it. They both knew she'd pulled a story about someone trying to break into their office through the emergency door out of her flat ass. She'd even done it with a straight face, but she could see it in his eyes. He didn't believe a word she said. Too bad. He wasn't Pack. Not her Pack. Therefore, it wasn't his problem to deal with. And the fact that she wouldn't tell him anything bugged the living holy hell out of him.

Jess didn't care, though. She had bigger issues to deal with at the moment.

May had not taken the news of the possible return of her ex very well. Bursting into frustrated, panicked tears, she took off running, heading out the back exit until Danny caught up with her. The five of them then stood in the cold doing their best to calm her down. The sock puppet seemed to help. Everyone loved Mr. Wizard.

After that, they'd discussed strategy and next steps. Informing the whole Pack at this stage was a bad move since it risked moving through the puppy rumor mill like lightning and ending up in Kristan's lap. So only the five of them would know at this point. They'd bring the rest of the Pack up to speed if necessary.

Now, however, they had a nosey wolf to deal with. A nosey

wolf who knew she was lying. Toe-to-toe they stood as he quizzed her, trying to trip her up so he could get the truth. She didn't trip up. She'd learned to lie back when the Pack still stole diapers and baby food for a newly arrived Kristan. Lying to protect her Pack didn't bother Jess, so if Smitty hoped to see some kind of guilt in her eyes, he might as well stop looking. She felt none.

Eventually, when he seemed to realize his questions weren't confusing her in the least, Smitty grabbed the cell phone hanging off his jeans pocket and flipped it open.

Frowning, Jess asked, "Who are you calling?"

"Mace. If people are trying to break in, and that is what you're telling me, right?" She nodded, even as they glared at each other. "Then we need to get this place locked down tight. Tonight."

"Locked down?" Locked down sounded expensive. "I don't remember saying we'd pay for that."

"You didn't. But you will."

Jess's eyes narrowed and she reached out to twist his nipples, but May slapped her hands down.

As always, May tried to diffuse the situation. With false cheeriness, she asked her daughter, who'd been watching the power play between Jess and Smitty with obvious eagerness, "And what are y'all doin' here?"

Kristan grabbed Johnny's jacket and yanked him forward. "Johnny has something to tell you guys."

But Johnny looked like he wanted to be a million miles away from here.

"Go on," Kristan urged. "Tell her."

With a sigh, Johnny pulled out an envelope from his pocket and handed it to Jess. She almost dreaded taking it. Not surprising when most envelopes from any of the kids usually came from their school and involved something they'd done or didn't do or said or should *never* had said.

Without looking at the envelope, Jess slipped the wrinkled but high-quality paper out and quickly read it.

Taking a deep breath, she looked up at Johnny. "You got in."

"Wait. What?" May grabbed the letter and the others leaned over to read it. "He not only got in," she finally said, "he got a full scholarship."

Refusing to look at any of them, Johnny gave a dismissive shrug. "It's just a summer program."

"You got in," Jess said again. Then she charged him.

"Okay. See you when you get here." Smitty closed his phone and clipped it back to his jeans. He turned to tell Jessie that Mace and the rest of his team would be along in the next thirty minutes when he found her, May, and Sabina all over the kid. Arms around him, hugging him. Part of him started to get kind of pissed about it until the kid looked at him. And he saw it in the boy's eyes—a definite plea for help.

He walked over and could hear Jessie saying, "I'm so proud of you."

"We all are," May added.

Johnny looked like he'd give anything to be able to wrench the women off him and make a run for it. Of course that would never work. They were fast. They'd just catch him.

"Mace is headed this way," he said to Jessie's back. "He said he's not surprised he has to step in and help y'all. Seein' as security is not your strong suit."

It took a second for Jess to realize what he'd said; then she pushed Johnny away and turned her complete attention on Smitty. May stepped between them, as always the peacemaker, and Sabina grinned, looking forward to a good fight.

"He said what?" Jessie demanded.

And behind their backs Johnny mouthed, "Thank you."

Jess had no idea how this spiraled out of control. She expected one big-haired lion, not an entire team of shifters taking over her building and them.

Mace kept walking into her office and asking her to authorize things. When she'd ask, "Authorize what?" he'd give her that annoyed cat look and she'd sign.

She sure was paying a lot for telling one lie.

Smitty walked into her office, leaning against the doorjamb. "You told Mitch you thought there might be another way in."

Jess let out a sigh and rubbed her forehead.

"Somethin' wrong, Jessie Ann?" Smitty asked, sounding way smugger than seemed necessary. "Something you need to tell me before this goes any further?"

Dropping her hands to her desk, Jess forced a smile. "Nope, nothing to tell."

Jess stood and led Smitty through the office and down the long hallway that led to the bathrooms and the emergency exit. She took him into one of the rooms that held secure servers. With his help, they pulled aside a metal case holding old computer parts and crouched down next to a vent.

She shrugged. "It's not huge but—"

"It's big enough."

Using one hand, he took hold of the grate blocking the vent and gave it an experimental tug. A tug that pulled out the grate and four inches of drywall all around the perimeter.

Smitty glanced at her. "Oops."

"Oops? The best you can come up with is oops?"

"I forgot about my mighty strength."

Snorting, feeling the strain between them from the past two hours lift, Jess playfully pushed Smitty's shoulder and she might as well have been pushing up against a brick wall.

"You would have had to close this off anyway," he said, placing the grate and drywall aside.

"Don't we need vents . . . you know, to breathe and all?"

"Yes, Miss Smarty Ass. But there are ways to make sure they are secure."

"Did you just call me Miss Smarty Ass?"

"That's what you are." Smitty pulled a small flashlight from his back pocket and leaned down to look into the vent. "Is there actually something here, in this building, that someone would feel the need to break in?"

"Computer equipment, I guess. But it would take a major effort to get the desktops out of here since each one is locked to its desk. And we don't allow anyone to use laptops in the office except Pack. And we take ours wherever we go."

"Hhhm. Then why would someone try and break in here, Jessie Ann? Since it don't look like y'all have much to steal that isn't locked down."

She didn't answer him and he wasn't shocked. Smitty knew when someone was lying to him, and Jessie Ann was lying her cute little ass off. Something was wrong. Really wrong. And the whole "locking down the office thing" was merely a way to push her hand. He had no idea she'd go through with it. As soon as she realized how much this would cost her, Smitty thought for sure she or one of her friends would put a stop to it. He'd tried to trip up each of them as this progressed, finally getting to meet the people so close to Jessie, including "dancing dog Phil." But they kept their mouths shut and signed whatever his team put in front of them until Sabina muttered something about putting Smitty's company on retainer.

Stubborn little SOBs, weren't they?

Letting out a tired breath, Jessie sat down on the floor, her back resting against the wall. "I should have gotten some coffee. Now I'm too tired to get up and get any."

"Want me to get you some?"

She gave a faint smile. "No, but thanks for offering."

Clicking off the flashlight and closing the door, Smitty sat down next to her. His leg brushed against hers and he felt her body tense the slightest bit.

"All right, Jessie Ann, cough it up. What aren't you telling me?"

"Nothing." And if he didn't know her, he'd probably believe her.

"Woman, you are lying to me. I can't help you if you lie to me."

"I didn't ask for your goddamn help."

Smitty leaned forward, resting his arms on his raised knees. "I'm fixin' to get mad, Jessie."

"You're *fixin'* to get mad?"

"Yeah."

"Why don't you just get mad?"

"I'm not there yet. But I will be if you don't start talking to me."

Jessie pushed herself to her feet. "I have nothing to say."

He watched that cute little ass walk across the room to the door. Was that what she'd been planning to wear out tonight with him? Ripped black jeans with gray thermal leggings underneath, a Chicago Blackhawks hockey jersey that reached to her knees, and white high-top sneakers.

Maybe she was trying a little too hard *not* to make an effort? Although now all he wanted to do was get those clothes off her and see what the hell she was hiding.

Why did she insist on driving him crazy? Well, hell . . . two canines could play this game of tug.

She had her hands on the door handle when he asked, "Does this have anything to do with the kiss?"

And he almost felt real bad when that door smacked her right in the face.

Jess gripped her forehead and spun around to stare at Smitty. "What kiss?"

He slowly got to those big wolf feet. "The kiss we almost had sixteen years ago."

"Why would anything have to do with that kiss that never happened?"

Smitty gave her an indulgent smile. "Now, Jessie Ann, we both know how you felt about me."

"How *I*—"

"And maybe you still feel that way so you're afraid to get too close to me. To trust me. To—now, Jessie, let's not start throwing things."

Jess held an old 60-gig external hard drive in her hand that she'd grabbed from one of the shelves. The thing weighed a ton. It would cave his head in quite nicely.

"I'm just trying to find out the truth."

"And you're doing that how?" She didn't want to talk about that night. The night he'd pushed her away. Always a late bloomer, sixteen-year-old Jess still hadn't had her first kiss by then mostly because she'd wanted that kiss to come from Smitty. But he'd hurt her that night when he pushed her away. Not physically, of course, but emotionally her young, way-too-romantic heart had been crushed.

Even now, sixteen years later, she still didn't want to have this discussion. She could already feel her cheeks heating from embarrassment, remembering how she wasn't cute or hot enough to get a drunk boy to kiss her. What girl couldn't manage something that simple from the weak? Apparently she couldn't.

Already she could feel her embarrassment turning to anger. No, she didn't want this discussion. She didn't want to hop down memory lane with Bobby Ray Smith. Not now, not ever.

"You know, Jessie, I'm of the mind if we get that kiss out of the way, maybe you could focus on the bigger issues right in front of you."

Huh. Look at that. Her leash just snapped.

Good thing he was fast because that heavy piece of metal came right for his head. Smitty stepped to one side and it went sailing by.

He stared at her. "*Woman, have you lost your mind?*"

"No, I think I'm getting it back." Her hand reached out and she blindly grabbed some other hunk of metal. Computer equipment it looked like. "Yeah, I'm feeling better each second." She pulled her arm back like a pro baseball player and Smitty took the three long steps over to her, grabbing hold of the thing in her hand and wrenching it away from her.

"Jessie Ann, calm down!"

"Go to hell," she snarled as she reached for that damn shelf again. Everything on it was a potential missile to take out his head.

Slamming down the thing already in his hand, Smitty reached out and grabbed Jessie by the back of the neck. Without thought, only wolf instinct, he yanked her over to him, determined to get her under control. To get her to submit. That's what Alpha Males did, and it didn't even occur to him that Jessie wasn't part of his Pack. Hell, she was barely part of his life. Just a blip in his week, really.

But when her body slammed up against his, everything but the wolf in him was wiped clean. All that calm, cool, rational logic he'd spent years and years refining until he moved only as fast as he wanted or needed slipped away from him, leaving the raw, demanding animal behind.

Jessie stared up at him, her hands slapping against his chest, trying to push him off. Too late for that, and he could tell by the way her eyes widened and her breath left her body in one rush that she realized it too.

His grip tightened on her neck and he lifted until she stood on her toes.

"Smitty, wait—"

He didn't. He cut off her next words by slamming his mouth down on hers, his tongue sliding into her already open mouth, and kissing her hard. He sensed her claws unleash, coming for his face or his chest, so he released her neck and grabbed her wrists, before turning them both and forcing Jessie up against the wall. Using his hold on her wrists, he pulled Jessie's arms above her head and pinned them in place.

She struggled against him, her knee trying to move so she could take out his nuts. Again, the rational voice in his head that he always listened to told him to let her go. Told him "nice Southern gentlemen" didn't do this sort of thing to sweet, innocent, wild dogs.

Then Jessie Ann groaned. It slid up the back of her throat, easing into his mouth, setting his nerve endings on fire. In that moment, his rational voice got shut down for the beast who ruled his heart.

And this . . . *this* right here was why he didn't kiss her that night all those years ago. If it had caused even a tenth of the lust pouring through his body this very second, his poor little eighteen-year-old brain would have crumpled from the pressure, and the two of them would still be stuck in Smithtown up to their armpits in Smith sons.

He didn't have to worry about that now, though. They were both adults with an excellent grasp of birth control. They could keep this simple and friendly and still have the time of their lives. Because he had to have her. Now. This very second.

Damn. Poorly planned, Smith. He didn't think to bring a condom with him. Unfortunate, since he'd love nothing more than to take her right here, right now, and right up against this wall. Then again with such weak drywall probably not a good idea. Of course, the floor had looked pretty clean . . .

"Hey, Aunt Jess, Mom's wondering if you guys are hun— Whoa!"

Jessie shoved so hard Smitty stumbled back from her. He knew Kristan stood in the doorway, but at the moment he couldn't really turn around. She was way too young for that visual.

Horrified. Of all the people in the world to catch her it had to be "Big Mouth, I have no filters" Kristan.

"I am *so* telling Mom!" she squealed.

The evil brat took off, laughing the whole way, and Jess shoved past the bastard wolf standing in front of her and went after her niece.

Kristan threw open the door and skidded into the main office. "You guys are not going to believe what I—"

Jess slapped her hand around Kristan's mouth and dragged her back into the hallway.

"Excuse us," Jess said to the room full of shifters staring at them.

Jess carried the pink-clad brat into the storage closet and slammed the door.

"Not a word!"

"Oh, come on! You can't expect me to keep this to myself. *You* making out with a wolf. I could sell this to *Sixty Minutes!*"

"I'm ordering you to keep your mouth shut."

Kristan snorted and Jess stepped up to her.

"You're sixteen. Almost an adult. It's time you learn how it works when you have an Alpha."

"Yeah, right."

Jess bared her fangs and took two dramatic steps forward. Frightened, Kristan stumbled back, slamming into the wall behind her. Jess moved in close and rested her cheek against Kristan's forehead, her snarls low and dangerous, her fangs brushing against the girl's skin.

"Okay, okay!"

"Are we clear?"

"Yes!"

Jess stepped back. "Not a word. Understand?"

Kristan nodded but wouldn't look Jess in the eye. Good. She was learning.

"Now get Johnny and you two go home."

The girl nodded her head again and took off running.

Jess gave herself a very brief moment to get her breath back and wipe shaky fingers over her bruised lips and through her hair, trying to get it back under control before following after Kristan since she wasn't entirely ready to trust the girl would keep her mouth shut.

But as she opened the door she practically collided with Smitty.

"Jessie Ann—"

"Don't."

"But—"

She walked away from him and into the main room. She forced a smile since everyone was still standing around looking confused. "The kids are going home. But I'm starving. What are we ordering for dinner?"

Smitty sat back and watched them stand around a menu for a local Chinese restaurant and place their orders. Jessie acted like butter wouldn't melt. Cold, indifferent, and trying to pretend like it didn't mean anything to her.

But it had meant a hell of a lot to the woman he had pinned up against that wall. And if Jessie Ann really thought it would be that easy to shake him, she had so very much to learn.

Chapter 10

Jess sat at her desk, staring out the big office window, her feet up and resting on the small ledge. She had no idea how long she'd been sitting there. How long she'd let herself waste precious business hours by thinking about the disaster that was her life. But she couldn't stop herself. She couldn't stop thinking about that goddamn kiss and the goddamn wolf who'd done this to her. She really should hate the man. If she had any sense, she'd keep as far away from him as humanly possible. But something told her it wouldn't be that easy. Smitty wouldn't let it be. Not because he cared about her or wanted her for his very own, but because his ego wouldn't allow for anything else. He had something to prove, and he seemed intent on proving it with her.

She knew she couldn't let that happen. She knew she couldn't let her heart take over here. Bobby Ray Smith was and always would be the one man who could break Jess's heart. He'd done it once; she wouldn't let him do it again.

"Jessica!"

Jess blinked and looked away from the window. She had no idea how long May had been standing there calling her name, probably a while. "Hey, hon. What's up? Are you okay?"

It had not been an easy night for May either, but Danny had taken care of her. Like he always had. The two of them fit to-

gether so perfectly Jess found herself happy for them and sometimes bitterly jealous. After all these years and five kids, they
still meant the world to each other. Jess, however, had a very
healthy relationship with the Pack's pet dogs. They were very
good snugglers.

"I'm fine. You scared my daughter to death, though."

Jess winced. "Sorry about that. I just . . . I just couldn't have
her yelling what she saw across the room in front of all those
people."

May dropped onto a chair. "What did you do?"

"The ol' snarl and snap. It's still quite effective."

"That it is."

"Sorry about that. Is she okay?"

May waved her concerns away. "Don't apologize. Y'all have
spoiled her. She needed a good snarl and snap. Of course my
question now is what exactly did my baby see . . . and should
we get her therapy?"

Jess cringed and looked down at her desk.

"That bad, huh?"

"Nothing she'll end up on *Jerry Springer* for, but . . ." Jess's
eyes crossed.

May rested her elbows on the desk and her chin on her fist.
"Can I make a suggestion?"

"Does it require me to humiliate myself any more than I already have?"

"Jessica Ann—we're dogs! Tolerating humiliation is what we
do."

And Jess knew May was only joking . . . a little.

"Do you think I'm pretty?"

Smitty glanced away from the computer screen he'd been
staring at for the last three hours, looked at his sister, and shook
his head. "No."

"What do ya mean no?"

"You asked. Sorry if you didn't like the answer. I always

thought you were funny lookin'. Asked momma, 'What is that thing laying in your bed?' And she said, 'I found it hiding under a car, you be nice to it now.'"

"Bobby Ray Smith! What is wrong with you? You're as mean as a cat."

"Is there a reason you're here, Sissy Mae? I thought we sent you out on a job."

He wasn't in a good mood. He'd been up all night thinking about Jessie. Worrying about her and what she might be hiding from him. And worst of all, thinking about that goddamn kiss. Not surprisingly, thoughts of that kiss led to all sorts of other thoughts about Jessie Ann and what she could do with that mouth of hers.

His sister stretched across his desk, heedless of the file folders under her, and reached into the Navy mug he had filled with Hershey's Kisses. "That job's boring. I want something more interesting than checking out some company's safety."

"That's our bread and butter. So stop whining and do your job."

"I did. It took me no time. And I'm bored. How come you don't give me anything more interesting?"

Smitty sighed and leaned back in his chair. "You don't want to have this conversation, Sissy Mae."

"Yes, I do. Spit it out. I can handle most of this bullshit better than you and Mace. So what's your problem?"

With a shrug, he answered, "You are."

"Me?"

"Yeah, you. I've never known anyone who could start shit faster than you do."

"That's not fair, Bobby Ray."

"Maybe not, but we both know it's accurate. I love you, baby sister. But you are trouble. I need people who can defuse situations and get everyone out safely. You, however, are an instigator. You turn complicated situations into national news."

"*That* was not my fault!"

"Whose fault was it?"

She didn't answer the question and instead said, "And I got everyone out safely."

"Yes, you did. After you got S.W.A.T. involved."

"Well, I—"

"And I really hope that wasn't so you'd be able to widen your dating pool. How many of those guys did you finally go out with? Four? Or was it five?"

"You act like I went out with them all at the same time."

Smitty held his hand up. "This conversation is over. What Mace and I have going here is too important for me and the Pack to let you screw it up by being yourself."

"That was just mean, Bobby Ray."

"Check with Mindy. She's got an assignment for you since you're finished with this last one."

"Yeah, yeah. She already gave it to me."

Mace walked by the open door and glanced in. He scowled. "Get off his desk. I've got an important client coming in to see your hick ass, Smitty, and I don't need this to look like we're at a local hoedown."

Sissy Mae slid off the desk before Smitty could push her off. "Okay, okay. Calm yourself," she said before she proceeded to eat his Hershey's Kisses.

Mace walked off, and Sissy Mae asked, "Who's this important client?"

"I have no idea. And would you like a shovel for the rest of that chocolate?"

"Why you mean old—" Sissy Mae stopped talking abruptly, her nose lifting in the air. "Hey. Does that smell familiar to you?"

It sure did. And Smitty felt his body come alive, images of Jessie pinned up against that wall ravaging his sleep-deprived brain. And exactly who taught her to kiss like that? Wait. Bad question. He didn't want to know. He *never* wanted to know.

His gaze rose from his desk and he watched Jessie Ann and Mace walk into view. She stopped in front of his office.

"Someone's here to see you," Mace announced.

Jessie gave a small smile. "Hiya."

"Hey." He stood. "Come on in."

"I'm sorry to bug you at the office," she said, stepping into the room, "but do you think you and I could—" She stopped abruptly, finally seeing Sissy Mae.

Sissy Mae's face lit up. "Well, Jessie Ann Ward. As I live and breathe."

Jessie stared at Sissy Mae for a good thirty seconds, a completely blank expression on her face.

He didn't know how to read that look, but he sensed flashbacks, and the last thing he needed was to have to track Jessie Ann down under the bleachers at Yankee Stadium. So quickly moving around his desk, Smitty reached for her, but his sweet, innocent, "can't survive without her Pack" Jessie Ann went and coldcocked his sister like a heavy-weight champ. Her small fist slammed into Sissy Mae's jaw and sent his sister flying over his desk, her body crashing into the wall behind him.

"Holy shit," Mace said softly in the silence that followed.

Jessie blinked, her hands covering her mouth. She'd shocked herself more than she'd shocked him or Mace.

"Oh, God. Oh . . . uh . . ."

Smitty motioned to Mace. "Take her to your office."

Mace gently took Jessie by the shoulders and led her out. Smitty knelt by his sister, grabbing a half-empty water bottle from his desk. He dumped the contents over her head and she woke up sputtering.

"Wha . . . what? Where . . . ?"

"You all right?"

She blinked up at him. "Yeah. Sure. I'm fine."

Smitty raised his hand and lifted three fingers. "How many fingers you see?"

Sissy Mae stared thoughtfully. "Eighty thousand."

Sighing, "Great."

Mace crouched down next to Jess's chair and handed her a bottle of water. "Here. Drink this."

Jess gripped the water bottle, feeling like it might be her only anchor at the moment. Good God, had she actually done that? Did she actually just hit someone who hadn't been threatening her or her pups or . . . *something?*

"I can't believe I did that," she finally managed, feeling like she had to say something with that lion crouching next to her and those scary gold eyes watching her.

"It's okay, Jessica."

"No, it's not. I should have more control than that." She looked at him. "But suddenly I was sixteen again, only this time . . ."

"You weren't afraid of her."

Jess shrugged. "She was Pack-less. So I attacked accordingly."

"If it's any comfort, my sisters would be quite impressed."

"Isn't it nice to hear that cats would be impressed by my violent actions? That gives me much ease."

Smiling, Mace stood. "Good point." He walked around his desk and sat down in the big leather chair.

"From what I hear, though, Sissy Mae definitely deserved that."

"That's not the point. I'm supposed to be above it all. Because I'm better than her."

"Oh, I see."

She closed her eyes, then shook her head. "I'm leaving. It was a bad idea to come here." Damn May for talking her into this. She should have stayed at the office and kept staring out the window until her Pack dragged her home.

Jess stood and reached out her hand.

"Thank you so much for having me," she said, then winced when she realized what a stupid thing it was too say. It's not like he'd invited her over for tea. Hell, no one had invited her anywhere.

"Are you going to be okay, Jessica?"

"Oh, yeah, I'll be fine. I just want to go home now. You know, before I get in a fistfight with your assistant or take on a school bus full of nuns."

"My assistant is a cheetah. You'll never be able to catch her."

"Gee. Thanks, Mace. That helps."

Jess turned and reached for the door, but it opened and Smitty walked in.

"Well, little Jessie Ann Ward, that's quite a right hook you've got on you, darlin'."

She wanted to get good and mad. She wanted to tell him to shut the hell up. But she couldn't do it. Not after decking his baby sister. To be honest, she was lucky he hadn't kicked her ass himself. She'd seen him do all sorts of terrible things to other wolves who'd hurt his sister.

"Oh, God!" she finally burst out. "Smitty, I'm so sorry. I don't know what came over me. You hate me, right? I can totally understand if you hate me."

"Darlin', I don't hate you." Smitty shrugged. "Even my momma says that every once in a while Sissy Mae needs to be punched in the head."

Jess frowned, seriously confused. "Um . . ."

"And don't worry," Mace added, "she has a really hard head."

"Uhhh . . ."

Mitch Shaw walked by the door, stopping and staring at the three of them. "Bruh, who decked Sissy Mae?"

"Little Jessie Ann here," Smitty said, motioning to her.

The lion grinned at her. "Nice work, Mighty Mite."

"Hey," Smitty demanded, "did you leave her alone?"

"You did."

"*I* have a guest."

Mitch shrugged. "Eh. Ronnie Lee's with her." Apparently already bored, Mitch wandered away.

Jess shook her head. "I better go." They were freaking her out. How was this sort of behavior okay? It wasn't. Then again . . . maybe it wasn't okay among the wild dogs but it was everyday livin' for the rest of them.

Thank you, but she'd stick with the dogs.

Jess stepped around Smitty, but his hand lightly gripped her forearm, halting her.

"I thought you came here to see me."

"Changed my mind. Running away now."

"You can't avoid me, darlin'."

And she knew he was not talking about the situation with his sister. The look in his eyes made it clear he really wasn't that worried about Sissy Mae.

"Yeah, Smitty, I can avoid you. Watch." Then she pretty much ran.

Smitty pushed out the front door and past the people coming out of the surrounding businesses on their way home. He caught sight of Jessie making a beeline for the subway. Typical. She couldn't be a little princess and wait for a freakin' cab. She had to be "everyday girl" and go for the public transportation. He took off after her, but by the time he made it to the stairs leading to the subway, she'd already gone inside.

At least that's what he thought until he was halfway down the stairs and Jessie's scent faded. He stopped and sniffed the air. She'd looped back around.

Tricky little She-dog.

Turning right around, Smitty headed back up the stairs and down another street. Midway along the second block he stopped—and let out a sigh.

"Tell me you're not hiding from me."

"I wouldn't call it hiding per se. More of a 'casually standing behind a pillar hoping you'd pass right on by' sort of thing."

Smitty grinned. She was just so dang cute. He waited and she reluctantly stepped out from behind that pillar.

"Jessie Ann, you know I've got the best nose in ten counties."

"I thought the lovely funk of the city would distract you."

"Nah, just makes you easier to find 'cause you smell so sweet."

Jessie, rarely fooled by his charm, sneered in disgust. "Oh, please."

"Fine. Don't believe me." He grabbed her hand. "Let's just go then."

Taking a step back, Jessie stared at him. "Let's just go then where?"

"You wanted to talk. We're gonna go talk."

"No, I said I changed my mind."

"Too bad."

Smitty took firm hold of her wrist and proceeded to drag her the ten blocks to his apartment. She didn't struggle and she kept quiet until they walked into the building and headed to the elevator.

"You know, we can talk another time."

"Nah, we'll talk now." He dragged her into the elevator and pushed the button for his floor. When the doors opened, he dragged her down the hall and to his apartment. He practically tossed her inside, slamming the door behind them and locking it.

Smitty leaned against the door and grinned. "Now, Jessica Ann . . . we can talk about that kiss that just melted your sweet heart."

Chapter 11

She'd love to slap that grin off his face. Melted her heart? Egotistical bastard. Instead of slapping him, though, she rubbed her suddenly itchy nose and growled, "There's nothing to talk about."

"Fine. We won't talk." When he started toward her, Jess jumped back, her hand held up in front of her to ward him off.

"Okay, okay! We'll talk."

"You don't wanna kiss me again?"

"No."

"Liar."

"Aaargh! You are so annoying!" Yet, he had gotten her mind off his sister.

Jess paced away from him, too angry to even appreciate his loft apartment with the big, comfortable furniture. A place like this, with its exposed brick and tons of space and light, didn't come cheap. Apparently business was damn good for Llewellyn and Smith Security.

"I'm only annoying you 'cause you like me."

"I do not—"

"Now, don't lie, Jessie Ann."

"I don't lie." *Unless absolutely necessary.*

"We both know you want me."

"We both . . . what?"

"You want me. It's okay. I totally understand the need."

"There is no need. There's only my hate for you."

"Again with the lyin'. Look," he said slowly, carefully, "if it makes you feel any better, I guess I'm of the same mind."

She stared at him. "You . . . You *guess* you're of the same mind?"

"You know me. I don't rush into these kinds of decisions—hey! Let's be calm here."

She wasn't. Not anymore. He'd snapped her leash again. How did he manage to do that? How could one man piss her off that much?

"Don't even think about it, Jessie Ann," he warned.

Jess held up a half-filled bottle of warm beer she'd grabbed off a side table. "The name is Jess-i-*ca*!" And that's when she let that beer bottle fly at Smitty's head. He ducked, the bottle barely missing him.

"Jessie Ann," he said smugly, taunting her, "you're simply proving what I already know. Can't stop thinking about me, can ya?"

Her anger good and frothy now, she grabbed a glass off a side table and flung it at the giant target he had the nerve to call a head.

"Jessie Ann! Stop it right—hey!" He barely avoided a plaque with the Navy emblem on it. "Dammit, woman! I nearly died to earn that plaque."

"If only!" She grabbed blindly.

"Whoa!" A coffee-table book on the history of the Navy nearly took his ear off.

"You said you wanted to talk, you asshole! *So let's talk!*" she yelled, grabbing a vase of dying flowers. "What are you going to . . . to . . ."

"Oh, Lord."

And that's when the sneezing started.

It came on so fast, all Smitty could do was grab the vase of flowers from her and quickly open his window and put them out on the fire escape. By the time he shut the window and turned back around, Jess was on her knees, the sneezes coming one after the other except when broken up by vicious coughing. Seemed nothing had changed. The girl had had bad allergies since he'd known her, and it seemed only worse now.

Crouching beside her, Smitty pulled the backpack off her shoulders and opened it. If she still operated the way she used to, he'd find her "works" buried somewhere in this unbelievably overpacked bag. Sure enough, he found her pills, nasal spray, and inhaler in one handy pouch. With that in hand, he quickly got her out of her cumbersome—and damn ugly—parka and scooped Jessie into his arms, taking her into the bathroom. Placing her on the counter, he opened the pouch and first took out her pills.

"Here." He put two pills in her hand and filled a cup with water. She popped the pills and he handed her the cup. She took a deep drink and then sneezed into the glass, water spraying back into her face.

"Dammit!"

"It's okay," he said, ordering himself not to laugh. He gave her the nasal spray after using a hand towel to quickly wipe off her face. "Use this."

She did, and when done he handed her several tissues.

"Do you need your inhaler?"

"No, no," she said around coughs. "That's for when I actually fall *into* the flowers. Which I've done on occasion."

Smitty grinned. "I know. I remember."

She let out a rough laugh. "I thought Miss Hazel was going to kill me."

"I think she wanted to. You know how she used to love her flowers."

Jess blew her nose and nodded.

"You all right now?"

"Oh, yeah." But she wouldn't look at him, and her cheeks were a bright red.

Using a knuckle, he lifted her face up to meet his. "Jessie Ann? Are you crying?"

She smirked. "No, you bonehead. My eyes are watering. If you spent the last five minutes coughing up a lung, your eyes would be watering too."

"Fair enough."

He stroked her cheek with one finger. "Can't you get allergy shots to help with that?"

Her appalled expression made him snort in surprise. "You're still afraid of needles?"

"I think afraid is a bit of a loaded word."

"I remember that year they had to inoculate us for something or other—"

"Distemper."

"Right. Distemper." He sure did love being canine. "And you just cried and cried. Like a baby. Did a lot for your reputation."

"Shut up."

On a whim, he lifted her hair a bit. "You still don't have earring holes."

She slapped his hands away. "I think I have enough holes in my head without adding to them, thank you very much."

"So nipple piercing completely out of order?"

She scrunched up her face and he had the feeling she wanted to cover her breasts to protect them. "Don't even go there!"

"Sorry, sorry," he said on a laugh. "Didn't mean to freak you out."

Jessie let out a shaky breath and pushed her hair off her face. That's when he saw her hand. "Your knuckles."

Jessie looked down at her hand. "Oh, God." Her eyes widened a bit as she remembered what she'd done. "Your sister. I hit your sister."

Although it seemed throwing things at his head didn't warrant any remorse since she'd done it twice already. "Don't worry about her. She's got the Smith hard head." He reached over and opened his medicine cabinet, taking out a first-aid kit. "And it's not like she didn't deserve it a bit."

"That's not the point. It was weak and pathetic and—"

"Jessie Ann, do me a favor. Cut yourself some slack." He lifted her hand and began to carefully clean it. "I know it's hard for you, but really. Give yourself a break."

"What's that supposed to mean?"

"It sure isn't hard to get you pissed off."

"I'll admit, I'm short on temper."

"Short like a Munchkin."

Her eyes narrowed dangerously. "You know what—owwww!"

Smitty glanced up from wiping her knuckles with an alcohol swab. "Oh. Did that hurt?"

"I am starting to hate you."

"No, you're not. But I know you're tryin'." He covered her knuckles in antiseptic cream and a loose bandage. "There. That should do it."

"Good." She tried to get up, but he wouldn't move. "Would you move?"

"In a second." He washed his hands in the sink and took his own damn time drying them. The longer he took, the crankier his little wild dog got.

"You know I have to get back to work."

"Liar."

"I am not lying."

"What? They'll beat ya?"

"Smitty."

He gave her a wicked smile. "You into that?"

She finally smiled even as she tried not to. "Bobby Ray!"

"It's all right. There's no shame in enjoying a firm hand. Especially if it's mine."

"Don't even think about it." She glanced down at her watch and he immediately covered it with his hand. "What are you doing?"

"Time is not of importance at the moment."

"Time is always of importance."

He removed the watch. "Not today."

"Hey. Give that back."

Smitty shoved it into his back pocket. "Nope."

"You do know that watch costs more than your body parts would earn on the black market."

Smitty placed his hands on either side of Jessie's legs, keeping her in place. "I'm not going to ask how you know that."

"That's for the best," she answered solemnly.

Smitty stared at her for so long she got nervous. "What? What are you staring at?"

"Your mouth is driving me crazy."

Jess wiped her mouth with the back of her hand. "Why? Do I have something on it?" she asked sincerely.

His hands gently gripped her jaw. "It will." Then his lips were on hers. Possessive. Demanding. His insistent tongue making her mouth his.

Smitty stepped closer, his legs butting up against her knees. When she didn't open to him, his hands slid between her thighs and pried them apart so he could move in. He didn't stop walking until the presence of the counter under her butt made him.

Once comfortable, those big hands moved up again and framed her face, holding her in place as Smitty kissed what sense she had left right out of her.

Jess tried to push him away . . . well, sort of. She slapped her hands against his shoulders really hard.

Unfortunately, she didn't shove him away. Her control snapped, and all that pent-up horniness took over.

She yanked off his jacket and tossed it across the room, her legs wrapping around his waist and her ankles locking at the base of his spine.

Smitty dragged his hands up her torso, gliding across her breasts. The feel of his hands on her breasts, even through her sweater and T-shirt, had her arching into him, her own hands scrambling to the snap of his jeans. She didn't know what had come over her, but she loved it. For once the only thing she could think about was this moment. Not tomorrow or ten years from now or ten years ago. No worries about the business or college funds or charity plans or anything else. She didn't have any of those worries as she released Smitty long enough for him to tear at her jeans, dragging them off her hips and down her legs. When he yanked them off, her sneakers went flying, slamming into the shower curtain and landing in the tub.

Jess went back to Smitty's fly, desperately yanking it down while Smitty leaned over and dug into the medicine cabinet. A box of condoms in his hand, he went back to kissing her, rocking her to her toes at the urgency she felt in his every move.

Like he simply had to have her.

Lord, she tasted good. He could kiss her for hours and never get tired of it. But his body was screaming at him. Screaming for him to take her. He'd never felt such urgency before. Not for any female. Usually, Smitty took his time, driving a woman crazy until she couldn't see straight. Until she was begging him.

But Jessie Ann didn't beg. She didn't have to. Instead, she snatched the box of condoms out of his hand and tore the cardboard open. When she had one, he caught her hand in his.

Panting, he said, "Wait, Jessie Ann. Just wait." He rested his forehead against hers, trying to get his breath back. Trying to get control.

"Okay," she said softly. "Okay."

Closing his eyes, grateful she gave him some breathing room, he thought about how he'd take his time, make this right. This was Jessie Ann, after all. Little Jessie Ann. She deserved this to be right and proper and . . . and . . .

Smitty let go a vicious snarl as Jessie's fingers scratched a little-known spot at the base of his scalp. One of his two "happy spots." *How* she knew, he had no idea. But almost immediately his right leg started to shake as his rational mind slipped away.

"Don't—"

But she did, clever fingers stroking, digging into that spot and scratching harder.

"Dammit, Jessie Ann!" was the last thing he said before he took hold of her panties and ripped them off with one yank.

Grinning as she tore open the condom packet, the tip of her tongue resting against her top lip, she lifted his cock from his jeans and rolled the latex on.

Smitty took firm hold of her thighs, yanking her to the edge of the counter. He fit his cock against her—amazed how wet and hot she was with so little effort on his part—and shoved home.

Both of them groaned, then Jessie wrapped her arms around his shoulders, pulling him closer. He gripped her ass tight in both hands and braced his legs apart to keep him steady. She held him like her life depended on it. He'd never had a woman hold him so tight, one arm around his shoulder, the other his waist while her ankles stayed locked behind the small of his back. He tipped her back, giving him the perfect angle.

Taking firm hold of her hips, Smitty fused his lips to hers before he slowly pulled out of her only to drive back in. She screamed into his mouth, but that did nothing except make him insane. He held still inside her for a minute, his cock throbbing as her pussy clenched around him. One more time he desperately tried for control, but Jessie rested her lips against his ear and whispered one word.

"Smitty."

The wolf in him took hold and he pulled out only to slam back in. Again and again—with a ferociousness that worried even him.

She thought they'd been bullshitting. Or bragging. Or both. All those giggling girls who'd said they'd been with one of the Smith brothers. Jess would sit under the bleachers in the gym or at the football field, or she'd hide in trees and listen to those stupid, silly girls go on and on about "going on a Smith ride."

But now she knew. As she gripped the man who fucked her senseless for, hell, she didn't know how long, Jess realized those girls hadn't been bullshitting. At least not about Smitty they hadn't been.

And when that Smitty-provided orgasm snuck up on her, she couldn't even scream or speak. Instead, it felt like her heart had stopped and her organs temporarily shut down as her head fell back and she gasped, her entire body sort of clenching around him, gripping him so tight she knew she would have broken a lesser man.

"Oh, yeah, Jessie Ann," Smitty panted against her sweat-drenched skin. "Oh, God, yeah."

Then he gave a shout and she felt him let go, his body giving a hard jerk as he came.

For a moment, she thought his knees would buckle as he leaned against her, breathing hard and holding her tight. But he held steady and strong, like always.

They stayed like that for several minutes, saying nothing but feeling each heartbeat, each ragged breath.

Jess finally gazed into Smitty's face. He smiled and started to say something, but she immediately cut him off. "Don't say anything that will annoy me."

Smitty stared off for a long moment, let out a breath, opened his mouth to say something, but shook his head. When he finally looked back at her, all he could manage was a shrug.

Chapter 12

Smitty dropped her on his bed, reaching down to help her off with the rest of her clothes. He shucked his just as quickly and stretched out on the bed next to her.

Resting on his side, Smitty propped his head up with one hand while dragging the other slowly down her body. Amazed at how soft her skin felt. *She must bathe in lotion*, he thought before gently taking her shoulder and turning her onto her stomach. His hand skimmed down her back, resting on her ass while he slowly kissed his way down her spine. Now he had some control. Now he'd keep it.

"I want you to stay tonight," he stated between lazy kisses.

"No," she replied firmly, her head resting on her folded arms. "But I'll stay for a while."

Smitty palmed her ass, turned his hand, and slowly thrust two fingers inside her. She groaned and rocked back against his hand. Wrapping her arms around the pillow, she buried her face and moaned his name.

It annoyed him more than was reasonable that she seemed so ready to walk out his door when they were done. He really should be grateful. Getting involved with Jessie Ann was just a quicker way to break her heart. He eventually would too. Jessie had "forever with pups" written all over her. She needed someone nice and sweet and completely nonthreatening to her or her Pack. He needed someone who could handle being around the females of the Smith Pack. No way would he spend the next forty years searching for Jessie under bleachers.

Still . . . she'd leave when he was ready for her to leave and not a damn minute before.

Smitty continued kissing her back, his hand busy between her thighs. Turning his fingers inside her, he found a spot that had her gasping and biting the pillow.

"You're beautiful, Jessie Ann," he sighed while rubbing that same spot, over and over until he heard a small sob break from her. "Always have been."

Jess turned her face away as if she couldn't handle his words while her body writhed on his bed.

He kept up the pressure with his hand, while leaving a trail of hickeys down her spine. She abruptly lost her breath and then tensed, her entire body pushing back. She came hard, her head thrown back and her hips pushing against his hand.

By the time she crash-landed on the bed, her entire body still shaking from release, Smitty had a condom on and raised to his knees behind her. Grabbing her hips, he lifted them up and slammed his cock inside her.

Startled and more than ready, Jessie raised herself up on her hands and let out a throaty laugh that drove him completely insane. Back to being out of control, Smitty pounded into her relentlessly, barely aware she pushed back on each brutal thrust. Hell, barely aware of his own damn name. So out of it, he didn't realize he had his fangs out and almost buried in the flesh of her shoulder—marking her as his until the end of time—until Jessie let out a desperate sob, her entire body unraveling under him.

That's when he pulled back, somehow getting control of the wolf inside him. Barely.

Desperate and, to be quite blunt, a little terrified, Smitty pushed Jessie forward, reaching around her and taking firm hold of her breasts with his hands. Then he fucked her hard and long and almost angry, until Jessie screamed into the pillow she'd buried her head in. Screamed and shook and came like crazy. That's when he finally let go, coming so hard it hurt.

Smitty dropped on top of her, trapping her under him. It wasn't until her arms sort of reached out and flailed wildly that he realized he might be suffocating her.

With a groan, he rolled off her, and Jessie's head popped up as she gasped for air.

Now, thoroughly exhausted and still, to continue being blunt, terrified, Smitty grabbed her around the waist and pulled her down next to him.

"Okay," she finally stated after they got their breath back. "So I really enjoyed that kiss. Just get over yourself."

Smitty chuckled and buried his face into the back of her neck. "That's real big of ya, Jessie Ann."

"I do try and bring joy wherever I go, however I can."

Yup—and that's what terrified him. For the first time in his life, he'd actually found joy in a woman's arms. Can't say as he liked it much, and he had no intention of losing control like that again.

Of course, he also thought as he drifted to sleep with Jessie in his arms, that didn't mean they couldn't have fun while it lasted. Nice, controlled, hot sex fun.

Yeah, that would work.

Jess opened her eyes, quickly realizing it was late evening. She must have slept hours.

Time to go.

Seriously. She had a crapload of work waiting for her, and although this had been a blast, she needed to get back to the office. Yet, she had every intention of doing this again. Hell, she'd do this again and again until a nice wild dog came along who could sweep her off her feet. But until then, sex with Bobby Ray Smith definitely had a place in her busy universe.

When she could fit him into her schedule, of course.

On his stomach, face buried in his pillow and snoring, Smitty seemed perfectly out of it. Jess eased toward the edge of the bed. Smitty's arm rested around her waist, but it would take nothing to slip out from under it and out of his apartment.

She kept thinking that, too, as she tried to get that arm off her. Jess finally dragged herself across the bed, Smitty still attached to her even as they both tumbled onto the floor.

"Where are you going?" he finally asked, his grip tightening around her waist, if that were possible.

"Home," she lied. She had a feeling he'd be upset if she went back to the office. Although she had no idea why she should care if he was.

"Stay." He yawned and rested his head on her back. "Stay the night."

A strange panic swept through her. Stay? The night? No. Bad idea. She needed to maintain as much distance as possible when they weren't having sex. Thousands of miles would be good.

"Can't. Gotta go." She again tried to drag herself away from him using her arms, but he held on, eventually yanking her back right by his side. Jess fell flat to the floor seconds before Smitty flipped her over.

She looked into that beautiful face with his brown hair a sexy mess falling into his eyes and that slow, wicked smile, and all she wanted to do was run.

He stared at her for a long moment, those dangerous wolf eyes trapping her.

"I bet I can make you stay," he finally murmured.

Yeah, he probably could.

"Smitty, no. Bad dog!"

Now he laughed, pulling her body toward him, pinning her legs down with his torso. She slapped her hands against his shoulders and pushed, but Smitty only stared at her breasts and sighed before leaning down to gently grip one of her nipples between his lips.

Desperate now, Jess pushed harder against his shoulders. She was running out of fight here. Fast. But her body arched into him as his mouth sucked on one nipple and his fingers teased the other.

She could feel herself losing the fight. Losing to her weakness.

Then he moved lower, and Jess again tried to struggle out of his grasp. Her last and only hope. But Smitty only gripped her thighs tight, keeping her in place. He gave her that lazy, wicked smile again before he slowly kissed his way to her pussy.

No! Not this! Anything but this. She'd been hearing about the man's skills in this area since before she could fully understand what the hell the girls were talking about. There were some men in the world who loved nothing more than to give a girl head. They'd feast on a pussy for days if you let them.

According to Smithtown lore, Bobby Ray Smith was one of those men.

She didn't even try to keep up the fight anymore. Not once his tongue speared between her lips, stroking against all that wetness he'd already created. He licked, he sucked, he nibbled. He drove her insane.

So lost, Jess could do nothing but ride his mouth while her hand reached out to grip the legs of the bed and the bedside table. The only way to hold her steady as the man took her right to the edge . . . right . . . *there*.

"So you'll stay?"

Jess's head snapped up. "What?"

"Stay?" he asked, apparently in no rush to get back to what he'd been doing. "Tonight? All night?"

She shouldn't. Really. So much to do, so much riding on her shoulders. But one look into those eyes and she was lost. In what universe did she actually think she could handle Smitty when it came to sex? Delusional. She'd become delusional.

Unfortunately, though, it was too late now. Too late for anything.

"Yes," she groaned out, her hand releasing the table and reaching down to grip his head, pushing him back to the job he was doing so very well. "Yes, I'll stay. Oh God! Yes!"

* * *

It was after midnight when Jess slipped out of bed, grabbed her phone, and stumbled to the bathroom. Stumbled because a body couldn't really be expected to walk after all *that*. Man oh man. Egotistical he might be but apparently with reason.

After a quick use of the facilities, Jess stood at the counter and sent a text message to May letting her know she'd be home in the morning. The last thing she needed was for her Pack to show up at Smitty's door, demanding to know if she was okay.

May wrote back immediately—which let Jess know she'd been waiting up for her—

RIDE HIM, GIRL!

Stretching like any good canine loved to do, she reveled in how relaxed she felt. She hadn't felt this relaxed in ages. She forgot how much she enjoyed it.

Jess grinned and pulled open the bathroom door. Smitty stood on the other side.

They stared at each other until Jess asked, "Can I help you?"

"I'm hungry."

"That sounds like a personal problem."

She would say he frowned, but he'd actually already been frowning when she opened the door.

"Feed me."

Did he expect her to cook for him? A few hours of fucking and suddenly she was responsible for managing his hunger?

She wiggled past him since he was blocking the entire doorway with that big wolf body of his. "I'm not cooking, Smith. If you're hungry, cook your own damn meal."

Jess tried to crawl back into bed, but Smitty swept her up in his arms.

"Put me down, you cretin!"

Smitty carried her into the kitchen with her flailing all the way until he sat down in a chair at the kitchen table and fixed Jess onto his lap facing him. That's when she realized he already had a big plate of leftover cold fried chicken, a pitcher of iced tea, a big bowl of barbeque potato chips, and a cherry cobbler laid out on the table.

Jess stared at the mini-feast in confusion until she felt Smitty push his way inside her. She gasped in surprise, looking away from the food and at Smitty. Whether he'd been wearing the condom already when he walked her over here or had one sitting at the table, she didn't know. All she did know was he took his time burrowing his way inside her pussy, his eyes focused on where they were joined. Once he'd seated himself completely inside her, he looked up and repeated, "Feed me."

"Now?"

His hands, tightly gripping her hips, raised her up and quickly slammed her back down. Her toes curled at the feel of him inside her, her breath coming out in hard little pants.

"Feed. Me."

"Okay, okay," she said between breaths.

Jess reached over to the plate of fried chicken and grabbed a drumstick. She held it in front of Smitty's mouth and, his eyes never leaving her face, he took a bite. He chewed and motioned to her with a slow lift of his chin. It wasn't until she ate that first bite of chicken that she realized exactly how hungry she was. Starving actually, since she'd barely touched breakfast and had missed lunch altogether.

She fed him chicken while he slipped her chips. They both drank their own tea. And the entire time he stayed inside her. Sometimes he'd use hands messy with chip grease to rock her on top of his cock. Other than that he didn't say a word. She found that strangely erotic. Maybe because most of those around her, including herself, never really shut up. Smitty didn't talk while he ate, though. He barely spoke while he fucked. The combination of the two practically made him a mute.

Yet, she had to admit to herself that never before in her entire thirty-two years had she *ever* been this turned on.

Sure, Smitty could have just fed her and taken her back to bed to fuck once they were done. That's what most people did.

But waking up and finding her gone had annoyed him more than he'd admit. Then immediately feeling relief when he realized she'd only gone to the bathroom did nothing but piss him off. There were few wolves who didn't wake up to find the She-wolves they'd bedded long gone. Most females didn't stick around unless physically tied to the bed, which often led to all sorts of enjoyments and trouble. Smitty, however, never bothered with that because he never really cared much if they were still there when he woke up.

To be honest, he avoided most full-human females because he usually woke up with them hanging on to him like a capsized boat after the Titanic went down. He'd wake up feeling smothered and annoyed.

Finding Jessie gone had annoyed him more than if he'd found her wrapped around him like a blanket.

He wouldn't think about that, though. He definitely wouldn't worry about it. He had her right where he wanted her. In his lap, on his cock, feeding him chicken. A man, any man, couldn't ask for much more.

They finished most of the chicken and chips, leaving only the cobbler.

Jessie examined the table. "You forgot plates and forks."

She had yet to realize he never forgot anything. Not with his training.

Smitty used two fingers to dig into the cobbler, raising them to Jessie's lips. She stared at his hand in surprise, the most adorable little smile on her lips.

"Open," he growled.

A soft almost-laugh, almost-moan slid from the back of her throat as she slowly licked her lips before opening her mouth. He placed his fingers inside and she closed her mouth around them. First her tongue cleaned off the pieces of cherry and cobbler crust; then she sucked hard to rid his fingers of the filling.

He didn't know what got to him more: the suction with which she sucked his fingers, the little sounds she made while she did it, or the way her eyes closed and her entire body rocked against him. Probably the last because it showed him how much this was turning her on.

Her pussy pulsed around his cock, making it harder than Smitty could ever remember it being.

She finished cleaning off his fingers and leaned back a bit. Holding his gaze, she licked her lips and said, "Yum." Then she smiled. That big, goofy Jessie Ann smile. It was silly and ridiculous and innocently sweet.

And made him want to fuck her so bad, he couldn't even see straight.

One second she'd been sitting on his lap, jokingly debating with herself whether she should go into porn with her fabulous new techniques. The next she was slammed to the floor with a growling Smitty on top of her.

Wow, she briefly thought as Smitty powered into her again and again, *I* am *good*. Then she stopped thinking altogether when Smitty kissed her, his forceful thrusts never stopping, the merciless rhythm never changing.

He felt so good inside her, filling her completely. Maybe even a tad too much. But she didn't care. She simply wrapped one arm around his neck, the other around his back, and held him tight against her as he fucked her. She groaned into his mouth during that first orgasm. Screamed into it during that second. And blacked out for a few seconds during that third one.

When she snapped back into the moment, Smitty was groaning into her hair, his body shaking and shuddering until he collapsed into her arms.

They stayed like that for a long while until Smitty slowly got to his feet, Jess tight against him. He stumbled across the room and back to bed. Together, they dropped onto the mattress and Jess fell right back to sleep, enjoying the scent of the wild wolf lying next to her.

Chapter 13

When the alarm blared to life at five, Smitty quickly shut it off and stumbled out of bed. No matter how many years he spent in the service, he never seemed to be able to grasp the whole early to bed, early to rise logic. He glanced back at Jessie Ann. She was still out cold, her head buried into his pillow, her naked ass peeking out from under the sheets she'd tried to kick off in the night.

One eyebrow raised, he debated about going back to bed and getting some more of that ass. Then he realized he couldn't do a damn thing without his coffee. So, he made his way into the kitchen, ground up his beans, and started the machine. Stopped by his bathroom and took care of some necessary functions and then went back out to the coffee machine to watch and wait.

He'd just poured himself a hot cup of coffee, his mouth already watering as he brought the mug to his lips.

"Oh, thanks, sweetie." And like that, the cup was gone.

He glared down at the female who dared take his coffee. The life-giving elixir was his! Then he noticed she was fully dressed.

"You're leaving?" Damn. And he really did have plans for that adorable little ass.

"Oh, yeah." She sipped the coffee and grimaced. "Geez. Battery acid." It suddenly occurred to him . . . She was perky. Who was perky at five-thirty in the morning?

Good Lord! *Morning people* were perky at five-thirty in the morning!

"I've got meetings all morning. I need to get to the office."

"Now?"

"Yup. In fact, I've gotta go." She gave him the half-full mug and shrugged into her coat, then hauled that nightmarish back-pack onto her shoulders. "I had a great time. I have to say all those slutty She-wolves were right. You're amazing." She stood on tiptoe and kissed his cheek. "And I *really* needed that. Thank you."

"My pleasure," he murmured with all honesty.

"Okay. Well . . . bye!" She turned and walked out of his apartment.

Wait. That was it? No passionate kiss? No promises of call-ing him later? Or making him promise to call her later? What the hell?

Confused and barely awake, Smitty stood staring at the closed door for at least a minute before he slammed the mug of coffee down on the counter and went after her. She stood patiently waiting for the elevator, her eyes bright and alert as she stared at the murals on the ceiling painted by the previous owner of his apartment. Smitty worked hard to ignore the fact that she was muttering to herself.

"So when will I see you again?" he heard himself asking.

She looked at him calmly. "Got me. I've got a hell of a sched-ule right now."

"Yeah, but—"

"But you can always text me."

And she said that just like she might have said, "I don't mind cheese on my salad if it's available."

He crossed his arms over his chest, barely aware he stood be-fore her butt naked. "Text you?"

"Yeah, but I know we're both busy." She smiled. "Don't worry. I won't call you crying hysterically if I don't hear from you. No shotgun wedding." Then she laughed.

The elevator doors opened and she immediately stepped in. "Bye, handsome."

Fifteen minutes later and he was still standing in the same exact spot.

Three meetings and one high-level firing and it was barely eleven A.M. Once in her office, Jess kicked off her pumps and threw herself into her chair.

She had to admit, paying attention to any of it had not been easy. She couldn't stop thinking about fried chicken and hard cock. Although those thoughts made that firing go a lot easier.

Christ, she was in too deep. She should be able to have sex with a man and then not think about it again. She knew women who did that all the time. But, as usual, Jess didn't really know how to separate her heart from her pussy. She hated it too. Hated what she considered a weakness. She had no doubts Smitty wasn't spending a second thinking about her. Although a big part of her wanted him to be. She wanted him as wound up and horny as she was.

"Why should I suffer alone?" she murmured to herself.

Hell, it didn't matter. She still had a lot of work to do. She spun her chair around and raised her wrist to look at her watch when she saw them all sitting there, filling up her couch and the available chairs—watching her.

"What?"

When her four friends all continued to stare, she snorted. "Forget it. I'm not telling you guys anything."

"Why not?"

She liked how Phil had the nerve to sound so indignant that she wasn't filling them in on all the details of her night with Smitty.

"Because it's none of your business."

"We told you about our first time," Phil coaxed.

"You didn't tell me anything. I was there. In a sleeping bag across the room desperately trying to mind my own business. But you, sir, are a screamer."

*   *   *

Smitty woke up the seventh time someone called. They wouldn't leave a message, they just kept calling back instead. He'd gone back to bed as soon as he'd walked back into his apartment. He didn't really have any intention of getting up before he was ready. Seemed someone else had other plans.

Snatching the phone off the receiver, he barked, "Yeah?"

" 'Bout time you picked up the damn phone, boy."

Smitty scowled. "Daddy?"

"Who did ya think it was? The Queen of Siam?"

Sitting up in bed, Smitty shook his head. It was too early for this. Too early to deal with the one man who still rattled him. And he'd been having such sweet dreams too. Well . . . sweet and damn dirty. He simply couldn't seem to get enough of Jessie Ann. He should have worked her out of his system last night. But pathetic wolf that he was, he simply had to have her again. He would too. He snorted when he realized all he had to do was *text* her. Lord, what he'd been reduced to.

"Are you there, boy?"

"Huh?" Smitty shook his head again. Damn, he'd completely forgotten about his father. That had to be a first. Must be his lack of coffee. Anything before noon and he couldn't focus without his coffee. "Oh, yeah. Sorry, Daddy." He scratched his head, yawned. "So why are you calling me?"

"I'm trying to figure out this bullshit your momma's been telling me. What does she mean you don't want anything to do with the Tennessee Smith territory?"

Yeah, he needed his coffee . . . *now*. "Momma told me y'all were revising territorial lines and I asked her not to include me." Smitty got out of bed and headed for his kitchen. "I'm not going to fight those idiots over Smithtown. Let them have it."

"You always were a fool, boy."

Faster. Make coffee faster. Cradling the phone between his neck and shoulder, Smitty tossed out the crappy coffee from earlier, ground up fresh beans, and poured water into the pot. His apartment didn't have a lot, but a reliable, sturdy coffeepot would always be an integral part.

"Why does that make me a fool? I'm not coming back there, Daddy. This is my home now. This is Sissy's. We'll make this work."

His father laughed. "Do you really believe that? Do you really think you'll be able to compete with all those fancy high-end companies? Do you think that *cat* will stay loyal to you? He'll be out as soon as he gets bored and you'll be left holding that bag. Be smart, boy, for once in your life. Come back to Smithtown where y'all belong. Before those other Packs get a sniff of you and try to force you out. Y'all ain't strong enough to fight off those bigger Packs, and we both know it."

Smitty pushed his empty mug away and leaned against the counter. "No," he finally stated.

"Dammit, boy! You never—"

"Bye, Daddy. Tell Momma I said hey."

He disconnected the phone while his daddy was still going off and sat in the silence of his apartment for several minutes.

Several long minutes before that phone went flying, smashing into the wall and breaking into way too many pieces for him to bother repairing.

Jess walked into her office. Another two meetings, one right after the other. Barely one o'clock and already exhausted.

Sitting at her desk, Jess speed dialed her assistant. Bets worked on the floor right beneath this one. Normally Jess would have an assistant right outside her office, but Betsy was full-human, so she didn't come to this floor without a special request. Jess knew the woman found it weird, but she got paid so much she overlooked it.

"Hey, Jess."

"Hey, Bets. Anything I need to know about?"

"I've e-mailed you a list of client callbacks you should make."

"Can you handle any of them?"

A long pause followed her statement. So long, Jess thought she'd lost her. "Bets?"

"I'm here."

"What's wrong?"

"I can handle most of the calls . . . if you want me to."

"I wouldn't have asked if I didn't want you to."

"It's not a problem, but usually you handle, well, pretty much everything."

"I'm tired today. Too tired for bullshit." It's not like she got much sleep the night before. "So anything you can handle—"

"Not a problem," Bets rushed in. Suddenly Jess wondered if she'd been holding the poor woman back. And if she had, why did Bets stay?

"I'll send you an updated callback list for people who really need to hear from you and not your lackey."

"You're not my lackey, Bets."

She chuckled. "Let's see. You also got a call from Kenshin Inu."

Jess immediately perked up. "Oh, Kenshin! How is he?"

"Sounds fine. He'll be in town in the next couple of weeks and he says he'll want to get together. I e-mailed you his new cell phone number."

"I see it. Thanks."

"And a Bobby Ray Smith called."

"He did?" Jess frowned. She told him to text her. Why would he call? And why was she so damn happy he did?

"Did he say what he wanted?"

"He wants to meet for lunch."

"Call him back and tell him—"

"And he said if you start, and I'm quoting here, 'Fussin' about it,' to tell you that his daddy called."

"His father called him?" That couldn't be good. To be honest, Jess thought the man such a Neanderthal that he didn't possess the necessary skill set to use a phone, much less dial out of the Tennessee region.

"I don't really know if his father called him. I'm just repeating what he said. But I did enjoy his use of 'fussing' in a sentence."

Jess went to look at her watch, and that's when she realized she didn't have it on. Christ, where did she leave it last?

"Jess?"

Panic flooded her system as she grabbed her backpack, tearing through it.

"Jess?"

"Give me a second, Bets."

"He also said to tell you if you're wondering where your watch is . . . he has it."

She closed her eyes, horrified at how relieved she felt. No one should be that attached to an inanimate object. "Oh."

"I won't ask what that means. I'm sure it's none of my business."

"You're right. When's my next meeting today?"

"Not until three, so you'll have some time. He's waiting at the diner around the corner."

"Okay. Is the meeting a call-in or face-to-face?"

"Call-in for the rest of the day. So you're okay to change."

"Thank God!" Jess kicked off the damn pumps again. "Thanks, Bets."

"No problem. I'll get back to you after I've spoken to the clients."

"Good."

Jess went to the small closet she had built into the wall and pulled out something much more comfortable to wear. Especially since she was only going to see Smitty. It's not like she wanted to impress him or anything.

Chapter 14

Smitty looked up from the newspaper in front of him and blinked. How could anyone look so ridiculous and cute at the same time?

His eyes narrowed. It had to be that stupid parka. It was too big for her, covering her from head to knees. She had to be able to afford something better than that. But clothes had never been Jessie's thing. Still, no matter what she wore and if she'd let him, he'd bend her over this table and fuck the living—

"Hi," she said when she stood at his table.

He cleared his throat, unable to stand up at the moment. Hopefully she didn't need that level of politeness his mother had taught him. "Hey, darlin'. Thanks for coming."

"No problem. I needed a break from the office anyway. And I want my watch back." He wondered how intense her panic had gotten when she realized she wasn't wearing it. A six or seven on the Richter scale?

She unzipped the parka and pulled it off, hanging it from the coat stand against the back wall. She slid into the booth and immediately his waitress showed up.

"Heya, Jess."

"Hi, Trish."

"The usual, sweetie?"

"Yeah, that'll be fine."

The older woman laughed. A wheezing sound that suggested Trish had been a smoker since she turned twelve. "You are such a creature of habit." She turned to Smitty. "What about you, handsome?"

"Whatever she's having . . . just double it."

Jess snorted. "Triple it, Trish. Thanks." She smirked at Smitty. "Double it, my ass. You'd be eating again in an hour."

"I didn't want to embarrass you."

"I have other clients I bring in here. Any time I show up with this tiger, Peter Greely, we have to quadruple the order. He practically shuts the place down."

Smitty chose to ignore the fact that she was hanging around tigers. Like those striped bastards could be trusted.

"So your dad called?"

Closing up his paper and placing it on the seat beside him, Smitty said, "Yup. He called all right."

"Why?"

"To tell me I'm making a mistake. To tell me I should bring my ass back home. To tell me what a loser I am."

Trish placed a Coke in front of Jessie and filled up Smitty's coffee mug. Jess sipped her pop through a bendy straw like a ten-year-old and stared off thoughtfully. He blew on his coffee, and as he brought the mug to his lips, barely tasting the strong brew, Jessie said matter-of-factly, "You do know your father can be an amazing prick, right?"

Good thing he wore dark colors today because he'd probably never get the coffee stains out.

Jessie winced, grabbing a napkin and leaning across the table to wipe the coffee off Smitty's chin and neck.

"Sorry."

"No, no. You're probably one of the few people who actually has the guts to say the words out loud."

"It just seems to be what he does. To keep control. Convince you guys, you and your brothers, that you're fuckups and that you can't survive without him. Besides," she added, "I think he really likes having you around."

Smitty snorted. "Oh, come on. Let's not bullshit a bullshitter."

"I'm serious. He was really sad the day you left. I saw him at the bus—"

She cut herself off and looked around the restaurant.

"You were at the bus station the day I left?"

"Well, uh . . ."

"Jessie Ann?"

"I was near it."

"Near it how?"

"Hiding in a utility closet that had a window so that I could see the bus."

She had no idea, did she? How much it meant to him to know she'd come that day. Knowing she'd risked being caught by his sister and her merry band of She-bitches.

"I thought I caught your scent, but I figured it was my imagination. I really wanted you to be there. It's nice to know you were."

"Yeah, well." She took another sip of her pop. "Anyway, your dad was real sad. He didn't want you to go. But I think he knew you had no choice."

"That's some mighty guessing you're doing there."

"When you spend most of your time watching people, you learn to pick up things." She rubbed her nose and frowned. Rubbed her nose and grimaced.

"Jessie Ann?"

Before she could answer, the sneezing started and didn't stop.

Leaning over a bit, he saw that the woman in the booth behind Jessie had a bouquet of flowers in her hand. The man sitting with her must have just given her the damn things.

"I'll be right back," he said to her before sliding out of the booth and walking over to the couple.

Jess hadn't brought her backpack, but she'd shoved her allergy stuff in the big pocket of her parka. God, she loved this coat!

By the time she'd pulled the little zipped plastic pouch out, Trish had brought her a glass of water. She swallowed two pills as best she could while sneezing and pulled her nasal spray out next. By the time she finished using that, her sneezing stopped and Smitty was sliding back into the booth. She thought for sure she'd have to use her inhaler and probably leave, but when she turned around, she saw that the couple with the offending flowers had moved to a table across the room.

"What did you say to get them to move?"

"I just asked 'em nice."

"This is New York. Nice does not exist here."

"It works for me. Must be my charm."

"And the fact you're built like a fullback for the Dallas Cowboys. You probably terrified them."

"That too." He smiled. "Feel better?"

"Yeah, sorry about that."

"Don't apologize, darlin'. I just can't believe you still have those allergies. I figured you'd grow out of them."

"I thought so too. But no such luck. Plants, not really a problem anymore. But flowers . . . my doom."

Smitty laughed and moved his arms off the table so Trish could put their food down.

Once she walked away, he said with what seemed like total honesty, "I'm glad I got to see you today."

"You're lucky my schedule allowed for it. My next meeting's not until three."

"So then we still have time to go back to my apartment and—"

"No, we don't." Although she was glad he actually suggested it. Did wonders for her ego.

"Fine. Guess we'll just have to talk then."

Jess put her usual quart of ketchup on her burger and over her fries. "I guess I fell right into that little trap, now didn't I?"

"Like an impala."

Before biting into her burger, Jess had to ask, "Talk about what?"

"Let's start off easy. Why did you leave?"

Easy. Yeah. Sure. "Well, after throwing Bertha off Otter's Hill, figured it would be in my best interest to get out of town."

Smitty stroked his chin. "I thought she got drunk and fell off."

"No, she was drunk when she came up there looking for me because apparently she hadn't kicked my ass enough earlier in the day. But when she went over—that was all me."

"My, my, Jessie Ann Ward. You sure are full of surprises."

"You have no idea."

Once she told him about Bertha—and wasn't *that* a surprise—she got comfortable enough to tell him more about her and her friends and some of what happened over the past sixteen years. She held a lot back, though. There were still holes she didn't seem ready to fill. Yet, how she and her four friends had lived this long, he had no idea. Between Phil shooting his mouth off at inopportune times; Sabina pissing off and physically threatening the wrong person—constantly; May walking down dark alleys by herself; Danny so paranoid by all of society he kept making the United States Secret Service nervous; and Jessie walking into buildings, cars, walls, telephone poles, small children, houses . . . whatever . . . they all should have ended up dead several times over.

Funny, he thought only cats had nine lives.

"You sure have been all over."

"In the States, yeah. Chicago, Flagstaff, Detroit, Seattle, San Diego, and Aberdeen. That's in Texas."

"You planning on moving again?"

"No, I want the kids to have a stable place to grow up. I did the cross-country thing with my parents before they got sick. It was great and I learned a lot, but when they died—there I was stuck in Tennessee with no one. When they're eighteen, they can do what they want and go where they want. But until then, their asses are staying right here."

"Seems like you've got good control over it all."

"I guess. But some days you wonder."

"Wonder what?"

"How much more you could fuck it up?"

Smitty pushed his empty plate away. "You're doing a great

job, Jessie. You're not fucking up a damn thing. Don't let anybody tell you different."

She rewarded him with a small smile. "Thank you."

"You're welcome." He rested his elbow on the table and his chin on his fist. "So you're coming by tonight."

"And wouldn't it be nice if you actually asked that?"

"If I asked, you might say no."

Laying her hands flat on the table, Jessie studied them. "I don't really know what we're doing, Smitty."

"Do you mean literally?"

"No." She gaped at him. "I know what we're doing literally."

"Just checking."

"I mean getting together for sex is one thing. But having lunches and talking about family and our Packs seems outside the realm of casual sex."

"We were friends, Jessie. I want that back. The sex is just a bonus." *A really hot, makes my legs tremble bonus.* "Why? Do you want more?" Did he just ask that? Had aliens invaded his body? What the hell was going on?

Even worse was her response. "No."

If she'd done the "Of course not!" or "Whatever gave you that idea?" and then tried to argue the point, well . . . he'd know she'd want more. But that one simple word, given in that simple Jessie Ann way, said she wanted exactly what she was getting.

Good. That made it nice and simple, now didn't it? And that empty feeling he got in the pit of his stomach when she said no all calm and casual was probably just from that last hamburger he ate. Nothing more.

"I gotta cash out, hon."

Jess, busy laughing at something Smitty said, looked up at Trish. "You're leaving early today."

The waitress smiled, glancing at Smitty. "No, I'm not."

Jess didn't understand. Trish clocked out at four-thirty, right before the dinner rush.

Glancing at the clock behind the counter, Jess's eyes grew. "Oh, good God! Look at the time!"

She frantically dug into her front pocket and pulled out a wad of bills. Since they were all rolled up, she had to unroll them to make sure she was putting out the right amount.

"Jessie Ann, I invited you. I'll pay."

"I can pay."

"It's too pathetic watching you with those crumpled bills. I'll take care of it."

"Okay." She quickly slid out of the booth. "I can't believe no one called me. I've already missed two meetings."

Smitty grabbed her arm before she could get to her coat. "Breathe."

"What?"

"Breathe. You stopped as soon as you saw the time."

Feeling stupid, Jess took in a deep breath.

"Now let it out."

She did, even though she kind of wanted to snarl at him. If it hadn't been for him and how comfortable he made her feel, she would have remembered she needed to get back to the office.

"Don't forget, Jessie. You're the boss. If you don't make a meeting, it's up to your staff to cover for you."

"Yeah, but—"

He gripped her lips with his fingertips. "Shush. I don't know why you argue with me when you know I'm always right."

She slapped his hand off her face and turned around before he could see her smile. "You're an idiot, Smith." She snatched her coat off the hook and shrugged it on. "I'll see you later."

"Tonight. You'll see me tonight."

Jess didn't have time to argue. "Fine. Tonight." Then she charged out the door, only to stop at the corner, spin around, and run right back in. Smitty still sat at their table, her watch in his hand.

Glaring at him, she grabbed it and headed back to the door. He made her forget her watch. She *never* forgot her watch.

"Jessie Ann."

She stopped at the door. "What?"

"Come here."

"I don't have—"

"Come. Here."

She stood there a second longer.

"Don't make me come over there and get you."

Dammit. Why did he have to sound so sexy when physically threatening her?

Letting out an exasperated sigh to cover up the slight trembling, she stormed back over to the table. "What?"

He crooked his finger at her.

Glancing around, Jess saw several people staring at them. "What?" she snarled at them all. "Can I help you with something?"

"Hey, Miss New York."

She looked back at Smitty. "What?"

"You done yelling at people?"

"They were staring."

He grinned. "Come here."

"I am here."

"Closer."

She leaned in a bit.

"Closer."

She leaned in again until their faces were mere inches apart.

"Now kiss me," he whispered, his breath caressing her mouth.

Unable to stop herself from following his orders—and not really wanting to stop anyway—Jess slid her hand behind his neck and pressed her lips against his. Smitty didn't automatically kiss her back. He didn't slip his tongue into her mouth; he didn't take over the kiss. He simply waited.

Jess tipped her head to the side, moving her lips across his. Then, softly, she drew her tongue across his mouth. His lips parted for her, but he did nothing else, still waiting for her. She closed her eyes, allowing herself to delve further. Her tongue stroked his slowly, firmly, until she felt him groan. Then his hands slid into her hair, holding her head steady as he finally kissed her back. She rested her knee on the booth seat, her arms around his neck.

She had no idea how long they were sitting there, making out like two teenagers, until Trish said, "Don't you have to get back to work, hon?"

Pulling away from Smitty, she looked at the waitress. Now Trish had on her coat, scarf, and hat. Meaning she'd cashed out, gotten her tips counted out and divvied up, and had time to change into warm clothes.

"Dammit!" Jess glared at Smitty and he shrugged.

"What did I do?"

She took off running but could hear him yelling behind her, "Tonight, darlin'."

She got back to her office in less than five minutes. And to her great annoyance, Smitty had been right. Her team had covered for her and didn't seem unhappy at all that she missed the meetings.

Man, she hated when he was right.

Smitty sauntered into the office and Mindy looked up, one eyebrow raised. "How nice of you to join us."

He grinned back at her. "I know how y'all miss me when I'm gone."

She laughed and went back to her paperwork while Smitty headed to his personal office.

Unlocking his office door, he flipped on the light and walked in.

"Look who finally showed up?" Mace yelled from his office.

"I know you missed me, hoss. But you know I can't handle it when you're needy."

"Shut up."

Smiling, looking forward to his evening, Smitty sat down and turned on his computer to check his e-mail. After a few moments, he tapped on the rich mahogany desk before asking, "Why are you under my desk?"

"No reason," his sister replied calmly.

"How's your face?"

"Fine. Who knew Jessie Ann Ward had such a killer right hook?"

Smitty decided it was in his best interest not to mention he'd taught Jessie that right hook. "She's just full of surprises."

"Yeah."

Pushing his chair back, he looked down at his baby sister. "Are you going to stay down there?"

Sissy checked her cell phone. "Just for a little while longer if that's all right with you."

"Sure," he sighed. "Why not?"

Chapter 15

"Have you seen Kristan?" Johnny froze with the sandwich in his hands halfway to his mouth. Jess stood at the table drinking a Coke and watching him.

He cleared his throat. "She's at the library."

"On a Friday night?"

"Paper due."

"Anything interesting?" And she seemed seriously interested.

Giving her complete eye contact, he replied, "I didn't care enough to ask."

She snorted in disgust. "I swear. You two. For all you know it could be a very fascinating topic." She took another sip of her soda. "What about rehearsal?"

Still staring her in the eye like a psychopath, "After I eat. Then I'll pick her up at the library."

"Good. I don't like her walking around the city alone."

Jess brushed his hair back and kissed his forehead. "Thanks for watching out for her, Johnny."

"That's what Packmates do, right?"

"You're learning, kid."

She grabbed her parka, and Johnny casually asked, "You going back to work?" Not unusual. She worked a lot of hours and sometimes would even sleep at her office if she needed to. But instead of her usual, "What do you think?" Jess stared at him, straight in the eye, and slowly responded, "Yes, I'm going back to work."

"Okay."

"I'm going to do that now."

"Okay."

She stared at him a moment longer, then said, "Bye," before escaping from the kitchen.

Weird, but Jess was weird. Pulling out his cell phone, he sent Kristan a text message:

U SO OWE ME.

In less than a minute she responded,

MEET U AT 9. BRINGING ICE CREAM.

He smiled and wrote back,

U BETTER.

Smitty opened his door. "You're late."

"You didn't give me a time."

"And what is it with you and that coat?"

"I love this coat."

"It's too big."

"It's not too big."

Smitty took hold of the hood and pulled it down until it covered her face completely. "See? Too big."

"Are you letting me in or are you going to keep abusing me in your doorway?"

Grabbing her by the too-big hood, he yanked her into his apartment.

"Hey!"

He unzipped her parka, spun her around, and yanked it off her back.

She stumbled forward. "What are you doing?"

"Abusing you inside my apartment instead of my doorway."
He grabbed her around the waist and tossed her across the
room. "And now I'm gonna abuse you on my couch."

Laughing, Jessie scrambled off the couch and took off running.

"You're just making it worse for yourself 'cause you know I
love the chase." Slowly, Smitty followed after her. "I guess it's
time to pull out that firm hand we were talking about yesterday."

Jess gripped the headboard, her knuckles turning white, her
entire body bowing. Good God! The man had the most talented
mouth she'd ever—

"God, Smitty." She panted and writhed under him. Feelings
so intense slamming through her, she tried to pull away. Smitty
gripped her legs tighter, bending them back toward her chest
and pushing them out so she was wide open to him.

Her hold on the headboard tightened, a sob catching in her
throat. He slid two fingers inside her as his mouth continued to
ravage her pussy. He found a spot inside her with his fingertips
and rubbed it again and again until she exploded, her body
quaking in climax, her muscles tightening.

She hadn't even finished coming when Smitty was suddenly
over her and in her. She gripped him tight, one arm around his
neck, the other encircling his back. She wrapped her legs around
his waist, locking her ankles at the base of his spine.

He kissed her, his body rocking against hers. His cock filling
her up, feeling so good inside her.

"Hold me tighter, Jessie Ann."

Jess did, enjoying the fact that he didn't mind. That he didn't
feel trapped by it.

Again, he kissed her, his tongue stroking her like his cock.
Their rhythm was effortless, like they'd been doing it forever.

Another climax tore through her, ripping her open, leaving
her a groaning, sweating, panting mess on Smitty's sheets.

When her eyes uncrossed, she found Smitty lying on top of her. Both of them drained. She stroked his sweat-drenched hair, enjoying his weight on top of her. His head on her breasts.

"Am I too heavy for you?" he was kind enough to ask.

"Nope."

"Good. 'Cause I'm real comfortable."

"Oh, well. As long as you're happy."

"Now you're learning."

She had no idea how long they stayed like that, holding each other. She drifted to sleep, and when she woke up a few hours later, they were on their sides, facing each other, their arms and legs intertwined.

Jess didn't think Smitty was awake until, with his eyes still closed, he asked her, "You hungry?"

"Starving."

Not bothering to open his eyes, he kissed her and placed his hand on top of her head. He started to push her under the covers and she slapped his hands away.

"I'm starving for food, you barbarian!"

Laughing, Smitty rolled onto his back. "You can't blame a guy for trying."

"Explain to me again why I can't wear clothes."

Smitty looked up from the steak he'd nearly finished devouring. "I find clothes distracting. You naked soothes me."

She snickered and went back to her food. Once they'd finished, Smitty leaned back in his chair. She seemed relaxed and comfortable. So he asked her what he'd been wanting to ask her for days.

"Jessie Ann?"

"Hhhm?"

"What's really going on with your Pack?"

She frowned. "What are you talking about?"

"You lied to me the other day. No one was trying to break in. So what really happened?"

Jessie picked up her plate and took it to the sink, trying to give herself enough time to come up with another suitable lie. He wouldn't let her do it this time. He wanted a straight answer.

When she turned around, the lie on her lips, he was standing right behind her. Startled, she jerked back against the counter.

"Tell me the truth, Jessie. No more bullshit."

She opened her mouth, and he said, "And I'll know if you're lying."

Her mouth closed and she peered up at him. She wanted to tell him. He could see it on her face, but she still didn't trust him. For some unknown reason that bothered him. He needed her to trust him.

"Whatever you tell me doesn't leave this apartment. It's just between you and me."

Finally, she said, "That could put you in a very awkward position."

"How do ya mean?"

Jessie stepped away from him and went to his freezer. She grabbed one of the pints of chocolate ice cream his sister kept there. She placed it in the microwave for fifteen seconds, grabbed a couple of spoons, and took the whole thing back to the kitchen table. She sat down, pulling her legs onto the chair. With a slight tilt of her head, she motioned for him to sit cattycorner to her.

"You met May's daughter, Kristan, that night at the office." She took off the top of the ice cream and immediately scooped up a spoonful.

"Yeah."

"Danny isn't her biological father. He met me and May when she was about seven months pregnant. Kristan's real father wanted nothing to do with May or his child."

"But now he's back."

"Now he's back."

She motioned for him to take some ice cream. He wasn't a big fan of ice cream, but it was kind of like being around a smoker or a drinker. If you wanted them to talk, to give you information, you sometimes had to join in.

"If we thought he really wanted to know his daughter, the Pack wouldn't have a problem. Danny probably wouldn't be happy, but he'd follow my lead. But we don't think that's what this guy wants. We think he wants money, and he's willing to use his daughter to get it."

"Jessie Ann, I'm not sure why you didn't tell me this in the first place."

"Because her father is Walt Wilson."

"Who?"

Jessie gave that soft smile that made him crazy. It was so misleadingly innocent. "Walt Wilson? Of the Wilson Pack? Your cousin?"

He shook his head. "Still drawing a blank."

"Out of Smithburg, Alabama."

Smitty thought real hard and then it hit him. "Oh. Oh, yeah. I remember." He grimaced. "Lord, I made him eat shit one time."

Jessie rubbed her eyes. "Tell me you didn't."

He stroked his jaw, trying to get so long ago into focus. "Yeah, I did. If I remember correctly, he was mean to Sissy. Made her cry. I don't think either one of us was more than eight or nine. She was only six or seven. I was gonna make him eat dirt . . . but they used to have a dog."

To his relief, Jessie laughed. "That is a horrible story."

"I know. I know. I'm not proud telling it. But it's the truth." He took another spoonful of ice cream, enjoying it more than he thought he would. "And you didn't want to tell me because you lived in Smithtown long enough to know the Smith credo."

"Family first," she recited. "Pack second. Everybody else dead last."

Or dead, his daddy would always add. A credo the old bastard drummed into the heads of his children growing up. Every Smith in every town lived by it. And that way, everyone knew if you messed with one Smith—really, truly messed with them— you messed with all the Smiths. And no one wanted that laid at their doorstep.

"The Wilsons are blood," she said.

"Barely."

"Still. I lived in Smithtown long enough to know how this works. I have no doubt my Pack could take on the Wilson Pack and win. But all the Smith Packs . . . ?" She let out a breath and treated herself to more ice cream.

"Okay. You've got a point. So how about I do this. I quietly take a look into this—"

"Bobby Ray, I don't want you involved."

"Or you could let me finish," he said gently. "I take a quiet look into this. Maybe with my help I can get him to back off. If all he wants is money. But if he just wants to see his daughter . . ."

"Then we're fine with that. We never lied to Kristan. She knows Danny isn't her blood, but he is her daddy. That little girl's got a big heart and I won't have anyone crushing it."

"Understood." He reached across the table and took her hand. "But let me help."

"Are you sure? I know how your father can be."

"Let me worry about my daddy. He's my cross to bear."

"That's a lovely way to see your father."

Smitty grinned. "You always liked my old man, didn't you?"

Jessie licked her spoon. "You know, he always made me laugh. And when he found me under tables—"

"Under tables?"

"At parties my foster parents made me go to. He'd never tell anybody I was there. Instead, he'd hand me a bottle of . . . well, a bottle of beer."

Smitty placed his elbows on the table and buried his face in his hands. "Good Lord."

"And he'd say, 'Don't worry none, little gal, you'll be just fine.' I had no idea what that meant, but it always made me giggle."

"That could have been the beer."

"Are you sure about this, Bobby Ray?" she asked after a few minutes of silence.

He dropped his hands back to the table. "I can always tell when you're serious because you call me Bobby Ray."

"This is serious. I won't get between you and your family."

"You're not, darlin'. This is what one friend does for another. And we're friends. Just like me and Mace."

She gave him a wicked little smile. "You fuck Mace too?"

"Only when he's feeling needy."

Jessie laughed, a wonderful sound that echoed around his home. Leaning forward, Smitty peeked into the ice cream container. "I wonder what use I can make of this leftover ice cream."

He gazed up at Jessie, raising one eyebrow. She gave a little squeal and made a run for it.

Sitting back in the chair, Smitty asked the cute ass dashing away, "Where are you always running to? It's a one-room apartment."

Jess turned over and looked at the clock. She'd overslept. It was nearly eight in the morning.

She sat up and Smitty's arm immediately wrapped around her waist. "Don't go."

"I'm supposed to make breakfast for the kids this morning and I've already missed that."

"It's Saturday. Stay the weekend."

"I can't do that."

"Why?"

"Um . . ."

"As she scrambles for an excuse," he mumbled under his breath.

"I am not scrambling for an excuse." Man, she really needed to stop lying. But what did he expect? Casual sex didn't involve whole weekends. At least they didn't if she hoped to have a prayer not to get too deep into this. "I just can't—"

"I know," he said, sitting up. "Let's ask the Pack."

And before she could stop him, he'd grabbed her cell phone off the bedside table.

"Give me that!"

"Not until we get an answer." Flipping her phone open, he went up on his knees and went through her contacts. Jess tried to get the phone from him but he kept moving so she couldn't get a grip.

Putting the phone to his ear, he asked, "And who is this? Well, hi, May, darlin'. I've got little Jessie Ann here—"

"Give me that goddamn phone!"

"—as you can hear, and I'm trying to get permission for her to stay the weekend at my house while my parents are out of town."

"I am not playing with you!"

"Yeah, she said she already missed breakfast, but I figure she can make that up during the week. Uh-huh. Yeah, she's still naked."

She gasped. "Bobby Ray!"

"Keep her naked the whole weekend? Yeah, I can do that. Yup. Naked and happy. I can handle that. Thanks, darlin'."

He looked over his shoulder at her. "May says you can stay."

Jess grabbed the phone from Smitty's hand, and as she brought it to her ear, she heard her Pack yell, "Have a good weekend, Jess!" before they hung up.

Slamming the phone shut, Jess turned to yell at Smitty but he'd disappeared—with her clothes!

It was a one-room apartment, but the man was crafty. And by the time Jess had spun in a circle looking for him, he'd suddenly appeared in front of her—without her clothes.

"Where are my clothes?"

"Safe." He reached for her. "Safer than you are."

Jess slapped at his hands and quickly stepped away. "I am *not* staying the weekend."

"You are if you want your clothes back."

"Blackmail!"

"Extortion. Now bring that pretty ass over here. You know I'm cranky in the mornings."

"Go to—hey!"

Smitty scooped her up and walked back over to the bed, throwing her on it. "I don't know why you insist on fighting me." His smile was slow and wicked. " 'Cause we both know you'll give me what I want."

"You are such an egotistical ass—"

He kissed her, pinning her to the bed with his body, his arms holding hers above her head. Before she knew it she was writhing and gasping beneath him.

"I wager," he panted in her ear when he finally pulled back a bit, "I can keep you in this bed all weekend long."

And much to her annoyance and enjoyment . . . he did.

Chapter 16

Smitty slammed open their bedroom door, thoroughly enjoying Ronnie Lee's squeal of surprise and Shaw's roar of anger. Especially when Shaw scrambled to pull the covers over their naked bodies.

"Hey, Ronnie Lee," he said casually. "I was wondering if you could help me with something kind of important."

Shaw went to say something, but Ronnie slapped her hand over his mouth. Smitty bit the inside of his cheek as he eyed the position of their bodies—Brendon on top of Ronnie. And, again, naked.

Lord, Bobby Ray Smith, sometimes you can be a real asshole.

"Bobby Ray, can you go out into the living room? I'll be out in two shakes of a dog's tail."

Fighting to hold in his laughter, he turned and moseyed on down the hallway. As promised, Ronnie suddenly appeared, a hotel robe wrapped tightly around her. She backed out of the bedroom, holding up her finger and pleading, "You just wait right there, darlin'. I'll be back in a few minutes. I promise."

She closed the door and headed down the hall toward Smitty. She held up that finger again, brought it to her lips to indicate silence, and flashed five fingers at him. Then she disappeared down another hallway.

Smitty wandered into the living room and dropped onto the

couch to wait. In about ten minutes, Ronnie reappeared. Freshly showered and dressed, she motioned to Smitty while grabbing her leather jacket.

Ronnie opened the front door and again motioned to Smitty. Knowing where this was going and wondering what exactly was wrong with his people, he stood and followed after her. He met her at the elevator. "What are you doing?"

"Same thing you're doing, only for a different reason." She pushed the elevator button again. It dinged its arrival and the doors slid open. Ronnie pushed Smitty inside as Shaw's roar rang out from their apartment.

"*Ronnie Lee Reed! Where the hell are you going?*"

"Lunch with Bobby Ray. I'll talk to you later tonight. Have a good day at work. Love you!"

Smitty watched Shaw snatch the front door open and, completely naked, charge right for the elevator, but the doors closed seconds before he reached it. His fist slamming against those doors, though, shook the suddenly small box they were riding in.

"Ronnie Lee . . . ?"

"You interrupted us in the middle of . . . well, ya know."

"And so you torture the man?"

"Oh, like you weren't trying to. Besides, I'd already gotten what I needed." She grinned in sexual satisfaction. "Twice. My poor kitty, however, had been holding out and was left a little frustrated." She rocked back on her heels. "Yeah, I left him hanging . . . I'll be paying for that tonight." And clearly she couldn't wait.

Smitty laughed with her. "You always did play with fire."

"I know. I know. But I can't help it."

The elevator doors opened and she grabbed Smitty's hand, pulling him out of the elevator, through the bustling lobby, and out to the busy Manhattan streets. Cutting between cars, she led him to a diner across the street and two blocks down.

They walked in and the cook behind the counter called out her name.

"Hey, Matty," she said with a smile.

"The usual, baby girl?"

"Yeah, and"—she pushed Smitty into an empty booth—"give him the same but triple it." Ronnie Lee sat down and let out a sigh. "All right. Spill it."

Jess was on her forty thousandth yawn when Phil walked in her office.

"Hacker."

It was such a common problem Phil didn't even bother creating full sentences about it anymore.

"Any good?"

"A little too good. Something familiar about it."

"Trace 'em," she said around another yawn. "I want a name."

"Already on it." He moved into the room. "Are you okay?"

"Yeah. Why?"

"Because you've been yawning all morning." He grinned. "Busy weekend?"

"Something like that."

He dropped into the chair across from her. The man never really *sat* as much as dropped, flopped, or dived onto furniture. "Is this getting serious?"

"No . . . maybe . . ." She sighed. "I don't know."

"Did you tell him about the Wilsons?"

"Yeah, he knew I was lying. I think he only pushed that security stuff on us trying to get me to admit it."

"So do we still have to pay for all that crap?"

Jess laughed. "You cheap bastard. Of course we have to pay for it. Besides, a little extra security couldn't hurt right now."

"Yeah, Sabina wants to up the ante at the den too."

"It's not a bad idea. I worry what she'll do if Wilson makes a move while she's human."

"And that worries you for good reason," Phil muttered under his breath. Unlike the rest of the wild dogs, Sabina was much more dangerous as human. She had this thing for knives . . .

"Call up Mace. See what they can do for the house."

"Will do. And the hillbilly?"

"I don't know, Phil. I keep telling myself not to get in deep with this guy, and then I find myself getting in deep with this guy. Wolves are notorious, ya know? Males and females. They fuck, fuck, fuck. Happily. Bouncing from bed to bed. Until one day they find *the one*. Their mate. I'm just a way station for this guy."

"Sweetie, you don't know that. You could be the one."

"I may be goofy, but I'm not delusional." She yawned, running her hands through her hair. "I am having a great time, though. I haven't been this relaxed in ages."

"Then we must hold on to him," Phil teased. "At least for a little while."

Jess giggled. "Yes, we must. Besides, he's being really cool. He's going to try and discreetly help us with this Wilson thing. And he didn't even get mad when I punched his sister."

The sound of chairs scraping and running feet had Jess's head snapping up. Her three friends charged in to join Phil.

Sabina literally dived onto her desk, knocking papers and pens onto the floor. "You punched her?"

"I was startled when I saw her. I didn't mean to."

"Did you make her cry? Bleed? Sob softly while begging you not to hurt her anymore?"

"What is wrong with you?"

Sabina took Jess's hand. "I just love you so much. I am so proud, my friend." She glanced over her shoulder. "Show her. Show her how proud!"

The other three ran out of the room and Jess jumped up, yelling, "*Dear God, no! Not the pom-poms!*"

Ronnie bit into her grilled cheese sandwich and said around a mouthful of gooey food, "Why do you want to know about the Wilsons?"

"Can you never just answer a question?"

Ronnie Lee Reed knew something about everybody. She didn't try to know these things, but she found out anyway. She was always a wealth of information when it came to the Smith Packs countrywide, and Smitty had used her knowledge time and time again.

"All right. All right. No need to get snappy. The Wilson Pack is small and ornery. They are distant cousins of the Smiths, but I don't know the bloodline."

"What about Walt?"

"Unpleasant. Rude. A real redneck. Last I heard he'd taken over his daddy's trucking company, but he ran that into the ground."

"You think he needs money?"

"He always needs money. He has a real nasty gambling habit. And he doesn't borrow from full-humans. He borrows from bears. Polar bears."

"That's stupid."

"Yeah, one time they broke both his legs when he didn't pay up. His mate finally had to borrow from her own kin."

"What do you know about his mate?"

Ronnie rolled her eyes. "Polly June Taylor. A most unpleasant woman. But she's loyal to him."

"Okay. Thanks."

"Anything I can help with?"

"Don't know yet."

"Well, you just let me know."

They ate in silence for a few minutes until Ronnie asked, "So that's her, huh?"

"That's who?"

"Jessie Ann. I saw her on the monitor at the museum, but I didn't have time to ask you about her."

With such a short amount of time to pull everything together for that museum job, Ronnie Lee offered to help out. Mostly she'd been handling their payroll, but she did a damn fine job of working the surveillance truck too.

"Yeah, that was Jessie Ann."

"And then she shows up at the office and decks your sister."

"Yup, she sure did."

"It seems you've been seeing a lot of Jessie Ann."

"Maybe."

"Even after she popped your sister?"

"Definitely after she popped my sister."

Ronnie laughed. "You Smith males do like 'em mean. So what's going on with you two, Bobby Ray?"

"I don't know. I like her."

"You always liked her."

"Yeah, but . . . It's different now."

"Of course it is. You're adults now. But don't play with her, Bobby Ray."

"Why do you think I would?"

"I don't think you'd mean to, but don't string her along. Since I can remember, when I'd see her in the school library reading those ridiculous romance books, that girl has had 'forever' written across her forehead. I'd hate to see her hurt 'cause you're just scratching an old itch."

"I can't promise anything."

"Then just don't be stupid."

Smitty smiled and winked. "I'll work on that."

"Stop. Please stop. For the love of all that's holy, *stop!*"

But they wouldn't. They just kept going.

While Jess sat on Phil's desk, the rest of them shook their pom-poms and cheered. May actually did a split. She was a very flexible gal. Thankfully, Jess hadn't brought the pets with her because the additional dog howls would have made her insane.

They wouldn't even have those stupid pom-poms if it hadn't been for her dumb idea after too many dark truffles one late night. "I know! Let's go to the Halloween party as Satan's cheerleaders!"

"I'm leaving," she warned her friends.

"One more," May begged. "Just one more."

They turned away from her and started another cheer that didn't remotely rhyme and involved way too much violence.

Placing her hands on the desk behind her, Jess relaxed back. "Hey, Smitty."

"Hey."

Then Jess screamed and scrambled off the desk. "*Where the hell did you come from?*"

"The Lord."

She glared at him. He stood there, that perfect ass resting against Phil's desk, his arms crossed over that massive chest. He'd even taken off his jacket. How could they not notice the man in the room?

Taking a deep breath to calm her shattered nerves, Jess demanded, "Why are you here?"

"Two reasons." He looked at her friends. "What y'all cheering about?"

"Nothing," they all automatically answered. All except Sabina who said, "Actually—"

But May slamming her heel into Sabina's instep elicited a lovely silent scream.

May gave her prettiest smile. "How are you, Bobby Ray?"

"Fine. And you?"

"Pretty good. Thank you kindly for asking."

Unable to tolerate the Southern politeness anymore, Jess snarled, "What two reasons?"

Taking his time answering, Smitty looked her up and down before saying, "First, I heard from Mace that y'all want us to secure your den. He went over to check out the location, but we have one problem."

"Which is?"

"The pups. The mobile ones are going to be a problem. Especially if we're going to do a top-to-bottom overhaul."

"A top to bottom?" She figured a couple of cameras and stronger doors. "Why are you doing that?"

" 'Cause y'all need it."

"And how much is that going to cost us?"

"A lot."

Jess's eyes narrowed. "So what do you want?"

"Any way you can give us complete access to your house for a few days. The less distractions, the quicker we can get this done."

"I'm sure there is. We'll come up with something and let you know. And the second thing you came here for?"

"When can I expect you tonight?"

Presumptuous timber wolf! "Who said I was coming over tonight?"

"I did."

Jess folded her arms across her chest. "So sorry to disappoint, but I have plans tonight."

"Plans?" She could see his entire body tense even though he never moved his ass from that desk. "What plans?"

"Plans with my Pack—"

"You should come," Phil cut in.

And all of them turned to him, shocked.

"I should?" Smitty asked.

"Yup, definitely."

The man truly was evil. Evil incarnate.

Smitty glanced at her. "Jessie Ann?"

"Sure," she said after clearing her throat. "You should come."

"No—"

But Sabina cut May's plea short by slapping her hand over the woman's face. "We'd love for you to come," Sabina chimed in, even while she struggled with May. "Yes, you will be there. Nine o'clock."

Phil jotted down the club information and handed it to Smitty. "Yup, nine o'clock."

Smitty stared at the piece of paper. "Caleb's Corner? Never heard of it."

"It's a nice place. You'll love it."

We're all going to hell.

Jess could tell by the look on his face that Smitty knew damn good and well they were setting him up, but he had no idea how. And Jess knew that after tonight, Smitty might actually end it all with her. He might never speak to her again. *Ever.*

Smitty slipped the paper into his pocket and slowly walked over to her. "See you tonight," he said.

"Yeah, see ya tonight."

Then his hands gently grasped her jaw, framing her face. No way. He wouldn't kiss her in front of her Pack, would he? They'd never said anything about keeping their sexual relationship secret, but Smitty had never been an outwardly affectionate male to the women he slept with. At least not when she knew him. But before she could analyze it anymore, he was kissing her. It was a sweet kiss but, at the same time, claiming. Making it clear to anyone within a thirty-mile radius exactly whom Jess belonged to. Whom she belonged to at the moment anyway.

After he'd completely melted her bones, Smitty stepped back and winked at her. He turned and headed to the elevator, glaring at Phil the entire time until the elevator doors closed.

An awkward and large silence followed his departure. Until Sabina stated the obvious, "He's worried about you and Phil?"

"I guess so," Jess replied, completely fascinated. "It was a definite Smith 'this is my bone' move."

Jess and Sabina stared at each other for several seconds before they burst out laughing.

"Me? *And Phil?*"

Sabina released May so she could bang on the desk. "That's hilarious!"

Phil cleared his throat. "I don't appreciate the humor here. I'm definitely a threat to the male population."

That just pulled more laughter from his wife and best friend.

"Maybe you should let it go," Danny suggested. "You're just embarrassing yourself."

"Wait!" May ordered. "Just wait. What about Smitty? You can't have him come tonight. It's not fair!"

Now all of them *but* May were laughing, leaving the poor She-dog to dramatically storm off on her own.

Chapter 17

"**W**hy am I here?"

Smitty didn't even spare a glance at Mitch. "Because I'm pretty sure this is a gay bar Jessie has me coming to. And you're much more gay-friendly than I am. You'll distract them from my amazing body."

"So . . . I'm your beard?"

"I don't know if you're using that term correctly, but I also don't care."

Smitty grabbed Mitch's jacket and pulled him to the bar called Caleb's Corner. There was a bouncer out front, but he barely looked at them. And there was no line waiting to get in. *What a lame-ass gay club.* Still, Jessie was here. Which meant he was going to be here.

But once they got inside, all Smitty wanted to do was turn around and run. Run for his very life. Lord in heaven, Jessica Ann Ward was the meanest female on the planet! And she should burn for this. *Burn!*

"Wait. I thought you said this was a gay bar?" Mitch sounded as horrified as Smitty felt.

"I thought it was."

"Well, it's not, and I'm out of here!"

Mitch tried to make a run for it, but Smitty grabbed his jacket collar and yanked the big cat back. "You're not deserting me, Shaw."

"Like hell I'm not. You may have that military connection with Llewellyn, but I'm from Philly. There's some things we won't do for *anyone*."

The two were seconds from pulling out claws and going at it in the middle of the bar when Jessie suddenly—and literally—jumped in front of them.

"Smitty!" She wrapped her arms around his neck and hugged him. And in that second he knew he wouldn't leave. She smelled too good.

When she pulled away, she looked over at Mitch. "Oh . . . you."

"And I'm happy to see you, too, beautiful."

Jessie stepped back and gestured around. "As you can see, we've pretty much taken over the place, but we've got some bears and a few jackals hanging out tonight, so you two shouldn't feel too out of place with all these dogs." She pointed toward an empty booth. "Why don't you guys grab a table and sit back and relax."

"Sure. After we stop at the bar first."

"Oh." Jessie scrunched up her face. The action annoyed him because she looked so goddamn cute doing it. "I forgot to mention. Caleb lost his liquor license a week ago. So, at least for now, soft drinks, virgin margaritas, and Shirley Temples only. But the Shirley Temples are to die for."

Smitty worked hard not to grit his teeth. "There's no liquor here?"

"Nope." And she grinned, evil female that she was. "I'm sorry, Smitty."

No, she wasn't. She wasn't sorry at all!

"Don't worry about it, darlin'," he lied. "We'll survive."

"We will?"

Smitty shoved Mitch into an empty booth. "We'll be just fine," he insisted, unwilling to show any weakness in the face of such travesty.

"Okay." Jessie's head snapped up. "Oh, there's my cue. I'll talk to you guys in a bit."

Smitty watched Jessie Ann run across the dance floor and up on the stage. The crowd roared her name; apparently this was not a once-in-a-blue-moon event. The Kuznetsov Pack were regulars.

The music for "Coal Miner's Daughter" started to play and Jess stepped up to the mic.

"Oh, Lord in heaven."

"A karaoke bar." Mitch glared at him. "You dragged us to a karaoke bar?"

"She didn't tell me it was karaoke."

"You know it's bad enough having to listen to you guys howl all the time. But this . . . this may be asking too much. Dogs. Singing." Mitch turned to the bar and lashed Smitty with another glare. "And no goddamn liquor. You know, as per shifter law, I could legally kill you."

He almost wished the whining cat would.

Jessie opened her mouth to start singing and Smitty cringed, waiting for those first tragic, painful notes . . . but he ended up blinking in surprise. Even Mitch looked shocked. Jessie Ann was good—and she sounded *exactly* like Loretta Lynn, the Grande Dame of Country Music.

"I never knew she liked country music," Smitty said in awe.

"Yeah, that must make her prime mate material for a Smith. She'll fit right in at one of your hootenannies."

Smitty glared across the booth. "Please. Give me one reason to kill you. Just one."

Jess belted out that last note of "Coal Miner's Daughter" and the crowd jumped to their feet, chanting her name. Okay, so she'd never make it to the Grand Ole Opry in this lifetime—her secret dream only her closest friends knew about—but who needed that when she had dogs barking for more?

She bowed to her adoring fans and jumped off the stage. Immediately Danny replaced her for his rendition of .38 Specials "Hang on Loosely," which always made his wife swoon.

To her surprise, Smitty and Mitch hadn't bailed yet. She thought for sure Smitty would run screaming into the night as soon as he realized it was a "dry" karaoke bar. Wolves may love to howl, but nothing they hated more than to hear dogs sing. And dogs *loved* to sing. Add in no tequila and that was not a wolf's idea of a good time. More like one of their nightmares.

Yet how he kept Mitch Shaw locked into place, she'd never know. Cats *really* hated hearing dogs sing. It rankled their fur.

Jess sat down next to Smitty and smiled.

"You could have warned me, Jessie Ann."

"I could have—but how would that be fun for me?"

Teeth gritted again and she even elicited a slight sneer. Feeling pretty good about that, Jess turned to Mitch. "How's that non-alcoholic beer doing it for ya, Mitch?"

Really, you haven't lived until you've been hissed at.

"So how long does this thing last anyway?" Smitty asked, probably trying to distract her from toying with Mitch.

"Until two. Usually."

"In the morning?"

Jess barely held in a laugh. He sounded so . . . despondent. "Would you prefer I said afternoon? Besides, you don't have to stay. In fact, feel free to go."

"Rock on." Mitch went to stand up and Smitty reached over and shoved him back in the seat.

"Is there a reason you're being mean to me, Jessie Ann?"

"Other than I'm enjoying it? Not really."

"You know, Jessie Ann," he growled, "when you're being mean like this you do nothing but make me hard."

Not exactly the response she expected.

Mitch shook his head. "Wolves are so weird, bruh."

Ignoring Mitch, Smitty took her hand, and in that one simple move had her wishing they were alone. With his thumb making lazy circles around her knuckles, he said, "Okay. You made your point. Now come home with me."

Jess swallowed. She'd never had a man seem so desperate to be with her before. She liked it.

"Uh . . ." she began awkwardly, but May jumped into the booth right behind her.

"Hey, Jess." On her knees, May leaned over the back of the booth. "Kenshin's here."

Kenshin Inu walked into the club with his Pack right behind him. An Asian wild dog, Ken had a family that moved around constantly. True nomads, the Inu Pack traveled all over the world. Their main den remained Tokyo, Japan—yes, all of it—but the world was their true home. Ken and Jess had been close since he'd saved her from getting arrested one summer in Chicago many, many years ago. And Ken had given her the seed money to start the company. The dot-com bubble had busted a long time ago, and giving their Pack money had been a risk. One he still made money off of. Jess was nearly as close to Kenshin as she was to Phil.

As soon as he saw her, his face lit up and Jess pulled her hand away from Smitty's grip, slid out of the booth, and ran over to her friend.

"Kenshin!" She threw her arms around his neck and Ken picked her up, swinging her around in a circle. They hadn't seen each other in over a year and she missed her bud. It had been ages since they stayed up watching bad seventies slasher films and mocking. She missed the mocking.

"How is my favorite wild dog?" he jokingly asked.

"Wonderful." She kissed his cheek and he lowered her but kept his hands on her waist. "How's your father and mother?" Jess had always liked Ken's parents. They were sweet and outrageously goofy.

"Tiresome." Ken leaned back the slightest bit and gazed down into her face. "You look very . . . happy." His eyes grew wide. "Did you get laid?"

"Kenshin!" She grabbed his hand and led him to a booth at the back of the club. "I swear I can't take you anywhere."

*   *   *

Smitty watched some scrawny Akita walk away with his woman.

"Uh . . . dude?"

He looked over at Mitch. "What?"

"You need to calm down."

"What are you talking about?"

"Your claws are out. So are your fangs."

Retracting the offending implements of death, he demanded, "Well, who the fuck is that guy?" Other than someone who had to die.

Mitch leaned in a bit, moving his nonalcoholic beer out of the way. "Wow. You're really hot for her."

"What?"

"Seriously. And this would explain why you're putting up with"—Mitch glanced at the stage in disgust—"the wild dog version of 'Strobe Light.' I used to love the B-52s. Now they've been ruined forever."

Mitch shrugged it off. "Anyway, I wish you'd just take her in the bathroom and do her so we could go."

Smitty didn't bother answering him, not when he couldn't stop staring at Jessie leaning way too close to that dog. She was practically in his lap!

"Unless you've already . . . Bruh, did you already fuck her?"

Snarling, Smitty swung back around. "Would you *shut up*?"

"And that's a yes." Mitch relaxed back in the booth, took a sip of his faux beer, grimaced, and dropped the bottle back on the table. "Bruh, just go over there and grab her. I mean, he's a wiry little guy. What's he going to do? Then we can go get a real beer."

"I'm not doing that." Jessie wasn't even his to claim. But did he want her to be? Did he want Jessie to be his? The way he had to struggle to stop himself from killing some scrawny little wild dog, he was starting to worry that could be the exact problem.

Great. Just great.

"Why not?" Mitch asked, oblivious to Smitty's internal struggle and panic. "You're a Smith Pack male. Isn't it part of your DNA?"

"Just 'cause I got the Smith name don't mean I'm not civilized."

"Oh. Good to know. And I hope that civilized living will keep you warm at night when your woman is off gettin' fucked twenty ways to Sunday by an Asian wild dog."

Smitty nearly had his hands around the cat's throat when Jessie appeared beside the booth. She caught his hand in hers and glared at him.

"Smitty, I'd like you to meet Kenshin Inu. Kenny, this is Bobby Ray Smith. But everybody calls him Smitty."

"My friends do anyway."

He winced a bit when small claws dug into the back of his hand. "Smitty," she spit out from between her teeth even while she kept that fake smile, "Kenshin wants to talk to you about your business."

Kenshin looked at Mitch. "And are you Mace Llewellyn?"

"As a matter of fact—"

"He's not." Jessie released Smitty's hand and grabbed Mitch's arm. "Why don't we leave you two to talk? Besides, Mitch has some singing to do."

"I . . . What? Wait a minute. I'm not singing!"

Somehow Jessie dragged a man more than twice her size away from the booth and Kenshin sat down across from Smitty.

The two males eyed each other up carefully.

"Jess had a lot of good things to say about you."

Kenshin's English had a slight British accent to it. Jess probably found that sexy. *British-sounding bastard.*

Getting disgusted with himself, Smitty grunted and waited for him to continue.

"I've heard about your security business. The thought of our own kind running something like that intrigues me. We don't have anything like that in Tokyo."

"Yeah . . . and?"

Smiling, Kenshin leaned over the table the way Mitch had. "Look, hillbilly, let's get this out on the table right now. First off, I'm here to talk business. Now, if you're worried about me and Jess . . . don't be. I blew my shot with her a long time ago, and I'm firmly and permanently in the 'best friend, like-a-brother' zone. But I'm sitting here, ready to discuss a possible deal that could bring you and your feline pal a lot of money based on Jessica's recommendation alone. So we can either discuss business or we can sit here and let you play rabid wolf over a woman who, at the moment, is barely tolerating you. Which is it gonna be?"

Smitty rested back in his seat, his fangs and claws receding. He let out a deep breath and nodded. "All right, pooch. What do you wanna know about my business?"

Jess covered her mouth with her hand. "Oh, God."

May rested her head on Jess's shoulder and kept her eyes down, but her entire body shook. Sabina simply stared . . . blindly.

When they'd first thrown Mitch up on the stage it was mostly to torture him. Dogs merely trying to embarrass the cat. Three power ballads later and Jess knew she'd created a monster.

"I don't think I'll ever listen to Bon Jovi the same way again."

" 'Dead or Alive' has taken on a whole new meaning to me," May got out between bouts of hysterical giggling.

"And let us not forget Whitesnake's 'Here I Go Again.' "

Sabina snorted. "I think that one made my ears bleed."

May wiped her eyes and sat up. "We have to have him back next time we come. It's an absolute must."

"I say we send him with the rest of the Pack next week. Kerri and the girls will love us forever." Because someone had to protect the pups at all times, the Pack rarely did these sorts of late-night events together. So this week it was the Original Five and about twenty other wild dogs. Next week, the rest of the Pack would go, and Jess and the others would stay home with the kids. It wasn't the best system, but it was the safest, and that's all that mattered.

"And," Jess added, "it does not hurt he's severely hot."

"No," May and Sabina sighed together, "it doesn't hurt at all."

Finally, probably because Phil shoved him, Mitch relinquished the stage. As he walked past the three of them, he gave them a big grin, a wink, and said "Ladies" with a smugness that rivaled Napoleon Bonaparte's.

Under the table, they each grabbed hold of the other's leg and dug their nails in so they wouldn't burst out laughing.

"Mitch," they said together.

"Oh, my God," May cleared her throat after Mitch walked by. "This is the best Karaoke night *ever.*"

Half an hour later and, as Kenshin Inu walked away from the table, Smitty realized he'd somehow worked himself into a business deal . . . maybe. To be honest, he still wasn't sure if he could trust this guy, and he had no idea if this would turn out to be anything. He certainly wouldn't worry about it. He had more important things on his mind.

Like the hot little wild dog walking back over to him. But before she could get close, Kenshin grabbed her hand and dragged her on stage. And when he sang "Love Me Tender" to her while holding Jessie tight against him and the rest of the females squealed at his Elvis impersonation, Smitty did seriously consider killing the man. Killing him a lot.

Lighters in hand, arms waving, the dogs enjoyed Phil's version of "No Woman, No Cry." Not exactly Bob Marley, but close enough.

Laughing and trying not to burn her hand, Jess glanced over her shoulder to see if Smitty had finally bailed—especially after one of her Pack mangled Poison's "Every Rose Has Its Thorns"— but to her eternal surprise, he was still in the same spot she'd left him. However, he wasn't alone.

Jess's eyes narrowed as she locked on to the four females from Kenshin's Pack happily settled into Smitty's booth with him and Mitch.

Disgusted, she turned back around and tried to force herself not to care. Didn't work, but she did try.

"What's wrong?" May asked against her ear so only she could hear.

"Nothing."

"Liar. Tell me."

Jess gave a small motion with her head and May glanced around behind them. When her eyes narrowed like Jess was sure hers had, she knew May saw it too.

"Bitches."

"No. No. They're friends."

"Bitch friends."

Sabina leaned over. "Who?"

May leaned over Jess and whispered, "Over at Smitty's table."

Surprisingly discreet, Sabina looked and her eyes narrowed. She gave a little sneer. "Those bitches."

Now Jess could only laugh. Could this get more ridiculous?

She knew it could when Phil leaned over his wife and asked, "Who's a bitch?"

Thankfully, they spoke English. Smitty's Japanese was rusty at best. And the words he could clearly remember would only get his face slapped. Besides, they seemed less than interested in him. Their focus locked right on Mitch. And Mitch lapped up every bit of it like the greedy, never-satisfied cat that he was.

Bored and wondering how much longer this would last, Smitty stared at his empty beer bottle. Nonalcoholic beer. Christ, could getting laid be worth all this?

"Hey."

Jessie stood at the edge of their table and he couldn't quite understand her expression.

"Hey."

"So"—she motioned to the stage—"what are you going to sing for me?"

"Sing?" Panic, cold and desperate, swept through his system. "I'm not singing."

"Why not?"

"I don't sing, Jessica Ann." Not after that school recital when he was nine. No. Never, ever, *ever* again.

"Oh." Jessie shrugged. "Okay, then."

She walked over to the table with her Packmates and grabbed her coat. She was leaving. Because he wouldn't sing?

"Jessie, wait—" He looked for a way around the lovely woman sitting next to him and he finally picked her up and handed her over to Mitch, who seemed more than happy to take her.

"Where are you going?" he asked while she zipped up her backpack. Why she felt the need to bring her laptop with her to a karaoke bar, he'd never know.

"Back to the office. I've got a ton of work to do."

He waited for the punch line, but it never came. "You're serious?"

"She's serious," Sabina sighed out. "Pathetic, isn't it?"

"Give me a break. I left a lot of stuff not done."

"And you'll sleep when?"

"I can use the couch in my office. And the engineering-coding floor has a Sleep Room. I'll crash there."

"I thought . . ."

"You thought what?"

Smitty glanced around at the Pack and he quickly figured out they had no intention of giving him and Jessie some privacy.

"I thought you'd come home with me tonight."

Sabina bumped her arm. "Sex is better than work. Go home with the wolf and use him like the dirty, vile whore he is."

Smitty frowned. He had no idea if the woman was helping him or not.

"Not tonight. He didn't make it worth it."

"Make it worth it?"

She looked up at him. "Yeah."

"If you come home with me, I'll make it worth it," he promised.

"Sex is sex, Smitty. I can get good sex from any unmated male here."

"She sure can!" someone from the crowd yelled out, proving they had everyone's attention.

"So what would make it worth it for you?"

She grinned. "Sing for me."

"I don't sing for anyone."

"So I'm anyone?" She snorted and picked up her backpack. Sad when she had to have Danny help her haul it on. But when she put that thing on, it meant she was leaving.

"You're serious?"

"Extremely," she muttered while trying to keep her balance. Why she didn't get a better bag or take some of that crap out, he'd never know.

"Fine."

Brushing past her, Smitty headed up to the stage.

Jess' eyes grew wide and she looked at her Pack. "No. Way." She turned, but did it so quickly her backpack threw her off and if Danny hadn't caught her, she'd have fallen flat on her ass.

Letting Danny put her back on her feet, she watched Smitty flip quickly through the song book, pick something, and plug the code into the machine.

She never thought he'd get on that stage. Not in a million years. Even his mother could never coax him into singing. Not even when he was drunk off his ass and he'd do pretty much anything else. Based on his reaction alone when she mentioned it, Jess thought nothing had changed.

Yet there he was, pulling his baseball cap a little lower on his head, hooking his thumbs into the front pocket of his jeans, and focusing on the monitor rolling the lyrics. It took her no time to recognize the music. She'd *always* had a thing for Randy Travis. No country singer she knew of had better down-home love songs. But it was the man's voice that got her every time. Yet, for the first time ever, she found a voice to rival the master. Low, smooth, and decadent, Smitty's voice rolled over her as he started singing "Deeper Than the Holler."

"Lord have mercy," May whispered next to her.

"Good God," Sabina said in shock.

Jess didn't say anything. She had no words. Nothing witty or dismissive. She could only stare—and pine.

It wasn't a long song, and before she knew it, Smitty finished. The crowd jumped to its feet—even the bears, who were notoriously snotty about that sort of thing—clapping and cheering.

Smitty, his eyes focused on the floor, walked off the stage and through the crowd, ignoring all the pats on his back and praise of his voice.

He walked right up to Jess, grabbed her hand, and kept on moving. He didn't even stop to say good night, check on his friend, or anything else people might do.

Smitty walked out of the club and dragged Jess down the street until he hit an alley. He pulled her inside, pushed her up against the wall, and kissed her. A desperate, yearning kiss she returned, her hands running up his back and shoulders until her fingers could dig into his hair.

He finally pulled back, after he had her like melted chocolate in his hands, and said, "You're coming home with me."

Definitely an order and she so didn't give a shit. "Yeah. I'm coming home with you."

He kissed her one more time until she groaned and clung to him. That's when he pulled away and, taking firm hold of her hand, dragged her to his truck.

Chapter 18

The cell phone woke him up Thursday morning. Not surprising. He'd meant to set his alarm but he kept forgetting. For the last three nights he'd had Jessie Ann in his bed and the last thing he worried about was time. After they left the Karaoke bar Monday night, they'd started making out in the elevator leading to his apartment, unable to keep their hands off each other. Nearly fucked in the hallway but she took off running and Lord knew he loved a good chase. The rest of the night they spent in bed, making each other come like crazy. It had been nice.

Hell. Who was he kidding? It had been amazing.

The next night she'd shown up at his door, extremely tipsy on champagne after dinner with a client, and dumped there by Phil. After getting her out of her skimpy dress, they'd dived under the covers and spent hours playing "what am I fondling now?"

Then last night he'd had a job that wouldn't end until late and he didn't think he'd see her. Done by two, he still found himself driving over to her office. He wasn't exactly shocked to see that the light in her office was on. Now that he and Mace handled all security for Jessie's company, he'd let himself in, gone up to the top floor, dumped her over his shoulder, and taken her back home with him. They'd both been exhausted and ended up doing nothing more than kissing and nuzzling before they both fell asleep in each other's arms.

He'd never slept so well before in his life.

And he'd had no intention of getting up early, until his damn phone went off.

Yawning, Smitty flipped open his phone but quickly realized it hadn't been his ringing.

By the time he turned around, Jessie had her phone to her ear and was scrambling over the bed and over him, heading to the bathroom.

Before the door closed all he heard from her was, "No. I'll handle this myself."

She didn't sound happy, but he figured he could dig into what was going on once she got out of the bathroom. He really hoped it didn't have to do with that idiot Wilson. He had Mitch tracking him down. The lion could find anyone once he set his mind to it. But until they tracked Wilson down and Smitty had a chance to talk to him, he wouldn't feel Jessie's Pack was safe. At least not safe enough.

He soon heard the shower start while he had the coffee brewing, when his own phone rang.

"Yeah?"

"Hey, buddy. It's Phil."

"Yeah?"

"Okay. Not a morning person. Good to know. Anyway, the Pack needs you to do us a favor."

"What?"

"Stay with Jess."

Smitty's lip curled back, he felt his incisors lengthen. Did he actually just have a dog tell him he should stay with Jess? *As in permanently?* Two things bothered him about that. One, he didn't want the little runts ordering him to do a damn thing. And two . . . that "permanently" didn't sound as bad as it should.

"Hello? Damn. I think I lost the connection."

"No. I'm right here."

"Oh. So you can do that?"

Taking a deep breath, "Don't you think that's up to me and Jessie Ann?"

"Well, she'll just say no."

And there went his hackles.

"What d'ya mean she'll say no?"

"She'll say she won't need you." The little runt said it so matter-of-factly too. Why wouldn't she need him? They got along real well. Didn't irritate each other too much, in his opinion. And had amazing sex.

Dammit. Now what was he doing?

"Are you there?"

Smitty ignored the pooch's exasperated tone. "If she doesn't need me why are you trying to force the issue?"

"Because we don't want her to go to Connecticut by herself. Since she's *our* Alpha Female we have to abide by her wishes. But you don't. And from what I can tell, you won't."

"Connecticut?"

"Yeah. What else have we been talking about?"

Annoyed, frustrated, and just downright pissy due to lack of coffee, Smitty slapped his phone closed and stalked to the bathroom, bursting into the room.

He snatched the shower curtain back, and got a lovely Jessie scream for his trouble.

"What?" she demanded, trying in vain to cover herself with a washcloth—although he didn't know why. He'd spent many hours licking her from head to toe, exactly what hadn't he seen? And tasted? And enjoyed?

"Why are you going to Connecticut?"

"Were you listening to my phone call?"

"No."

She gave an adorable little snarl. "Damn Phil."

"Answer my question."

"No."

She yanked the curtain closed. But Smitty just yanked it back open.

"Why are you going to Connecticut?"

"I need to check on something out there. Something that has nothing to do with *you*."

She yanked the curtain closed again. Smitty yanked it back.

At this point he kind of guessed he was being a bit ridiculous, but that didn't stop him from finding something else to go off about. "What is that on your head?"

Jessie glared. "It's a shower cap."

"I didn't even know I had one of those."

"It's probably your sister's. Now will you piss off?"

"I'm coming with you."

"Like hell you are."

"This isn't up for debate." He forced a smile. "Just think of me as your protection for when you're not paying attention. Which is, from what I can tell, all the time."

"I'll make you regret this. I will talk. A lot. Just to piss you off."

Smitty nodded slowly. "So all those other times you talked a lot, you weren't trying to piss me off?"

"You son of a—now you asked for it. I'm so going to annoy you."

He grinned and this time he didn't have to force it. "Leave the shower cap on. That'll do the job."

"Oh!" She closed the shower curtain. "I hate you!"

"Now, Jessie Ann—"

"Shut up!"

"Come on now. I'm just jokin'."

"Oh? Really?" She pulled the curtain back again, standing there beautifully naked, except for that cap and her washcloth. "Then fuck me while I'm wearing this cap."

"Do I have to?" he whined and ready to run if his survival instincts deemed it necessary.

"Fuck me with the cap or I go *alone*."

"Well . . ." He stepped into the shower. "I guess if I have to."

"It was an accident."

Jess slammed the truck door, refusing to believe that line of bullshit. "Don't speak to me."

Smitty buckled up his seatbelt. "I don't know how it happened. That cap just went flyin'."

Crossing her arms over her chest, "Shut. Up." Jess scowled. "And who doesn't have a blow dryer?"

"Me. I don't need it."

Jess pushed her frizzed mass of curls out of her face. "Clearly you do."

"Not really. I just get out of the shower and my hair dries like this."

It was the triumphant smile that insulted her most.

Jess held her hand out. "Hat."

Smitty reached into his backseat and pulled out a baseball cap with the football team logo for the Tennessee Titans embroidered on the front. She pulled the cap on, yanking it low over her face, tucking her hair back behind her ears.

"Now don't you look cute as the dickens?"

She had uncontrolled hair, a baseball cap for a team she didn't even know, Smitty's way-too-big bomber jacket because the man detested her much beloved parka, and the same clothes from last night except her panties, which she refused to put back on since she simply found that disgusting. So, all in all, she found that compliment damn rude.

"We don't discuss this again. You don't tell me how cute I look. And you get a goddamn blow dryer. Now drive."

Clearing his throat, Smitty started the truck. "Yes'm."

"And I need more coffee."

"Darlin', I think that's a given."

The trip should have felt a hell of a lot longer since Jessie Ann never actually shut up the entire time. She'd been pretty cranky until he got her some coffee. Then she cheered up and started talking . . . and talking . . . and talking.

Thankfully, Smitty found her pretty amusing. Downright funny, sometimes. The woman could definitely tell a story. And she had lots of those.

Around noon, as the radio news predicted rain, they finally arrived at a small, tidy white house that even included a white picket fence.

"What's here?" he asked.

Jessie shrugged. "We found the hacker."

Smitty tensed. "What do you mean you found the hacker? What hacker?"

"We had a hacker problem. And we've had this problem before. I'm dealing with it."

"Should we call the cops?"

"Not yet. Not unless I have to."

"You should have told me. I'm not prepped for this."

"You don't need to be."

Smitty stared into her eyes. "You know this guy?"

"Yup."

"Jessie, this isn't safe."

"It's safe." She grinned. That big, innocent, goddamn goofy grin. "Come on."

Before he could stop her, she was out the truck and heading up the walkway. Cursing under his breath, Smitty followed her.

As he walked up behind her, the front door opened. A woman not much older than him smiled at them but as she recognized Jessie, her smile faded.

After several moments, she stepped back and yelled, "Carol Marie Haier! *Get your ass down here this minute!*"

Jess sat in a chair across from a pouting thirteen-year-old. Her mother's head had nearly exploded when she realized her daughter had gone back to her old habits. Habits that had cost her mother dearly once before.

Marie Haier placed a glass of water in front of Jess. "Are you sure you wouldn't like some coffee or something?"

"No. Thank you. Just a few minutes with your daughter."

Marie glanced up at Smitty, looking a little nervous.

He gave her a slow, sweet smile. "Actually, ma'am, I wouldn't mind a cup of coffee."

"Sure. Of course." She seemed relieved to have something to do and walked out of the room.

Jess looked at Carol. "So we're back here again."

"I don't know what you're talking about."

"Carol. Let's not play this game. We both know how it'll end. One call and this is all done."

She shrugged. "Do whatever you want."

"How will that sit with your mom? When she has to hire lawyers again, pay your fines. You're not even supposed to be near a computer."

Staring at the floor, "So what do you want?"

"The truth. What happened?"

"There's a company. In Spain or something. They've offered more than five thousand dollars to anyone who can hack your systems."

Well, that explained the recent increase in assaults on their system. With her team and less-than-law-abiding friends, Jess was able to keep the wolf from the door, so to speak. But Carol had always been really good. She could hack damn near anything and had already broken into their system four years ago. A lesson they only had to learn once. Especially since it was a nine-year-old that had done it, their competition had loved every moment of their situation. The laughter died, though, when the same companies realized Carol had already been and gone from their systems, taking whatever she wanted with her.

"Where did you get access to a computer?"

"Internet coffee shop."

Jess nodded. "So while you're sucking down those non-fat lattes you're trying to break into my system?"

"I wasn't going to take anything from you. But we need the money."

Jess let out a breath. "I understand, Carol. But this isn't the way to go about it."

Carol looked between her and Smitty. "So now what? Drag me off to jail?"

"You're thirteen. The best I can hope you get is some time in juvey. And maybe a public caning."

Confused, she asked, "You're not going to turn me in?"

"No. I don't think your mother deserves that. Do you?"

Smitty drank weak coffee and forced down a sub par muffin because that's how he'd been raised. After twenty minutes of Marie Haier nervously fluttering around them, Jess made their excuses to leave. She said goodbye to the little girl and Marie walked them to his truck.

"I'm so very sorry about all this."

"Don't be. There's only so much you can do when you've got a genius for a daughter." Jess opened her door. "So how's work going?"

Marie shrugged, looking just like her daughter. "Not bad."

"Still working at the grocery store?"

"Yes."

"Ever consider secretarial work?"

"Uh . . . sure."

"I'll have my assistant call you. We just set up a system for Lathan Industries. They're not far from here. They're expanding and I think there are openings if you're interested. They'll give you on-site training."

He could see Marie working hard to not get overexcited. She'd been let down before. A lot, he'd reckon. "Yes. I'm interested."

"Good. My assistant will call you later today with the information."

"Thank you."

"Sure."

Jessie climbed into his truck and closed the door.

"Thank you for the coffee and muffin, Mrs. Haier."

She smiled at Smitty. "You're more than welcome."

Smitty stepped into his truck, started her up, and pulled out. As soon as they got to the corner, Jessie called into her office.

First she called Phil. It had to be the strangest conversation he'd heard in a long time.

"The Spanish have sent their Armada to destroy us. Yes. It's time to call in the fleet. I want them blasted out of the water by the end of next week. Good. Thank you, Admiral."

When he glanced at her while sitting at a light, she gave him that big dog grin, before dialing her assistant. That, thankfully, was a much more logical discussion. Jessie went over messages, gave instructions on who to call back and who to ignore. As they finished their conversation, Jessie instructed her assistant to contact the CEO of Lathan Industries and to remind him of how he'd said, " 'I owe you one'. Now it's time for him to pay up."

She shut off the phone and Smitty stopped at another light. "I don't get it."

"Don't get what?"

"Why are you helping the Haiers?"

"That poor woman is blissfully average like the rest of us. And she has a daughter with a one hundred and ninety-five IQ."

Smitty blew out a breath. "Wow."

"She has no idea what to do with her. And the kid is bitter because her old man bailed. Blah, blah, blah. Let me tell you, nothing is worse than a bored, bitter genius." Jess stuck her phone back into the pocket of the jacket she wore. "I figure we get the mom straight. Then we can get that kid into some program that will keep that brain of hers occupied. Then when she turns eighteen—that brain will belong to me."

He glanced at her in surprise. "What?"

"That kid is going to make my company a fortune. I just have to keep her out of federal prison long enough." She snorted. "What? Did you think I was doing all this out of the goodness of my heart?"

"Well . . . yeah. I did."

"She's not a stray puppy, Smitty."

"Puppies. Kids. They're all the same to you when they're needy."

She grinned. "Quiet yourself."

He reached for her with one arm. "Come here, darlin'. Let ol' Smitty show you how much you're appreciated."

"Shut up," she said again, slapping at his arm.

Laughing, Smitty turned onto the main highway. And as they drove out of town, the skies opened up.

Chapter 19

So busy responding to an e-mail from her phone, Jess didn't realize that Smitty had pulled over until he said, "Do you ever live outside your head?"

"What?" She looked up and around. "Why did we stop? Wow, it's really raining."

"Yeah, it's really raining. Thought we'd get some lunch and hope that the worst of it will blow over. Interested?"

"Yeah, sure." She looked around again, getting her bearings. "Uh . . . not sure we want to stop in this town, though."

"Why?"

"It's bear run."

"The sign said 'Martin County.' "

"That's not the name. It's a bear-run town. Literally, bears run it."

Smitty shrugged. "So?"

"This isn't like Smithville. They're not friendly bears, Smitty. Not friendly at all. They don't like outsiders."

"Darlin', we're stopping for lunch. Not taking over territory."

"Yeah, but—"

"Woman, you know how I get when I'm hungry."

"Okay. Okay.

Still thinking this was a bad idea, Jess stepped out of the truck and followed Smitty inside the steakhouse restaurant.

*   *   *

It took a while to get her comfortable. But when she realized the place was run by full-humans she seemed to relax.

They ordered two inhumanly large steaks, rare, and several side orders they shared. Once they finished eating, they relaxed back and just talked. It was nice.

"You're actually going to adopt Johnny?"

"That's the plan."

"Didn't you say he was going to be seventeen soon?"

"This upcoming weekend."

"Then doesn't that make him a little old?"

Jess sipped her coffee. "He has to know he belongs. That he's got family. I don't want him leaving at eighteen and thinking he doesn't have anybody."

"What does he say about it?"

Jessie stared at him so long, he finally asked, "You did ask him about this, didn't you?"

"I thought I did." She squinted, trying to remember. "But I think we got sidetracked by brownies."

Smitty rubbed his eyes with his fingertips. "Okay. Let's try this. He's wolf."

"So?"

"He doesn't really belong in a dog Pack, darlin'."

"Who says?"

"Look, I'm not trying to get you upset. And I'm sure you guys can be pretty tough when you wanna be, but you need to be realistic. He's a wolf. At eighteen those genes are gonna kick in full force."

"And you don't think we can handle it?"

"I think you can try."

"Unfortunately, Smitty, no wolf Packs wanted him. Children's Services tried to place him with wolves and they wouldn't take him in. We were the only ones who would."

"What about his parents' Packs?"

"Don't know who they are. His mom had some . . . troubles. She cut herself off from her family."

"His father?"

"No idea who he is and we've tried to track him down. Bottom line, all he's got is us."

Smitty cleared his throat. "You know, I can help."

"Help? With what?"

"With the boy. You know, if he needs advice or something. I can help."

Jessie stared at him again.

"Hello?"

She put her coffee cup down on the table. "I'll keep that in mind." She said it very politely and with a wariness he didn't much like.

"Is there a problem?"

"No." She glanced out the window. "Rain stopped."

"Looks that way."

"You ready to go?"

"Yeah, sure."

He motioned to the waitress for the check.

"Since you took care of lunch last time, I'll get this."

Jessie threw down a black credit card on the silver-plated bill holder the waitress brought by.

She did it casually, without a thought. No worries there about her last big purchase.

They finished paying up and headed outside.

"Think we can stop by that Starbucks up the road before we head home?" she asked.

Smitty dug into his jacket pocket to fish out his keys. "Yeah, sure." He'd just snagged the keys from his pocket when he walked right into the back of her.

"Jessie?"

He looked up and that's when he saw them, leaning against and resting on his pickup truck.

Bears. About eight of them, none of them smaller than seven feet. Great. Just what he needed. Really big, really cranky bears.

Jess had been afraid of this. The local bear population was not friendly. They actually didn't get along with each other either, but they teamed up in a heartbeat against outsiders. They welcomed full-humans, but cats and canines had no place in Martin County.

Smitty gently swiped his hand down her back before stepping around her.

"Can I help y'all?"

The one lying directly on top of Smitty's hood seemed to be the biggest problem, his seven-five stature not withstanding. A polar bear, he had his hands behind his head as he stared up at the sky.

"I just gotta wonder, what brings a couple of dogs to our territory."

"Just stopping to have lunch until the rains passed." Smitty shrugged. "They've passed."

"Yeah, that's true. But I have to say I'm getting pretty tired of you people traipsing through our town."

Smitty stood next to his truck. He looked calm, cool, completely rational, so Jess stepped behind a tree and out of the line of fire.

The problem was these Northerners had never experienced a true Smith wolf attack. They didn't play like the other Packs. Besides, the dumb bastard had fucked with Smitty's truck. You never fucked with a man's truck.

"You know, dog," the bear continued, "I'm thinking it's about time we made an examp—"

Smitty didn't even bother to let him finish. He just grabbed the bear by his foot and yanked all seven feet five inches and probably a good three hundred or more pounds of him off the hood of his truck, slamming the man face down on the concrete. Jess distinctly heard bone breaking. Probably the bear's nose. Maybe some ribs.

Calmly, Smitty explained, "That's for trying to threaten me."

Before the polar's companions could move, Smitty unleashed the claws of his right hand and brought it down on the bear's Achilles tendon—shredding it with one swipe.

"And that's for denting the hood of my truck with your fat

ass," he added, still calm, over the bear's howls of unspeakable pain.

One of the females stared at Smitty as he stood up. She towered over him, but the fear on her face matched everyone else's. "You . . . You're a Smith, aren't you?"

Smitty flicked his hand, the blood flying pretty much everywhere. "Why do you ask?"

"I met you people before. Smiths." She said it with disgust and undeniable fear.

"Yeah, I'm a Smith. Out of Tennessee. And I want y'all off my truck."

They got off his truck all right. They moved like lightning.

"Jessie Ann."

She walked out from behind the tree and over to the truck. She didn't run. She didn't have to. The Smith name alone had put the fear of God into these people, parting them like the Red Sea.

Smitty held the door open for her and she stepped into the truck. He closed the door and walked around to his side. He got in, started her up, and backed out.

No one stopped them. No one did anything. And she had no doubt no one would.

Smitty drove about five miles until he saw an old gas station. So old it was still full service. He told the kid pumping gas to fill his tank and then disappeared into the bathroom.

After ten minutes, Jess followed him. She knew that look on his face. Remembered it clearly. He got it anytime he had to use the brutal tactics drummed into him by Bubba Smith. The bear had forced that on Smitty, and now she had one less-than-happy wolf on her hands.

When she opened the bathroom door, which he hadn't bothered to lock, she found him standing at the sink and staring into it. He hadn't turned on the water, and blood still covered his right hand.

Jess slowly walked up to him, knowing better than to startle him or make any sudden moves. When she felt confident he knew she was standing next to him, she turned on the water in the sink and took his right hand in both of hers. She held them under the water, slowly washing the bear's blood from his fingers. She took her time, grateful they had liquid soap from a pump rather than a bar she'd be loathe to use. Especially since this place didn't scream "antibacterial clean" to her.

When she removed all the blood from his right hand, she washed his left for the hell of it. Then she took paper towels from the stack on the counter and dried his hands. Once done with that, she dried her own hands and tossed the paper towels away. She grabbed the sleeve of his jacket and forced him to face her.

"Smitty?" When he didn't answer her, she said, "Bobby Ray. Look at me."

He did and she literally forced herself not to run. This was Bobby Ray. He'd never hurt her. Even with his eyes shifted to wolf, he'd never hurt her. She knew that.

So when his hand whipped out and grabbed her by the back of the neck, she didn't even scream.

He had to stop. He had to stop now. But, Lord knew, he couldn't. He couldn't make himself stop. All she'd shown him was the ultimate kindness in the last ten minutes. The kind of kindness only a dog could show. She should be terrified of him. She should be screaming and fighting him. But she wasn't. She just kept staring up at him with those big, brown, innocent eyes. Those innocent eyes trusting him to do the right thing.

He didn't. Instead, he slammed her back against the wall and forced his mouth on hers. Her arms flailed for a moment, but instead of fighting him off, she wrapped them around his neck and pulled him closer. He kissed Jessie hard, his tongue pushing its way in, demanding she respond. She did. She moaned and gasped and held him tighter.

Her hands dug into his hair and one leg wrapped around his

waist. She writhed against him, letting him know she was all his. To do with as he would. Anything. She trusted him enough to give him anything and everything.

Snarling, Smitty pulled back, spun her around so she faced the wall. His hands unsnapped and unzipped her jeans in seconds, pulling them down until they were around her knees. He slipped his hands between her legs, his fingers sliding inside her. He growled like a rabid animal when he found her already wet and hot. He pulled his fingers back and stroked her clit. In less than thirty seconds he had her coming, crying out his name as he took her over again. With his other hand he yanked her jacket past her shoulder. He licked his lips, his fangs bursting from his gums. He leaned over her, wrapping his jaw around her exposed flesh.

She trembled in his arms. Trembled and panted and waited. Waited for him to take her like this. To do what the females of the Smith Pack referred to as the Smith mate-maul. Was he really going to do this to Jessie Ann? The woman who'd just washed the blood off his hands and accepted the fact that he'd mercilessly ripped the Achilles tendon off another being?

No. She deserved better than this.

Using absolutely everything he'd learned from his military training, he let her go.

He pulled his hands away and stepped away from her, like a recovering addict stepping away from his heroin.

Jessie looked over her shoulder at him. "Smitty?"

"Get dressed. I'm taking you home." He walked to the sink and washed his own damn hands this time. By the time he dried them and turned around, she'd already walked out.

She wanted to cry. She really did. But she learned early on from her days in Smithtown that the quickest way to lose respect was to cry. So she kept her tears for her Pack because they understood her and they accepted her.

She couldn't wait to get home. She wanted her people. She wanted out of this truck. She wanted away from the bastard who just broke her heart.

Because no one wanted to find out they weren't good enough. Especially when she had to find out like that. Her body still shaking from climaxing, her pants around her knees like a goddamn truckstop whore.

The truck door opened and Smitty got in. She didn't say anything. There was nothing to say. Instead, she placed her hands between her knees to control the trembling, prayed there would be no traffic on the freeways home, and wished with all her geeky might that she could portal her black, wild-dog ass out of here.

Chapter 20

Whed about her Pack was that she really didn't have to tell them anything. They might not know exactly what was wrong, but they knew when she needed them.

As soon as she stepped out of the truck, May opened the front door for her. Jess walked in without bothering to look back. Smitty had barely spoken two words to her on the way into the city; she doubted he'd have anything to say now. Once inside, she shifted and went out the back. She sat in the cold, staring out across the yard trying to figure out how everything went bad so damn fast.

Before she could get a really good wallow going, Phil whistled for her and she trotted back in the house, up the stairs to her top-floor apartment, and into her bathroom. They had the bubble bath waiting for her and a box of her favorite chocolates. She went into the water as dog, but when she came up, she was human again. They let her soak in silence for a few minutes before Sabina asked what happened. As her four friends sat on the bathroom floor, she told them pretty much everything.

"Aw, sweetie. I'm sorry." May leaned against the tub, handing Jess chocolates.

"I don't know what happened. Maybe I don't want to know."

"You should talk to him," May prompted, pushing gently. "Find out what's really going on."

"That would be the logical thing to do—and why start that ugly trend now?"

"He panicked, Jess." Phil sat with his back against the sink cabinet and his wife resting between his legs. "Men do it all the time."

"Smitty doesn't panic."

"They may not panic in a firefight in a foreign country, but a woman they care about makes them positively unglued. It's a man thing. Don't try and rationalize it."

"So what are you going to do now?"

Jess shrugged at Danny's question. "What is there to do? I'll be honest, guys. I don't think I can face him. Not right now."

"Not a problem," May reminded her. "We're going away for the long weekend tomorrow."

"Johnny's birthday party. I completely forgot. I'm a horrible mother."

Phil let out a long sigh. "You know, sweetie, if you want, I can start kicking your ass over bullshit if you're getting tired of doing it yourself."

"I hear sarcasm." Jess opened her mouth and caught the chocolate May tossed into the air. "I'm not trying to be hard on myself."

"But it comes so naturally?"

"Pretty much." Jess's cell phone rang, the tune letting her know she had a text message waiting, and Danny went into the bedroom to grab it out of her pile of clothes.

When he walked back in, he was staring at the caller ID and frowning.

She didn't even dare to hope it was Smitty. "Who is it?"

He handed the phone to May, who flipped it open and held it up so Jess could see the screen.

"Oh . . . fuck."

May shook her head. "You don't have to see her tonight."

"No, I better. I can stop by the office, grab the papers, and take them to her."

"Why can't we conduct business like we normally do with this woman?" Phil complained.

" 'Cause she's crazy," his wife stated. "Like a rabid dog."

"I like her," May admitted. "She's definitely crazy, but she makes me laugh."

"It doesn't matter. This deal could bring us a lot of money. That and our connection to these guys will keep us in the happy, shiny place for quite a while. So I've gotta go."

Sabina pulled away from her husband and stood. "Then we go with you."

"You guys don't have to do that."

Dramatically, Sabina took the phone from May's hand and stared at the small screen. "Do you really think we'd let you go *here* alone?"

"Or you could just admit that you really want to hit a club tonight."

"True. I could admit that. But it would only make me look like a bad wife and mother. Give me ten minutes to put on something sexy and then we'll go."

"I guess you're going too?" Jess asked May after Sabina walked out.

"Sure. It'll be fun." She kissed her husband and followed after Sabina, leaving Jess alone with Phil and Danny while she sat in a bathtub with dwindling bubbles. She didn't care. It wasn't like the two of them hadn't seen her naked before. And had been duly unimpressed.

"And you guys?"

"You know we'd love to come, Jess," Phil said.

"Really we would," Danny added.

"But we don't want to take away from you ladies getting in some nice girl bonding."

"You just want to stay home and watch that documentary on the Roman Empire again, don't you?"

"You know how much we love Nero. We have to see the scene where he fiddles while Rome burns."

Jess chuckled. Honestly, the male dog obsession with the History Channel was simply not normal. "Go. Enjoy your carnage."

Scratching her head affectionately, Phil asked, "You going to be okay, kid?"

"Yeah, I've survived worse. Although I have to admit, Smitty's rejections are getting much more intense."

Mace stared at the top of his friend's head. It wasn't that he was so much taller, it was that Smitty had his head on the desk. "Didn't think you'd be in today."

"Didn't want to go home," he grumbled into the desk. "It all smells like her."

"That bad?"

"That good."

"You going to tell me what happened or burrow your head into the desk like a badger?"

"There's nothing to tell. I blew it. I blew everything."

"Do you mind talking to me directly? I'm starting to think you find the desk more interesting than me."

"It is," Smitty muttered even as he sat up. "I don't know, hoss. Maybe my daddy was right. Maybe I am an idiot."

"Your daddy is certifiably insane."

"In the South we call that eccentric."

"Well, in New York, we call the cops to get 'em away from the front of our building." Mace relaxed against the door frame. "Is this about Jessica?"

"I almost marked her today. In a gas station bathroom." Elbows on the table, he buried his face in his hands. "The woman is rich, beautiful, goes to all these fancy charity parties no Smith would ever be invited to, and I nearly mount her like a bitch in heat right by the bathroom condom machine."

"Did she seem to mind?"

He dropped his hands to the desk. "That's not the point. I don't want her thinking . . ."

"Thinking what?"

Smitty let out one of those soul-deep sighs that used to drive Mace crazy when they were on duty together. "When I was eleven, I walked in the kitchen just as my momma slammed one of the Thanksgiving Day turkeys into the back of the old man's head. She dropped his ass too. Like two tons of garbage. The sad thing was I knew whatever he'd done—he'd deserved it."

"And?"

"I just don't want the next forty years to be filled with flying turkeys."

Mace laughed. He couldn't help it. "Smitty, I think you're worrying over nothing. Jessica Ward isn't the type to start throwing things."

When Smitty only stared at him, Mace asked, "She throws things?"

"Only at me, it seems."

"Did you deserve it?"

Smitty smirked. "Kind of."

"Sitting around the office whining about it isn't going to fix it. Let's go to dinner. You can whine over a rare steak and cold beer."

"Yeah, okay."

Smitty pushed his chair back when Mace said, "So I got a call today. From a Kenshin Inu."

"Who?"

"Asian wild dog who said he met you at a karaoke bar?"

"Yeah, right. The dog. What did he want?"

"To discuss a business offer with him. Next week. My cat senses are tingling. I'm sensing money."

"How do you know?"

Mace stared at Smitty. "You do know who Kenshin Inu is, don't you?"

"Not a clue."

"Well, he's many things. Mad scientist, ladies' man . . . billionaire."

Smitty stopped in the middle of pulling his jacket on. "Billionaire?"

"Yeah."

"Well, I hope you were nice to him 'cause I was kind of an asshole."

"I'm still trying to get my mind around you singing at a karaoke bar."

"Don't start."

His friend laughed. "Man, what you'll do for pussy."

"Is that right . . . *dog owner?*" Smitty met Mace's glare head-on. "How is the new puppy doing anyway?"

Mace let out an exasperated sigh. "It's bad enough we have the baby. Which I was accepting of because he's mine."

"That's real big of ya, hoss."

Mace thought so.

"But then she gets a puppy. So now we got the two stupid ones and the damn puppy. Who isn't too bad," he grudgingly admitted.

Smitty finally chuckled. "Everybody loves a puppy, hoss."

Johnny put his violin and bow down and answered the door to his rehearsal room. He expected one of the other musicians or singers using the other rooms were stopping by. Sometimes they did, although he rarely had anything to say to anyone. What he didn't expect was to find Kristan Putowski standing outside his door with a couple bags of McDonald's.

"Hungry?" she asked, pushing her way past him.

"Always." He watched her go to the baby grand piano that his instructor sometimes used during their practices and drop the bags of food on the bench. "Why are you here? I thought I was covering for you tonight."

"You were. Yeah. Quarter Pounder or Big Mac?"

"Either. And I hope you brought more than one of each or you're shit out of luck, Twinkles."

She flashed those goddamn dimples he kept dreaming about. "Of course. I've seen you eat before. Shame is so not in your vocabulary."

He closed the door, hoping none of the management stopped

by since he wasn't supposed to have food in the room, and walked over to Kristan. "What's wrong, Kristan?"

"Nothing." But she wouldn't look at him. She looked everyone in the eye. Even when you tried to avoid it. She practically turned herself into a pretzel sometimes to get you to look her in the eye.

"Bullshit. What's wrong?"

She placed napkins down and the food on top before asking, "Did you ever meet your dad?"

"No."

"Do you ever think about it? Think about what it would be like when you do?"

"Yeah, I guess. Why?"

She ignored his question and asked her own. "When you think about meeting him, do you like him?"

Johnny didn't really enjoy talking about this. His father was one of those sore points of his—Jess said he had many "sore points"—but he couldn't shake the feeling that Kristan asked him these questions for a reason. So he answered honestly, "It depends. If I'm thinking about how he treated my mother, then, no, I don't like him. But if I'm just thinking in general or thinking maybe there'd been a mistake, a misunderstanding between him and my mom, then I think I might like him. Stupid, huh?"

"No." She turned and faced him. "Not at all. I thought I'd like my father. I dreamed about it."

"You met your father? When?"

"Couple of weeks ago. I should like him. He's my father. I should like him, right?"

"Not necessarily. I've noticed the majority of human beings are assholes and don't deserve to breathe, much less procreate."

She smiled, flashing those damn dimples again. "Not that you have any strong opinions on the topic or anything."

"You asked me a question. I'm giving you an answer." He grabbed a fry. "Is that who you've been going off to see?"

"Yeah, I didn't tell my parents 'cause I knew Mom would be pissed. Now I wish I had told her."

"Why?"

"Because when she finds out she'll *definitely* be pissed." She grabbed one of the metal folding chairs and sat down. "I was supposed to see him and his Pack tonight." She rolled her eyes. "Not one of my top-ten fun things to do."

"Wolf Packs are different from wild dogs."

"I know that. But they weren't like the other wolves I've met." She looked up at him with those big, light brown eyes. "They weren't like you."

Ignore. Ignore. Ignore. "So what are you going to do now?" he asked, grabbing a Big Mac.

"Avoid for as long as I can manage."

"You've gotta tell your parents."

"I know. I know. Thought maybe I could tell them this weekend. They're always in a good mood when they get some hunting in."

"Yeah, nothing says spa-equivalent relaxation like taking down a deer and ripping its throat open."

Kristan nodded solemnly, seemingly missing his sarcasm. "Exactly."

Jess sat on the ratty old couch with Sabina on one side of her and May on the other. They sat shoulder to shoulder, thigh to thigh, needing the strength of their Packmate to soothe their rattled nerves. Rattled nerves that got worse as they watched the woman they'd come to see pace around the dingy back office of a hot Manhattan club while reading the documents they'd given her. Jess had to keep reminding herself that being here was worth it. That being around this female was worth it. It would bring in a lot of money to their Pack if this worked out like she thought it would.

Her only problem . . . the She-wolf she had to deal with. Right now, all three of the wild dogs kept looking at her wondering if they could get out of the room before the She-wolf could catch them. And if she caught them . . . what would she do?

When this all started out, Jess had only met with the surly Alpha Male of this Pack. He wasn't friendly, but he seemed sane. Then he'd handed off the fine points of all this to his Alpha Female.

Jess wished she could say the woman was mean to her. She wasn't. In fact, Jess had the distinct feeling the She-wolf liked her. A lot. Jess wasn't sure if that was a good place to be or a bad place.

Reading the end of the last page, the female walked over to the worn table in the middle of the room and popped back onto it like a spring. She pulled off her black cowboy hat, shook out her long dark hair, and said, "I'm not real happy about this split."

Sabina opened her mouth to say something and Jess nudged her with her knee.

Then Jess answered, "Uh-huh."

"I think we'll need to haggle on that a bit more. And a few of these other details."

"Okay." *Don't startle the rabid dog,* she kept reminding herself. *Don't startle the rabid dog.*

"But overall . . . I think this will work. Hot gaming clubs. It's great music, hot games—It's a good idea."

Jess nodded slowly. "Great."

She stared at them with those cold brown eyes for several excruciatingly long seconds. "Y'all are dogs, right?"

"Yeah, African Wild Dogs."

Her gaze moved from May to Jess to Sabina and back to Jess. "African? But you're the only one who's black."

May's back snapped straight and she opened her mouth to say something. Jess slapped her hand on May's knee to keep her quiet. Letting her know without words . . . *Don't startle the rabid dog!*

Slowly, Jess explained, "Think of Africa as the cradle of all civilization. So the wild dogs encompass a full range of, uh, races."

"Huh. Is it true you don't have dewclaws? You know, when you shift?"

"Right. We don't."

"Weird. Do you have thumbs?"

Don't freak out. No matter how weird this gets, don't freak out.

"Yes, we have thumbs."

"Huh." Long fingers scratched the brutal scar that marred one side of her face. She didn't seem bothered by it, but Jess had to force herself not to stare. Her natural curiosity made her want to ask all sorts of questions about how she got it, but logic told Jess to keep her damn mouth shut. "You know, I don't like . . . well . . . anybody. Except a select few. But I think we'll get along 'cause I am a dog person."

Apparently that was all May could stand. She snorted first, her head immediately dropping. But as soon as Jess and Sabina heard that snort, they couldn't control themselves. The fear taking an immediate backseat to the hysterical laughter.

Jess had been hearing rumors about the Alpha Female of the Magnus Pack for a couple of years now. She'd taken over after completely wiping out an entire Pride of lions. She'd earned a lot of respect from the canines for doing it, but it soon became apparent she might be a couple dog biscuits short of a full box of Milkbones.

She thought the woman would snap, show that ugly insanity Jess kept hearing about. Instead, Sara Morrighan merely tossed her hair back over her shoulder and drank her beer.

"We're sorry," Jess said when she'd finally gotten some control back. "That was rude."

Sara frowned in confusion. "It was?"

Best not to push it. "So I'll have our lawyers get in touch about finalizing the contract and agreement."

"Yeah, sure." Sara finished off her beer. "One other thing."

Damn. She'd thought they were out.

"The Wilson Pack. You know 'em?"

The three of them tensed. How much do they let Sara Morrighan know?

"Yes," May answered. "Their Alpha is my first daughter's father."

One She-dog dragged the other away and Jessie Ann forced a smile. "I just wanted to say that I'm sorry . . . about the other day. When I . . . uh . . ."

"Slapped the shit out of her?" Ronnie volunteered.

"Made her cry like a girl?" Marty asked while popping another beer, using her claws to rip off the cap.

"Made her rethink her existence on this planet?"

"Made her find the Lord?"

Jessie Ann let out a sigh. "Well . . . as always it's been fun to talk to you guys. So if you ladies will excuse me." She turned around and walked right into the Amazon.

"Sara? Uh—"

The Alpha Female stared directly at Sissy. "Sabina says this bitch used to beat you up."

"Sara, that was a long time ago. I can assure you I can take care of myself now."

Over the years, Sissy had found there were several types of wolves. There were the wolves like Smitty, who lived to hunt, fuck, and sleep—the typical wolf existence. There were the ones like the Reed boys, who were more junkyard dogs than wolves, always looking for the next fuck or fight. And then there were the few like Sara Morrighan—silent but deadly attackers who went for the throat first and probably didn't even bother to ask questions later.

And that's exactly what the crazed She-wolf did. She pushed Jessie Ann out of her way and went right for Sissy with claws and fangs unleashed.

Sissy never took her eyes off her and braced herself for the hit. She hated fighting crazy people, but she would.

The She-bitch never even got near her, though. What Sissy assumed to be the Alpha Male of the Magnus Pack was there, catching hold of his mate in midair before her claws could dig into Sissy's face. Sissy had heard about this guy but never had the pleasure of meeting him.

Zach Sheridan lifted Sara up with one arm while holding his cell phone in his free hand. Even better, he kept a running conversation going with whoever was on the other end of that phone without missing a beat. He simply caught hold of his mate and carried her away. Sissy would bet cold, hard cash that this was *not* the first time he'd had to do this.

Hanging over her mate's shoulder, Sara Morrighan waved at Jess and grinned. "Bye, Jess! Call me!" she said, while making the universal sign for "call me" with her fingers in the shape of a phone.

"Friend of yours?" Sissy asked Jessie after Sheridan tossed his female into the back of a limo and drove off.

The She-dog cleared her throat. "Business partner."

She headed back to her friends, and Sissy asked her, "Did you ever get a chance to talk to my brother, Jessie Ann? You were looking to talk to him the other day, right?"

Jessie stopped walking, her entire body one rigid line. "Yeah," she said without turning around. "I did. Thanks."

Sissy watched the She-dog head off with her friends. "What don't I know?" she asked anyone who'd listen.

"A lot," Ronnie Lee answered, "based on your old report cards."

"Incoming!" someone yelled and the three women stepped apart seconds before Sissy's cousin Gemma rammed headfirst into the car they'd been leaning against.

Staring down at her cousin, Sissy made a *tsking* sound. "You're going to let a supermodel beat the shit out of you? Have you no pride?"

Gemma dragged herself to her feet and went after the supermodel again.

"You're going to hell," Ronnie said for the millionth time.

"Don't worry. I've picked up a lovely property overlooking the lake of fire. We're set."

Chapter 21

Halfway through a bottle of tequila, Smitty had a nice "wallow" going on. His dinner with Mace had gone fine and chances were high they'd make a fortune off this Kenshin guy. But so what? None of this fixed his problem with Jessie Ann.

He should have gone home, but he still couldn't face that bed alone, so he ended up here. At the Kingston Arms. It didn't surprise him either when his baby sister tracked him down in the back bar the Pack favored. Like him, she had a good nose. It ran in the family.

Laughing, Ronnie and Marty with her, Sissy Mae dropped into a chair across from him and put her feet up on the table.

"Well, you missed a fun time had by all."

"Doubt I missed much of anything."

"I wouldn't say that." Marty motioned to one of the waiters with a mere tilt of her head and a shot of vodka appeared before her in seconds. "Your sister almost got mauled by a rabid animal."

A lot less interested than he should be, Smitty still asked, "What?"

"The Alpha Female of the Magnus Pack tried to take a chunk out of me."

Smitty shook his head in disgust. Only his baby sister. "What did you do?"

"Nothing."

Letting out a tired sigh, Smitty tilted his head to the side and looked at her.

"I didn't! Tell 'em, Marty. 'Cause he'll never believe you, Ronnie Lee."

"It's true. She didn't do anything."

"You didn't say something? Do something? Start something?"

"Just hanging outside a club, minding my own business."

"That's a first. So what set her off?"

"Got me. But she was with Jessie Ann Ward at the time."

Using every bit of control he had, Smitty kept his face completely neutral and simply replied, "Is that right?"

His sister stared at him for so long he almost started to squirm. He hadn't felt like that since his momma found that still he'd built when he was fourteen.

"Oh, my Lord," Sissy finally said. "*You're fucking her!*"

Ronnie grimaced. "Sissy Mae! You know Shaw hates when you yell stuff like that in the hotel."

Suddenly, his sister laughed. "I always knew you had a thing for her," Sissy accused good-naturedly. "Barely ninety pounds soaking wet, all that acne, and weird, but I knew those big dumb dog eyes of hers would get ya."

"Let it go, Sissy Mae."

"Now I'll have to be an aunt to wolfdogs. And aren't they a fun hybrid?"

"I said let it go."

"And I hope this doesn't mean we have to start hanging around that little yipping Pack of hers. That might be asking—"

His hand slamming down on the table silenced his sister. Actually, it silenced the whole room. Ronnie looked down at her hands, and Marty merely glanced away.

His sister, however, only glared at him.

"What is wrong with you? I was just jokin'."

"I said—let it go."

Sissy tapped her forefinger against the table, her gaze never leaving his face. Finally, she said, "Could y'all excuse us?"

"Yup."

"See ya."

Then they were gone.

Grabbing the bottle, Sissy poured them both another shot of tequila. "All right, big brother. Talk to me."

Johnny knew the only way to get some alone time with Jess was to wait for her on the stairs leading to her apartment on the top floor of the Pack den. He read while he waited, having grabbed another Tolkien book from Jess's personal bookshelf.

When Jess finally headed up the stairs toward him, she walked slow, her head down—obviously exhausted. But when she saw him, her eyes lit up, her energy jumped. She seemed so happy to see him. He didn't know how to handle that. Since his mother died all those years ago, he'd never had anyone happy to see him.

"Hey!"

"Hi."

Jess sat down next to him and visibly cringed when he marked off his place in the Tolkien book by folding the edge of the page. He could almost hear her internal scream of "*Sacrilege!*"

"What's up, Boo?"

She always called him that when they were alone. Her personal nickname for him. He should find it annoying, but it had been so long since anyone had mothered him.

"I think there's something I need to tell you."

"Then tell me."

He stared at her. This is when it could get awkward. But before he could say a word, Jess grabbed his arm and demanded, "Please tell me you didn't sleep with Kristan."

"*What?*"

"Isn't that what you're afraid to tell me?"

"No!"

Jess released his arm. "Whew! Had me worried."

"Can I go on?"

"Sure."

"Although this is about Kristan."

"What about her?"

"She's been meeting with her biological father. For a couple of weeks now."

Slowly, Jess's gaze locked on him. "And how is that possible, when she's been with you or the library every time I or her mother asked?"

"I've been kind of covering for her."

"So you lied to me."

"Yes." He'd never felt guilty about lying before until this very moment. With those caring brown eyes staring at him. She'd definitely kick him out now. Kristan was top dog among the pups. They would have expected him to protect her, not help her get away with shit. "I'm . . . I'm sorry."

"You should be. You're the oldest, you're supposed to be protecting the pups."

"I know." No big deal. He could get someplace else to live. He had lots of contingency plans. He'd be seventeen this weekend. Not a full adult, but with a fake ID, he could get a job and—

"Say good-bye to your allowance for two weeks, bucko. And this better never happen again."

He frowned, confused. Where was the rage? The disgust? The orders to get the fuck out of her house.

"Why are you staring at me like that, Boo?"

"To be honest, I thought you'd kick me out."

"For what? I mean, you definitely screwed up, hence the loss of allowance, but you're not going anywhere. Besides, we've already started the adoption process."

Johnny's heart literally skipped several beats. "Adoption?"

"Yeah."

"You guys are adopting me?"

"Yeah. We didn't talk to you about this?"

"No."

"Yeah, must have been the brownies." Jess stared off for a second and then smiled. "They were really good brownies. Dark chocolate."

When he only stared at her, Jess said, "Wait. Don't you want us to adopt you?"

"I'm seventeen on Saturday. I thought that when I was eighteen I'd be gone." The system kicked foster kids out at eighteen. He had contingency plans for that, too, if the Pack showed him the door a year from now.

But, to his horror, Jess's big eyes filled with tears.

"Don't . . . don't cry. I didn't mean I didn't want you guys to adopt me."

She sniffled. "Then what did you mean?"

"I meant no one has ever wanted to adopt me before. I figured that when I was eighteen you'd expect me to leave."

"No, we don't expect you to leave. We expect you to go to college. I'm assuming, to get your degree in music. Which reminds me, we need to sit down and figure out what schools you want to apply to."

"I . . . I guess wherever I get a scholarship."

"Scholarships are nice and good on résumés. But if you don't get one to a favored school, we've already got your college fund set up so you're covered there. So it's a matter of where you *want* to go."

"I have a college fund?"

"Of course. Every one of you little brats are going to college. Even if you don't want to," she finished on a snarl. "Do you understand me?"

"Yes, ma'am."

"All right, then. Any other questions?"

"No."

"Anything else you're keeping from me?"

"No."

"Good. Thanks for coming to me now, though. We're not sure of the deal with Walt Wilson, so I needed to know this."

"You're welcome."

Johnny leaned to the side a bit, his shoulder pressing against Jess's. He'd learned to bury his emotions over the years. He definitely didn't feel comfortable with them coming back up. But he had to say something. He just prayed she didn't cry again. "Thank you."

"You're welcome." Thankfully she didn't cry. "But you're still losing your allowance, bub. Nice try, though." She winked at him, but her expression changed in a second as her head lifted and she scented the air.

"What's wrong?" he asked, still learning to hone the skills the adults took for granted.

Jess didn't answer him, simply jumped to her feet and charged up the stairs to her apartment. Johnny followed behind her, nearly crashing into her when she stopped right in her doorway.

Hands on hips, Jess snapped, "What the hell are you doing here?"

Smitty folded his arms across his chest. "Came to see you, my little sweet tart."

Sweet tart?

Why was there a drunken wolf in her apartment? How did he even get in? The only way to the second entrance to her apartment was to get over the Pack house fence and cut through their backyard.

A house full of dogs and no one scented a *wolf* wandering by? A *drunk* wolf?

"I thought we said all that needed to be said this afternoon."

"Nah." He spotted Johnny over her shoulder. "Boy."

"Idiot."

Smitty took a step forward and Jess pushed Johnny out the door. "We'll talk more tomorrow."

The concern on Johnny's face warmed her heart. "Jess, are you sure?"

"Yeah, it'll be fine."

He didn't look happy about it, but he left anyway.

Jess closed the door and turned around to find Smitty standing mere inches away from her.

"You look real pretty tonight."

"Thanks."

"I missed you something horrible."

"It's been eight hours."

"*That's too long!*"

"Ssssh." Jess pushed Smitty away from the door. "Keep it down."

"I want to stay here with you tonight."

"No."

"Why not? Don't you care about me at all?"

"Smitty, this isn't fair."

"All's fair in love and fucking."

"I'm pretty sure that's not the exact quote. How did you even get here?" Christ, she hoped he hadn't been driving.

"Sissy shoved me into a cab. She said we should talk. So I'm here to talk."

Damn that woman!

"You pushed me away, Smitty. That's the second time. There won't be a third."

"Okay," he said way too calmly. Then added, "So you'll let me stay?"

Jess gritted her teeth. "No, I'll call you a cab."

"Fine. Be evil." He took her arm and pulled her into his body. "At least give me a kiss, evil woman."

"Smitty—"

"Kiss. Me. Now."

"You'll leave quietly if I kiss you?"

"Yes."

Resigned and kind of wanting to anyway, Jess slid her hand behind Smitty's neck and pulled him down so she could kiss him. He tasted like tequila, the wolf drink of choice. But, truly, tequila never tasted so damn good. His hands stroked her neck, his tongue making lazy circles around hers. The kiss seemed endless and she wished it could be. When Smitty kissed her, she could forget nearly everything else.

His hands slipped from her neck and reached for her breasts. She caught them and pulled away.

"That's enough."

Smitty licked his lips. "I knew it."

"Knew what?"

"You're not over me."

Jess took a deep breath, looking around for something to throw at that big head when Smitty's next words stopped her in her tracks.

"Don't feel bad," he said, wandering into the bedroom, "I'm never gettin' over you."

Jess followed after him, her heart soaring. "What?"

"You're dug in . . . like a tic."

Running her hands through her hair, she asked, "You're comparing me to a parasite?"

"That's a negative way to see it."

She snatched the cordless phone off her chest of drawers. "I'm calling you a cab."

"Okay." Smitty stumbled to the bed. "I'll just lay down until the cab comes."

"No, no. Don't—"

Too late. As she knew, as soon as his big fat head hit her mattress he was out like a light. She hung up the phone. She would not force a cabbie to endure pouring a Smith into the back of his vehicle.

Giving up, Jess turned off all the lights in her apartment and kicked off her sneakers. Fully dressed, she got into bed beside Smitty. As soon as the bed dipped, his arm reached out and pulled her close to his body.

"Let me go."

He muttered something and went back to snoring.

"Trifling," she growled. "Absolutely trifling."

Chapter 22

He sensed the danger before he fully awoke. Could feel it running up to him, flying at him. All he could do was brace himself for impact . . . and then *bam!*

"Wake up! Wake up!"

"He's pretty. When I grow up I want one just like him."

"He smells like Uncle Petey after Thanksgiving dinner."

"He looks mean."

"*Waaaake uuuuuuuuuuuuuuuupppp!*"

Smitty raised his head and looked at the six pups crawling all over his back and legs. Jessie Ann would definitely go down in history as the meanest woman to ever walk the planet.

A tiny fist banged against his forehead, causing immeasurable pain. "Auntie Jess wanted us to tell you to get your butt out of bed." The little girl grinned now that she'd delivered her message.

Smitty cleared his throat. "Thank you. I'm on it."

"Great!" she yelled, causing his head to split open and all the contents to fall out. Or so it felt like.

"There's waffles waiting. But you better come on. Once the older kids start feeding, forget it."

"Any chance you'll go away while I get up?"

"No," they all answered in unison.

"Of course."

"Auntie Jess wants us to make sure you get up. But you need to hurry because we're leaving soon."

Yawning, Smitty forced himself up. "Leaving?"

"Yup, for the weekend." She gave him that pretty smile again. "It's Johnny's birthday. So you need to go. After you eat. Because we're leaving. And no one seems to like you."

Smitty stared at the little blond girl. "Your momma's Sabina, isn't she?"

"How did you know?"

"Wild guess."

Jess finished her waffle and took her plate to the sink. She'd filled the adults in on the entire Walt Wilson situation, including everything she'd learned since the day before. Once done they'd gone on to pack and get their kids ready. From the main four, she'd gotten the reactions she'd learn to expect over the years. Sabina wanted to stalk and decimate the entire Wilson Pack. May took full responsibility for something that wasn't her fault. Danny saw doom. And Phil said nothing, which meant he'd already plotted and planned the violent death of Walt Wilson.

That's the thing about the Kuznetsov Pack that many didn't understand. They weren't a sweet dog Pack who had grown up among their own kind. Nearly every one of them was a street dog. Pit fighters who'd kept their Pack together and alive by doing whatever necessary. They were survivors and they protected their own.

"What do you want us to do?" Phil asked.

"I want him tracked down. Smitty's got someone on it, but call in some of our old buddies." She turned from the sink and faced her friends. "If he really just wants to see his daughter, I won't stop him. But if he's just using her—all bets are off. Understand me?"

Her Pack nodded, even though she could see May on the verge of tears. Jess walked over to her, stroked her hair, and kissed the top of her head. "Don't cry, May. We'll handle this."

"I don't want any of you to go to prison, and y'all are plotting something that will send you to prison."

Jess grinned, knowing May was right. "We'll worry about all that next week, sweetie. We've got plans this weekend. And Kristan will be with us. Safe. So let's get to it. We've gotta get these bratty-brats dressed, packed, and buckled up before we can even think about getting on the road. And pack enough for after the weekend. Don't forget we're not coming straight home. Mace's team will be setting up den security next week."

As they all stood Smitty wandered into the kitchen, pups hanging off him like monkeys.

He glared at her with bloodshot eyes. "Jessie Ann." Her name had never been filled with such accusation before.

All sweetness, "Morning, Bobby Ray."

"Think you can help me out here?"

"But you look like you're handling it so well."

"Jessie Ann," he snarled through clenched teeth, making the pups giggle.

May and Danny removed the children from Smitty's body and sent them to their rooms to start packing. Sabina sat Smitty down at the kitchen table while Phil pulled waffles out of the warmer. May filled up two glasses, one with milk and one with orange juice. Sabina brought him coffee.

"Kind of got this down to a science," Smitty noted as he clung to the coffee mug like his life depended on it.

"So many kids," Jess said, "we have no choice."

Jess poured herself a mug of coffee, and as she placed the pot back in the machine, she said, "I'm going upstairs to pack. When I come down, you'll be gone." She patted his cheek. "See ya."

One stubby Russian finger poked him in the head. "How did you screw up? Are you slow?"

"Don't poke my head."

"Don't pick on him." May topped off his coffee. "I'm sure it's just a misunderstanding."

"No, Jess is quite sure he is fool. And I think I agree with her."

"Why are y'all picking on me?"

"Because," Phil snapped, "if you screw this up, we're stuck with Sherman Landry or an equivalent." Phil glared at him. "That is unacceptable to me."

"Sorry I'm screwing up *your* life."

"Just get it right." Danny let out a deep breath. "You've got one more shot here. We're going to our Long Island house."

"And?"

"Marissa Shaw's property butts ours. Do the math, hillbilly," Phil snarled between clenched teeth.

"That'll work," May said with that constant cheerfulness. It was annoying. "You can 'accidentally' meet up with us at some point." She winked at him.

"I'll see what I can do."

"You better," Phil bit out. "Because if I have to deal with Landry on a regular basis, there will be hell to pay."

"Mornin', sunshine."

Brendon, dressed in only a towel and fresh from his shower, slowly turned away from his kitchen sink and faced the man who had quickly become the bane of his existence. His sister had been right, it seemed. She said you take on one Packmate, you take on them all. Now, nearly every day, he found some wolf wandering around his home, eating his food, watching his TV— and he wouldn't even discuss the bathtub incident.

"Why are you here?"

Smitty held up a bowl of plain yogurt. "I was hungry."

"This is a hotel. You can get room service. In another room. Even better, another hotel—in another state."

"True enough. True enough. But I do have a question for you."

Brendon took a deep, cleansing breath. "Okay."

"Your sister has property near the Kuznetsov Pack's, right?"

"The one out on Long Island?"

"Yeah."

"Yeah. So?"

"Any plans for this weekend?"

Brendon folded his arms in front of his chest, his patience sprinting out of the room. "Spit it out, canine."

"Thought we could bring the Pack there, maybe Mace and Dez, since we have this long weekend coming up. Make it a family thing."

"And you want to take them to the property that just happens to butt up against your girlfriend's Pack's?"

"She's not my girlfriend."

Yet.

Brendon had been there. He knew the possessive look in the man's eye. Poor idiot. He had no idea. None. But Smitty had given Brendon's boneheaded brother a job that kept him in New York and out of trouble. More important, Smitty had brought him Ronnie Lee. For that alone he owed the man, although under torture he'd never admit that out loud. "All right, little puppy, we can go. Besides, it'll be fun watching her ignore you."

"That's real kind of you, hoss."

"Well, ya know . . ." Brendon grinned. "I do try."

Chapter 23

Jess loved this. Loved coming to this place. To this sanctuary. To relax and be at peace.

"So you gonna marry this guy?"

Jess sighed loud and long. Of course, when you brought the pups along, one risked the whole sanctuary thing.

"Why," Jess asked while sitting on the front porch of the Long Island Pack house staring out at the woods dusted in snow, "must you ruin my weekend with your incessant questions?"

"I asked one." Johnny sat down in a chair next to her, a cup of hot chocolate in his hands. "After what Kristan told me and now seeing him in your apartment, I was just wondering—"

"Kristan was supposed to keep her mouth shut."

"Yeah, good luck with that."

"And you didn't see anything." Jess took Johnny's hot chocolate and sipped it. "So what are you wondering anyway?"

"If you marry this guy—"

"I'm not going to marry him."

"—will that change the whole adoption thing?"

Jess turned in her chair and stared at Johnny. And she kept staring until the boy twisted uncomfortably in his chair. "What?"

"See this?" Jess pointed at her face. "This is my unhappy expression."

Johnny's lips turned up a bit at the corners. "Your unhappy expression?"

"Yes, this is the expression I get when I'm unhappy."

"Oh. And you're unhappy because . . ."

"Because you actually think that some man, any man, could make me change any of my decisions. I didn't know you saw me as such a wuss."

"I don't. It's just . . ." Johnny shrugged. "My mom changed her whole life over a guy, and she was one of the toughest women I knew."

"She was also seventeen when she had you. I'm thirty-two. Big difference, kid."

Johnny smiled. "I guess you don't get all this by being a wuss, huh?"

"Nope."

Jess happily breathed in the fresh air. "Might as well suck it up, Johnny. As I told you before, you're stuck with us."

"Right. Like the Mafia." Seventeen this weekend but still a smart-ass kid as far as Jess was concerned. "So am I going to go hunting this weekend with the others? Or are you still gonna treat me like a pup who hasn't cut his teeth?"

Jess placed her feet up on the railing and relaxed back. "We'll see. The Stark Clan is here this weekend too."

"So?"

"Those hyenas tend to come on our territory unasked."

"Hence the fistfight at the grocery store."

"They started it. And it wasn't a fistfight—it was a shoving match." Jess handed the mug back to Johnny. "No marshmallows?"

"I don't like marshmallows."

"Philistine."

"Fascist."

The pair stared off into the surrounding woods. It snowed all last night and now the entire property had a healthy bit of snow for them to enjoy. Jess had every intention of snowboarding this

weekend. She'd completely recovered, physically and emotionally, from her ugly run-in with that rutting male elk last year.

Good thing wild dogs were fast runners.

Smitty did really well until the young cub climbed up onto his
shoulders and bit into the back of his head. Slowly, he faced
Ronnie Lee, who seemed engrossed in a gossip magazine.

"Ow," he said.

Ronnie Lee glanced at him, but her eyes widened when she
saw Brendon Shaw's son trying to turn him into a meal.

"Oh, crap!" She tossed the magazine, pulled herself to her
knees on the couch, and grabbed the cub off Smitty's head.
"Erik! We discussed this. Wolves are not for eating."

When she pulled him away, Erik screamed and fought to get
back to Smitty.

"I think he likes you."

Smitty held his arms out. "Give him here."

Before Ronnie could do anything, Erik charged back over to
him, slamming his small body right into his chest.

Smiling, Ronnie said, "Kids love you."

"It must be my charm."

Unprompted, the cub in his lap began to howl. Loudly.

Ronnie placed her hand over Erik's mouth. "Shush!" she ordered in a loud whisper. "I told you not to do that when your
daddy's in the house."

"Ronnie Lee, what have you been teachin' this cat?"

She shook her head. "Nothin'."

"Ronnie Lee . . ."

Ronnie grabbed her magazine and settled back into the
couch, ignoring his chastising tone. "So what's your grand plan
here, Bobby Ray?"

"My grand plan?"

"To trap you a wild dog this weekend. That is why we're
here, isn't it?"

"Lord, Ronnie Lee. I don't know. I don't know what I'm
doing."

She turned on the couch to face him, pulling her feet up so her toes grazed his thigh. Neither was too surprised when Erik grabbed them. For a toddler, he already seemed to have quite a few fetishes. "What do you mean?"

"I mean, one second I'm thinking, 'She's mine. She's always been mine and I'm taking her.' Then the next I think, 'She's not strong enough. Not to be part of the Smiths'.'"

"You don't know that, Smitty."

"When I went after that bear, she hid behind a tree."

Ronnie snorted. "I would have hid behind a tree unless you needed me."

"No, you wouldn't."

"Smitty, every female in Smithtown knows—you never get between a Smith male and a regular fight. Ever. Sounds to me she was smart. Not weak. I won't say it's easy being part of the Smiths. But if she's the right girl for you, neither of you may have a choice."

"I know that."

"I do have to say, she's grown up real pretty, Bobby Ray."

"That she has."

"Pretty and still innocent enough to shame the angels."

Smitty smirked. "Not all that innocent."

"Why, Bobby Ray Smith, you're gonna make me blush—Ow! Erik! That's my toe, boy. Watch those teeth."

As wolf, Sissy Mae sauntered into the room, the females behind her. She yipped at Ronnie Lee and motioned to the door with her head.

"Y'all go on now." Smitty pulled Erik off Ronnie Lee's feet. "I'll watch Erik."

"Are you sure?" She raised her eyebrows, letting him know she could still talk but not saying it because then Sissy Mae would demand to know what they were talking about. And even worse, she'd try to "help." Nothing worse than Sissy Mae trying to help. She'd thought she'd helped last night when she sent him to Jessie's apartment.

"Go. I'll hunt tomorrow."

"Thanks, darlin'." She kissed his cheek and walked over to the door, opening it and letting the other She-wolves out. Then she shifted, shook off her clothes, and followed them outside.

"You sure are good with cats—for a canine."

Dez sat down on the couch opposite Smitty, her son asleep in her arms.

"Not as good as you, my sweet Dez."

"Well, *darlin'*, you lack the equipment for that."

He laughed and the boy in his arms laughed with him.

Smitty looked down at the toddler in his lap and grinned at him. "You really are cute for a Shaw, ain'tcha?"

In response, the boy threw back his head and howled again. Seemed he liked doing that a lot.

Unfortunately, the snarl of rage behind him suggested to Smitty that Brendon Shaw did not agree.

Smitty smiled up at the male lion standing behind the couch—seething. "Hey, Shaw. Nice house you've got here."

Arms crossed over that massive chest, the lion looked down his nose at Smitty as only a cat could. "What else have you taught my son? How to chase his tail? Lick his ass?"

"Nah, I stuck with the cat basics. Park lazy ass under tree, sleep twenty hours, eat all the food after the females do all the hunting, take a few minutes to roar, then sleep another twenty hours."

When the cat flashed those fangs, Smitty was smart enough to shut the hell up even while Dez burst out laughing.

Sitting out here on the porch, staring at the snow, Jess asked Johnny her usual litany of questions. How was school? Did he like it? Was he getting along better with the other pups? Did he need new boots? A new violin? Exactly how much did those Stradivarius ones cost? And how exactly did he get past the killer orc on level fifteen without having the plus-twelve dexterity magick armor?

She really never stopped talking, his Jess. Of course, none of them did. Even the males talked—constantly. Johnny liked his quiet time. He liked to sit and think. Just be. He didn't think the wild dogs had it in them to just be. They either slept or talked. No in between for the wild dogs.

But they were his, weren't they? His family now. His Pack. True, when he shifted he was already about two times bigger than the biggest wild dog, but that didn't change what he knew.

He was home.

Johnny turned to the woman he'd come to quietly care so much about, silently debating whether he should actually tell Jess that when she suddenly sat up straight in her chair. Her eyes scanned the woods; her ears twitched.

She'd heard something she didn't like. Wild dogs had killer hearing. They should. When shifted, they had the biggest ears imaginable considering their slight size.

Jess growled, her gaze locked on the forest in front of them. "I want you inside, Johnny."

Christ. He was seventeen tomorrow. Maybe it was time to start treating him like an adult. "Yeah, but—"

"*Now!*"

Startled by Jess's yell, Johnny headed into the house. As he went in, a majority of the Pack adults ran out, already shifted. The adults who stayed behind shifted and stood on the porch or directly in front of the house. A few took up positions in the back.

Johnny knelt on the couch with the other pups and watched through the big picture window as the adults charged off into the woods.

"Someone," Kristan muttered next to him—smelling delightful as always—"is going to get their ass kicked."

Sissy Mae got her teeth in the deer's neck and flipped over, taking the animal with her. Ronnie Lee wrapped her jaw around the throat and crushed the windpipe. It eventually stopped moving, and the She-wolves settled down to enjoy an early lunch.

They didn't plan to linger. They'd crossed into wild-dog territory, and although Sissy didn't really worry, she still knew in her gut that her brother had come here for another shot at Jessie Ann. She wouldn't ruin that by embarrassing the dogs on their own property.

So when Ronnie Lee lifted her head and scented the air, Sissy assumed it was the dogs coming to investigate. But then she caught the scent, too, and heard the sound. That laugh-howl. Her head snapped up and she saw them come out of the trees. Not a full Clan, only about ten, but enough to cause a problem. She snarled and the She-wolves left off their meal, surrounding it. The hyenas came for the food. But they'd have to fight for it. Sissy Mae Smith didn't give up her kills to anybody.

She stepped forward and snarled, and the hyenas dodged in and out, making that annoying sound that set her nerves on edge. They were looking for a way past the wolves to get to the deer. Sissy glanced at one of the younger She-wolves and sent her off to round up the males.

Focusing back on the hyenas, Sissy pulled her lips back, baring her fangs. One of the hyenas danced close and Sissy leaped forward, her teeth just grazing the hyena's jaw. It jumped back, surprised by the aggression but not ready to back off yet.

But before the hyena could make another move, wild dogs burst out of the trees from the other side.

Sissy watched in fascination as Jessie Ann's Pack went after a breed more than twice the wild dogs' size. And hyenas had jaws that could easily crush bone.

Even more surprising, the hyenas ran off. Maybe because they were on dog territory. Maybe because there were only ten of them or they were a weak Clan. Whatever.

Once the hyenas disappeared back into the woods, the wild-dog Pack turned to Sissy and her She-wolves. Hhhm. This could prove awkward. But, again, she'd respect her brother and let this alone. Sissy looked back and guesstimated the territorial line between the dogs' property and Shaw's was about three miles. No big deal, they'd make that without any—

The bark cut off her thought and she turned around to see that the dogs had moved closer, barking constantly and moving out in a circle around them.

If she were human, she would have laughed. The hyenas may have run off, but not the wolves. Smith wolves didn't run. They'd leave, but they wouldn't run. She nodded her head, letting the dogs know without words that her Pack would leave of its own accord. No reason to make this nasty.

Jessie Ann stepped forward; her eyes locked on Sissy's. She snarled, baring her fangs. In that split second Sissy realized Jessie Ann was unbelievably pissed off that the wolves dared to cross territorial lines.

Refusing to believe Jessie Ann would be stupid enough to challenge her, Sissy gave a warning growl. Warning Jessie Ann not to even try it. Not to even think it. She sucker punched Sissy once, but that wouldn't happen again.

Sissy motioned to Ronnie Lee, who took several steps back before turning completely around and trotting off, the other She-wolves right behind her. Sissy growled and barked one last time before she turned and slowly followed after her She-wolves. Once again, Smith wolves didn't run. Besides, she only had to get to the territorial line between the dogs' and Shaw's properties.

That's exactly what she kept thinking as she came in sight of that territorial line. Then Jessie Ann Ward dug painfully sharp fangs into Sissy's left thigh and flung her nose over tail back into dog territory.

Smitty laughed as Shaw backed away from Ricky Lee and the moonshine-filled Mason jar.

"Keep that crap away from me!"

"Now don't go turnin' into a big pussy. Drink up, boy!" Ricky Lee winked at Smitty. "Trust me, Bobby Ray. We'll turn this Yankee into a good ol' Southern boy in no time."

"Hell you will!" Shaw laughed.

Watching the Reed boys torture Ronnie Lee's mate, Smitty

debated about whether to get some food from the fridge or go take a nap. A good sleep often did wonders when he needed to figure out a problem. But before he could do either, the scent hit him first.

The scent of panic.

By the time he made it down the front porch stairs, a She-wolf slid to a stop in front of him. She barked and turned, running off. The others shifted and followed after her. Smitty took a second to look back at Mace standing on the porch stairs. "Stay here. Protect Erik."

"Got it. Go."

He did, running and shifting simultaneously. He caught up with the rest of them as they neared a ridge.

Smitty could smell they were nearing another breed's territory. Wild dog. Jessie Ann's territory.

Lord, what had Sissy Mae been thinking?

As Smitty and the others made it over a small ridge, they saw them. There were about three dogs to every wolf, and there were at least four dogs on Sissy.

Shaw roared in anger and charged toward the dogs tag teaming Ronnie Lee. Smitty headed right for his sister and Jessie Ann, immediately recognizing her scent and markings.

Besides, only a dog with a grudge would go after Sissy Mae the way she was. Sissy held her own, but she was weakening fast. Still, Jessie Ann kept at her. Sissy would turn and try to take a chunk out of her and Jessie would dance away from her. Then another dog would attack her flank, and when Sissy would turn to fight them, Jessie Ann would come back.

Smitty knew he had to get his sister and the She-wolves over the territorial boundaries they were mere feet from. He had to do it fast.

But the wild dogs cut in front of him, zigzagging past, blocking him. Blocking him from Jessie Ann.

Pissed, he batted the dogs out of his way, barreling through them when he could, and, without hesitation, went straight for Jessie Ann. Fangs sank past fur and into vulnerable flesh and muscle. She let out a cry of pain and twisted away from him, releasing Sissy Mae in the process. Jessie Ann jumped back several feet and stared at him. Then she tried to dodge around him to get back to Sissy. Smitty cut her off, baring his fangs in warning. She snarled back and again tried to go around him.

His Packmates were desperately trying to get the other dogs off Sissy Mae so she could limp her way back to Shaw territory, but the dogs wouldn't let her go. When two were knocked off, two more attacked.

When Jessie Ann tried to go around him again, he batted her back. She stared at him and he wondered if she'd run off. Lord, what if he made her cry?

Then, in a moment that he'd remember until the day he died, sweet, innocent Jessie Ann Ward charged him head-on.

They went up on hind legs and clawed at each other while biting at the most vulnerable areas. She bit into his muzzle and he clawed her throat.

Her Pack, hearing their Alpha's fight, came running. Smitty let them. He let them go at him, tearing into him. He let them, but he didn't back off Jessie Ann. Not until he knew his sister was safe.

And Jessie Ann never backed off him. Not once. She went after him like she would have any other predator. Coldly.

When Brendon Shaw roared again, Smitty knew his Pack had gotten Sissy over the boundary. He snapped at the dogs on his ass and shoulders, and backed up until he made it back into Shaw territory. The dogs came right up to that line, one long row of them. That's how they attacked—in a line, until they slipped off to surround their prey, ran it down, and ripped it apart.

Smitty knew this was part message, part revenge. The message letting the Smith Pack know that, without an invite, traipsing onto wild-dog land would get them killed. But the revenge . . . Well, apparently eighteen years of resentment had just exploded way past that punch in the face.

Brendon stepped forward and stared at Jessie. Her eyes moved from Smitty to Brendon and back again. Finally, she gave a brief yip, turned, and trotted back into her territory. Bushy white, brown, black, and blond tail up and swishing proudly. With another yip, Jessie's Pack followed.

With one last shake of his head, Smitty turned and followed after his Pack and wounded sister.

Chapter 24

With all those stitches covering a good portion of her body, Sissy looked sewn together. The dogs had done a lot of damage but none of it lethal. Just painful. She probably wouldn't even get the fever, that important step their bodies took when fighting infection, but she would definitely have scars. A lot of them.

Yeah, Jessie Ann had known *exactly* what she'd been doing.

"I warned you," Brendon said again to Ronnie Lee. "I warned you not to go into dog territory."

"Yeah," Ronnie said with a shrug, and a wince from her own pain, her own stitches, "but I thought you were being sarcastic. I mean . . . they're *dogs*."

"True. And they kicked your ass."

"There were two thousand of them," Sissy shot back.

"I told you they had their pups this weekend. It doesn't matter if there's one million or one, wild dogs will do whatever necessary to protect their pups. End of story."

"Yeah, but—"

Shaw slammed his hand down on the metal kitchen table, nearly buckling it. "No buts! I don't even have room to complain about this. Or demand retribution. Their attack was completely warranted. I told you I hadn't gotten permission for you guys to go off my territory. And Marissa and I can only go within a mile of their den. Even Mitch doesn't go over there and he's a dumb-ass!"

"I heard that!" Mitch yelled from the living room.

"Shut up!"

Sissy sighed. "Look, y'all, I'm sorry. Okay? I didn't think it would be a big deal. Now I know." She looked at him. "Sorry, Bobby Ray."

"Don't apologize, Sissy Mae. It's something any of us might have done when we're running down lunch."

"I wouldn't have done it," Shaw muttered, but quieted down when Ronnie Lee glared at him.

"This changes everything, don't it, Bobby Ray?" Sissy asked softly.

Smitty sipped his beer before speaking. He hoped the beer would deaden the pain around his stitches. He had far less than Sissy Mae but enough to cause discomfort. Yet, due to their biological makeup, in a few hours they'd have to remove the stitches or risk the skin healing over them.

"Yup," he finally answered. "I reckon it does."

"You're a Smith male, Bobby Ray. It's not like you can do any different."

"I know."

Sissy poured herself more orange juice. "Then I guess you better get on over there."

"Yup."

Shaw looked between them. "What are you two talking about?"

"Make it quick, Bobby Ray. Like Daddy would."

Bobby Ray grimaced, but nodded. "I'll do my best."

"Wait. What are you two planning?" Shaw demanded.

Ronnie sighed. "Mind your own, Brendon Shaw. This is Smith business."

"You're kidding, right?"

When they all stared at him, he threw his hands up. "Fine. But I gotta tell you, I praise the day I was born a cat."

* * *

Jess literally tore the still-beating heart from her opponent's chest and forced him to look at it.

Her twelve-year-old nephew glared at her. "You are *mean*," he accused.

"Suck it up, Boy Scout."

He threw down his controller and stormed off.

"Next!"

Sabina and Phil's fourteen-year-old son jumped into the vacated seat on the couch.

"Nice facial lacerations there, by the way." The boy had his father's sarcasm, coupled with his mother's brutal sense of humor. Smart-ass.

"Like these lacerations, do you?" she asked. "Good. You'll look like this when I'm done."

The bell for the next round rang, but before she could recover from an aerial kick to the head, Danny called for her from the front porch.

She paused the game. "Don't even try and cheat, brat."

"I don't have to. I'll destroy you without it."

"Dreamer."

Jess grinned and walked through the living room, her Pack involved in different forms of relaxing activities. From chess and checkers to role-playing games with pen, paper, dice, and their imaginations to video and computer games to yoga . . . which just seemed weird.

But her grin faded when she walked out onto the porch and found a human and clearly brutalized Smitty waiting for her. Okay, so maybe she'd done more damage than she'd given herself credit for.

He leaned against his truck, arms crossed over his chest. To the untrained eye, he looked relaxed. Composed. But she knew that look. She saw it once, years ago, seconds before Smitty beat the living hell out of his older and larger brother for sleeping with Smitty's whore girlfriend at the time.

"What do you want, Smith?"

"We need to talk."

If he thought she was getting off this porch, he was high.

"So talk."

When he realized she wouldn't come to him, he pushed himself off his truck and walked up the stairs. He stared down at her and she fought the urge to stroke his face, do whatever she could to help take away the pain she knew he suffered.

He didn't say anything, and she quickly grew impatient with the long Smitty-silence. "Well? I'm waiting."

Big arms crossed over his chest, Smitty gave a sad sigh. "I underestimated you all along, didn't I?"

Jess shrugged. "Probably." Everyone else had, why should he be different?

"What happened this morning . . ." He gazed off into the woods, then shook his head. "I have to say, I never saw that coming."

"Your sister was on my territory. I have pups here. What did she or you expect?"

"I expected you to let her get over territorial lines. I expected you to let her walk away. The Jessie Ann I thought you were would have done that. Because you didn't, do you know what that makes you?"

Jess knew she didn't want to hear this. She didn't want any more hurtful words or, even worse, hurtful silences between her and Smitty, but there was no avoiding it now. "What, Smitty? What does that make me?"

Amber wolf eyes locked on her and she saw fangs as he opened his mouth to speak. Her own claws slowly slid into place, prepared to tear and render as necessary.

"Mine, Jessie Ann," he finally said. "That makes you mine."

Jessie stared up at him like he'd grown a second head. Even her claws had receded. He'd seen them slide out, and that had only confirmed what he already knew. She would have ripped him apart if he'd made a move on her. Jessie Ann had a vicious streak a mile long and ten miles deep and nothing turned him on more.

"I'm sorry . . ." she said softly. "What?"

"What did you think would happen, Jessie Ann?" Smitty asked calmly. "You attacked my She-wolves when they were trying to leave your territory. Mauled my sister after just apologizing to her the other day for punching her in the eye. And tore open my face with your teeth when I tried to protect her. And you did it without pity or remorse or a lick of conscience. Sorry, darlin', but that makes you prime Smith-mate material."

Looking away from that beautiful face and those big shocked eyes, Smitty examined the surrounding acres. He immediately spotted a big unused barn. Perfect.

"Come on, Jessie." He took hold of her wrist and kissed her palm gently. "Let's do this right, darlin'."

Yeah. He'd do this right. Slow and easy. Just the way Jessie Ann deserved. No Smith mate-mauling for her. Even if that's what he wanted to do, he'd give her what she needed.

Smitty walked to the top of the porch stairs with Jessie behind him when she stopped abruptly, bringing him up short. He turned and saw that Jessie had secured one foot against the porch railing, locking her in place. Then she jerked him back and slammed that small fist of hers right into his already abused face.

He dropped her arm and covered his bleeding nose.

"*What in the holy hell was that for?*"

"Oh, you don't know? Well, let me do it again until you figure it out!"

Grabbing her under the arms, Smitty lifted her up until they were eye to eye. "What the hell is wrong with you?"

"*The barn?* You were going to take me off to the barn like we're walking to the local store?"

He smiled and let out a breath. "Jessie Ann, if you wanted something fancy, you just had to say."

"Fancy?"

"Yeah." He carefully placed her back on the porch. "We can wait until we get back to the city, and then we can go somewhere real nice. Just what you'd want. I know you're used to better now, and I should have thought of that before. I'm sorry."

When she plowed that fist into his stomach, all he could do was stare at her.

"*What was that for?*"

"You think it's all about money? Is that what you think?"

"Woman—"

"Don't you 'woman' me. For you to think I'm that shallow and insipid and that it's all about money *is just rude!*"

"*Then what do you want?*"

She threw up her hands. "*Everything!*" She stepped away from him. "And until you can give me that, we have nothing else to say to each other."

Without another word or punch, she walked around him and headed back to the house.

He followed. "Jessie Ann—" But she slammed the door in his face, leaving him standing outside in the cold.

Jess leaned back against the door, fighting tears she'd never allow to come. He wasn't worth one damn tear. Not one.

She glanced around the room and every dog stared at her. Pup and adult. All she saw was sympathy and warmth. They all loved her as only dogs could. *They* knew what she wanted. What she needed from Bobby Ray Smith. Because they understood her completely. Even if he didn't.

Sabina walked up to her and handed her a bag of dark chocolate chips.

"Here, my friend."

"Thanks."

"You want hug?"

Jess nodded, feeling particularly pathetic but not caring. Sabina hugged her tight, then her Pack was there in one massive group hug that would completely freak out most people.

Ronnie jumped when the front door slammed open, and she blinked in surprise when she heard Bobby Ray Smith of all people yell, "*She is driving me insane!*"

He yanked off his jacket, threw it across the room, and

stormed into the kitchen. She scrambled over Shaw and the back of the couch, making it to the kitchen as Smitty grabbed hold of a bottle of tequila from one of the cabinets.

"Oh, no, you don't." She took hold of the top and yanked. He yanked back. "Bobby Ray, you give me that bottle this minute."

Bobby Ray snarled at her—he'd never snarled at her before—and yanked the bottle with one hand while shoving her back with the other. Ronnie stumbled back and watched as he unscrewed the cap. He almost had it to his lips when his sister walked up behind him, slammed her foot into his instep and, when he gasped in pain, snatched the bottle from his hand.

"What happened?" she asked, walking to the other side of the kitchen.

"None of your damn business." He stormed toward her. "Now give me—"

Sissy Mae held the bottle up, aiming right for her brother's head. "Just try it."

Smitty stared at his sister, probably debating whether she'd really hit him with it. He had to know she would.

"I'm out of here."

They watched him storm out the back door, strip, shift, and take off into the woods behind Shaw's house.

Ronnie let out a breath and looked at her friend.

"What?" Sissy asked. "You think I'd waste all this good tequila on that fat head?"

"Well, you did have me worried."

The rest of the day went by slowly and uneventfully. Jess mostly stayed in the kitchen with May under the pretense of helping her bake cakes for Johnny's birthday the following day; but since she couldn't bake anything but chocolate chip cookies, she really stayed in there because no one would bother her. May said little and Jess sat in a corner and re-read Tolkien's *The Two Towers* for perhaps the ninety millionth time.

But even J.R.R. couldn't distract her from thoughts of Smitty.

It hadn't been easy walking away earlier. But she knew she had to. Knew she had to walk away and not look back. Not if she wanted all of him. The man who came to her that afternoon might as well have been a full-human for all the passion he showed her. A Beta with extremely low expectations of his mate.

As soon as he took her hand, she could see their lives played out in front of her. Nice quiet, simple lives with about as much passion and love as you could get out of a vibrator. She'd rather be alone than live that way. She'd only known her parents fourteen years, but what she always felt certain in was their love of each other. It was passionate and wild and beautiful, and she was the product of that.

If she wanted a solid but passionless relationship, she'd start returning Sherman Landry's calls. But she didn't want Sherman Landry or the boring relationship he could offer. Jess wanted more. And in that disgusting bathroom off the turnpike, she really thought she'd found that with Smitty. Then he'd pushed her away. Not comfortable with what he'd felt. With the Smith inside him.

Sure, she could tell him what her problem was. She could tell him how she wanted a true Smith mating because that's how she'd know she meant everything to him. But she knew Smitty enough to know he'd simply fake it to make her happy. He'd take her to bed, fuck her stupid, maybe get a little rough with her, and mark her. But it wouldn't change a damn thing. It wouldn't make him okay with who he was and always would be simply due to his DNA strain.

Jess now realized, as she dragged herself up to her room on the top floor, that she'd never have him—hell, never want him—until he could accept who and what he was. You had to accept it before you could go beyond it. Instead, Smitty probably spent more time fighting his desires than moving to the next stage of his life.

It broke her heart, but to be blunt, it wasn't her problem. As her mother used to say, "Some things a body just has to figure out on their own."

Jess walked into her room and closed the door. She really hoped she could shake this by tomorrow morning. They had a full day planned for Johnny and she wanted his seventeenth birthday to be a blast for him. What she definitely didn't want was to bring the whole thing down by being a sad sack.

She sat on her bed, untying and toeing off her boots. She briefly debated changing into night clothes, but she simply lacked the energy or desire. So she flipped off the light and stretched out on the bed.

After a few minutes, she caught his scent. She hadn't noticed it before since she'd been unable to get the essence of it out of her head in the first place.

She sighed. "What do you want, Smitty?"

He stepped out of the shadows. At least he looked as miserable as she felt.

"I know you don't want to see me right now."

"You're right."

"But I don't want to sleep alone again tonight. I miss you, Jessie Ann."

"The same way I miss my dogs after I dropped them off at the kennel yesterday?"

He went from miserable to angry in about two seconds. "What the hell does that mean?"

Too tired to argue, she turned on her side. "Forget it. It doesn't mean anything."

She heard him take a deep breath, trying to calm that temper he insisted on hiding from her. "Do you mind if I stay?" he asked.

"Whatever."

She heard his coat drop to the floor, followed by his boots. Then, fully dressed, he crawled into bed with her. He spooned her from behind, one arm tight around her waist, the other curving over her head on the pillow. She reached down and pulled the comforter over them before she settled back in.

He snuggled in closer, burying his face in the back of her neck. She placed her hand over the one on her waist, her fingers sliding between his. He closed his hand, locking his fingers around hers.

Like that they fell asleep and Jess realized nothing in her life had ever felt so right before.

In the morning, when she woke up to the pups banging on her door, he was gone.

Chapter 25

It had taken her second in command getting between them to separate Brendon Shaw from Bobby Ray.

It had started off like any other morning hunt. The Smith Pack wolves tracking down a deer and taking it down. And just like every other hunt now that lions had become a constant part of their lives, the cats happened on by to steal their meal. If there was only one, Mace or Brendon, they usually put up a fight. But with Mace, Brendon, and Mitch, Sissy thought they'd just let them have the damn thing and go after another one. But Bobby Ray had fought back with a vengeance. Mace backed off immediately, understanding Bobby Ray better than any of them did. She had no doubts you learned a lot about a man when you were stationed with him in a war zone. Mitch enjoyed his job, and Sissy even had the sense he was seriously considering not going back to his police job in Philly, so he'd backed off pretty quick too.

But Brendon seemed more than happy to give Smitty the fight he'd been looking for, the two of them going after each other like the deer at their feet couldn't simply be replaced by a drive-through run to McDonald's.

Of course, this had nothing to do with the damn deer. Or the fact that the lions always stole their meals. It was all about that damn She-dog.

It still boggled Sissy's mind that the little heifer had the nerve to turn down *her* brother. The best of the batch, in her estimation. Maybe if it had been one of the other four, Sissy could understand Jessie Ann pushing him away. But Bobby Ray wasn't like her other brothers. And her other brothers probably wouldn't have given Jessie Ann the option. They would have taken her down like they had that deer.

But Smitty wouldn't tell Sissy more than, "She don't want me. That's all you need to know."

Sissy doubted that. Actually, she *knew* that to be wrong. That little geek had wanted her brother since the first time she'd set eyes on him. And it hadn't changed. Really, in Sissy's opinion, it would never change. Jessie Ann Ward would always love Bobby Ray Smith. And now that she'd seen him so miserable, Sissy knew that Bobby Ray would always love Jessie Ann.

Yet, for some unknown reason, the two of them insisted on fighting it. So the question for her was how to fix this. She was Alpha Female. She needed to fix this.

By her third fight with Bobby Ray—this time over potatoes— Ronnie Lee dragged her off to the town bar. Lots of cute local talent, but she couldn't even enjoy flirting since she had Bobby Ray's drama on her mind. So she and Ronnie sat at the bar, nursing their beers, and occasionally muttering to each other.

Near four o'clock she heard a soft voice with a thick Southern accent say, "Two glasses of champagne, please, Charlie."

Sissy raised her head and stared at the two females lounging at the end of the bar. She recognized them both from the night at the club when she'd had that run-in with the Magnus Pack Alphas. One of them pulled out a box of high-end chocolate from a glossy shopping bag and placed it on the bar. Their drinks arrived and they sat down on stools and opened the box.

"Let it go," Ronnie Lee muttered before Sissy had done anything.

"But look at 'em. Sittin' over there like nothing's wrong."

"Sissy, let it go."

She should. But she couldn't. She banged her fist on the bar and both She-dogs looked up at her.

"Think you can explain to me what the hell is wrong with your Alpha Female?"

They both stared at her, but neither said a word.

"Does she really think she's too good for my brother? Because she's damn wrong."

Again, the blank stare and the silence.

"What? Something wrong with your mouth? Can't ya speak?"

The Asian one leaned forward a bit, her hands flat on the bar, her head tilting to the side. After a long moment, she said, "Woof."

Sissy leaned back a bit, her gaze sliding over to Ronnie's. As soon as they looked at each other, though, they lost it. Bursting into surprised laughter.

The two She-dogs walked down to their side of the bar, bringing their drinks and chocolates with them.

"Another two glasses of champagne, Charlie." The Asian one held her hand out and Sissy shook it. "I'm Maylin. Y'all can call me May. This is Sabina."

"Nice to meet ya."

"So," she said, plunking herself down on the bar stool, "what are we gonna do about these two idiots?"

Yup. Sissy liked this one already.

Lord, could he get more pathetic? Sitting in the snow, in the woods, watching Jessie's house. He couldn't help it. She spent most of her time out on that back porch watching the pups play in the snow. Sometimes jumping in with a well-placed snowball.

Of course, it wasn't like Smitty had anywhere else to go. He'd alienated nearly everyone else at Shaw's house except Dez, who knew how to get a cranky male to back up off her with only a look.

To avoid losing his friends and Pack forever, Smitty had shifted and taken off into the woods. Sometimes he focused on problems much better as wolf. He'd chased a couple of rabbits and a couple of crows. Although that had been a bad idea after they dive-bombed him and tried to shit on his head. Then he'd ended up back here, trying to figure out what the hell Jessie Ann wanted from him.

Okay, so the barn had been a bad idea, but he'd merely been trying to expedite the situation. Once he knew what he wanted, no need to fight it anymore. But when he offered her a soft bed and a romantic marking in the city, she'd acted like he'd offered to take her to an execution in the town square.

Why wouldn't she just tell him what she wanted? Jessie had never seemed like "other girls" who wanted you to guess everything. When you asked how they were, they'd respond, "Fine." If Jessie was mad, she sure as shit let you know it in no uncertain terms. But she always told him the reason. Now she wouldn't and he didn't know what to do to fix this. And he had to fix it.

He loved her. Maybe he'd loved her forever. But he knew it for sure when he'd wrapped himself around her last night. She'd felt so good in his arms, so perfect. Like she'd been made to order just for him.

Lord, he couldn't lose her now. But, for once, he was at a loss on how to handle this and her. Years of training to handle nearly any and all situations, but the United States Navy never saw Jessie Ann Ward coming.

Smitty laid his head down on his paws and watched Jessie lob snowballs at Johnny. It must be his birthday since she insisted on his wearing a crown, and Smitty could see through the glass doors and windows the other wild dogs decorating the house and fixing a huge meal.

Jessie squealed and he watched Danny toss her over his shoulder, spinning around until Phil took her and hung her upside down by her ankles. Smitty's lips pulled back over his fangs and he thought about tearing the little bastards into several pieces.

Snow crunched near him and he glanced over his shoulder to see Mace walking toward him. The big cat lay down beside him. As lion, Mace beat him in weight and size by more than double.

But they were friends more than they were predators. Nothing had ever come between them and nothing ever would.

Mace didn't do anything. He didn't shift and try to talk to him or drag him out to get drunk and find another girl. He didn't do anything because he didn't have to.

They'd had to lie to Jess to explain why they were leaving the house in the middle of the afternoon and just before Johnny's party. But watching her pretend not to be miserable was hard on them all. May, having grown up around Smiths, had a pretty good idea where she could track down the Smith Pack Alpha Female. And although her idea sounded improbable—why would a couple of afternoon-boozing She-wolves help them or Jess?— Sabina was desperate enough to try anything.

Now, after talking to these females for over an hour, it seemed like there was only one option at this point. An option Ronnie Lee Reed kept trying to talk her friend out of.

Most things people stressed over Sabina didn't understand. But this, this she understood. It was something she'd never do. Not for all the dark chocolate in the world.

"Phone, Ronnie Lee."

The She-wolf dug the phone out of her small backpack, then stopped and asked again, "Are you *sure* you want to do this? Are you really sure, Sissy Mae?"

"Do I have a choice? Do any of us?"

To Sabina's surprise, she actually didn't despise Sissy or her pouty-lipped friend. They both cared about Smitty the way she and May cared about Jess. They were family and they were willing to do anything to make these two assholes happy even if it killed them all!

"Give me the phone."

Ronnie slapped the small cell phone in her hand. "I sure hope you know what you're doin'."

Sissy chuckled and dialed. "When have I ever?"

* * *

First they sang "Happy Birthday to You," as they were traditionalists. Then they sang, "Please, Please, Please Let Me Get What I Want," which made Johnny laugh out loud.

He did seem overwhelmed by his gifts and, okay, maybe the dirt bike and new violin based on his teacher's recommendations—and which he could return if he wanted a different one—was spoiling him a little, but she knew what it was like to be spoiled and then not to be. Johnny was a good kid. He deserved a little spoiling now and again. Although she didn't agree with the dirt bike. Why would you give someone with hands blessed with musical talent a goddamn dirt bike? But when she argued the point, Phil shoved a piece of chocolate cake in her mouth.

Jess knew when Johnny suddenly hugged her while she poured glasses of milk for the kids that she'd made him happy.

Now, while her Pack danced to old seventies and eighties music in the living room, Jess wandered out to the back porch and sat on the steps. She'd brought with her a piece of May's dark chocolate cake and a glass of milk. She wasn't really hungry, especially not after all that food, but having it would keep everyone off her back about "sulking."

Really, there was nothing like having forty wild dogs asking you if you're "okay"—constantly.

Jess wasn't surprised when she saw Smitty walk out of the dark woods toward her. She'd known he'd been in the woods earlier in the day, only as wolf. If she hadn't been able to scent him or hear his breathing—she had—she would have simply known. She felt his presence like a warm blanket around her shoulders. Protecting her, soothing her.

Now, as a fully dressed human, he sat between her legs on the lower step. She handed him the slice of cake and then the milk.

They sat like that for a long while, not saying anything, simply enjoying the land they felt a part of.

When Jess heard her Pack in the kitchen, putting food away and cleaning up, she took the empty plate and glass and stood. By the time she walked to the back door, Smitty had walked off.

But she knew he'd be back. When she went to bed, she'd find him in her room, waiting for her.

And, again, she'd let him snuggle up to her, snoring lightly in her ear. Why? Because she loved him and didn't want to sleep away from him.

Unfortunately, none of that changed a goddamn thing.

She knew Smitty; he was still floundering. Still trying to figure out what she wanted. It would take something extreme to get him to wake up. Something he'd never see coming.

She simply prayed it was before she gave up hope entirely. She had only so much.

Chapter 26

Smitty climbed down the tree that he'd been using to get in and out of Jessie's room. Once he figured out how to make her his for good, he'd cut down this goddamn tree. Too easy for scumbags to get in and out of her room. But it definitely served its purpose this weekend.

As he dropped to the ground, he scented a wolf and quickly turned to find Johnny leaning against the trunk of another tree, watching him.

"Boy."

"Loser."

Smitty's eyes narrowed. No, no. Not a good idea to kick the shit out of the kid yet. No matter how much he deserved it.

They stared at each other, and Smitty was impressed the kid didn't look away. But he did speak first.

"Don't hurt her."

"I'm trying not to."

"Well, you're doing a shitty job."

"Maybe you should stay out of this, son. Until you actually have some fangs."

Johnny glanced at Jessie's window. "That woman means the world to me. Fuck her life up at your own peril, hillbilly."

He walked off and Smitty gave a little smile. That kid would be dangerous once he grew into his paws.

*   *   *

Jess sat on the front porch, her feet up on the railing and a mug of May's hot and delicious coffee gripped between her hands. They were heading home today. Back to work. Back to her life. What she still didn't know—whether her life included Smitty. They'd slept together again the night before. Literally. Fully clothed. Simply holding on to each other. To be honest, Jess slept like a baby, feeling safe and loved in Smitty's arms.

Clearly, she'd have to help this idiot out. If she waited for him, she'd be old and gray by the time he bought a goddamn clue.

So annoyed by the whole thing, Jess answered her phone without even checking caller ID.

"This is Jess."

"Yes, it is."

Jess's feet dropped to the ground and she frowned, the southern accent that slithered through the phone making her hackles rise.

When she didn't speak, the male voice continued, "I thought about calling Maylin directly, but she couldn't decide her way out of a wet paper bag. And I need decisions."

Jess slowly stood and walked down the porch steps. "Decisions about what?"

"About how my daughter will spend the next two years of her life. With y'all? Or with me and mine?"

Jess continued to walk away from the house, a potent rage singing through her veins. "You don't want her."

"No, but I'll take her. The courts are real kind about that sort of thing. Especially when a father's been kept from his child."

She didn't bother to argue the point with him. They both knew it was a lie, arguing would waste her breath.

"So what do you want?"

"A lot. I want a lot."

"That's awfully vague."

"I can be much more specific . . . in person."

She stopped walking. "I'm sure you can."

"We can keep this nice and simple, you and me. Just between us."

Jess gave a short snort.

"What's so funny?"

Turning, she faced the Pack house. Not surprisingly, a good majority of the adults stood there, listening. Their wild-dog hearing clueing them in, their loyalty to each other leading them.

"You really don't know what you've done, do you?"

He laughed. "Ain't no little runt dogs gonna scare me."

"I know," Jess sighed out. "But that's because you're stupid."

She hung up before he could say anything else, her gaze focusing on her Pack. She had one shot to fix this before all hell broke loose. Then it wouldn't matter who Wilson's Pack was tied to, who his kin was.

None of it would matter once the damage was done.

"Move that ass, Sissy Mae."

"Hold your damn horses, Bobby Ray."

Sissy Mae ran down the stairs, her traveling bag slung over her shoulder. "I don't see what the big rush is."

"It's a rush when I say it's rush. Now move!"

She muttered something mighty offensive and stormed out of the house. Smitty started to follow when his phone rang.

"Yeah?"

"Hi. It's Jess."

His very soul immediately soothed just from the sound of her voice, Smitty smiled. "Hey, darlin'. What's up?"

"I hate to bother you and you can say no—"

"What do you need, Jessie Ann?"

"Wilson contacted me."

Smitty let out a breath. "And?"

"And we either pay him or he's going to try and take Kristan. That can't happen."

No, it couldn't. He'd met the Wilsons and he'd met Kristan. No way would he let that sweet little gal spend ten seconds in Wilson territory.

"Background noise when he called makes me think he's in New York."

"But Mitch has had a hell of a time finding him."

"I know. So has Phil. But if our best trackers can't find him . . ." He could hear her pacing, sense her anxiety through the phone. "And it worries me that we can't find him. It means he's hiding. Why?"

"We both know why, Jessie Ann."

"Yeah," she said with deep resignation. "We both know why."

"Tell me what you need, Jessie."

"Look, I wouldn't bug you about this—"

"You're not bugging me, Jessie."

"—but my Pack is about three minutes from doing something really . . . not good. Something I think the Smiths will never be able to forgive us for. Either I stop this now or I let them off-leash."

"Don't do that. I can help." He just didn't know how. But knowing her Pack as he now did, he had no doubts they could and would do some serious damage that would and could cause a Pack war between the Smiths and the Kuznetsovs. He couldn't let that happen. He had to come up with something fast or . . .

Ronnie Lee rushed back into the living room. "Would you stop barking at me!" she yelled toward the front door. "I'll be right out!" She smiled at Smitty before digging through the couch cushions. In a few seconds she found her MP3 player and headed back the way she came.

"Hey, Ronnie Lee?"

She stopped, staring at him expectantly.

"Your aunt still live out here?"

"Yeah, but she's in Nassau County."

"Think she'd mind if I dropped by?"

"Of course not! She's always loved her some Smiths, Bobby Ray." Ronnie grinned and grabbed a pen and piece of paper.

"Jessie Ann?"

"Yeah?"

"Wanna go for a ride, darlin'?"

* * *

"*Bobby Ray Smith!*"

Jess stepped out of the way as the forty-something woman threw herself into Smitty's big arms.

"Morning, Annie Jo."

The infamous Annie Jo Lucas. Jess remembered her fondly. Why? Because the other females hated the She-wolf. She'd worked her way through every Smith male in at least four counties in three states. She took what she wanted, and she always walked away without looking back. A few males tried to get her, but none of them could handle her. And once their mates found out they'd been with Annie Jo at one time or another, jealousy made for a few nights in a cold bed.

On the drive over, Smitty had explained how a nasty argument between Annie Jo and her older half-sister and Ronnie Lee's mother, Tala Lee Evans, had led to Annie Jo's break from the Pack and her move to Long Island, of all places. But Annie Jo never forgot family or the Pack she left behind. Except for her sister, all Smith Pack members had open invites to stop on in and say "Hey." But you couldn't stay. Not for longer than a night. As always, Annie Jo remained the classic lone wolf.

"I should have thought about talking to her in the first place," Smitty had said as they'd sped down the Southern State Parkway, "but I had this hot little wild dog on my mind. So I was distracted."

For a long second she wondered what "hot little wild dog" he was talking about and how long before she could track the bitch down and tear out her long intestine. Then he smiled at her and she realized he was talking about her.

Duh.

Now they stood on the doorstep of Annie Jo's house and the She-wolf didn't seem to be in any great hurry to let Smitty go. Jess normally wouldn't mind all the hugging if the woman wasn't still unreasonably hot.

"Look at you," Annie Jo finally said, leaning back to get a good look at Smitty but not actually releasing him. "Don't you look good? Remind me of your Uncle Eustice. Handsome, handsome, handsome. How is handsome Eustice?"

"Doing twenty-five to life in West Tennessee State Penitentiary."

Annie Jo blinked. "Oh. Well. Somehow that doesn't surprise me." She *finally* released him and stepped back. "Now y'all come right on in this second. Come on."

They walked into a small but tidy house with comfortable, well-worn furniture and lots of pictures on the mantels and bookshelves. A small piano filled one corner of the living room and Jess remembered how Annie Jo used to give lessons. Once she left town, the number of boys taking piano lessons dropped dramatically.

"Annie Jo, this is—"

"Jessica Ann Ward. How could I forget such a pretty face?" Annie Jo hugged her and Jess grudgingly let her. "I see you've grown up even prettier."

"Thank you."

"Y'all want some coffee or hot chocolate?"

"Love some."

Annie Jo led them to her kitchen and sat them down at the breakfast table. She put out fresh cinnamon rolls while she brewed up some coffee and made Jess hot chocolate from scratch.

When Jess took that first sip all she could think was, *Marry me.*

"So what can I do you for, my darlin' Bobby Ray?"

Smitty put down his coffee. He'd already devoured three sweet rolls in the time it took her to brew the pot. Now he was reaching for a fourth.

God, the man is a bottomless pit.

"I need your help," he said.

"Help with what?"

"I'm trying to track someone down."

Amber eyes that were so light they looked more yellow and doglike than Jess remembered watched Smitty closely. "You mean Walt Wilson?"

Smitty stopped in the middle of licking icing off his fingers, which did nothing but drive Jess crazy. How was she supposed to focus when he insisted on doing that? "You've heard from him?"

With a sigh, Annie Jo got up and went to her refrigerator, pulling out cream and sugar from her cupboard. She offered some to Smitty, who passed, and put a small amount in hers before she spoke again. "About four weeks ago he and that mate of his showed up here looking like they've seen better days. I know he was hoping I'd let him stay, but I got one rule. You can spend one night and one night only. Otherwise, I'd never get rid of any of 'em. I'd have Smiths acting like this was a bed and breakfast while they were visiting New York." She returned the cream to the refrigerator before dropping back into her chair and focusing on Jess. "I know his daddy, you see? Took a turn with him when I was eighteen or nineteen." She shrugged. "It wasn't the best ride I had, but it wasn't the worst. At least Walt Junior is smarter than his daddy. But not by much. Anyway, the next morning, about three She-wolves and a male showed up and off they went."

"Do you know where?"

She sipped her coffee, those shrewd eyes watching Smitty. "Why you askin'?"

"Because of me," Jess cut in. "Because I need to find him."

"You know, he left something behind." She stood and disappeared from the room, but she yelled back through the doorway, "He called about it a day later and I said I'd already thrown it out because I didn't want him back here."

Annie Jo came back in. "I thought it was strange he'd call about something like this, so I went through it. And found this."

She placed the issue of *Wired* Magazine on the table. "Isn't that you, Jessie Ann? In the background? With the sword?"

Jess cringed. That damn article! They'd been pretty successful keeping their names and info out of the paper until about six months ago when *Wired* did an article on the company. Far in the background of one of the candid shots, if you looked really close, you could see Phil and Jess sword fighting with the Roman short swords they'd just ordered. Watching and laughing were Danny, May, and Sabina. When they saw the photo they all figured no one would notice them in the back like that.

Then the woman in Human Resources said they were getting in a ton of résumés because of that one article. Why? Because everyone saw the "owners" sword fighting in the background. In other words, "What a cool place to work!"

Great for their employee pool, but bad now that they had losers like Walt Wilson coming into their lives.

"Yes, ma'am. That's me."

"But he circled her." She pointed at the black marker circle around May. "Why?"

If they needed her help, they'd have to be honest with her. Annie Jo needed to know why she should rat out family.

"That's Maylin. She's part of my Pack. She got pregnant sixteen years ago by Wilson. But he doesn't care. He wants money and he's using her daughter as leverage."

Annie Jo sat down again. "Yeah, I was afraid you were gonna say that. The Wilson males are notorious. They'll knock a girl up and walk away in a heartbeat. Then they won't have anything to do with her. See I was real careful because I had a scare once, when I was fifteen, and I swore never again. All I needed was for that bitchy sister of mine to find out I was pregnant and all hell would break loose. Besides, I never wanted children. So I always made sure I was on birth control and that any man I ever had sex with wore condoms. One thing you've gotta remember about wolf males, Smith or otherwise, is they can impregnate sand. As a female, you've gotta protect yourself. Isn't that right, Bobby Ray?"

"She's right. Which reminds me." He patted Jess's arm. "I need to have a condom conversation with Johnny."

Jess's back snapped straight. "I'm sorry. What?"

"Who's Johnny?"

"Her foster son. A wolf. She's gonna adopt him. But he just turned seventeen."

"Oh, Lord!" Annie Jo exclaimed with a laugh. "Yeah, darlin'. He has to have that conversation with him. And soon. The Smith mantra—condoms, condoms, condoms."

"Thank you, but *I* can have that conversation with my son."

Annie Jo rolled her eyes. "Darlin', you cannot talk to that boy about fucking. You just can't. It will freak him out. Let Bobby Ray do it. Y'all are together, aren't ya?"

"Yes."

"No."

Now Annie Jo's expressive eyes crossed in exasperation. "Whatever."

"I don't see why we need to discuss this now."

"We don't. But I need to talk to him soon." Smitty smirked at Annie Jo. "Maylin's daughter is sixteen and a cutie."

"Oh, Lord!" Annie Jo exclaimed again. "Darlin', you better let him talk to that boy or y'all are gonna have yourself a nine-pound, eight-ounce problem."

"Phil and Danny can do it."

"They're wild dogs, too, right? They can't tell that boy what he needs to know. You need Bobby Ray to do it."

"Why?"

"Wolves are different. From, oh, let's say, fifteen to seventeen, their aggression kicks in."

"Johnny's not aggressive."

"He growled at me in the elevator," Smitty told her out of nowhere.

"He did what?"

"If little Kristan hadn't been there, he'd have gone for my throat."

"Why didn't you tell me?"

"What was there to tell?"

Jess opened her mouth to start yelling when Annie Jo put a calming hand on her forearm.

"Before you tear his head off, you need to understand that the wolves and the wild dogs are different. They grow up different. You, of course, don't count because you were the only dog in a town of wolves. But it goes like this, from fifteen to seventeen, male pups are aggressive to adult male wolves. They'll take 'em on in a heartbeat and get their ass kicked every time. They actually need that sort of discipline and they don't really mind. Of course, Bubba was . . . oh, never mind. But when they hit eighteen, their aggression turns to a level of horniness the likes of which you've never seen. They'll fuck damn near anything."

Jess snorted. "That's not entirely true."

Smitty growled. "I walked away *for a reason.*"

"Don't bark at me."

"He probably walked away for two reasons." Annie Jo cut in. "One, because he didn't have condoms. Bubba Smith beat into every one of his sons the condom, condom, condom rule. He made sure they had condoms in their trucks, in their school bags, stuck in books. Any place he could think of, and Lord love ya, but you better use 'em. Bubba didn't want a bunch of grandkids running around since he knew his sons would breed a ton once they were mated. Unfortunately, the Wilsons just didn't have that same philosophy. "

"And what, pray tell, is the second reason?"

Annie Jo smiled. "The second reason is, you were special, Jessie Ann. Everybody in town knew that. Why you think the She-pups kept coming after you? But none of that is here or there. Y'all can work that out yourselves because one of my students will be here in about five more minutes."

Smitty nodded. "Where is he, Annie Jo?"

"The Bronx." She stood and opened one of the kitchen drawers, extracting a pad. She tore off the top sheet. "Here. Take it. I don't want that boy back here. But let me tell you something, Jessie Ann. The best thing Walt Junior probably ever did was throw that little Maylin away. Wilson's mate, she can't be more than late twenties, early thirties. But damn if she don't look closer to mid-forties. They ride their females hard and put 'em up wet, with very little payoff."

"She's married now," Jess said with true pride. "And her husband loves her and their daughter."

"There you go. That's all that matters."

The doorbell rang and Annie Jo stood. "All right, y'all. Time to go."

She couldn't hustle them to the door fast enough. But when Jess saw Annie Jo's "student" she could see why.

Jess didn't know a lot of virile-looking twenty-five-year-old males who went for piano lessons in the middle of a suburb.

"Curtis, why don't you go on in the living room and wait for me there. I'll be right in."

Devouring the woman with his eyes, he nodded. "Yes, ma'am."

Annie Jo walked them out to Smitty's truck. "Now, if y'all need anything else from me, you just let me know. And of course, y'all can stop by anytime."

She kissed and hugged Smitty, then kissed and hugged Jess. But before they could get in the truck and drive away, she added, "And you be careful, Bobby Ray. That boy is a lot like his daddy, and you can say what you want about Bubba Smith, he fights fair. I can't say that for the Wilsons. But don't you forget they're family." She pointed at Jess. "And she ain't."

"Thanks, Annie Jo."

"You're very welcome. Y'all get on now. Good luck."

Chapter 27

After parking a couple blocks away from the rundown hotel Wilson and his Pack stayed in, Smitty asked, "Should I bother telling you to stay out here until I'm done?"

Jessie shrugged, dug into her backpack, and pulled out a book, settling back into her seat. "Sure. I'll wait."

He grinned. "Now most females of my Pack would be itching to go up there with me."

"Because they look for a fight. I don't. I'm more than happy to keep my wild-dog butt right down here until you're done. Unless we're talking about a sword fight. Or a fight to the death in the Roman Coliseum."

"And you just lost me."

"Like that's new."

Smitty gripped her chin, lifting her face so he could kiss her. "Smitty—"

He didn't let her finish, kissing her hard, demanding her tongue come out to play. When he finally pulled back they were both panting and Jessie had her eyes closed.

"When we get this done, you and I are going to talk."

He stepped out of the truck and he heard her mutter, "Great. More talking."

"What?"

She opened her book. "I said good luck."

* * *

Walt Davis Wilson, Jr., was tired of the bullshit. Tired of the wait. Playing caring daddy to that cheery little snot-nose brat did nothing but wear on his nerves. He already had seven kids— pure wolves, not freaky tiny half-breeds—and he didn't need an eighth.

But he'd run out of patience and time. He had bears watching his house back home, wanting their goddamn money, and he needed to get it to them sooner rather than later. So he'd pushed it with that wild dog. He had no choice. Especially when the kid stopped returning his phone calls. Usually she responded to his messages right away, meeting him all over the city for dinners mostly. But she'd missed their last dinner date and he hadn't heard from her since. Bad sign. So he'd put his call in to that Alpha Female, letting her experience a little fear. He hoped she'd pay him off outright. But if she didn't, he'd take the kid back to Alabama. They'd never follow him into Smithburg. They couldn't be that stupid. The Smiths protected their own, that was a fact, and the Wilsons were connected to them by blood. In the end, they'd be better off paying him what he wanted so they could get the little brat back.

That money would change everything for him.

Once he paid off his debt and used whatever money was left—he had every intention of asking for way more money than he actually needed to pay off the bears—to start a business, he'd have wolves from all over Alabama itching to join his Pack. He planned to make the Wilson Pack as big as them snobby Van Holtzs or trash-talkin' Magnus bastards. And he'd definitely make his Pack more important than any Smith. He'd show 'em all. Show 'em all just how powerful he was.

But first he had to find that little bitch. He'd try nice first. If that didn't work . . . well, best not think on that right now.

He stepped out of the bathroom, closing the door behind him to block the smell, and stopped dead when he saw Bobby Ray Smith leaning back against the worn dresser.

"Bobby Ray."

"Walt."

"What are you doing here? I thought you were in the Navy."

"I was. Been out for a while. I'd heard you were in town." The big bastard shrugged. "And that don't work for me."

Walt didn't know if Bobby Ray's words pissed him off or the fact that the bastard seemed to still have a full head of hair. Wilson males went bald pretty early, but those damn Smiths seemed to go to their graves grizzled, mean, and with full heads of hair.

"It don't work for you?"

"Uptown, Fifth Avenue, and Park Avenue belong to the Van Holtzs. The Bronx and Harlem are split up between the Vega Pride and the Armstrong bears. But Downtown belongs to the Smiths now."

"And?"

"And I don't want you here. I don't want you on my territory. I don't want you near my territory. And I can assure you the Van Holtzs, the Vegas, and the Armstrongs ain't gonna want you on theirs."

"They don't know—"

"They do now."

Walt took a step back in shock. "You son of a bitch."

"Now, now. Let's not get nasty."

"We're family."

Bobby Ray stood to his full height, a good four inches over Walt's, and casually walked over to him.

"I wouldn't let my brothers come here either. Only them I'd hurt. So you're getting off lucky."

"I'll need some time to—"

"No. Tickets are bought. Sissy took care of all that. Think of it as my Pack's gift to yours. All you gotta do is head on over to JFK and you'll be back in Birmingham before the stores close."

He wouldn't let the bastard push him around. No way. He wasn't nine years old anymore.

"Look, Bobby Ray, we're taking care of some other business first and—"

That big hand wrapped around his neck, shoving him back into the wall. His teeth rattled and his spine ached. Walt felt claws dig into the skin of his throat, and they kept digging until blood trickled down to Walt's collarbone.

"Since you've never been known as a bright boy, I'll say this one more time. You get your ass and your Pack's ass to JFK airport within the next hour or I'll hunt you down again and then I won't be so nice. Do you understand me, boy?"

Walt stared at him, trying to think of any way out of this. He needed that money. He needed it more than anyone realized.

Bobby Ray didn't say another word. He let his claws do the talking for him. When Walt felt one claw get dangerously close to a major artery, he turned his eyes away—since he couldn't move his neck—and relaxed back. Submissive.

"Good." Bobby Ray wiped his blood-covered hands on Walt's yellow sweatshirt. "Now you tell your momma I said hi."

Bobby Ray Smith turned and walked out the door. He didn't even feel threatened enough not to turn his back on Walt. The ultimate insult.

Two minutes later, while he was trying to wipe the blood off his neck and chest, Polly June stormed in.

"Why did I see Bobby Ray Smith leaving here?"

"That bastard came here to push me out."

"What?"

"Telling me he didn't want our Pack on his territory."

"Really?"

It was the tone his mate had. Not fear—something else.
"What?"

"I'm just wondering why I saw that dog sitting up in his truck like she owned the damn thing."

"Which dog?"

"Jessica Ann Ward. I figured you'd convinced her to come here and bring us the money."

"She hung up on me. I was going to call back later after she let it all sink in. Are you sure it was her?"

"Yeah, it was her. I wondered why she'd parked three blocks away. And I wouldn't have seen her if I hadn't gone up the block to that little store on the corner."

Walt slammed down the blood-stained cloth in his hands. "Where's the rest of the Pack?"

"They're still at the store getting some junk food and tequila."

"Did you find the kid?"

"Yup, found all of 'em. They're at this real fancy hotel in the city."

"Good. Now get my momma on the phone."

"I don't understand. Why don't we need to pay them any money?"

"Because y'all be paying them until Kristan turns eighteen. This was a better way to go."

"The ol' 'get out of my territory' move?"

"Yeah. You forget. There's a hierarchy among the Smiths. I have the Smith name. Walt doesn't. And if he messes with me, he'll not only be messing with all the Smiths, he'll be messing with all the Packs connected to us. The Reeds. The Lewis Pack out of Smithville. The Evans." He shrugged. "Marty."

Jess laughed. "God, we don't want that."

"Trust me. You don't. Leaving you and your Pack out of this altogether was the best thing."

"Okay." She had no problem with that logic. The less involved her Pack, the better for Kristan in the long run.

"Thanks for this, Smitty. I mean it."

"Anytime, darlin'." He took her hand, holding it gently in his. "Now let's talk about us."

"Okay."

"I've been thinking long and hard on this." Christ, again with the thinking! "And I know what I need to do."

"And that is?" she asked, her heart pounding in her chest, praying he'd figured it out. Praying he'd get it right.

"Court ya proper."

And there went her heart, plummeting to earth, through the floor of his truck, and into hell.

"Court me?"

"Yeah, proper Smith courtin'. It's just what you deserve. Proper dates, an official announcement about us to all the Smiths. We'll just take this slow and easy until we *both* know it's the right time."

"You . . . you . . . *bastard!*" Jess snatched her hand away.

"What? What's wrong?"

"That's what I deserve? *That?* You know what? The biggest mistake I ever made was falling in love with your hick ass."

"Jessie Ann—"

"No, we're done. I'm done. Done, done, done. I'm cutting you out of my heart. Because you don't deserve me."

"Now you're making me angry."

"Really? That's fascinating."

"If you'd just talk to me—"

"I'm done talking."

"*Jessie* . . ." he warned through gritted teeth.

She stared straight ahead, the book gripped tightly in her hands. "Unless you want me to shift right here, and start pissing all over this lovely interior, including the dashboard, you'll . . . stop . . . talking."

Both hands tight on the wheel, Smitty focused back on the road. She'd made him mad but, as always, not nearly mad enough. And if she couldn't make that happen, they had no business being together in the first place.

Chapter 28

Smitty barely stopped himself from snatching the keycards from the poor woman at the front desk. He had no idea what he looked like, but after three minutes, her hand started to shake and she couldn't get him through the check-in process fast enough. He stormed away from the desk and toward the elevators, brushing past his sister and Ronnie Lee as he stalked toward the elevators.

"Bobby Ray, wait."

"Leave me be, Sissy."

He slammed his fist against the elevator button and the doors smoothly slid open. He walked inside and his sister's hand slapped against the frame. "There's something I need to—"

He barked and snapped at her fingers, almost taking them off, and his sister jumped back about ten feet. The doors closed and he hit the button for his floor.

He couldn't believe it. Couldn't believe her. What the hell did she want from him anyway? He'd offered her a proper Smith courting. He risked abuse at every family reunion for that, but he was willing to do it. *For her!* And what does she do? She throws it back in his face like it meant nothing.

She also had the nerve to be angry at him. She won't tell him what's wrong. Won't tell him why she's so mad. And doesn't want him to mark her. But while she's fighting him, in the same goddamn conversation, she admits she loves him.

"That's it," he snarled to himself. "That is goddamn it." He'd throw his crap into his room; then he'd find that little gal and he'd find out exactly what the hell was going on. He'd hit the end of his leash, and she'd damn well know it.

Smitty opened the door to the hotel room he'd gotten himself so he could be near the crazy woman he loved while his team secured the wild-dog's den and tossed his bags and jacket inside.

Busy kicking the sleeve of his jacket away from the door so he could close it and go search out Jessie, for the first time in his entire life, Smitty never saw it coming. Didn't scent it. Didn't hear it.

He just never saw it—or *him*—coming.

"Boy."

At the gruff words, Smitty froze.

"So your sister called and said you're fucking up your life again. And why does this not surprise me? You were always a little bit dumber than the others."

Smitty closed his eyes and thought of all the wonderful ways he'd eviscerate his baby sister, before turning to face Bubba Ray Smith. His daddy.

Jess stood on the corner on the far side of the hotel and seethed. She didn't even need her coat she was so goddamn mad. Courting her? And what? Dinners? Dancing? Dates? What in all holy hell led him to believe she wanted to be courted?

She needed to score some chocolate. She needed it so goddamn bad she might actually shut down a Godiva store at this point.

She looked up the street. *There has to be a goddamn chocolate store somewhere on this street. Or maybe inside.* But Bobby Ray was inside. No, she'd have to go find it down the street or freeze to death trying.

But before Jess could take a step, before she could hope to make a run for it, a voice behind her froze her in her tracks.

"Well, well, well. Jessie Ann Ward. As I live and breathe."

Jess closed her eyes. *No, no, no.* Anyone but this. Smitty. Sissy Mae. Even Big-Boned Bertha. But not *her.*

"I'm not gonna bite, suga. You can turn around."

She did—and faced Smitty's momma. Janie Mae Lewis, originally of the Lewis Pack out of Smithville, North Carolina. Built like a first-string linebacker for the Dallas Cowboys and quite beautiful, the female smoked a rolled cigarette and stared at Jess through the smoke. Smitty had gotten his mother's eyes. Only hers were harder. Colder. Even Sissy's eyes weren't that cold.

"Miss Janie . . . I . . . uh . . ."

"Lord, stop your stuttering, girl." She smiled . . . sort of. "I always did make you nervous. The dog in you just wants to run away, don't it?"

She was right. Where Jess ran from the other She-pups because they'd outnumbered her and she'd gotten tired of getting her ass kicked, she outright avoided Miss Janie. Even though the female had never been anything but polite and somewhat kind, there'd always been something about her—that lone lioness separated from the Pride because she threatened the others' cubs.

"My, my. Jessie Ann Ward. Look at you." She took a long drag on her dwindling cigarette. "You've always been adorable but now . . ." She smiled . . . sort of. "I wasn't surprised to hear my youngest boy locked on to you. He'd always had a mighty hunger for little Jessie. Went out of his way to protect you, course it always backfired. Set some of them girls against you somethin' fierce knowin' he wanted you and not them. At least he didn't want them for the long haul. Just a quick fuck in the back of that old pickup truck he used to drive. But you were special. He wanted to give you much more than that."

Oh, God. Please make her stop. But she knew Miss Janie wouldn't stop until Miss Janie was damn good and ready.

"Daddy."

"Boy."

Must he continue to call him that? The older four at least

had adequate nicknames—"Stupid," "Idiot," "Fuckhead," and Smitty's personal favorite, "Shit for Brains." But Smitty always remained "Boy."

"So is it true?" his daddy grumbled.

"Is what true?"

"That you're too much of a pussy to take your woman? To take what's yours?"

The old man had been saying that to him since the day Smitty had graciously—at least he'd thought it gracious—let Rory Reed take his Big Wheel. He knew he'd get it back, but he didn't see a point in dragging the boy off it and beating him to death for spending more than five minutes on the damn thing. But his daddy had a fit. Calling him weak and telling him, "What? You're too scared to take it, you big pussy?" Yes. *Every* seven-year-old boy should be called "pussy."

Smitty didn't "take it" because the Reeds were like family. Especially with Sissy Mae and Ronnie Lee being thick as thieves. But reason and logic meant nothing to Bubba Smith. Never had, never will.

"Exactly how do you think you'll grow this Pack when you don't even have the guts to claim your woman? Do you think them Reed boys will let you lead when they know they can take it from you at any time?"

Smitty had two options here: tear his father's throat out and do twenty-five to life in a state-run prison like his Uncle Eustice, or spend the rest of the day arguing with the man for no reason.

As Smitty wondered how tough Sing Sing prison could really be, it suddenly occurred to him that he did have a third option. An option he'd never tried before.

"I don't have to explain a damn thing to you."

His father stared at him blandly. "What?"

"You heard me. I don't have to explain anything to you. I don't answer to you. Or anyone. This is *my* Pack. *My* woman. I can handle this any damn way I please. So you need to move your fat ass out of my way."

Smitty didn't wait for his father to do that; instead, he calmly walked around him, heading toward the elevators. Even as he felt rage, he also felt like he'd turned a corner. Like now everything in his life was different.

He needed to find Jessie Ann. He needed to find her now.

"You know, boy," his father said behind him and Smitty didn't stop to hear the old coot out, "it's about time you figured that out. I guess the Navy smarted you up some, huh?"

Smitty didn't turn around until he got on the elevator. His father still stood there, watching him. Then, the old wolf grinned at him and winked before ambling away.

The doors closed and Smitty snarled, "*Bastard!*" Completely terrifying the rich couple standing next to him.

The older female dropped her cigarette to the ground and pulled out papers and tobacco to roll another.

Not knowing what else to say, Jess went with polite. "And how are you doing, Miss Janie?"

"Can't complain. Not that anyone would listen if I did."

"And you're just visiting? Here to see Bobby Ray and Sissy?"

"Darlin'," she said on an annoyed sigh, "must we really stand around in this cold bullshittin' each other. I am so not in the mood." A surprisingly dainty tongue lashed out and swiped along the paper before she sealed it. "We both know why I'm here."

"Uh . . . we do?"

Those cold wolf eyes sized Jess up in a heartbeat. "I thought by now you would have gotten my boy to mark you. What exactly are you waitin' for?"

Feeling her temper—and that desire to throw things at Miss Janie's big, fat head—sliding out of her, Jess said softly, "I am so positive this isn't your business."

"All my sons are my business, little girl. Don't you forget it."

"Smitty's taking his time," Jess finally answered in the face of those cold wolf eyes daring her for a challenge. "Apparently he's not big on rushing."

Miss Janie gave one of those sorta-smiles. "No, he's not. He likes to think. Likes to plan, my boy does. Still . . ."

Jess looked up as a plume of smoke hit her dead in the face. *Bitch.*

"Still?" Jess asked around several coughs.

"Everyone thinks the Smith males are all the same, but they're not." Miss Janie leaned back against the brick wall of the hotel. "Each of my boys is different. And the same with Bubba and his brothers."

There went that sorta-smile again. "But even the slowest movin' wolf don't wanna hunt some prey that's just sittin' there starin' at him. Waitin' for him to notice her. Sure, he'll eat it. But it won't be half as satisfying as the one he has to chase over miles of untouched land, until he runs her down."

Jess blinked. "All right then."

"I can tell ya what my boy's planning 'cause I do know him so well." She took another long drag on her cigarette, knowing she had a rapt audience. "You see he'll wanna do it right. This is Jessie Ann we're talking about after all. Sweet little innocent with her big dumb dog eyes, just beggin' for someone to scratch her belly."

"Hey."

"His biggest worry will be scaring you off. He never wants to see regret in those big brown eyes. That's probably why he's taking so long. Fighting his instincts. Fighting his own needs. Maybe he even thought about courtin' you. Like that'll go down well with the family. But it won't matter 'cause it's you. But to get this movin', he'll suck up enough until you accept his apology, and then today, tomorrow . . . next *year* . . . when he thinks the time is right, he'll take you to a real nice hotel. Some place he can't afford, but he'll put it on his card. He'll make sure there are clean sheets and champagne. Flowers, if you've a mind for that. Or chocolates, if that's more your style. He'll take ya nice and sweet on those clean sheets. And that'll be your life for the next forty or fifty years. Nice and sweet and oh-so-clean."

If I set myself on fire . . . would she stop talking?

Besides, Jess already knew this. She'd known this from the beginning.

"I don't know you all that well, but I do know dogs. And dogs like it rough and tumble just like the wolves, unless you're one of those prissy little pillow dogs. If that's the case, maybe he'll put some bows in your hair and give you a pink studded collar." She laughed at her own joke and didn't seem to mind that Jess didn't.

"Look at this." Miss Janie finally said, tugging her down jacket off her shoulder and pulling her thick pink cableknit sweater aside, revealing an age-old wound. Flesh that had been torn and ripped, more than once based on the healed-over scars on top of scars. "That first time, when he made me his, bastard nearly tore my shoulder out. Best night of my life, though. And we've repeated that night—often."

She dropped the remains of her cigarette—no more than a stub now—at her feet. "Mind if I give you a little advice, suga?"

"I'm relatively certain I could cut your throat and you *still* wouldn't stop talking."

The older woman threw back her head and laughed. A rich, deep, somewhat frightening sound. "You're probably very right about that. Bubba always said nothing he loves and hates more about me than my directness. But I promise. Last bit and then I'm done."

Shrugging, Jess knew she had to let the female finish. No matter what happened between Bubba Smith and his sons in the eternal Smith fight for dominance, Jess didn't see Miss Janie giving over her mantle of power to another female anytime soon.

"Make him chase you down, suga. Make him hunt for you." Miss Janie stepped toward her until they were barely a few inches apart and whispered, "Because we both know . . . you are just *achin'* to be caught."

Jess slowly looked up at the woman Smitty endearingly called "Momma." They didn't say another word to each other. They didn't have to.

The automatic hotel doors slid open and four older She-wolves walked out.

"Janie Mae," one of them called out, "I thought we were goin' shoppin'."

"Oh, we are. I've got Bubba's credit card and miles of jewelry stores to explore before the night falls."

"He'll be mad," one of the females reminded her with a smile, "when he finds out you spent money."

"Guess he'll just have to punish me then, won't he."

I could make a run for it. I might be able to lose them in the city traffic.

Miss Janie pointed at Jess. "Y'all, you remember little Jessie Ann Ward, don't ya?"

The women stood around her now and Jess, at her cool five-nine, felt surrounded by giants.

"Of course!"

"How are you, darlin'?"

"Isn't she just the prettiest little thing?"

Jess smiled and nodded and tried to wish them all away. Miss Janie must have seen it in her eyes because she suddenly walked toward the corner. "Come on, y'all."

"They say a snowstorm's comin', Janie Mae," one of them informed her.

"Then we better get a move on. I'm thinkin' there's a diamond necklace with my name on it."

Miss Janie stopped at the corner and looked at Jess. She smiled. A big one and real. Almost warm. "Don't forget what we talked about, suga. I won't say being with a Smith is easy—" the older She-wolves snorted and laughed at her statement— "but it'll be the best ride you *ever* have."

Chapter 29

Smitty stood in front of the Kingston Arms. He couldn't seem to track his little wild dog down, and she wasn't answering her cell phone. He had to find her. He'd make her take his apology, although he still wasn't sure what he'd done wrong. And once he had all that settled, he'd take her to the Ritz-Carlton tonight. Get her the best room his credit card could afford and he'd make her his. He'd do this right. She'd never regret being his.

"She's gone."

Turning around, Smitty stared at Johnny DeSerio.

"What do you mean she's gone?"

"She left."

"Went back to the den? Or the Long Island house?"

"Neither. The Pack has this little house in Jersey. The adults' little love shack when they need some away time from the pups."

"Where is it?"

The boy shrugged.

"You don't know?"

"Oh, I know. I'm just not telling you."

Smitty had his hand around the boy's throat and had him slammed against the wall in less time than it took to say "Ow."

"Listen up close, boy, 'cause I'll only say this once. These dogs may protect you, but I'm wolf. Just like you. And we both know I'll rip the flesh from your bones if you don't tell me what I wanna know."

A delicate throat clearing had Smitty looking over his shoulder even as he tightened his grip a bit more on the boy's throat.

Kristan smiled up at him. "Take your hand off his throat," she said softly.

If this had been one of the adults, he would have ignored them, but sweet little Kristan . . . well, he simply didn't have the heart. So, grudgingly, he let the boy go.

"Here." She took hold of his hand and wrote on his palm with a pink felt-tip pen that had a fluffy kitty on the top. "This is where Jess went if it's the place in Jersey. But you didn't get it from me because the pups aren't supposed to know about it."

Smitty stared at the address. "How do you know she'll be here?"

"I heard her talking to my mom and Sabina."

"Can you tell me why she left?"

"She said she needed some time to think, which isn't necessarily a bad thing. Thinking's good."

Not in his case. In that moment, Smitty realized this would be his last chance to get Jessie Ann. If he didn't make her his now, he'd lose her to the Sherman Landrys of the world. "Thanks, Kristan."

He walked toward the valets in order to get his truck when Kristan called to him. He looked at her and she held up both thumbs. "Good luck!"

Smitty smiled. Johnny DeSerio didn't stand a chance with this one. "Thanks, darlin'."

Hands on hips, Kristan turned around and glared at Johnny, one foot tapping. She could see the bruises on the idiot's throat, and she knew he'd be wearing them proudly for as long as they lasted. "You enjoyed that, didn't you?"

Johnny smirked, embarrassed, and said, "Well, it kind of made me feel like, ya know . . . a wolf. It was cool."

Kristan rolled her eyes and, walking away, sighed out, "You're an idiot."

Jess paused her game and pulled off her headphones. Someone was knocking.

She yawned and dropped the headphones on the desk, pushing her seat back by bracing her hands against it and shoving. The chair rolled back and then spun around. She stood and headed toward the front door.

Assuming the groceries she'd ordered had arrived, Jess pulled open the door and stared.

"Afternoon, Jessie Ann."

Wow. Apparently his mother had been right. Especially with that barely controlled anger on his face. He even had a whole ticking jaw thing going on. She'd seen Smitty annoyed, exasperated, frustrated—but never pissed. Not like this.

Smitty didn't even wait for her response, he simply walked in.

"What are you doing here?"

"Came to see you." He looked around the hallway and whistled. "Y'all have the nicest homes."

Jess closed the door. "You weren't invited."

"Wolves rarely are, darlin'."

He turned and faced her. "You look real casual."

Her sweatpants had holes, as did her nearly twenty-year-old *Raiders of the Lost Ark* T-shirt. She wore heavy socks to keep her feet warm and, for some unknown reason, had put her hair in two pigtails.

"I wasn't expecting company." *This soon.*

"Then you shouldn't have opened the door without asking who it was."

Jess bit back her retort and watched Smitty wander off down the hall and into the kitchen. She followed and found him staring into her refrigerator.

"You sure don't have much," he chastised. "And there's a storm coming."

"I know. I'm waiting on a grocery delivery. And I know

there's a storm coming. That's why you should get back to the city before you get trapped out on the road. 'Cause you're not staying here."

Smitty sighed, loudly, and slammed the refrigerator door shut. "I have to say, Jessie Ann, I am running out of patience."

Jess laughed. "Really? Are you?"

"I'm not leaving, Jessie Ann. Not until we talk this out. Nice and proper."

"Nice and proper? Uh-huh." She turned and headed back up the hall.

"Where are you going?" he demanded from behind her.

"If you won't leave—I will."

She found her discarded sneakers by the couch and reached down to grab them, but big fingers wrapped around her bicep and yanked her up.

"You're not going anywhere."

"I'm not?" Jess pushed up against him. "And how are you going to stop me?"

He let her go so abruptly, she stumbled back a bit.

"No, we're not doin' this. When you've calmed down, we'll talk."

She followed him to the front door. He snatched it open and marched outside.

"Yeah, yeah," she said with a glibness she didn't feel. Not when the only man she'd ever love was walking out of her life. Maybe forever. "Go on and run."

She watched him walk down the stairs and toward his truck. "I guess your daddy was right all those years ago—you are afraid to take what's yours."

He froze beside his truck, his body one rigid line of rippling muscles. And in that instant she knew she'd said the one thing that might push her wolf over the edge.

Slowly, as if he had all the time in the world, Smitty opened the passenger side of the truck. He took off his baseball cap and tossed it inside. Then he did the same with his heavy winter coat, shrugging it off his big shoulders. He carefully closed the door shut and turned to face her. All Jess saw were cold wolf eyes and fangs.

That's when she made a run for it.

He never expected her to shift, but it didn't stop him. He simply shifted to wolf and went after her. Wild dogs and wolves were equally fast, but wild dogs could run for hours before running out of steam. Wolves could run for miles and lope for hours. But the weather worked in his favor. Wolves could maneuver in the snow easily; wild dogs not so much. They'd been built for hunting in grasslands, not the uneven terrain of North America. He'd take advantage of that weakness. Because nothing would stop him now. Nothing would hold him back.

Smitty looped around and came at her from the front. She spotted him and made a fast change, her small paws slipping slightly on the snowy ground, losing momentum.

He quickly backtracked and looped around again, cutting her off from the new angle. She dashed off in another direction and he stayed right behind her, pushing her through the woods.

For a moment, he thought he had her. His front paws slamming against her hips. But she easily spun and slapped him with her paw, ripping into one side of his muzzle.

Jessie didn't even stop, merely ran off in a different direction. Smitty turned and followed. Again pushing her where he wanted her. This time toward snow-covered rocks.

She leaped up but couldn't keep her footing and slid across, then off the big stones. She quickly scrambled to her feet, but she'd lost precious time. Smitty tackled her from behind, shoving her hard to the ground. She kept fighting him, though. Her paws slashing at him as she tried to get out from under him, her jaw snapping at his. Not a fake fight. Not a show of a struggle. She fought him like her life depended on it—because it did. Her future life. Their lives together. Which was why he didn't give up. He'd never give up where Jessie Ann was concerned.

It took some doing and a lot of slashes to his chest and side, but he finally forced her onto her back. He immediately wrapped his maw around her throat, the additional fur protecting her throat tickling his nose. He bit down hard and shook her.

Jess wiggled, trying to get out of his grasp, but he growled and bit down harder, shaking her one more time. Making his intentions, his *demands*, very clear.

Jessie Ann stopped moving, stopped fighting. She panted. She waited.

He held on a little longer. Long enough to make sure she wouldn't run again. Not merely at this moment, but ever.

She let out a sigh and her body relaxed beneath his. That's when he knew.

Smitty unhinged his jaw and nuzzled her neck, licking the blood off where he'd buried his fangs.

At the same moment, they shifted back to human. She had faint bite marks in her throat and blood on her cheek where it had dripped from his face. Her claws had ripped a rather healthy chunk out of his flesh. He dragged his hand across his cheek, wiping off the blood. He ignored the rips in his chest—they weren't that deep.

It hurt, what she did to him. Physically, it hurt like a bitch. But emotionally, it only proved what he'd already known. Only Jessie Ann could push him like this. Only Jessie Ann could bring out the wolf inside him and face it head-on. He'd been fighting it so hard, for years. Afraid that by letting out the wolf, he'd be letting out the Smith. But he wasn't his daddy. He wasn't his brothers. He was Bobby Ray, and he'd be damned if he didn't take the woman he wanted, who loved him more than anything, and make her his the only way predators could.

No wonder she'd been so mad. A Smith courting must have seemed an insult to her when she'd known damn good and well how Smiths took their mates. They didn't call it a Smith mate-maul jokingly.

But that's what she'd deserved. Because no one else matched him as perfectly as Jessie Ann. As different as they were, they still belonged together. She'd challenge him again, and next time . . . hell, next time she'd probably win.

*   *   *

Jess forced herself not to wince when she saw how badly she'd fucked up his face. Thank God the Smith wolves weren't so much pretty as hot. The scar that would leave might make some guys look less attractive. Not Smitty. It would make him look even hotter.

As he flashed his fangs at her, Jess felt no fear. No regret. Nothing but a need to be fucked and marked by her mate that went deeper than anything inside her had before.

He turned her over roughly, forcing her onto all fours. Nope. There'd be no going back to the bed for this coupling. There'd be no romance, soft lights, jazz music, and high threadcount sheets. There'd be no condoms.

She wasn't in heat and she was on the pill. Chances were low to nonexistent she'd get pregnant. But that didn't matter. Not to the Smith males. When they claimed a female, they *claimed* a female. And like the canines they were, they'd do it out here. In nature. Something both of them were elementally a part of.

Smitty leaned over her, his lips dragging across her back, his tongue licking her spine. One hand slid beneath her and rested against her stomach, holding her in place; the other hand braced Smitty above her. Like most things when it came to Smitty, he didn't rush this. Her wolf took his time. Brushing his head against her shoulders, his nose against the back of her neck. Strong, powerful thighs pressed against the back of hers and she could feel his hard cock resting against her ass.

He kissed her neck, moving down until he reached her shoulder. He licked a spot there. Once, twice. Then his mouth opened and wrapped around the muscle. She closed her eyes, preparing for the pain.

And it hurt. God, it hurt! This wasn't soft and gentle and sweet. Fangs brutally tore through flesh and muscle, digging against bone. Her yelp of pain didn't stop him. She didn't expect it to.

Jess gasped and whimpered, instinctively trying to pull away, but the more she struggled the harder Smitty held on. His arms wrapped around her, keeping her tight against him, trying to keep her still. Then his cock pushed against her, demanding entrance inside her pussy. Demanding and receiving.

It wasn't until he pushed home that she realized how wet she was. How ready for him. So ready that as soon as he slammed inside her, the first orgasm washed over her without his having to do much of anything. He held on to her as her body shook and she cried out, the sound echoing off the leafless trees.

Smitty waited until she shook and groaned through that first one, until the panting slowed down. He waited until she realized it wasn't over. Then he used his body to force the top half of her close to the ground while pushing her ass up higher. He readjusted his grip on her shoulder, dragging another cry of pain from her when he settled his fangs back inside her flesh; then he drove into her body without pity, without mercy. A Smith wolf claiming his mate in absolutely no uncertain terms.

And with each vicious, nearly cruel thrust, she felt how much he loved her. It was weird. Something a full-human would never understand. Yet Jess knew. Knew that as surely as he'd always call her Jessie Ann—no matter how much she hated it—he would always love her. He'd die for her. Protect their pups. Protect her Pack while protecting his own. He'd do whatever he could to make her happy.

One of the arms gripping her tight loosened and the fingers slid down her belly, between her legs. He stroked her clit several times until he gripped it and squeezed. Jess broke again, this time her gasps turning into sobs. Sobs of release. Sobs of triumph. She'd finally gotten him. She'd gotten her wolf.

Yet even as she knew they were perfect for each other, she also knew that she'd always drive him crazy. She'd always confuse him. Confound him. Make him wonder, "What the hell is she going on about now?" She'd never give him a moment's peace. And he'd always annoy her, talk as slowly as humanly possible, if he said anything at all. He'd always think she was weird. And he'd laugh at her more often than not. Their pups would grow up to be crazed wolfdogs. Part of a group of hybrids so dangerously unstable, Prides and wolf Packs all over the country went out of their way to keep them out of the shifter-only towns and resorts.

But they'd be theirs. Ward-Smith "freaky little bastards," as Sabina often called her own children. They'd be theirs and no other pups would ever be as loved or as confused as they.

Jess braced her forearms against the freezing cold ground, balancing her body so Smitty could drive inside her harder, faster. So he could make her come again.

And he did.

She screamed out, the sounds of her release echoing off the snow-covered trees as her body pushed back into his every thrust. Meeting him, stroke for stroke. Squeezing his cock until he thought both his heads would explode.

Then she spoke the words. The words he'd been waiting for her to say without anger. And, most important, without regret. What he would have continued fucking her in the cold for until he heard them.

"I love you, Smitty. God, I love you so much!"

That's what he'd needed to hear. What he expected to keep hearing until the Lord called them both home.

Again, Smitty unhinged his jaw where he'd marked her as his for eternity. He grabbed tight hold of her hips and yanked her back as he drove into her. Taking what was his, giving her everything he had. Because as much as she belonged to him, he belonged to her. He always would. His soul, their lives, all wound together in a wonderfully messy knot. Nothing in their lives would ever be normal or quiet, and that made him happier than he ever thought possible.

He dug in deeper, gripped her hips tighter, and pounded into her harder, until he threw his head back and roared his release, rivaling any lion he knew.

Her pussy spasmed around his cock, milking him dry as she whimpered out another orgasm, her body shaking as badly as his.

Smitty came deep inside her, making sure she took all of it, all of him before collapsing against her back and the two of them landed on the hard ground.

Fighting for breath, Smitty looked up at the overcast sky. The storm had come and it suddenly occurred to him they were completely covered in snow. Then he glanced down at Jessie . . . and that's when he saw it. As clear as he could see Jessie Ann's trembling form, he could see this. There'd be no Smith sons for him and Jessie. No males he'd have to spend his whole life watching his back over. No males to try to maul him during family hunts.

No, there'd be no Smith males for Smitty and Jessie Ann— there'd be daughters.

A lot of them. Practically their own Pack. All of them like their mother in varying degrees . . . except for one. One would be just like him. They'd all mean the world to him, but that one would hold a special place in his heart.

But with Smith females came a whole new crop of problems. The majority of those problems involving other males.

Smiling, already longing for and dreading the day those daughters of theirs started growing up and torturing them as only Smith females could, he forced himself to sit up. He slipped his arms under Jessie and lifted her until she rested against his chest.

He stood on shaky legs, thankful for her smaller wild-dog size, and carried her back to the house.

Chapter 30

Smitty placed her on the living room rug, her back braced against the couch. She shivered uncontrollably, mostly due to freezing to death but also recovering from orgasms so strong she thought she might pass out in the middle of them. She sat and waited for Smitty to return. He carefully placed two blankets around her, tucking them behind her, his fingers brushing against her skin. It made her shiver more.

Soon the fireplace blazed to life and she stared at the male crouched in front of it, trying to make the flames higher. His body astounded her. The Smiths weren't the largest wolves around. On the West Coast there were Viking arctic wolves who were enormous. But the Smiths were still what her mom would have called "healthy sized." She stared at his wide shoulders and muscular back, tapering down into a narrow waist and rock-hard thighs. The man had the *best* legs. Always had. Now they were even better.

A knock at the front door startled them both and Smitty glared at the door.

"Probably groceries," she said through chattering teeth.

His expression cleared. "Oh. Good. I'm starved." Grabbing another blanket and the wallet from his jeans, Smitty walked to the front door. She heard him open it, some conversation about payment, and then the door closed. She heard her wolf walk down the hallway and go into her kitchen.

"There's no meat," he finally called out.

"Freezer. There's at least three cows' worth in there."

"Oh. Good."

She grinned. They'd have to start doubling up on food orders now.

Several minutes went by, then Smitty walked back into the room. "I put perishables in the fridge."

"Thanks."

He again crouched in front of the fireplace, the blanket wrapped around his hips, and stirred the fire again. He glanced at her over his shoulder. "Warming up?"

"Yeah, a bit."

He nodded, laid down the poker, and walked over to her. He reached down and picked her up, lifting her easily now that he'd gotten his strength back.

Smitty sat her down by the fire. "Wait here." And where exactly would she be going?

He returned in five minutes with the first-aid kit from the first-floor bathroom near the kitchen. He sat across from her and pulled the blanket down until it hung around her hips.

"How's your shoulder, darlin'?"

"Like some big wolf tore into it."

She couldn't read his expression as he opened the first-aid kit and proceeded to clean her wounds.

"Jessie Ann?"

"Yeah?" Jess asked through gritted teeth, pain ripping through her shoulder.

"What did you think you were doing?"

She knew what he was asking. Why did she push him? Why did she let the genie out of the bottle, so to speak? "Getting what was mine," she answered honestly, letting the pain flow through her.

Slowly, methodically, the way Smitty did most things, he continued to clean the wounds and bruises on her body. He didn't say anything and she didn't want him backing off now. Not now, not ever.

Jess reached out, yanked the blanket off his hips, and gripped his cock tight. In that split second, his eyes shifted from human to wolf.

"Mine," she growled, baring her fangs.

Then he had her on her back, the first-aid kit strewn across the floor. He dug his hands into her hair and pushed her legs apart with his own.

"All yours," he snarled back, his hard cock pushing inside her. "And I'm gonna make damn sure you never forget it."

Jessie picked up the phone on the third ring. "Yeah?" she answered. "Really?" She slipped out from under the blankets and walked to the front door. Smitty heard the door open, followed by a "Huh. Look at that." Then the door closed and he could hear her feet slapping against the floor as she walked back into the room. "Yeah, yeah. Everything's fine. Yup. Talk to you later."

She slipped back under the blanket and Smitty immediately reached for her, pulling her close to his side.

"What was that about?"

"We're snowed in."

"Snowed in?"

"Yup."

"How bad?"

"If it doesn't thaw soon, we're gonna die out here."

Smitty raised up enough to stare down into her face and she grinned. Big, cheesy, goofy dog grin. He couldn't help it, he grinned back.

"You're more than a little crazy, aren't ya?"

"Yep."

Smitty stroked her cheek. "I love you, Jessie Ann."

"Because I'm a little crazy?"

"No, that just proves I love you because I put up with it."

As he expected that little fist came winging toward his chest and he caught it, yanking Jess across his lap, making her straddle him. He held her by her waist and smiled up into that pretty face.

"I'm serious, Jessie Ann. I love you. Darlin', I think I've always loved you."

"Good." And her uncomfortable smile made him nervous. "Then you won't mind when we get married."

"Married?"

"Uh-huh."

"Wolves don't marry."

"Wild dogs do."

"An elopement kind of thing?" he asked hopefully.

"Don't get me wrong, I'd love that. Really. But the Pack will never let me get away with that. There has to be a wedding. We never had money for a really nice one before. It'll be our first, and I'm the Alpha Female. Trust me, they won't accept less."

"Uh-huh. With like, what? Ten, twenty people?"

"Ten, twenty . . . three hundred. Whatever."

Smitty groaned. "Forget it, Jessie Ann."

"Smitty—"

"I don't need a piece of paper telling me I love you and that we're together forever." He reached up and brushed the already-healing wound on her shoulder. Her eyes closing, Jessie gave a pain-filled grunt. So he brushed his fingers across it again. This time Jessie snarled and went to grab his hand. He caught her wrists instead and yanked her close.

"I don't need some preacher to make real what we have."

"But—"

He released her hands only to grip both sides of her face and yank her down for a kiss. His tongue invaded her mouth and Jessie pulled hers back so he had to reach for it. That's when she bit down.

Smitty jerked and she raised a single, challenging eyebrow. He flipped her onto her back, pinning her arms above her head. Jessie stared up at him with no fear, no regret. Only lust. She didn't fear the rabid Smith side she'd unleashed and could come out at any minute. In fact, she continued to egg that side of him on. Daring him to take her on a hard, fast, rough ride.

And what kind of Southern gentlemen would he be if he ignored the lady's request?

In the future, she might want to consider the consequences of calling a Smith wolf's bluff. Because one second he had her wrists pinned to the floor, the next they were tied to the couch leg by utilizing the straps of her backpack. She had to give it to the man, SEAL training definitely taught him how to make the best of what he had at his disposal.

Once he had her wrists tied, he had free rein of the rest of her body. And he took full advantage of that fact. Keeping her on edge for what felt like forever. Teasing her, torturing her. Making her legs shake and then pulling back and leaving her hanging. His mother's last words to her came back to haunt her: "... the best ride you'll *ever* have." And it was. The best, the roughest, the most demanding.

Jess loved every second of it. And when he finally let her come, she couldn't even scream. Instead, her entire body bowed and she could only shake and gasp, the orgasm rolling and rolling until she thought she'd lose her mind.

When her body stopped shaking and her eyes uncrossed, she discovered he'd already untied her and was sleeping beside her. Snoring. His arm wrapped around her waist, holding on to her like he thought she might try to sneak away.

And she might have—if she could actually walk.

With all that late-night tusslin', Smitty thought he'd worn her out. He should have known better.

Her naked body landed right on his stomach and she slapped her hands against his chest like she was playing bongo drums.

"What?" he groaned, trying to turn over and go back to sleep.

"It's morning!" she cheered.

"And?"

"Let's go hunting! You and me taking down a deer or elk. Wouldn't that be romantic?"

"No, go back to sleep, Jessie Ann."

Those hands slapped at his chest again and he snarled. Unfortunately, Jessie didn't seem too put off by that.

"Come on, Smitty! It's a beautiful morning. Everything is covered in snow and the sun is shining bright. But it may snow again later, so let's do this now."

"What time is it?"

"It's morning," she insisted.

"Jessie Ann."

"Six-thirty."

His eyes popped open and he glared at the beautiful naked woman on his chest. "You woke me up at six-thirty in the morning? Woman, have you lost your mind?"

"Come on, Smitty," she whined. "I need my wild dog morning greeting."

"Which is?"

"Ummm . . . let's see. Hugs, chaste kisses, and nose rubs between Packmates."

Smitty shook his head. "Nah, I can't do all that." She pouted, looking more adorable than was fair. In resignation, he offered, "I can fuck you until you pass out."

Jessie shrugged and sighed. "Well . . . if that's the *best* you can do."

Smitty turned his muzzle away, refusing to participate. Jess tapped him again, forcing the issue. Her Pack wasn't here, so he'd have to do for now. He still tried to ignore her, so she slapped the deer's femur against his head and whined just enough to be annoying but not make him storm away.

Growling, Smitty looked around like he expected to find someone watching them. When he seemed to conclude the coast was clear, he gripped the other end of the bone between his massive jaws and pulled. Jess pulled back and Smitty dug his feet in, forcing Jess to work.

It was true. Somehow, some way, she'd gotten Bobby Ray

Smith to play tug in the snow with the remnants of their morning meal.

She gave herself another month before she'd have the snobby wolf bastard chasing his tail too.

It wasn't until her elbow hit his ribs that he woke up.

"You're missing the best part."

"There's a best part?"

Jessie sighed. "See? Once again proving my point we have nothing in common."

"I'm sorry. I just can't get past the ears."

She turned off the DVD. "They're elves. They're supposed to have pointy ears."

Smitty yawned and sat up straight. "There's gotta be something we can both agree to watch."

"Like?"

"Uh . . . westerns?"

"You're kidding, right?" Jessie finger-combed her hair behind her ear. "What about a good British mystery?"

"British? Isn't that like the elves?"

"Forget the British."

"How about horror movies?"

"You mean like scary ones that are psychological in nature, taking you to the ultimate brink of fear?"

"Nah, I meant zombie ones."

"Zombies?" Jessie shrugged. "I never got the zombie thing. I mean, they're already dead. Why do they need blood?"

"Forget the zombies." Smitty glanced at the bookshelf holding one of the Pack's DVD collections. Floor to ceiling and three cases deep, it seemed to have every geek movie ever made. Amazing. All those movies and nothing they could agree on. On a sigh, hope gone, he mumbled, "*The Godfather?*"

"One, two, or three?"

"That third one doesn't exist for me."

Jessie turned to face him, her eyes wide in shock. "The third one doesn't exist for me either."

Afraid to hold out hope, Smitty asked, "*Goodfellas?*"

"In my top five. But anything by Scorsese or Coppolla is a must-see. If not a must-see two thousand times." She took his hand, held it against her chest. "What about the old black and white ones? From the thirties and forties?"

"*Anything* with Jimmy Cagney."

"I love Jimmy Cagney." Her grip on his hand tightened. "We actually have something in common, Bobby Ray. I'm so happy I'm gonna cry."

"And if we have one thing in common, I'm sure we have others."

Jessie patted his hand. "Let's not push it, baby."

"Good point."

Jess sat on the couch by the window, staring out at the snow-covered trees just outside the house. Except for the fire blazing in the fireplace, the house was dark and quiet. She'd called in earlier, made sure her Pack was okay. They were and apparently having a great time during the storm. Although Shaw had been heard muttering, "I'm so calling a zoo for those pups."

Strong fingers stroked down the column of her neck. "You all right, darlin'?"

"I'm fine."

Smitty sat on the other end of the couch and they stared at each other. Jess had no idea for how long, until Smitty opened his arms. "Come here, darlin'." She did, crawling over to him and settling in between his legs, her back to his chest. He held her tight, his chin resting on her now-healed shoulder, although she had no doubt it wouldn't be the last time he tore into it. She expected it to look like his mother's one day.

They fell asleep like that, holding on to each other. Surprisingly early in the morning, Jess woke up to Smitty kissing her body. They enjoyed each other for hours, took a break to eat, then went back at it.

The storms had ended and they decided to have a late lunch/early dinner in town. But when Jess walked out of the bathroom in a pair of panties and nothing else, she found Smitty getting dressed.

"What's wrong?"

"Get dressed, Jessie Ann."

"What's wrong?

"I figured with all the snow, Wilson's plane out of JFK would be grounded until the storm passed, but he'd be forced to stay inside. I sent the Reed boys to watch out for him. Put your Pack and mine on alert. But he's gone. So's his Pack."

She dropped to a crouch and dug into her duffle bag. "And?" She knew there was an and.

"He knows I'm with you. His momma has already got word to my daddy's cousin."

"Eggie?"

"Yup."

Eggie Smith was a hardcore Smith who spent the majority of his time as wolf in the hills outside of Smithtown. The man hated everybody and everything except his mate of twenty years and being a Smith. Eggie was the one you called in when a Smith got crossed. He had no boundaries and no problem taking down anyone he deemed a threat to his family.

She felt panic slither down her spine. "I'll be dressed in two minutes."

"It'll be okay, Jessie Ann. My daddy and momma are still here. We'll talk to 'em."

For some reason, she really didn't think that would help.

Chapter 31

"It's nothing personal," Kristan said firmly. "I really just don't like you." She nodded. "What do you think?"

Johnny shrugged. "Seems rude."

"You think?" She bit into her candy apple. Mr. Shaw had told them where to find the staff kitchen. And the staff at this hotel had the hookup. She couldn't tell her mom or Jess. They'd finish off the cabinet filled with chocolates in less than thirty minutes.

"Maybe you could tell him you've got some school things coming up and you changed your mind about visiting this summer. You know, blow him off. Like you did that kid who helped you with biology."

She glared at him over her apple. "I did not blow him off."

"Yeah, yeah. Sure. I found him sobbing in the locker room before gym because he was PMSing."

She laughed. "You did not."

"How's the candy apple?"

"Good. How's the caramel?"

He held it out for her and she leaned over the counter to bite it while holding hers up for him so he could do the same. Johnny DeSerio really was cute. She knew quite a few girls in her class who thought the whole deep-thinking-artist thing really sexy.

Not her, of course. She liked football players and she adored basketball players. All that height. She'd inherited very little from the wolf side of her DNA. Even shifted she was simply shaggier than the rest of them, but still mostly wild dog. She didn't mind. Wolves were a little too cranky for her. She liked being happy. Liked enjoying her life. After knowing her biological father she had absolutely no regrets about the fact he'd wanted nothing to do with her or her mother. He'd only made her realize how wonderful her real father was. Danny might not be blood, but it didn't matter. He loved her, took care of her, and treated her like his own. Nothing else mattered.

Johnny slowly chewed his bite of apple while staring at her. He wanted to kiss her. She knew the signs. She wouldn't, though. Not yet. Not until the time was absolutely perfect.

"Good?"

His gaze snapped away from her lips to stare into her eyes. "Yeah. Yeah, it's really good."

"So is yours."

She licked caramel off her bottom lip and watched in fascination as Johnny turned an interesting shade of red.

"Kristan?"

Kristan spun around. Walt Wilson stood in the doorway of the staff kitchen. When he stopped trying to contact her, she'd prayed he'd given up and gone back to Alabama. Apparently no such luck for her. *Shit, shit, shit!*

"What are you doing here?"

"You haven't returned any of my messages."

She hadn't. She hadn't wanted to talk to him. And she didn't even want to think about how he tracked her down. She'd finally had to admit to herself that the man simply creeped her the hell out. Danny was her dad. He'd always be her dad. And he *never* creeped her out.

"Sorry. With the snowstorm and all, I haven't really touched my cell phone."

"Fine." And he truly seemed not to care. Danny worried when she was ten minutes late getting home from school. "But I'm thinking, little girl, you need to come with me."

She felt Johnny tense behind her at the man's coldly stated words.

"Come with you?" she asked, stalling for time.

She had to get out of this and not let Johnny get hurt. He was dumb enough to do something heroic, and she had no doubts the man standing across from them would kill Johnny without even thinking about it. With Smitty it had been a mere show of strength, putting Johnny in his place among the Pack. But Walt Wilson would kill him, and it would be all her fault because she'd allowed the man into their lives.

Still not comfortable shifting for battle, her eyes strayed over to the block of kitchen knives.

He laughed. "Don't even think about it, little girl."

As panic began to set into her bones, the other set of kitchen doors opened and Smitty's mom, whom everyone called "Miss Janie," walked into the room.

"There you two are. And eating that bad food when dinner will be ready in another hour." She took the apples by their sticks and tossed them into the garbage. "Now I want you two to get on upstairs and change into something nice."

"Why are we doing this again?" Johnny asked, clearly relaxing now that the older She-wolf was in the room.

"Because, little man, this is for your momma and my son. Now move that skinny ass upstairs before I take a switch to ya."

"It's New York. We don't have any switches."

Miss Janie raised one eyebrow and Johnny held his hands up. "We're going. We're going."

Johnny took her hand and dragged her toward the door. Kristan looked back once at Walt Wilson. Something told her she wouldn't be seeing the man again.

The sad thing was . . . she felt relieved.

Janie Mae Lewis faced her very distant kin. "Well, well, well. Walt Wilson."

"Miss Janie."

"Your momma told me you were in town. She was very upset. Upset because my son was choosing that little wild dog over kin."

"I just want to see my daughter."

"Is that right?" Janie walked toward him and she watched Walt's body tense at her approach. "That's funny. 'Cause your momma also said you're having some money problems and that Bobby Ray should help."

Walt took several steps back at her approach, but he didn't break eye contact. "I never asked for that, but I ain't sure what it has to do with anything?"

"Everything if Kristan's momma is right and you're just using that little girl because you're hoping her Pack will pay you to go away."

"I'm doing no such—" The boy nearly jumped out of his skin as the swinging door opened behind her and Bubba strolled into the room. She didn't even have to turn around to recognize his scent, the way his work boots dragged on the floor, the way he growled every time he looked at her ass. Lord, she did love that man.

"Why are you in here?" Janie demanded, hiding her smile.

"Heard there's candy apples."

"Bubba Smith! We are eatin' in another hour."

"So? Trust me, woman. I'll eat again."

Shaking her head in disgust, she looked back at Walt. "Do you believe him? Man has the worst sweet tooth. Now, where was I . . . oh, yes! The girl."

"My daughter's not your concern, Miss Janie."

"Real funny how she's your daughter now when not six months ago she was that lie some wild dog told on you."

"A man can't change his mind about getting to know his own blood?"

"Of course he can. But my cousin, Micah Lewis, did notice how your desire to meet Kristan seemed to coincide with this

magazine coming out. . . . What was it called again, Bubba?"
she asked over her shoulder.

"Cables or something."

"Not cables. *Wired.* That was it! *Wired* Magazine. They were
buried inside, is my understanding, but you saw 'em fast enough,
didn't you? And then suddenly you wanted to know your kin."

Walt's nostrils flared the tiniest bit, and that mean streak his
daddy always had came out with a vengeance. "Maybe you
should mind your own, Miss Janie."

"You brought it to my table. *You* did."

"I wanted to warn you that your idiot boy was—"

She moved so fast, he never saw it coming. He underestimated
her because of her age. Foolish boy.

Janie slapped her hand against Walt's mouth, her fingers sliding in to grip hold of his bottom lip and jaw while staying away
from his teeth. Then she shoved him back until she had him
pinned to the wall. They both knew all she had to do was twist
and she could either tear his bottom lip off or break his jaw,
whichever she might be in the mood for this late afternoon.

"Do you really think Bubba Smith only keeps me around
'cause he likes fuckin' me?"

"Although I do," Bubba said while downing that caramel
apple.

"I am the meanest woman you'll ever meet, boy, so listen
close. You leave. Tonight. You leave this town and you leave
that little girl alone. She don't like you much anyway from what
I can reckon. You leave and you never look back."

Walt twisted his head around until he could get Janie's fingers
from his mouth. "You can't keep me away from my own daughter," he snarled. "Not you and not these weak little dogs. I'll
take Maylin to court to get my rights—"

Not liking what she was hearing at all, Janie wrapped her hand
around Walt's neck, pulled him forward, and quickly slammed
him back. She knocked the wind right out of the man too.

"You ain't listening, boy. I'm giving you one chance here. And only one. You stay away from this Pack; you stay away from that darlin' little girl or there will be hell to pay."

"I'm family!" he argued.

Janie tipped her head to the side and slowly unleashed her claws, digging them into Walt's neck. She avoided major arteries by tearing into scars that looked recently born—seems her Bobby Ray learned well from his momma.

"You're *distant* family. You and your scrawny little Pack. But Jessie Ann Ward will be the momma of Smith babies. That means she takes precedence over you idiots. That means she and her Pack are now blood." Janie stepped closer, her nose right next to Walt's neck.

"You cross her or my son," she said in a low whisper, her fangs brushing against his jaw as she spit out the words, "and there won't be a place in this universe where you'll be safe from the Smiths. No place where we won't find you." She tightened her grip. "We'll hunt you down. We'll tear you apart. We will wipe your Pack from the face of the earth. And I won't miss a moment's sleep about it. Do you understand me?"

When he didn't answer in five seconds or less, she dug her claws in and Walt let out a panicked yelp.

"Do. You. *Understand?*"

"Yes," he bit out between clenched teeth.

"Good. I want y'all back in Alabama by tomorrow morning or I'm sending Eggie for you. He's been looking for a good fight, and you know how he is about family. You know, he always did like little Jessie Ann. Said he never knew a dog who could climb trees. Now the Reed boys are going to be kind enough to take you and your Pack to the airport. They're waitin' outside for ya right now." Janie released his neck and Walt let out a breath as she stepped back. "Now you're gonna leave these dogs alone. No more questions. No more being nosey. Yeah, I heard you were asking around about them. About their past. Well, their past is their business. Not yours. Although I'd wager none of them would ever use their own babies to get money. Right?"

"Damn right they wouldn't," Bubba muttered. The Smiths and Kuznetsovs had been trapped in this fancy hotel for nearly three days during the snowstorm and they'd gotten along like a house on fire. Even Bubba, who didn't like much of anyone but her, had found himself a warm spot for little Maylin and her baby girl. Although Phil wore on Bubba's nerves pretty fast. Janie herself had grown fond of Sabina. A mean girl after her own heart.

When he didn't answer in three seconds or less, Janie snapped her fingers right by his ear and Walt jumped.

"I asked you a question, boy."

"Yes! You're right. They wouldn't use their own babies to get money."

"Good. Now you need to learn from that." Janie carefully took hold of Walt's scarf, enjoying the way the boy cringed away from her, and gently wrapped it around his throat to hide the blood and claw marks. "There." She patted his chest. "Now get on outside. The Reed boys are waiting for you out front. And you know how they get when you keep 'em waitin' for too long."

Walt nodded and headed toward the door.

"Tell your momma I said hi," she called after him, enjoying the way his entire body jumped at the sound of her voice.

"Yes'm."

The door closed and Janie turned toward her mate. "Bubba Ray Smith! You are not eating another one of those."

Bubba reached for a bright red candy apple. "Don't bark at me, woman."

"But we're going to have dinner in a little while!"

"I'll eat." He took a bite and chewed. "Why are we having this dinner anyway?"

She walked around the counter to stand next to Bubba. "To celebrate your boy finding his mate. It's a happy time."

"Foolish girl if you ask me."

"Well, no one did."

He held up the candy apple for her and she stared at it. "Go on. You know you want to."

She leaned forward and took a bite.

"I wonder where they find these apples," he grumbled, staring at her mouth. "They're huge. As big as my head."

"No," she said after swallowing. "Nothing quite that big."

"Keep it up and we won't make that dinner."

Janie licked her lips. "Is that right?"

"Uh-huh." He took another bite, chewed, and said, "You know they'll have wolfdogs."

"So? They'll be our grandbabies."

"Our crazy wolfdog grandbabies."

"Not always crazy. Look at little Kristan," Janie argued.

"Yeah, but you know it's only a matter of time before that little girl snaps. She'll go off like a rocket and take everyone in a twenty-five-mile radius with her."

"Bubba Smith! You stop that kind of talk right now."

"I didn't say I didn't like her. I'm just warning the general populace." He finished off that giant apple in seconds and dropped the stick and core on the counter. "Now . . . come here."

He reached for her and Janie grabbed his wrists. "Your hands are sticky."

"They're gonna be stickier in a second."

She laughed while she tried to hold him back. "You always get like this after I have to deal with family business."

"I love seeing you get mean."

"Is that the only reason you came in here? To watch me scare that little boy?"

He finally had his arms around her, pulling her close against his body. "Damn right. Wouldn't miss it for the world."

"That's what I thought," she said on a giggle as he teased her neck.

"Now, darlin'," he murmured in her ear, "give your sugar some sugar."

Chapter 32

Smitty handed his truck keys to one of only two valets at Shaw's hotel that he trusted and took Jessie's hand. Together, they headed toward the automatic front doors of the Kingston Arms. He had to do some damage control and do it fast. He'd promised Jessie he'd fix this. He didn't break promises, and he sure as hell wouldn't let Walt Wilson make him break a promise.

The doors slid open, but Jessie stopped cold, bringing Smitty up short.

"What?" he asked, when he found her staring at the corner. "What's wrong?"

She raised her hand and pointed. His gaze followed and they watched as Ronnie Lee's daddy dragged Walt Wilson to a waiting SUV. Ronnie's two uncles behind them.

"Lord, they've brought in the original Reed boys."

"The *original* Reed boys?"

"Yeah, the Reed boys before the Reed boys. They invented the junkyard dog." Smitty shook his head. "This isn't good."

As he said the words, Clifton Reed slammed Wilson headfirst into the SUV door frame.

Jessie jerked in surprise. "Oh, my God."

"Yeah."

"Smitty, what's going on?"

"I don't know. Come on." He moved toward the door, pulling

Jessie behind him. As they walked into the lobby, Kristan charged up to them, throwing her arms around Jessie first and then Smitty.

"I'm so happy for you guys!"

Johnny walked up behind her, his eyes mid-roll.

Examining the pair, Jessie asked, "Why are you guys dressed up?"

The boy had on the makings of a suit, although he looked downright miserable. And Kristan had on a little cocktail dress.

"We can't tell," Kristan said with way too much enthusiasm before grabbing the boy's hand and dragging him off.

"This can't be good," Jessie said.

"I know, darlin'."

"Something's going on."

"I know."

"I say we make a run for it."

He nodded. "Yup."

They headed right back to the front door, but sturdy hands used to raising five sons and one out-of-control daughter grabbed the back of their necks and held tight.

"And where are y'all runnin' off to?" Janie Mae Lewis demanded while pulling him and Jessie back around. "You gonna leave without saying hello to your own momma?"

Resigned to his fate, Smitty smiled. "No, no, 'course not."

"Then give your momma a hug."

He did, enjoying her warmth. No matter how tough she was on the rest of the world, she always took good care of her boys.

Sissy Mae, however, was another matter altogether.

"Look at you," she said when she finally pulled back. "So handsome."

"Momma, come on."

She hugged Jessie Ann before raising an eyebrow at her. "Don't you look well tended, my little wild dog."

Jessie's cheeks reddened a bit and she shrugged.

"Now y'all come on." She took his hand and Jessie's and led them to the elevator.

"What's going on, Momma?"

"Don't you trust me?"

Smitty shook his head. "Trick question. I'm not answering that."

"Smart boy."

A quick elevator ride to the top floor of the hotel and the five-star restaurant it held. When they walked in, the room erupted into applause and whoops. They were all there—his Pack, much of his Daddy's who'd come with them on their trip, and Jessie Ann's. And all of them applauded and yelled out congratulations.

"Took you long enough!" one of his Daddy's cousins yelled from the back of the room.

For the first time since he'd met her again, Jessie looked like she'd give anything to have some bleachers to hide under.

"Momma," Smitty said, taking Jessie's hand with his own, "you didn't have to do all this."

"Of course I did. Your daddy's family did it for us. It was downright humiliating. Now it's y'all's turn." She slapped Smitty's hand and he let Jessie loose. "Now, Jessie Ann, you go on down to that end of the table and sit with me and Bubba."

Smitty reached for Jessie when he saw the panic in her eyes, but his daddy caught hold of her arm and pulled her away.

"And you'll sit down here with some of Jessie's people." *Jessie's people?* Sure enough, his momma led him over to sit beside Phil and Sabina, as well as Sissy Mae and, oddly enough, Mitch Shaw.

As they walked Smitty said under his breath, "What about Wilson?"

"Oh," his momma waved her hand dismissively, "don't y'all worry about him no more."

Smitty didn't understand. "He's family."

She stopped at the end of the table and looked up at her son. She ran her hand down his cheek, her smile warm. "Yes, and your Jessie Ann is the mother of my grandbabies. Who do you think really wins that pissing contest, darlin'?"

He kissed his mother's hand, knowing exactly what she'd done for them. "And what if we decided not to have any kids?"

"Don't even play, Robert Ray Smith. Lord knows, if I have to wait for this one"—she shoved Sissy Mae's chair with her knee, knocking his baby sister's chest into the table—"I'll be in my grave before I see my grandbabies."

"One can only hope," Sissy muttered, getting herself a nice slap to the back of the head.

Fangs bared, his momma snarled, "Watch your mouth, little girl." When she turned back to Smitty, her warm smile had returned. "Now you sit right on down and enjoy your meal. And I'll go and get to know my baby's mate."

Smitty sat down and Sissy glared at him from between Sabina and Dez. " 'And I'll get to know my baby's mate,' " she mimicked with a sneer.

"Now, now, Sissy Mae. Don't be jealous 'cause you're barren and lonely."

Mitch laughed until that basket of hot dinner rolls hit him right in the head.

"I guess my question is, why a pretty little thing like you would want anything to do with my big-headed boy?"

Jess snorted as Miss Janie glared across the table at her mate. "Look who's throwing stones from that glass house."

"My head ain't *that* big."

The older woman held her hands up at least two feet apart. "Huge," she mouthed at her, making Jess laugh harder.

Smitty would probably never forgive her, but she found his parents thoroughly entertaining. At first, she'd admit, she thought she was being set up Mafia style. Lull her into a false sense of security with a wonderful dinner and champagne until someone took a baseball bat to the back of her head. But the more she talked to them, the more she realized Walt Wilson was out of the picture—permanently. She looked around the room filled with her people and Smitty's. They all enjoyed their meal while talking and laughing. Even the cats were invited and, seemingly, accepted. Only one full-human made the cut, but they all seemed to love Dez.

"You haven't answered my question," Bubba reminded her.

"Oh. Um . . . I guess 'cause I love him."

"Why?"

Slamming her fork down, Miss Janie snarled, "Bubba Ray Smith!"

"It's a simple question. Don't yell at me, woman."

In order to head off what could be an interesting fight, Jess answered quickly, "Because Bobby Ray made me smile—when I had nothing to smile about."

Miss Janie put her hand to her more-than-ample chest. "That is the most darlin' thing I've ever heard." She smiled. Not one of her scary sorta-smiles either, but a real one. Nice and warm and caring. "So . . . when can I expect some grandbabies?"

Of course, that didn't mean the woman wouldn't *say* something scary.

"What about Uncle Eggie?" Smitty asked his sister while debating whether to gag Phil since he wouldn't shut the hell up.

"You know he don't do shit until he checks in with Daddy. And then Daddy don't make a move until he checks in with Momma. Who checked in with Miss Tala Lee—that's Ronnie's momma," she quickly explained to Dez before turning back to him, "who grudgingly checked in with Annie Jo."

"And a dosie-do," Mitch muttered.

Sissy reached for another bread basket, but Dez snatched it up first. "Would you stop throwing food at him. I'm eating this stuff, ya know."

"Does this mean I don't get to kill the balding wolf?" Sabina pouted. "I was so planning to kill him."

"It's okay, baby," Phil soothed. "I'm sure someone will piss you off enough one day to garner a reason for you to pull out your knives."

"You always promise and then they sit around . . . unused."

Smitty leaned forward and said to his sister, "I never thought

I'd say this to you, but if anything happens to me and Jessie, *you* get the kids."

"They were going at it on the floor like animals."

Jess kept her head down and her hand over her mouth trying to stifle her hysterical laughter as waiters passed around dessert and everyone got up to mingle. Of course, hard to hide the laughter when Sabina wouldn't stop telling this story.

"There was growling and snarling and barking."

May pointed her mousse-covered spoon at Sabina. "How long were you watching them exactly?"

"Long enough to know that old wolves still fuck."

"Stop it. Please." Jess couldn't even eat she was laughing so hard.

"I'm just trying to warn you. What they say about Smith wolf males is true. They fuck well into old age. You have quite the years of horniness ahead of you, my friend."

Jess sank lower in her seat, but she made the mistake of looking up at Danny and Phil—then they all lost it.

"Think Jessie knows?"

Sissy whispered back, "Knows what?"

"That every one of us is insane."

"Oh, darlin', yeah . . . she knows."

They looked down the table and watched Jessie and her wild-dog friends.

"What do you think they're laughing at?" Mitch asked.

"Something tells me I don't wanna know." Smitty picked up his fork and dug into his piece of cherry pie. "And I'm okay with that."

Smitty had a bite of pie in his mouth when a slap to the back almost had him choking to death.

His sister slapped his back attempting to dislodge whatever got caught. "Spit it," she ordered. "Spit it!"

He finally did, cherries flying onto his plate, and glared up at his father. "Must you do that?"

"Ain't my fault you got a weak back."

Smitty's grip tightened around his fork, but Sissy's hand on his arm kept him from using the damn thing to take out his daddy's eye.

Bubba looked down at Mitch. "Cat in my chair."

Mitch chuckled, then realized Bubba was serious. "Oh." He moved over a seat.

Sitting down, Bubba said, "I'm taking the men out for a drink tonight. You'll come."

"I don't think so, Daddy."

"Don't be weak, boy. You'll come. One drink won't kill ya. You can even bring your cat friends if you want. If you'll feel safer," he taunted.

Smitty took the kind of deep breath he took only around his daddy. "Fine."

"You'll regret it," Sissy sang under her breath.

"One drink, Sissy. That's all I'm having."

She heard her full name yelled at the same time that big hand cracked right across her ass, snapping her out of a sound sleep.

"What? What's wrong?" Jess sat up straight and saw Smitty standing at the end of the bed, sort of swaying. "Smitty? Christ, what time is it?"

"It doesn't matter."

"It's three in the morning? Why are you waking me up at three in the morning?"

He muttered something that sounded like "The hypocrisy." But Jess chose to ignore it.

"Bobby Ray Smith . . . are you drunk?"

"Maybe."

"Maybe? Maybe you're drunk?"

"Don't try and distract me, woman."

"What happened to 'I'm only having one drink. I'll be back in an hour'? Isn't that what you said to me five hours ago?"

"I'm drunk because my daddy is still in town. We started off in Uncle Bart's room. Went to Momma's. And then we left the building. At some point, I believe we left Daddy passed out somewhere in Battery Park—but I'm not really sure."

"Isn't your mom going to take care of him?"

"Her exact words were 'Leave his big drunk ass right there.' "

"Oh." Her head cocked to the side as she stared at him. "Did you know someone scrawled 'Omega' on your forehead?"

He growled. "Damn, Mace." He rubbed at his forehead, which only managed to smear but not wipe away the wolf-offending words.

"Did I get it?"

"Sure," she lied.

"So," he said, still swaying, "my daddy says I ain't good enough for you."

Jess blinked in shock, her hackles rising. "He said what?"

"He says you're a nice little gal with a lot of class. He says someone cultured like you deserves better. He says—"

Fed up, Jess cut in, "Your daddy fucked your momma on the hotel staff kitchen floor."

Smitty stared at her for a very long time. She stared back.

"I'm sorry?" he finally said.

Jess leaned forward a bit and slowly repeated, "Your daddy fucked your momma on the hotel staff kitchen floor."

Another long silence, then, "And you know this because . . ."

"Sabina saw them. My Sabina is many things, but a liar is not one of them. Besides, I don't think she could make that up. Do you?"

"Nah."

"So I wouldn't really worry about whether your daddy thinks you're good enough for me. You should only worry whether *I* think you're good enough for me. And I don't. But I'm willing to lower my standards." She gave him a big, cheesy grin. She'd perfected it over the years.

"That's real big of ya, Jessie Ann."

"It is, isn't it? 'Cause that's how cultured and classy I am. I'm all about the class. And don't you forget it."

He glared down at her, or the tequila was hampering his eyesight. She couldn't really tell.

"Why ain't you naked?"

"I could be."

"Get naked."

Jess pulled off her T-shirt, the only thing she'd worn to bed. "This work for ya?"

"Yup."

Smitty proceeded to start stripping off his clothes. When he got his elbows caught in his sweater and started to turn in circles, Jess sighed and crawled to the edge of the bed. She grabbed hold of Smitty's sweater, trying to get it off him. Whatever the man was doing, however, was not helping. And when she finally yanked the damn thing off, they both fell back on the bed, Smitty on top of her.

"Ain't you just the prettiest little thing?" he mumbled, gently pushing her hair off her face.

"Thanks. You're not half bad yourself."

He kissed her, lips moving slowly over hers. She knew she'd never get tired of kissing this man. When he pulled away, he asked, "Jessie Ann?"

"Yeah?"

She never heard what he had to say, though, as the wolf dropped his head in the crook of her neck and started snoring instead.

Smitty woke up with a dog on his chest. Not a wild dog, but a mutt he did not recognize. For some unknown reason the damn thing seemed real comfortable lying on Smitty, staring at him like he held the keys to the universe.

Hell, he didn't even hold the keys to getting rid of this hangover.

"You mind gettin' off me, hoss?"

The dog "moofed" at him but didn't move.

Smitty patted Jessie's bare thigh. She was naked. Good. He liked that. "Could you call off this animal?"

Jessie's eyes slowly opened. "Which one?"

"Do I throw him across the room or do you?"

"Okay. Okay. Calm down." Jessie reached over and picked up the dog. He clearly liked Jessie too. Couldn't blame him, though, with the way she seemed to enjoy cuddling the little bastard.

"Where did he come from?"

"Found him behind the hotel last night digging for food in the trash. I couldn't leave him."

"You and strays."

"Yeah. Look at you."

Smitty bared a fang and sat up, dropping his legs over the side. Immediately everything in the room spun and he carefully stood, heading toward the bathroom. He managed to use the toilet, brush his teeth, and not throw up, but that was about it.

When he returned to the bed, he sat down on the edge and placed his head in his hands, moaning in defeat.

"Oh, my poor baby."

He thought Jess had been talking to the dog. She-wolves had no sympathy for drunks. But then Jessie's arms went around his shoulders and she kissed his neck. "I'm so sorry you feel miserable."

Smitty tensed, waiting for it. He didn't know what, but "it." She-wolves came to you with sugar, but then made sure you ate a mouthful of salt. But Jessie simply rested her head against his and her soft hands stroked his chest. Then he looked down and saw the mutt had placed his head on Smitty's thigh, staring up at him with big eyes, not expecting anything but giving himself completely. Just like Jessie.

Putting one hand on her arm and the other hand on the dog's head, Smitty said, "Marry me, Jessie Ann."

The stroking hands stopped and Jessie pulled back enough to look him in the eye. "Pardon?"

"Marry me."

She scrunched up her face in that way she had when totally confused. "I thought you were dead set against it. Something about 'not as long as I breathe' was muttered."

"I did not say that." Smitty brought Jessie's hand to his mouth and kissed her palm.

"Then why?"

"Two reasons. One, because you deserve everything you want."

She shrugged. "All I ever wanted was you."

He rested his forehead against hers. "And you've got me, darlin'. You've always had me."

Smitty kissed her. She groaned and pressed her delicious sheet-covered body against him.

"And the second reason?" she asked, breathless.

"Because you're crazy about me and I'm afraid it'll crush your delicate little heart if I don't marry you."

"You are such an arrogant ass—"

He kissed her again, both of them laughing.

"Marry me," he repeated, against her lips. "Marry me, Jessie Ann."

"Okay. I'll marry you."

"Good."

Smitty slid his hands around her waist, pulling her toward him, when the sound of bodies colliding with the door cut into his next move.

"Auntie Jess! Are you up yet? Mom said to come for breakfast."

"O—"

Smitty covered her mouth with his hand.

"Tell your momma we'll be down later."

Jess pulled his hand away. "What are you doing?"

"Gettin' my morning Smith greeting." He tugged on the sheet covering her body and Jess slapped at his hands.

"Stop that! They're right outside!" she squeaked.

"Y'all get away from that door!" he yelled.

"They must be tusslin'," a pup complained.

"Well, hurry up," another barked.

"We'll be down in a minute," he promised, giving her a

healthy leer as he went to his hands and knees and rose over her. "As soon as we're done tusslin'."

Jess slapped at his hands again. "Tussling? Have you been teaching them that?"

"Oh, you want me to be more specific?" he asked, finally snatching the sheet from her body and sighing happily as he stared down at her. "Lord, you look good in the mornings."

"I thought you had a hangover."

"It's gone," he said, pushing her onto her back. He brushed his fingers against her mark, unable to stop touching it. She arched into his touch, her arms reaching out for him.

"We can't do this now, Smitty," she protested, even as she opened to him. Even as she took him into her body. "They're waiting for us for breakfast."

"They can wait," he groaned against her neck.

Poor thing, she had no idea he'd be waking her up most mornings like this.

Jess wrapped her arms around his neck and her legs around his waist. He rocked into her slowly, taking his time, his lips resting against her temple.

"Mornin', Jessie Ann," he murmured against her soft skin.

He felt her smile, her breath catching in her throat. "Mornin', Bobby Ray."

Epilogue

It was bad enough he was in a tux. It was bad enough they made him cut his hair. But the sobbing had to stop, and it had to stop now.

Smitty started to stalk across the room, but Mace stepped in front of him and held him back. "No, you'll regret it in the morning."

"But it'll make me happy now."

"As soon as the wedding is over, I'm sure he'll stop." They both looked at Smitty's father. Bubba had been crying for nearly two days straight. He said it was because the "boy" was bringing shame on the Smith Pack by actually *marrying* someone. But at the same time he clearly adored Jessie Ann. He kept hugging her, telling her how pretty she looked. Then Jessie assured herself the lifelong love and protection of Bubba Smith when she asked him to walk her down the aisle because her own daddy wasn't there to do it. After that everything had to be perfect for Jessie Ann, and anyone who looked like they might even *think* about annoying her had to face off against Bubba Smith. They'd already changed caterers three times. At least one was filing charges for assault.

Lord, the man would be an absolute mess during the ceremony.

"Why don't we get your mom to handle him and you go for a walk. The ceremony doesn't start for another thirty minutes."

"Yeah, okay." Smitty glared again at his father before walking out through the sliding glass doors of the lower floor bedroom. The dog, he'd named him Shit-starter after Sissy Mae, right by his side. He finally had to start bringing the damn mutt to the job since wherever Smitty went the dog went too. He seemed to think of himself as more wolf than dog and refused to hang out much with the other dogs of the Pack house. As far as Shit-starter was concerned, he was a Smith Packmate and expected to be treated as such.

Not that Smitty minded. He liked the little bastard, although he'd never say it out loud.

He had no idea how this wedding got so out of control. He'd thought Jessie had been exaggerating the first time they talked about it when she said 300 guests. She hadn't been. Between the Kuznetsov Pack's business contacts, the Smiths from all over the Southeast, nearly half of Kenshin's entire Pack, and an unhealthy number of geeks, they were nearing 400. They actually had to rent a castle on Long Island. A real, honest-to-God castle. Smitty thought you had to go to England to find those.

In the end, though, Jessie and Smitty had little to say about the entire event. Momma, Sabina, and May had taken over, the three of them getting along like they'd known each other for the past century. They went mostly for traditional except they couldn't have grooms*men* or brides*maids*. Sissy and Ronnie Lee had every intention of standing up with him. Phil and Danny with Jess. They ended up with the more politically correct "groomspeople" and "bridespeople." Smitty still thought it sounded ridiculous, but he was glad his sister would be with him while he stood there in this stupid monkey suit waiting for the torture to end.

Mace, not surprisingly, was his best man, but Jess couldn't and wouldn't decide between May and Sabina. So both would be her matrons of honor, although they hated the "matron" thing. Said it made them feel old.

Lord, he just wanted this thing over with.

He rounded one of the giant bushes dotting the property and Smitty smiled when he saw Jessie Ann sitting on one of the white stone benches. She leaned back, her hands propping her up. Her face lifted to catch the bright afternoon summer sun, her eyes closed.

She wore her wedding gown and looked beautiful in it. She had two. This one would be for the ceremony, styled after some medieval gown she saw in a movie. Only his Jessie Ann. The other, which would be easier to move and dance around in, was a sexy little strapless number he told her to buy.

Smitty didn't worry about seeing the bride before the wedding. True, he could be a superstitious man when necessary, but at the same time he didn't really believe in marriage. No piece of paper would make him any more committed to his Jessie Ann. The woman meant everything to him. Absolutely everything.

And last Thursday, when they woke up and realized she'd gotten pregnant the night before, everything became perfect . . . and just the beginning.

He sat down next to her and kissed her cheek. "Hey, darlin'."

"Hey." She opened her eyes and smiled at him.

"Couldn't take it, huh?"

"All the fussing . . . and the crying."

"Who? Momma?"

"Are you kidding? That woman is a Marine. Ordering everybody around. Keeping everybody in line. It's been quite a sight to see. And Sissy Mae looks like she's a few hours away from going after her with one of your team's guns."

"If there's one thing my momma knows how to do it's push Sissy's buttons."

"She wasn't pushing, Smitty. It was much more of a stabbing Sissy's buttons." Jess smiled. "I've really been enjoying it."

"If Momma's not crying, who is?"

"Ronnie Lee."

"You're kidding?" he demanded on a laugh.

"I wish I was, but that woman is balling like a baby. I couldn't take it; I had to go before I punched her."

"I'm sure Sissy punched her after you left."

"That I believe. She looked pretty fed up between Ronnie Lee and your mother."

He leaned back on the stone bench, his hands braced to keep him up, just like Jessie Ann.

"Tell me again this is almost over," she practically begged.

"It's almost over, darlin'. Tonight we go on our honeymoon, and I have every intention of fucking you silly. Startin' on the plane."

"Sweet talker."

"How are you feeling otherwise?"

"A little cranky."

"I'm guessing it's going to be that way until she's here."

"Well, I remember my mom telling me that when she was pregnant she glowed and was unbelievably happy." Jessie squinted at him, the sun full in her eyes. "But my daddy said she was a liar."

They laughed, and Jessie added, "So buckle up, cowboy. It looks like it's going to be a wild ride."

"And I can't wait."

"You always were a glutton for abuse."

Smitty rested his head against Jessie's. As different as they were, he always felt right when she was around. Centered. Without even trying, she made his life so much better and it hadn't been that bad in the first place.

"Explain to me how I'm supposed to get through the next six hours."

At first Smitty didn't really hear her, too busy nuzzling her neck and kissing her cheek. She always smelled so damn good.

"Well?"

"Well what?"

"I'm trying to figure out how I'm supposed to get through the next few hours."

They looked at each other at the same time and, after a good three minutes of mutual staring, they shook their heads and moved to opposite ends of the bench.

"We can't," she said.

"You're right," Smitty said, even as his cock begged him to argue with her.

"You have to be in there in, like, what? Ten more minutes?"

"Somethin' like that."

"And then the whole thing starts in another half an hour with my dumb butt walking down the aisle."

"Right."

"So we'll just have to wait. It's no big deal. It's like an hour."

"Right."

She stared up at the trees for a while until she finally said, "But you know, there's all the toasts and the dinner and the dancing and the photographs, and it's not like we'll actually have any time alone for quite a while."

"That's true."

She grabbed his hand. "That's asking too much of me." She yanked him off the bench with a strength he had no idea she possessed and dragged him behind the bushes. She slammed him up against a tree; then her hands were making real short work of his pants.

"Jessie Ann—"

"You're not going to stop me, are you?" she snarled, her brown eyes burning into his. "I'm a pregnant female predator. The most dangerous animal on the planet. Give me what I want or I'll show you how dangerous I really am."

He'd never had a woman tell him how much she wanted him in such an artful way before.

"No, no. Not going to stop you, just thinking we need to watch out for your dress or I'll never hear the end of it from the nightmare trio." Their nickname for Momma, Sabina, and May.

"Good point." She yanked up her dress to get it out of her way. "I'd give anything to be in my jeans," she muttered.

"Nice shoes, darlin'."

She lifted up her foot so he could get a better look. Another pair of gorgeous "hooker shoes." Five-inch heels with thick white laces that strapped around her ankle and up her calf.

"You like? Phil picked 'em out for me."

"That boy's got some interesting ways about him." He'd learned to tolerate Jessie's relationship with Phil and Danny. They were simply too weird for Smitty to see them as a valid threat.

"I don't question Phil and Sabina's male–female dynamic. They're happy and he dresses me in the best clothes—that's all that counts." She unzipped his pants, and as she pushed them down to his ankles she glanced at the dog and said, "Go keep watch."

And Shit-starter did just that. Yup. She had a way with canines.

Her hand wrapped around his cock and Smitty let out a sigh, his head dropping back against the tree. "Damn, girl."

She leaned in and nipped his neck. "Bobby Ray, don't make me wait."

He had no intention of it. That would be later. When they were on that little island out in the Pacific somewhere. Just the two of them, the dog, and lots of prey. Then he'd tie her to the bed and make her wait for hours. Oh, yeah. He had some serious plans for their honeymoon.

But at the moment, the only thing they both had on their minds was fulfilling their needs before they had to put on this dog-and-lion show. So Smitty tore off her panties and slid his hands up and under her legs, lifting her until he had her at the right angle. He slid his cock inside her and Jessie let out that moan that drove him absolutely crazy while she wrapped her arms around his neck, gripping him tight. She braced those shoes against the tree and squeezed her muscles until his eyes crossed. He gripped her ass hard, pulling her in snug against him. They kissed, tongues teasing, breaths mingling, as he used his hands to rock her back and forth on his cock. He didn't rush it. Didn't want to. This had to last them for a while.

Jessie gasped, her body stiffening. Her legs shaking as she

came hard. She sobbed into his mouth, dragging him with her when her spasming muscles locked around his cock like a vise.

He shot hard into her, everything draining from his body into hers. Then, weak and sated, they held on to each other for long, long minutes until they heard Shit-starter bark, followed by the words, "I knew you two were up to this."

Smitty dropped Jessie's dress to cover her ass, but he loved the fact she didn't jump anymore when his mother came out of nowhere.

Panting, they looked at her and she smiled.

"Everybody's looking for you. You're already ten minutes late."

"We are?" Jessie asked, shocked. She looked at her wrist and saw only the bracelet Smitty had given her on her birthday. "Shit. I forgot my watch again." She frowned in thought. "I think I threw it at somebody's head."

"Well," his momma cut in, "we don't have time to look for it now. That preacher looks fit to be tied."

"We'll be along in a minute, Momma."

"All right. I'll try and stall. Shouldn't be too hard. That preacher's been checking my ass out for the past two hours."

Jessie buried her face in his neck and giggled quietly out of respect for—and most likely some fear of—his mother.

When he knew they were alone again, he lifted her chin and smiled. "I love you."

"I love you."

"Come on, woman. Let's legally make you a Smith."

Smiling, Jessie said, "You know, Smitty, I'm never sure if that's a promise or a threat."

He shrugged. "It's a little bit of both, I suppose."

And Smitty let out a prayer of thanks when she laughed, kissed his cheek, and went through with the wedding anyway.

Tensions mount in
DON'T TEMPT ME,
the latest from Sylvia Day,
available now from Brava . . .

"What game are you playing?" he asked gruffly.

"I was staring," she admitted, turning to face him. She appreciated having the light behind her, which shielded her features in shadow while revealing the whole of his. "But then, every woman here was doing the same."

"But you are not just any woman, are you?" he growled, coming toward her.

So . . . he knew who she was. That surprised her. Her mother had insisted they hide their identities. They stayed with a friend instead of at their own property and were using an assumed surname. Her mother said it would prevent her father from becoming angry with them for deviating from their stated destination—Spain. She would have agreed to anything in order to come to Paris. In all of her life, her family had never visited here.

But then . . . If Quinn knew her true identity, why would he pull her away from the festivities in such a public manner?

"*You* approached *me*," she pointed out. "You could have kept your distance."

"I am here because of you." He caught her elbows and jerked her roughly into him. "If you had stayed out of mischief for a few days longer, I would have been far from France now."

She frowned. What was he talking about? She would have asked if he had not placed his hands on her. No man had ever been so bold as to accost the daughter of the Vicomte de Grenier. She could hardly believe Quinn had done it, but she could not jerk away because the sensations elicited by his proximity stunned her. He was so hard, like stone. She could not have expected that.

As her breathing quickened, she felt herself sway into him, her chest pressing into his. It was madness. He was a stranger and he seemed to be angry.

But she felt safe with him, regardless.

For a long taut moment Quinn did not move. Then he yanked her toward the window, impatiently pushing the sheer curtain aside so the moonlight touched her face. With a tug of his fingers, he untied the ribbons of her mask and it fell away, leaving her exposed. She suddenly felt naked, but not nearly naked enough. She felt a reckless, goading need to strip off every article of clothing while he watched. It was heady to be the focus of such heated, avid interest from so handsome a man.

He loomed over her, scowling, his mouth set in a grim line. "Why are you looking at me like that?" he snapped.

She swallowed hard. "Like what?"

Quinn made an aggravated noise, dropped the curtain, and caught her about the waist. "As if you want me in your bed."

Mon Dieu, what did one say to that?

"You are . . . very attractive, Mr. Quinn."

" 'Mr. Quinn,' is it?" he purred, his large hands cupping her spine, making her feel tiny and delicate. Conquered. "I always knew you were mad."

Her tongue darted out to wet her dry lips and he froze, his gaze burning.

"What game are you playing?" he asked again. This time, she heard something else in his tone. Something darker. Undeniably arousing.

"I-I think we are both c-confused," she said.

He moved, cupping the back of her neck and the side of her hip, melding her body with his. "I'm bloody well confused, curse you." He tugged, forcing her spine to arch, leaning over her so that she had no leverage to move.

Every inhale was his exhale. Every movement was an enticement, their bodies sliding against each other in a wanton dance. She felt a fever in her blood, a conflagration that had started with that first smoldering glance in the ballroom.

"Do you want to be fucked?" he purred, his head lowering so that his lips touched her jaw. The caress was divine and wicked at once, making her shiver with delighted apprehension. "Because you are begging for it, witch, and I am insane enough in this moment to indulge you."

"I-I . . ."

Quinn turned his head and kissed her, hard, his lips mashing against hers. There was no finesse, no tenderness. Her mouth was bruised by his volatility and ardor. She should have been frightened. He seemed barely leashed, his emotions swaying from irritation to consuming desire.

She whimpered, her hands fisting in his jacket to keep him close. Enamored with the taste of him, she licked his lips and he groaned, his hips grinding restlessly into her. She surrendered weakly and he gentled his approach, seemingly soothed by her capitulation.

"Tell me what you are involved in," he murmured, his teeth nipping at her swollen lower lip.

"You," she breathed, tilting her head to deepen the contact.

Don't miss Dianne Castell's
HOT AND BOTHERED,
out this month from Brava . . .

His neck snapped as someone grabbed his tie and yanked him inside the carriage house, the dark interior making it impossible to see who did the yanking.

"What the . . . !" he gasped as the wood door clicked closed. He stumbled, his body flattening a woman's against the wall, giving him a soft landing that made the choking worth it. He caught the faint aroma of coffee and doughnuts as breasts swelled against his chest, his body reacting as if he hadn't had sex in months. Hell, maybe he hadn't. "Charlotte?" he croaked through a shrinking trachea.

"We need to talk."

"Wish I could." He loosened his tie and gave a quick glance around the narrow hall, his eyes adjusting to the dim light. "Consider using a telephone?"

"Someone might overhear and I know you don't want that, and I was heading for my house to change and I saw you coming and . . ." She took a deep breath, her face scrunched in question as she peered up at him. "So why did you really come to the office?"

"The will? The missing daughter? Keeping things quiet? Stop me if you've heard this before. You sure you didn't whack your head when you fell off that chair?"

Her breath came fast and was getting faster. Her eye was lit with fire, he could tell even in the dim light. "Why me?" she whispered, the implication having nothing to do with the case but with the two of them together now in this hallway after all these years of dancing around.

His brain refused to function, probably because the part of his anatomy below his belt was over-functioning. "You run an ad in the yellow pages." Maybe. He had no idea about anything right now except Charlotte and wanting to kiss her and knowing he shouldn't. Things between them were complicated—always had been and getting worse by the minute. He studied her delicious mouth, wanting and waiting for his. Make that getting more complicated by the second, and if his plan worked, *complicated* would be a huge understatement and their lives would be totally fucked.

He touched Charlotte's cheek, her skin soft and smooth, as her body leaned into his, setting him on fire.

"We don't have an ad." She bit her bottom lip. "You're right, I should have phoned," she said with a shiver. "But we're here now." She yanked his tie again, bringing his face to hers, and she kissed him right on the mouth, her lips full and moist and delicious and opening. Did they have to open? Closed lips were a lot easier to dismiss, but this was not a dismiss, kind of kiss especially since he'd wanted it for so many damn years, he'd lost count.

She released his tie, her arms sliding around his neck as his tongue touched hers and he lost his mind. Dumbass!

Their tongues mated, and his hands dropped to her sweet round bottom, pressing her softness to his hardening dick. There'd always been an attraction between them, but this was pure jump-her-bones-and-do-her-right-now lust . . . and he liked it more than he ever imagined.

She sucked his bottom lip into her mouth, the motion suggestive as hell as her legs parted, nesting his erection tight against her heat. God, she had great heat! He slid his hands into the waistband of her skirt, her firm rump fitting so well into his palms. His mind warped, there was a ringing sound . . . no kiss or ass-grabbing had ever made his head ring before, especially to the tune of "Moon River"—a Johnny Mercer song—his favorite. Ah fuck! His cell!

Meet more sexy shifters in Cynthia Eden's
HOTTER AFTER MIDNIGHT,
coming next month from Brava . . .

"I'm an empath, Colin. My gift is that I sense things. I sense the *Other*. I can sense their feelings, their thoughts."

Oh, yeah, he'd definitely tensed up on her. "You're telling me that you can read my thoughts?"

The temperature seemed to drop about ten degrees. "I'm telling you that *sometimes* I can tell the thoughts of supernaturals." She'd known he wouldn't be thrilled by this news, that was why she hadn't told him the full truth the other night. But now that they were working together, now that her talent was coming in to play, well, she figured he had the right to know.

Colin grabbed her arms, jerked her forward against his chest. "So this whole time, you've been playing with me."

The sharp edge of his canines gleamed behind his lips. "No, Colin, it's not like that—"

"You've been looking into my head and seeing how much I want you?"

"Colin, no, I—" *Seeing how much I want you.* Had he really just said that?

His cheeks flushed. "While I tried to play the dumbass gentleman."

Since when?

"Well, screw that." His lips were right over hers, his fingers tight on her arms.

"If you've been in my head, then you know what I want to do to you."

Uh, no she didn't. Her shields had been firmly in place with him all day. Her heart was pounding so fast now, the dull drumming filled her ears. She licked her lips, tried once more to tell him the truth, "It's not like that—"

Too late. His mouth claimed hers, swallowing her words and igniting the hungry desire she'd been trying so hard to fight.

CPSIA information can be obtained
at www.ICGtesting.com
Printed in the USA
FSHW021850180820
73084FS

9 780758 220370